"So, you kissed me because...?"

"I'm here on vacation. And you are my sexy sailing instructor. Does it have to be more complicated than that?" Jenna asked. "And, by the way, I'd still like to buy you lunch."

Jude didn't trust her, but if she was willing to pay him five hundred dollars an hour for sailing lessons, then maybe he should go with the flow for once. But did he want to go to lunch with her? Hell yeah. After that kiss, he'd like to do a lot of things with her.

She stepped closer but didn't touch him. Just being near her seemed to make the air different. It came into his lungs charged with energy. It was hard to be rational in Jenna's presence. Would it be so wrong to have an end-of-summer fling?

Maybe. But the reality was that he'd never figure her out if he sent her packing. His gut said she hadn't been totally honest with him. And he wanted her honesty for some unfathomable reason.

"I could do lunch," Jude said.

Praise for Hope Ramsay

The Bride Next Door

"[A] laugh-out-loud, play-on-words dramathon...It won't take long for fans to be sucked in while Ramsay weaves her latest tale of falling in love."
—**RTBookReviews.com**

"Ramsay spins a thoroughly entertaining story for her fourth Chapel of Love contemporary. The clever plotting and skillful characterization lend an appealing depth to this story. Readers will want to come back again and again."
—*Publishers Weekly*

Here Comes the Bride

"Getting hitched was never funnier."
—**FreshFiction.com**

"A satisfying tale about finding love by finding yourself. This is a well-paced, expertly characterized, and fun story."
—*Publishers Weekly*

A Small-Town Bride

"My favorite read of April 2017 is the sparkling gem *A Small-Town Bride* by Hope Ramsay. How Amy makes it on her own AND finds the man of her dreams is a fast-paced, occasionally poignant, always enjoyable story."
—**HeroesandHeartbreakers.com**

Last Chance Family

"4 stars! Ramsay uses a light-toned plot and sweet characters to illustrate some important truths in this entry in the series."
—RT Book Reviews

"[This book] has the humor and heartwarming quality that have characterized the series...Mike and Charlene are appealing characters—unconsciously funny, vulnerable, and genuinely likable—and Rainbow will touch readers' hearts."
—TheRomanceDish.com

Inn at Last Chance

"5 stars! I really enjoyed this book. I love a little mystery with my romance, and that is exactly what I got with *Inn at Last Chance*."
—HarlequinJunkie.com

"5 stars! The suspense and mystery behind it all kept me on the edge of my seat. I just could not put this book down."
—LongandShortReviews.com

Last Chance Knit and Stitch

"Hope Ramsay is going on my auto-read list for sure. *Last Chance Knit & Stitch* may be my first Last Chance book, but it won't be my last."
—HeroesandHeartbreakers.com

"Ramsay writes with heart and humor. Truly a book to be treasured and [a] heartwarming foray into a great series."
—NightOwlReviews.com

Last Chance Book Club

"The ladies of the Last Chance Book Club keep the gossip flowing in this story graced with abundant Southern charm and quirky, caring people. Another welcome chapter to Ramsay's engaging, funny, hope-filled series."
—Library Journal

"Last Chance is a place we've come to know as well as we know our own hometowns. It's become real, filled with people who could be our aunts, uncles, cousins, friends, or the crazy cat lady down the street. It's familiar, comfortable, welcoming."
—RubySlipperedSisterhood.com

Last Chance Christmas

"Amazing... This story spoke to me on so many levels about faith, strength, courage, and choices. If you're looking for a good Christmas story with a few angels, then *Last Chance Christmas* is a must-read."
—TheSeasonforRomance.com

"Visiting Last Chance is always a joy, but Hope Ramsay has outdone herself this time. She took a difficult hero, a wounded heroine, familiar characters, added a little Christmas magic, and—voilà!—gave us a story sure to touch the Scroogiest of hearts."
—RubySlipperedSisterhood.com

Last Chance Beauty Queen

"4½ stars! Enchantingly funny and heartwarmingly charming."
—RT Book Reviews

THE COTTAGE
ON ROSE LANE

THE
COTTAGE
ON ROSE
LANE

HOPE RAMSAY

FOREVER

NEW YORK   BOSTON

Copyright © 2018 by Robin Lanier
Excerpt from *Welcome to Last Chance* copyright © 2011 by Robin Lanier
Bonus short story "A Wedding on Lavender Hill" copyright © 2018 by Annie Rains
Cover illustration and design by Elizabeth Turner Stokes.
Cover copyright © 2018 by Hachette Book Group, Inc.

Forever
Hachette Book Group
1290 Avenue of the Americas, New York, NY 10104
forever-romance.com
twitter.com/foreverromance

First Edition: December 2018

Forever is an imprint of Grand Central Publishing. The Forever name and logo are trademarks of Hachette Book Group, Inc.

The publisher is not responsible for websites (or their content) that are not owned by the publisher.

The Hachette Speakers Bureau provides a wide range of authors for speaking events. To find out more, go to www.hachettespeakersbureau.com or call (866) 376-6591.

ISBNs: 978-1-5387-1289-4 (mass market); 978-1-5387-1288-7 (ebook)

Printed in the United States of America

OPM

10 9 8 7 6 5 4 3 2 1

ATTENTION CORPORATIONS AND ORGANIZATIONS:

Most Hachette Book Group books are available at quantity discounts with bulk purchase for educational, business, or sales promotional use. For information, please call or write:

Special Markets Department, Hachette Book Group
1290 Avenue of the Americas, New York, NY 10104
Telephone: 1-800-222-6747 Fax: 1-800-477-5925

For the members of the Potomac River Sailing Association's Buccaneer Fleet und In remembrance of the man who made that fleet possible, my dear husband Bryan

Acknowledgments

I wrote this book during the months when my husband was diagnosed and became gravely ill with cancer. The manuscript wasn't finished until a few weeks before he passed away. At times, writing this novel became quite difficult, and yet my dear husband is all over this book in so many happy and fun ways.

While I was writing the book, he would remind me of the fun times we had traveling around the country racing our little eighteen-foot Buccaneer. Many of the funny and unexpected sailing events in this book are based on the misadventures Bryan and I had in our little sailing dinghy. It seemed that my husband had a knack for finding ways to capsize our boat, and I was not nearly as dexterous or as fit as the heroine of this book. When our boat broached, I usually ended up in the drink, not on the centerboard with the jib sheet in hand! I was a very bad sailor, but we had fun nevertheless—a testament to his patience and his character.

I would also like to give my deepest thanks to Queen Quet, Chieftess of the Gullah/Geechee Nation and founder of the Gullah/Geechee Sea Island Coalition. Queen Quet helped unsnarl my disastrous attempts at translating English into Gullah.

As a child, I spent time in the South Carolina Low Country, and was lucky enough to hear the islanders speak in their lyrical language. It made a huge impression on me, and I always knew I wanted to write a book about the people of those beautiful islands and the contribution they have made to southern culture generally.

The Gullah/Geechee Sea Island coalition is working diligently to preserve this culture, the language, and the unique history of these people. You can learn more about their efforts and Gullah culture by visiting www.GullahGeechee.net. Any mistakes I've made in representing the Gullah culture of the South Carolina sea islands are mine alone.

Finally, I'd like to thank the morning writers in the Ruby Slippered Sisterhood's chat room who kept me going every day and who encouraged me to take the plunge and write about a hero from a culture that is not my own.

I'd also like to thank my editor, Alex Logan, who put up with my grumpy self as we worked through the many issues with this manuscript.

THE COTTAGE
ON ROSE LANE

Chapter One

Was this her father's boat? The one he'd been sailing the day he died?

Jenna Fossey stood on the sidewalk, shading her eyes against the early-September sun, studying the boat. It was small, maybe fifteen feet from end to end. It sat on cinder blocks, hull up in the South Carolina sunshine, its paint blistered and cracked. Much of the color had faded or peeled away, leaving long gray planks of wood. Even the boat's name had bleached away; only the shadow of a capital *I* on the boat's stern remained. Some kind of vine—was that kudzu?—had twisted up the cinder blocks and crawled across the boat's hull, setting suckers into the wood and giving the impression that only the overgrown vegetation held the pieces together.

A thick, hard knot formed in Jenna's chest. She held her breath and closed her eyes, imagining the father she'd never known. In her thirty years on this planet, she'd imagined him so many times. In her fantasies, he'd been a fireman, a detective, a handsome prince, a super-hero, a scoundrel, a bastard, and an asshole. That last role had stuck for most of her life because, before she died of breast cancer three years ago, Mom had refused to talk about him. In fact, by her omission, Mom had made it plain that Jenna's father had been a mistake, or a one-night stand, or someone Mom had met in college but hardly knew.

And then, one day out of the blue, Milo Stracham, the executor of her grandfather's will, arrived at her front door and told Jenna the truth. Her father had been the son of a wealthy man, a passionate sailor, and he'd died before she was born.

She took another breath, redolent with the tropical scents of the South Carolina Low Country. Musty and mossy and salty. This was an alien place to a girl who'd grown up in Boston. It was too lush here. Too hot for September.

She shifted her gaze to the house where Uncle Harry lived. It was a white clapboard building bristling with dormer windows and a square cupola on top. Its wrap-around veranda, shaded by a grove of palmettos at the corner, epitomized the architecture of the South. She stood there listening to the buzz of cicadas as she studied the house, as if it would tell her something about the man who owned it.

At least Uncle Harry didn't live in a big, pretentious monstrosity like her grandfather's house on the Hudson. She would never live in her grandfather's house. She'd told Milo, who had become the sole trustee of her trust fund, to sell the place. But, of course, her grandfather's will restricted such a sale, just as it had restricted her ability to sell her grandfather's stock in iWear, Inc., the company he had founded and which now was the largest manufacturer and retailer of optics in the world, including sunglasses that regularly retailed for two hundred dollars or more a pair.

The *Wall Street Journal* may have dubbed Jenna the Sunglass Heiress once the details of Robert Bauman's will had become public, but that was so not who she was.

She'd been raised in Dorchester, a neighborhood in Boston, the daughter of a single mother who'd worked two jobs to keep her in shoes and school uniforms. She'd been a good student, but even with scholarships, Jenna had taken out huge loans for college and graduate school. But she'd earned her MBA from Harvard, and landed a job in business development with Aviation Engineering, a Fortune 500 company.

But her inheritance had cost her the job she loved, because iWear was a direct competitor in the advanced heads-up optics market that was so important to Aviation Engineering's bottom line.

The company she'd devoted eight years of her life to had made her sign a nondisclosure agreement and had booted her out within a day of learning of her good fortune. It was as if the universe were sending her a message that just ignoring the money or refusing to accept it was not sufficient.

So she did what she'd been thinking about doing for years—she took a year-long trip to the Near and Far East, intent on deepening her understanding of meditation and Buddhism. Her goal had been to learn how to handle the karmic consequence of the inheritance her stranger of a grandfather had given her.

She needed something meaningful to do. But what? She needed a cause. Or a reason. Or something.

After a year spent mostly in India, she'd come to the conclusion that she could never build a new life for herself without confronting the secrets of the old one.

Which was why she'd come to Magnolia Harbor, South Carolina, with a million questions about her father, seeking the one person who might be able to answer them—her uncle Harry, Robert Bauman's younger brother.

She crossed the street and leaned on the picket fence. It would be so easy to ascend the porch steps, knock on the door, and explain herself to the uncle she had never known. But it wasn't that simple. The rift between Robert and Harry had been decades wide and deep, and she didn't understand the pitfalls. She couldn't afford to screw this up. She'd have to gain Harry's trust before she told him who she was.

She walked away from the house and continued down Harbor Drive until she reached downtown Magnolia Harbor. The business district comprised a four-block area with upscale gift shops, restaurants, and a half-mile boardwalk lined with floating docks.

On the south side of town, an open-air fish market bustled with customers lining up to buy shrimp right off the trawlers that had gone out that morning. On the north side stood a marina catering to a fleet of deep-sea fishing boats and yachts. In between was a public fishing pier and a boat launch accessed from a dry dock filled with small boat trailers.

Presiding over this central activity stood Rafferty's Raw Bar, a building with weathered siding and a shed roof clad in galvanized metal. Jenna found a seat on the restaurant's terrace, where the scent of fried shrimp hung heavy on the air. She ordered a glass of chardonnay and some spinach dip and settled in to watch the sailboats out on the bay.

"The Buccaneers are always fun to watch," the waitress said as she placed Jenna's chardonnay in front of her.

"Buccaneers? You mean like pirates?"

"Well, they're obviously not pirates, but they do pretend sometimes. Some of them love to say *arrrgh* at appropriate moments. They also regard Talk Like a Pirate Day as a holy day of obligation."

Jenna must have let her confusion show because the waitress winked and rolled her eyes. "Oh, don't mind me. I'm a sailing nerd. Those sailboats are all Buccaneer Eighteens, a kind of racing dinghy. The Bucc fleet always goes out on Tuesday afternoons for practice races."

"So, sailing is a big thing here, huh?"

"It always has been. Jonquil Island used to be a hangout for pirates back in the day. And the yacht club is, like, a hundred and fifty years old."

Had her father belonged to the yacht club? Probably. It was the sort of thing the son of a rich man would do.

"Oh, look," the waitress said, pointing. "They're done for the day, and *Bonney Rose* is leading them in. Her skipper is a crazy man, but so cute. He's got a chest to die for." She giggled. "My friends and I sometimes refer to it as 'the Treasure Chest.'" The waitress pointed at the lead boat with a navy-blue hull and crisp white sails.

The boat was heading toward the floating dock with the others behind it. The two sailors sat with their legs extended and their bodies leaning hard over the water in an impressive display of core strength. The guy in the back of the boat was shirtless with his life vest open to expose an impressive six-pack. His skin was berry brown, and his curly dark hair riffled in the wind.

Jenna caught her breath as a deep, visceral longing clutched her core. He resembled a marauding pirate. Dark and handsome with a swath of masculine brow, high cheekbones, and a full mouth. Like someone with Spanish blood and a little Native American or Creole mixed in. Or maybe African too.

Had they met before? Perhaps in a past life?

She watched in rapt attention as the boat came toward the dock at a sharp angle. He was going to crash. But at the last moment, the boat turned away, stalling in the water, allowing the second sailor, a man with a salt-and-pepper beard, to step onto the dock in one fluid motion, carrying a mooring line. The big sail flapped noisily in the wind as the shirtless sailor began pulling it down into the boat, his biceps flexing in the late-afternoon sun.

Five more sailboats arrived in the same noisy manner, and for the next few minutes, an orderly chaos ensued as boats arrived and dropped sail and got in line for the launch. Jenna had trouble keeping her eyes off the man with the too-curly hair and the dark skin.

It was probably because she'd spent the day thinking about her father and the way he'd sailed here, and died here. Had her father been like a dashing pirate ready to buckle some swash? She pulled her gaze away and allowed a wistful smile. She was doing it again. Inventing a father for herself instead of seeking the real one.

"Can I get you anything else?" the waitress, whose name tag said Abigail, asked.

"Yes. What's his name? And why is the name of his boat misspelled?" She pointed to the man and the boat, where BONNEY ROSE was painted in gold letters along the stern.

"That's Jude St. Pierre. And the boat's name is a tribute to Anne Bonney, a female pirate from back in the day. It's also a tribute to Gentleman Bill Teel's boat, which broke up over near the inlet back in the 1700s. That boat was named the *Bonnie Rose*, after Rose Howland."

"And who is that?"

"She's the lady who planted jonquils all over the island in memory of Gentleman Bill, the pirate."

"I sense a story."

"It's basically the town myth. Explains all the pirate stores in town. You can pick up a free Historical Society pamphlet almost anywhere. I'd give you one, but we're out of them. It's the end of the summer, you know. Things are starting to wind down here."

"Do many boats go down in the inlet?" Jenna asked, a little shiver running up her spine. Is that what had happened to her father?

Abigail nodded. "The currents can be treacherous there if you don't know what you're doing or you get caught in a squall. Can I get you anything else?"

Jenna shook her head. "Just the check."

As Abigail walked away, Jenna turned to study the man named Jude St. Pierre. Her skin puckered up, and her mouth went bone dry. She pushed the attraction aside. That was not what she wanted from him.

She wanted a sailboat ride to the place where her father had died. But since she didn't know where that might be in the vastness of Moonlight Bay, maybe the best she could do was a sailing lesson so she could find it later herself.

"You've got an admirer," Tim Meyer said, nodding in the general direction of Rafferty's terrace. "Easy on the eyes, dirty blond, with big brown eyes."

Jude didn't follow Tim's glance. Instead, he concentrated on the job of securing the mast to its cradle with a couple of bungee cords. He didn't have time to flirt with tourists.

"She's a cutie. Aren't you even going to look?" Tim, newly divorced and constantly on the make, had spent the entire summer chasing female tourists who were too young for him, so this comment rolled right off Jude's back.

He'd learned the hard way that tourists always went home. Besides, he had a rule about blondes. His mother had been a white woman with blond hair, and she'd abandoned the family when Jude was fourteen. He could do better than a blonde. He wanted a Clair Huxtable who could also speak Gullah, the Creole language of his ancestors.

"I can't believe you aren't even going to check her out," Tim said. "She's got a hungry look in her big brown eyes."

Jude raised his head without meaning to.

Big mistake. The woman's gaze wasn't hungry exactly. It was steady and direct and measuring. It knocked him back, especially when her mouth quirked up on one side to reveal a hint of a dimple, or maybe a laugh line. And she wasn't blond. Not exactly. It was more cinnamon than brown with streaks of honey that dazzled in the late-afternoon sun. Her hair spilled over her shoulders, slightly messy and windblown, as if she'd spent the day sailing. She was cute and fresh, and he had this eerie feeling that he'd met her before.

Her stare burned a hole in his chest, and he turned away slightly breathless. Damn. He was too busy for a fling. And never with a woman like that.

"See what I mean? She's maybe a little skinny but… kind of hot," Tim said.

Jude ignored the sudden rushing of blood in his head and focused on snapping up the boat's canvas cover. "Stop objectifying. Haven't you heard? It's no longer PC."

Tim chuckled. "Objectifying is a scientific fact."

"So says the science teacher. If the parents of your students could hear you now, they'd—"

"Come on. Let's go get a drink and say hey," Tim interrupted.

"No. I have a meeting tonight."

Tim rolled his eyes. "With that group of history nuts again?"

"They aren't nuts. Dr. Rushford is a history professor." And he'd donated his time and that of his grad students to help Jude get several old homes listed on the historic register. Jude's last chance to preserve those buildings was the petition he and several of his cousins and relatives had made to the town council, asking for a rezoning of the land north of town that white folks called "Gullah Town." The area wasn't really a town at all, but a collection of small farms out in the scrub pine and live oak that had been settled by his ancestors right after the Civil War. Jude's people never used the term "Gullah Town." To them, the land north of Magnolia Harbor was just simply home.

The council was having a hearing this week. Jude had been working on this issue for more than a year with the professor's help. He wasn't about to miss a meeting to flirt with a tourist. An almost-blond tourist at that.

"Okay. It's your loss." Tim slapped him on the back. "But thanks for leaving the field of play. You're hard to compete with, dude." Tim strode off while Jude finished securing the last bungee cord. When he glanced up again, the woman with the honey hair was still staring at him, even as Tim moved in.

Tim was going to crash and burn. Again.

Jude turned away. He wanted nothing to do with another one of Tim's failed pickup attempts. Instead, he headed down the boardwalk toward the offices of Barrier Island Charters, his father's company, where Jude had parked his truck. He needed to get on home and take a shower before the meeting.

"Can I have a minute of your time, Mr. St. Pierre?" someone asked from behind him.

Jude turned. Damn. It was the woman with the honey hair. She had a low, sexy voice that vibrated inside his core in a weird, but not unpleasant, way. "Do I know you?" he asked.

"Um, no. Abigail. The waitress? At the raw bar? She told me your name."

"Can I help you with something?" he asked.

"Well," she said, rolling her eyes in a surprisingly awkward way. Almost as if she was shy or something. Which she was not, since she'd chased him down the boardwalk. "I was wondering if you might be willing to give me sailing lessons."

"What?" That had to be the oddest request he'd gotten in a long time. He was not a sailing instructor.

"I'd like to learn how to sail a small boat."

"Did Abby put you up to this?"

She shook her head. "No. Of course not. I was watching you sail, and, well, you seem to know what you're doing out there." A telltale blush crawled up her cheeks as she talked a mile a minute. She was a Yankee, all right, from Boston. He didn't need the Red Sox T-shirt to tell him that either. She had a broad Boston accent. She must be here soaking up the last of the summer sun before going back north.

She'd be gone in a week.

"I don't give sailing lessons," he said in a curt tone and then checked his watch. He really needed to go.

"Oh. Okay. I'm sorry I bothered you," the woman said in an oddly wounded tone. Her shoulders slumped a little as she started to turn away.

Damn.

He'd been rude. And stupid too. If she really wanted sailing lessons, it was an opportunity to earn a few extra bucks doing the thing he loved most. Barrier Island Charters could use all the income it could get this time of year. "No, uh, wait," he said. "How many sailing lessons do you want?"

She stopped, midturn. "I don't know. How many would it take?"

"To do what?"

"Learn how to sail? On my own, you know."

"No one sails by themselves. I mean, even in a small boat like *Bonney Rose* you need a crew."

"Oh?" She frowned.

"Unless you're learning on an Opti or a Laser. But I don't have an Opti or a Laser."

The frown deepened. "Oh."

"Optis and Lasers are one-person boats. They capsize. A lot."

"Oh."

"If you want to learn on a bigger boat, you know, with a keel, you should check out the group courses in Georgetown."

"What's a keel?" she asked, cocking her head a little like an adorable brown-eyed puppy.

He fought against the urge to roll his eyes. "A keel boat has a... Never mind. It's bigger and more comfortable. And safer."

"Okay, then I want to learn how to sail the other kind. Does *Bonney Rose* have a keel?"

"No. She has a centerboard."

"Perfect." Her mouth broadened.

"I'm not a certified teacher. In Georgetown, you can—"

"So you've already said. But I'm not interested in group classes in Georgetown. I don't want that kind of thing. I want to learn how to take risks. Live on the edge. Sail fast."

"Look, sailing can be dangerous, and I don't do thrill rides."

She folded her arms across her chest, her eyebrows lowering a little and her hip jutting out, the picture of a ticked-off female. "I'm not looking for a thrill ride."

"No?" He gave her his best levelheaded stare.

She blushed a little. "Okay. I know nothing about sailing. But I want to learn."

"Go to the sailing school in Georgetown."

"Is that where you learned?"

Damn. She had him there. He'd learned from one of the best sailors on the island. He shook his head.

"Okay. So, can you give me the name of your teacher?"

"No. My teacher is retired now."

"Oh." She seemed crestfallen. Damn.

He checked his watch again and huffed out a breath. He was going to be late to the meeting. "Okay, look, I don't know if I'd be any good teaching you how to sail, but if you want to charter *Bonney Rose* for a couple of hours, the going rate is two hundred fifty an hour." That should shut her up. Judging by her worn-out flip-flops and threadbare camp pants, she didn't look like someone who could afford that kind of rate.

Her face brightened. "Okay."

"Okay?"

She nodded. "Tomorrow?"

Damn. "Yeah. I guess. At the public pier. Four o'clock." He turned away before she could argue.

"Hey. Wait," she called as he scooted down the boardwalk.

He didn't wait.

"Hey. Don't you even want to know my name?" she hollered at his back.

He turned around and backpedaled. "Why? I'll recognize you if you show up tomorrow. Oh, and bring cash."

Chapter Two —————————————

True to its name, Rose Cottage stood in the middle of a formal rose garden traversed by a crushed-shell footpath that separated it from the innkeeper's house, an antebellum mini-mansion named Howland House.

The mansion was a little run-down, but the cottage in its backyard looked like a cover photo from *Southern Living*. Its wraparound porch, festooned with hanging flower baskets and rocking chairs, was the perfect place for sipping lemonade or mint juleps or whatever one sipped in South Carolina while watching the sun set over the bay.

"It's quiet out here," Ashley Scott, the innkeeper, said as she opened the cottage's front door onto a living room with nine-foot ceilings, light-colored wood floors, and neutral decor punctuated by pops of chintz on the pillows and a beautiful hand-stitched quilt tossed over the back of the sofa.

Jenna dropped her backpack on the floor inside the

door, prompting the innkeeper to give the luggage a quick glance. The ragged pack was hardly the sort of baggage that belonged in a place like Rose Cottage. But then, she didn't belong here either, wearing her worn cargo pants and favorite BoSox shirt.

"That quilt's gorgeous," Jenna said. "Is it handmade?"

The innkeeper's dark-brown eyes sparked with pleasure. "Yes, it is. It's one of my grandmother's. She was a devout quilter. Started a quilting club way back, right after Pearl Harbor was bombed. We still meet on Thursdays up at the main house. But don't worry. We don't make much noise and won't disturb you. Your assistant said you wanted peace and quiet. And Rose Cottage will give you that."

Her assistant. Boy, that was a laugh. Milo Stracham, the trustee for her grandfather's estate, had taken care of these arrangements as well as the phony driver's license in her wallet, an Amex platinum credit card in her assumed name, and a bank account, also under the name of Jenna Fairchild. If Jenna ever needed to disappear, she knew exactly who to call. Milo, for all his formality, would have made a great fix-it man for a mob boss.

And wasn't it like Milo to tell Ashley that Jenna wanted privacy when that couldn't be further from the truth. Jenna needed to worm her way into the local Magnolia Harbor scene in order to determine what kind of person Uncle Harry was without revealing her true identity.

"The bedroom's this way," Ashley said as she turned and walked away.

Jenna followed her into the bedroom with its Bahama shutters and a romantic gas fireplace. Another quilt, this one in a wedding-band pattern, covered the bed, which was made up with sumptuous linens and throw pillows. "It's beautiful," Jenna said.

The corners of the innkeeper's dark eyes turned up in an uncertain smile. "I think this is my favorite room." She let go of a long sigh. "What brings you to Magnolia Harbor for a whole month, Ms. Fairchild?"

The fake last name startled Jenna for a moment. "This is my vacation from my vacation," she said. "I spent the last year traveling in the Near and Far East, with a few other excursions along the way."

"Really? Where did you go?"

"I spent many months in India, and also I traveled to China and Tibet. I came home via Australia and took a long ocean trip to the Galápagos and then South America for just a few days. It's been enlightening, but tiring."

"Well, if you're looking for quiet relaxation, Magnolia Harbor is the place," Ashley said, her mouth widening in a chamber-of-commerce smile. "Especially this time of year. School's back in session, so we get fewer tourists in town during the week. It's a little busier on—"

"Hey, Mom, you won't believe what Cap'n Bill said." The rapid-fire thud of sneakers through the sitting room announced the arrival of a little boy, maybe six years old, with unruly dark hair and a pair of up-to-no-good blue eyes set in a freckled face.

"Jackie Scott, how many times have I told you not to run in the cottage? And you know good and well we have guests checking in today, which means the cottage is off-limits." Ashley gave her child a motherly scowl and then turned toward Jenna, her cheeks reddening. "I'm really sorry. This won't happen again." She turned back toward Jackie and said, "Will it?"

The boy stared down at his dirty sneakers. "I'm sorry. I forgetted." The boy's contrition lasted less than a nanosecond before he glanced up again, his eyes alive with mischief. "Mom, listen. This is important. The cap'n says there's a mystery afoot. You think someone's gonna die like in that TV show we watched about Sherlock?"

"I hope not." Ashley turned toward Jenna, lowering her head and speaking in a near whisper. "He's got a big imagination. We were watching *Sherlock* last night. It made a big impression evidently. He's been talking about becoming a private investigator all day."

"Really, Ms. Scott, I don't mind kids or quilters," Jenna said, trying to put Ashley at ease.

"Maybe so, but Jackie knows better. So, if he pesters you, you let me know right away, you hear? And you're welcome in the big house. We always have cookies out in the kitchen. There's a single-serve coffeemaker as well. And the library, which is down the hall from the kitchen, has lots of books. Of course, there's a kitchenette here in the cottage if you want to settle in and be alone."

"Thanks."

"Come on, Jackie," the innkeeper said, gathering her son by the shoulders. "Let's give our guest her privacy. We'll go get supper, and you can tell me all about what the cap'n says." Ashley spun Jackie around and marched him through the front door.

Jenna returned to the sitting room and sank down into the sofa, pulling the quilt around her. It was a work of art. Every patch of cloth had a rose motif. Calico and chintz, large and small, red, yellow, and pink. The quilter had made a pattern within the pattern because the dark and light patches also formed the outline of a single rose. A truly skillful hand had made this quilt. It almost seemed too special to use.

And yet, as Jenna wrapped the fabric around her, an easy peace settled over her. She laid her head back on a soft sofa pillow and fell asleep, dreaming of a dark-skinned pirate with odd, amber eyes, his curly hair ruffled by the wind as he steered his ship across the sea.

Jenna rose early on Wednesday morning, spread her yoga mat on the porch, and then stretched and meditated as the sun rose. Rose Cottage had a peaceful vibe that she could almost taste as she settled in for her daily rituals.

It was still early when those rituals were finished. She showered and dressed and walked down into town, picking up a copy of the *Harbor Times* at Planet Health, the local drugstore on the corner of Harbor Drive and Dogwood Street and settling down at a sidewalk table at Bread, Butter, and Beans with a scone and a cup of coffee to read it.

When she'd finished absorbing the local news, she got to work planning her day. She'd already decided to start her search at the public library, but when she googled Magnolia Harbor Public Library, she discovered that the local branch of the Georgetown County Library was not open on Wednesdays. Once upon a time, before she left Boston, the idea of a library not being open on Wednesday would have struck her as odd. But she'd lived in Mumbai, and she'd learned to leave expectations behind. She reminded her impatient heart that she'd been waiting her whole life to unravel the mystery of her father, so she could wait another day to look for newspaper accounts of the accident that took his life.

She turned her attention to her second problem, finding a way to meet Uncle Harry. She'd saved a few ideas in the notes app on her phone. She sipped her coffee and stared at the list. It wasn't very long.

Where can I meet Uncle Harry?
1) At church—Grandfather was a devout Methodist. Start there.
2) At a community event—check the newspaper for upcoming events.
3) At a chamber of commerce meeting—Milo says Uncle Harry was a banker before he retired. Maybe he still hung out with the business crowd.
4) ?????

She'd have to wait until Sunday for item number one. And her quick read of the *Harbor Times* had revealed that the next big town event was scheduled three weeks from now. Even so, the Last Gasp of Summer Festival sounded like the sort of pre-Oktoberfest event that attracted young people looking for a party, not seventy-year-old, retired bankers.

So she googled the Magnolia Harbor Chamber of Commerce, only to discover that there was no such entity. Business executives in this region belonged to the Georgetown County Chamber, located on the mainland. She surfed their website for a while, turning up nothing much of interest until she found a link to the Town of Magnolia Harbor's web page.

She followed the link and hit pay dirt. Harry Bauman's name appeared on the opening page because he was a member of the town council. Better yet, the council, which usually met the second Wednesday of every month, was holding a special hearing on a zoning issue tomorrow evening at five o'clock. The hearing was public. She could go and at least discover what her uncle looked like.

She leaned back in her chair, sipping her coffee. As her teacher at the ashram would say, she needed to cool it, relax, lose the impatience. Let the answers come to her, instead of forcing them. And besides, she had a sailing lesson later today. It might not solve the mystery of her father, but it was a starting point in her journey of understanding and discovery.

Jamie Bauman had loved to sail. She needed to figure out why.

Jude should have gotten the woman's telephone number and name, or where she was staying, or something. That way he would have been able to cancel the sailing lesson he'd rashly agreed to yesterday evening. Dr. Rushford's grad students were canvassing neighborhoods this afternoon, dropping literature urging citizens to show up at tomorrow's public hearing and express their support for the efforts to designate the land north of town as a historic preservation district.

As the man most responsible for ginning up the public debate on this issue, he ought to be with them instead of bailing out early for this client, who probably wouldn't even show up. He almost hadn't shown up himself. But Barrier Island Charters couldn't afford any more negative reviews on Yelp.

Daddy had screwed up a couple of times over the last year. A few months back, he'd taken out a part of the mooring slip at the marina where they kept *Reel Therapy*, the aging Striker 54, which was the backbone of their charter business. That had cost a bundle in boat and slip repairs. And had jacked up their insurance costs, which had required them to reduce their advertising expenditures this season. These mistakes combined with declining business put Barrier Island Charters in jeopardy.

Bad news gets around. And since there were plenty of captains with newer boats loaded with the latest electronic fish-finding equipment, the competition had become fierce. A lot of tourists thought technology was king when it came to finding fish. But they were wrong about that. The new radar could find fish, but Jude would never believe that it could find them better than someone like him or his daddy.

Their ancestors had been fishing these waters for generations. And not just for the fun of it. The fish his ancestors had caught had been food for their tables.

He checked his watch. The woman had exactly two minutes before he blew her off. He drummed his fingers on the sailboat's hull as he scanned the bay. It was a nice day for sailing. Light winds, smooth water.

"Hello. You actually showed up."

He turned, finding the woman with the pretty hair standing behind him. How the hell had she sneaked up on him? And was she wearing the same clothes she'd worn yesterday? "Of course I showed up," he said, annoyed that she'd been thinking the same thing he'd been thinking.

Her mouth twitched at one corner, and the sun glittered in her eyes. "But you didn't set up the boat."

Sure enough, she was onto him. Like maybe she could read his mind or something. "Did you bring cash?" was his lame and rude comeback.

The comma at the corner of her mouth deepened. "I did, as a matter of fact." She dug into the pocket of her shiny, threadbare pants and pulled out a small collection of bills. "I assume hundreds are okay with you?" She counted out five crisp one-hundred-dollar bills.

Well, damn. She was not what she appeared to be. Which opened up a whole passel of questions, starting with: who was she really, why did she want to go out to the inlet, and why was she wearing clothes that looked as if she'd found them in the Salvation Army's giveaway bin? And how could she afford to pay five hundred dollars in cash for a two-hour sailing lesson that would have cost her a fraction of that on the mainland?

He took the money and stuffed it into the zippered pocket of his board shorts. "I reckon I should know your name, then."

"Jenna. Jenna...Fairchild."

Interesting. She'd hesitated between the first and last names, as if she didn't want to give up that last name or something.

"Okay, Jenna Fairchild, you can help me get the canvas off the boat. And I need you to pay attention. Because I'm not really a sailing instructor. I've never taught anyone how to sail. So I may not be very good at it. I'm going to start by teaching you how to crew."

"Crew?" She seemed unhappy about that.

"Yeah. The person in the front of the boat who sails the jib."

"Oh."

"I can teach you a lot about sail trimming up there. Stuff you'll need to know before you get in the back of the boat and manage the tiller."

"Oh. Okay."

"And the thing is, if you took lessons over in George-town, you'd get the handouts with all the written instruc-tions about points of sail and boat rigging. I didn't have time to put that stuff together. I help my daddy run a charter business, but mostly we take people out to fish, not to sail."

"Okay. That's fine. No need to apologize."

"I wasn't apologizing. I was just saying."

She nodded and smiled. He liked her smile, dammit.

"I like to learn by doing," she said. "I think it's some-times the best way to learn. You know, like being thrown into deep water in order to learn the dog paddle."

"Well, I guess there is something to be said for that. But sailing is a lot more complicated than the dog paddle."

"I'm sure it is."

"Okay, let's get *Bonney* out on the water as fast as we can. Your two hours starts when the hull hits the water."

Something deep inside Jenna recognized Jude St. Pierre, as if she'd known him in a past life. Not that Jenna completely believed the whole reincarnation part of Bud-dhism, even if she had come to embrace the idea that there was an order to the world and that her actions and intent affected her future. But gazing at Jude St. Pierre, she was willing to suspend her disbelief.

She followed his directions as they set up the boat while simultaneously admiring him. The tight band of his white golf shirt displayed his dark bronze biceps. His baggy blue board shorts hung provocatively on his hips while simultaneously exposing a pair of sturdy legs cov-ered with wiry but sun-bleached hair. His wraparound iWear Sport sunglasses fit his face as if they'd been made for it. In fact, he looked so good in those glasses she ought to phone Milo and tell him that she'd found the perfect sunglass model for the Sport line.

With all that beauty on display, it was hard to concentrate on the information he rattled off in a delightful drawl. He had an odd accent. Not merely Southern but overlaid with a lilt and rhythm that sounded almost Caribbean.

She could listen to him talk for hours and not get bored.

He pointed from one rope to another and named them all. There were sheets and lines and shrouds and a thingy in the bottom of the boat that moved up and down that he called the centerboard. It was almost too much when he started explaining port and starboard and something called points of sail.

"You getting all this?" he asked, almost as if he could read her confused and overloaded mind.

"Yup," she said with false confidence.

"Okay, let's put her in the water. But first you need a PFD."

"A what?"

"Personal flotation device, otherwise known as a life vest." He reached into the cubby in the front of the boat and pulled out a bright yellow vest. "Here, try that on."

She pulled the big puffy life vest on and zipped up the front. Jude stepped closer, sending her body into awareness hyperdrive as he grabbed the shoulders of the vest and gave them an upward yank.

She almost came off the ground.

"Not tight enough," he said, and began messing with the plastic buckles around her chest and waist. As he fiddled, tightening down the straps until the vest hugged her chest, she got a chance to breathe in Jude St. Pierre's scent, salty, overlaid with sunblock and something else she couldn't quite name. Whatever it was, someone should bottle it because it was an aphrodisiac.

For an instant, she felt like the awkward teenager she'd once been on that day when Randy Gordon, the gorgeous, popular, suntanned lifeguard at the public pool, had smiled at her. She wanted to giggle as Jude gave her PFD another tug, nodded, and stepped away from her.

Like Randy Gordon, he hadn't noticed that she was having a full-core meltdown. He was a professional boatman, and she was a paying client. She needed to get a grip, and not on him.

"Let's go," he said, pulling his own life vest on and zipping it up.

Jenna helped Jude push *Bonney Rose*'s trailer down the boat ramp, and in a matter of moments, she found herself standing on the pier, holding the mooring line, pulling the boat along while he raised the mainsail. The wind caught the canvas, and the boat responded, giving the mooring line a sharp yank, as if to say *Bonney Rose* was ready to go. The pull on the rope tugged at her heart in a strange way. A prickly excitement jumped in her belly and sent goose bumps up her arms.

When the sail was all the way up the mast, Jude turned toward her, the sun reflecting in the mirrored surface of his sunglasses. She longed to see his eyes in that moment. To connect with him, the way she was trying to connect with the sailboat. "Okay," he said, "I'll need you to give the bow a push and then step off the dock and get to the cockpit quick. This is a Buccaneer Eighteen; she's a tippy boat—almost as bad as a canoe. So don't hang out for too long on the edge. You got that?"

She bit her lip as her heart rate spiraled. The jump from dock to boat seemed ginormous, but she wasn't going to wimp out now. She shoved the boat away from the dock and jumped with eyes open. Somehow she managed to get into the forward portion of the cockpit without mishap. Wow. There wasn't much room up in the front of the boat. She had to straddle the doohickey in the bottom of the boat. And every surface seemed to bristle with equipment and thingies that held ropes that she didn't have names for.

The sails stopped flapping, and the boat turned, heading out into the harbor, the wind trying to blow it over.

"Remember what I told you," Jude said from the back of the boat. "Get to the high side."

It made sense now, since the boat was leaning over. She shifted her weight to the molded seat on the side of the boat that was raised up in the water. Her weight immediately helped the boat to sit flatter in the water.

"Tuck your feet under the straps," he directed. She studied the bottom of the boat until she found the three-inch webbed strap. She tucked her feet under it.

"That's it," he said. "Now put your butt over the side."

"What?"

"You heard me. No one sits on the seat unless it's a windless day. You need to hike out."

She did as she was told, extending her legs and sitting up on the edge. The boat flattened even more, and the wind caught her hair. It was almost like flying.

God.

No wonder her father had loved sailing.

Chapter Three

Jude stifled a smile as he watched Jenna tentatively sit her butt up on the gunwale. Good thing the winds were light this afternoon. She probably didn't weigh more than a hundred pounds soaking wet. So he wouldn't want her crewing for him in a big wind. She didn't have enough counterweight to throw around.

She was cuter than Tim though, with all that glorious hair, unbound and flying in the breeze. He pushed that thought out of his head as he adjusted the main sheet and headed out into the harbor on a starboard reach.

He'd already given her the dry-land explanation of points of sail—a topic no one really understood until out on the water.

"Okay, Jenna, it's time to unfurl the jib."

She turned over her shoulder with an adorable frown. "Is that the sail up there?" She pointed over her shoulder with her thumb.

Damn. She really knew absolutely nothing about sailing. "This is your first time in a sailboat, isn't it?"

Her Mona Lisa smile reappeared, so enigmatic and mysterious. But her eyes lit up and she nodded. "It's wonderful."

That look tugged at him. What the hell was it about this woman? She had a kind of magic. So much so that his Old Granny might have said she'd bewitched him. But then Old Granny'd been the daughter of a root doctor and believed in all that Hoodoo stuff.

"The jib?" he asked again. "That's the little sail out there. In the front."

"Oh. That. Oh. Okay." She shifted her gaze to study the jib sheets coiled in the bottom of the boat. "That's these ropes down here, right?"

"Yes. But the ropes are never called ropes. In this case, they are called sheets."

"Sheets?"

"Yeah, I know. Makes no sense. But on a sailboat, a rope is a 'line' or a 'sheet.' So grab those ropes, which are called sheets, and unfurl the little sail out there in the front, which is called a jib."

She glanced around. "To unfurl the sail, I uncleat this...sheet?" She pointed to the correct cleat for unfurling the jib.

"Yup. But that's a line, not a sheet." He smiled.

She scowled back at him but uncleated the line, and the jib unfurled but on the windward side, so it didn't catch the wind. The boat rocked, and Jenna blew her cool. "Yikes," she squeaked. "What did I do wrong?"

He adjusted the tiller so the boat rode a little flatter in the water. "No worries. Just flip it so it opens on the same side as the big sail, which is called the mainsail. And, by the way, the mainsail is on the starboard side."

A muscle pulsed in her cheek. "Um, I forget which is port and starboard?"

He explained port and starboard again while she messed around with the jib sheets, getting slightly tangled up in them at one point, but eventually she managed to get the jib unfurled on the correct side. Once she figured that out, he gave her a short lesson in how to check the wind vane at the top of the mast and the telltales, which were small tassels attached to the jib that aided sailors in trimming the sails to make the most of whatever breeze might be blowing.

She listened intently and seemed to soak up every word. Teaching her wasn't nearly the chore he'd thought it might be.

"We need to come about. Are you ready to tack?"

"Uh, yeah, maybe. I guess."

He explained tacking again and then said, "When I ask the question 'ready to come about?' you are supposed to say, 'ready, aye,' but only when you're really ready."

"Okay."

"All right. Let's try it. Ready to come about?" he said.

"Um, ready, aye?"

He pushed the tiller away from him. The mainsail boom slid from the starboard to port side, almost knocking Jenna out of the boat. "Ack!" she squealed as she sprawled across the centerboard cap, the jib flapping wildly in the wind.

"Well, that needs improvement," he said.

She gave him an adorably mutinous look. "You should have warned me."

He stifled a smile. "I did warn you. That's why I asked if you were—"

"Okay, I was ready with the ropes, but not for the whatever that is."

"The boom."

"The boom. You didn't warn me about the boom almost taking my head off."

Maybe he hadn't warned her. "Sorry. That's what happens when you come about."

She clambered to the starboard side and started untangling the jib sheets again. She eventually got the jib out where it belonged.

"Want to try it again?" he asked.

"Coming about?" Her big brown eyes grew wide.

"Gotta tack to get from one place to another. It's a fact of life in a sailboat. Most of the time you can't sail in a straight line from here to there."

She nodded, and he verbally walked her through the tacking lesson one more time. They tacked again, and this time she made it from the starboard to the port side without risking her head. She even managed to get the jib over.

"Good work," he said, and she gave him a smile that lit up his day.

The breeze filled in as they practiced their tacks, so much so that he had to get Jenna to hike all the way out, letting her butt hang way over the side of the boat.

It was a beautiful afternoon with a steady wind and not too many wind shifts. Before too long, his love of the sport took over, and he forgot about everything but the wind and the water and the woman learning fast in the front of the boat. That was the thing about sailing. You could find balance out here. Even tranquility in a spot that was never quite tranquil.

But all good things come to an end sometime. When

they'd been out for about an hour and forty-five minutes, he tacked toward the dock in a lazy sail while he enjoyed the view of his crew from the back of the boat. They were both hiked out, and *Bonney Rose* was making her easy way across the bay when suddenly his hiking strap let go, and he found himself tumbling backward heels over ass into the drink.

He surfaced, his PFD doing its job. He still held the main sheet, which momentarily acted like a towline, dragging him through the water like a wakeboarder as *Bonney Rose* sailed on. Jenna sat in the front, still hiked out and flying the jib as if nothing were wrong.

Until she turned around and realized she was alone in the boat.

"Shit!" she hollered in a panicked voice. "Shit."

"Uncleat the mainsail sheet," he hollered, but the moment these words left his mouth he realized she didn't have a clue what the mainsail sheet was, and in any case, he still had the sheet in his hand, so uncleating it would be impossible. As this thought crossed his mind, a small wind shift caught the boat, and she went over.

Jenna hadn't gone through a capsize drill, so she didn't have any clue what to do. Instead of climbing over the gunwale and trying to stand on the centerboard, she fell forward, into the mainsail, her weight pushing the sail and the mast down.

Damn, damn, damn. *Bonney Rose* hadn't merely blown over in only eight-knot winds; she'd gone all the way mast-down within sight of the Magnolia Harbor dock and a fairly large afternoon crowd watching from Rafferty's terrace.

He was never going to live this down.

* * *

Riding *Bonney Rose* with her feet tucked into the hiking straps and her body flung over the water thrilled Jenna in a deep, personal way. Was this written in her genes? Is this how her father felt the first time he sailed in a boat?

But when bay water began spilling over the edge of the boat across from her, Jenna's sense of connection and joy disappeared. When she looked over her shoulder and discovered that Jude had fallen out of the boat, all her joy transformed into absolute terror.

Just then, the boat heeled all the way up on its side and flipped over, tossing her into the big sail. She would have been okay if the boat had simply stayed on its side. But no. The minute her body hit the sail, the mast continued its downward rotation, bringing the boat over on top of her.

Ironically, the buoyancy of her life vest made it hard for her to escape the capsizing boat. The PFD pushed her up in the water while the weight of the boat pushed her down. The only way out of this conundrum was to dive deep and swim away—an impossibility wearing the big life vest.

She knew a moment of dizzying panic before time slowed and a deep inner voice that came from somewhere inside her whispered that she needed to unzip the PFD in order to save herself.

She did what the voice told her, and it worked. Once the vest was off, she could dive under the boat and the rigging and swim clear. When she surfaced, she put the vest back on and zipped it up.

Boy, bad things could happen fast in a sailboat. Is this what had happened to her father?

The thought was chilling, even though the water in the

bay was quite warm. She lay there in the water, letting the PFD keep her above the surface, lost in her thoughts for a moment until she realized Jude was calling her name, a note of panic in his voice.

"I'm all right," she called.

"Thank God. Do you have the jib sheet?"

What the hell was a jib sheet? Oh, wait, it was that rope she used to control the jib. What made him think she still had the rope? She'd just almost drowned.

"No," she yelled, her annoyance bleeding through.

"It's okay," he called back.

She caught sight of him then, swimming around the boat, trying to get the mast to come back up, which had to be a hopeless task for one man. "What happened?" she asked. "Why did you leave me alone in the boat?"

"My hiking strap broke," he said as he unzipped his PFD. "Here. Take this. I need to swim under the boat and uncleat the main sheet and see if I can find the jib sheet." He floated his life vest in her direction, and she had to stifle the urge to tell him to put it back on.

Her already racing heart revved up when his head disappeared below the water. She forced herself to take several deep, calming breaths in a vain attempt to slow it down. It wasn't until his head popped back above the surface that she truly exhaled all the way.

He laughed. "Relax, Jenna. It's okay. This happens all the time. And besides, help is on the way." He nodded toward the shore.

Jenna turned in the water just as a small powerboat left the dock and sped in their direction.

"When they get here, I want you to get into the boat," Jude said in a commanding voice. "You're no help to me in getting *Bonney Rose* righted. And, for the record, I'm going to refund your money. The last thing I need is a negative review on Yelp."

"But I—"

"Just do as I ask, please."

She shut her mouth and decided to write the best review should could for him. He had made it clear that he wasn't a sailing instructor and yet, until this disaster, he'd been terrific.

Still, it irked her to be floating alongside the boat unable to help. One day she wanted to be useful in a sailboat. She wondered how her father might regard this situation. Would he be pleased with her or disgusted?

The powerboat arrived with the bearded guy she'd seen with Jude yesterday. He was standing in the front of the boat wearing a shirt featuring a skull, crossed sabers, and the words SURRENDER YER BOOTY. He had a gigantic grin on his face, as if he found their mishap amusing.

The powerboat's driver, a woman with short brown hair, swung around so that Jenna could reach a ladder built into its stern. Jenna did as she'd been told and climbed out of the bay, almost losing her waterlogged camp pants in the process. She needed to get some new clothes. She'd lost a lot of weight on the vegetarian diet she'd adopted in India. Nothing fit anymore.

"Hi. I'm Jenna," she said to the people in the boat. "I've never been on a sailboat before, and Jude was giving me a sailing lesson until he fell out of the boat, and I didn't know what to do." There. She'd confronted the truth and admitted her shortcomings. Self-assessment and truth were one of the life lessons she'd learned at the ashram in Mumbai. Too bad that self-assessment didn't make her feel any better about herself.

The bearded guy's grin widened. "Yeah, we saw it happen from Rafferty's patio. Name's Tim." He extended a big hand. "I'm Jude's regular crew, and don't worry about it. Sometimes we capsize *Bonney Rose* for the fun of getting her righted again. We'll have her mast up in a New York minute."

"I'm Kyra," the woman at the wheel said. "Sit, watch, and learn. You should see these guys when they're racing. They can capsize a boat and still beat everyone else to the finish line." She grinned and gave Tim a starry-eyed glance that suggested a bad case of hero worship. Then Kyra showed off a few skills of her own, maneuvering the powerboat alongside *Bonney Rose*'s upside-down hull.

Tim climbed over the powerboat's side and jumped onto the sailboat's upside-down hull. A moment later, Jude tossed him a rope that came from the boat's rigging, which was all down in the water.

"That's the jib sheet," Kyra explained. "Now, watch. Jude's going to dive under the boat and push up the centerboard."

She watched as the four-foot piece of wood, like a shark's fin, suddenly appeared. Tim grabbed it, and Jude resurfaced. At that point, Tim began to rock the boat, throwing his impressive body mass around to encourage the mast to rotate up toward the surface while Jude tugged on rigging hidden by the water. As the boat began to roll over, Tim jumped onto the centerboard and continued to throw his weight around. Wonder of wonders, *Bonney Rose*'s mast lifted out of the water.

As the boat rolled, Tim walked down the centerboard

and right into the waterlogged cockpit. To Jenna's surprise, Jude ended up in cockpit too, although she had no idea how that had happened.

Of course, the boat was filled with bay water and the sails flapped noisily in the wind, all the ropes in disarray. It didn't look as if the sailboat would do any more sailing today. So when Kyra said, "Last one back buys the beer," and turned the powerboat away, Jenna was surprised.

"Aren't you going to give them a tow?" Jenna asked.

"What for? I left a perfectly good order of loaded potato skins to rescue you guys. I'm sure the gang will have eaten them by the time I get back, and I'll have to get the boys to buy me another order."

Jenna craned her neck as the powerboat sped away. To her astonishment, Tim and Jude actually had *Bonney Rose* underway as if nothing untoward had happened. "How did they get the water out of it?" she asked.

"Oh, the Bucc has self-bailers," Kyra said, as if that explained everything.

Jenna decided not to ask any more questions that would display her complete ignorance of sailing. This incident hadn't quelled her desire to learn how to sail. Quite the contrary.

In fact, the partnership between Jude and Tim impressed the hell out of her. As did the fact that Kyra had left happy hour to come to Jude's rescue. Jude St. Pierre had a group of committed friends who cared about him. She had friends, of course. Back in Boston. But they were mostly work friends. Not the kind who would drop everything to come to her rescue.

"So, I guess you've had enough sailing to last you a

lifetime, huh?" Kyra asked, pulling Jenna away from her thoughts.

Jenna turned around. "Why would you say that? Until the boat tipped over, I was having the time of my life. I only wish I knew enough to have stopped the disaster when Jude fell overboard."

Kyra grinned. "Atta girl. In a racing dinghy like a Bucc, capsizing is a way of life."

By the time Jude and Tim got *Bonney Rose* out of the water and squared away on her trailer, it was nearly seven o'clock. Jude's board shorts were almost dry, and his stomach was growling.

"I heard that," Tim said. "Come on, let's go eat. Everyone's up at Rafferty's tonight. It's Jimmy's birthday."

"It is? Why didn't I know that?"

"Because you have your head up your butt and probably missed the e-mail. Either that or you were distracted by the cutie you said you weren't interested in last night."

"She's a client, Tim. She hired me to give her lessons."

"At what, getting wet?" Tim gave him a playful punch to the shoulder.

"No, sailing."

"Good one, Jude. I'm sure she's up there waiting on you."

"You think?"

"She's into you, bro. Come *on*." Tim took him by the arm and steered him toward Rafferty's.

Half the members of the Buccaneer Class Association were sitting at a long table on Rafferty's patio. But Jenna wasn't among them. "Where's Jenna?" he asked as he dragged a chair over to the table.

"She left," Kyra said.

"Oh." He sank into the chair, his bones suddenly heavy. "Why'd she leave?" he asked, doing a piss-poor job of masking his disappointment. He'd been thinking about asking her to join him for a bite when the hiking strap snapped. Maybe that was a good thing. Maybe the Lord was telling him to cool it.

"I think she was a little embarrassed. Not to mention wet as a drowned rat," Kyra said. "You know how we women are when our hair gets wet. I wouldn't be surprised if she goes home tonight and googles sailing terms. She seemed annoyed with herself that she didn't have the vocabulary to understand what was happening."

"You think?"

"I know. She said so."

Was he happy about that? Maybe. Would she want another lesson? Damn. He really needed to return her money before she nailed him on Yelp, but he didn't know where she was staying. Maybe he shouldn't have made her pay cash for the lesson. The money, still zipped in the pocket of his sailing shorts, seemed to burn against the skin of his thigh.

"Wanna explain how you managed to turtle a boat in eight-knot winds?" Jimmy, the birthday boy, asked, pulling Jude's thoughts away from Jenna Fairchild.

"The hiking strap broke," Jude said.

"A likely story," Tim said with a laugh, right before he went on to explain how he'd seen Jenna ogling Jude last night after they got back from practice racing. "Guess you figured out a way to send her packing, huh? I know you hate tourists, Jude, but capsizing a boat on purpose...?"

"And it's not going to work," Kyra countered with one of her devilish grins.

"No?" Tim asked, eyebrows raised. "She was terrified when we pulled up."

"I told you. She was dripping wet, and those clothes were going to fall off at any moment. She told me to tell you that she's sorry she didn't know what to do when the boat broached. I'll bet she's back tomorrow wanting another lesson."

"No way that happens," Tim said.

"You want to bet twenty-five on that?" Kyra asked.

"Wow, that's kind of steep."

"That's because I have the confidence of my convictions."

"Done. But she has to contact Jude tomorrow." Tim turned toward Jude. "And you're not allowed to call her."

"I wouldn't anyway," Jude said, leaning back in his chair as Abby Cuthbert came by. He was just about to order one of Rafferty's beef burgers when his older brother Colton came up the steps from the boardwalk wearing his burgundy St. Pierre Construction Company shirt and a hard expression on his face. Colton stood there for a long moment scanning the patio until his gaze landed on Jude like a stinger missile.

Something wasn't right.

"Hold that thought," he said to Abby, right before he got up from the table and headed in his brother's direction.

"Is Daddy okay?"

"As far as I know. Where the hell have you been? I've been calling you all afternoon."

"I was out on the water in the sailboat." He didn't feel the need to explain that he'd been paid for the time out in the boat. Colton seemed to believe that any activities out on the water classified as goofing off. Colton also thought it was time for Jude to stop working for Daddy's charter business and use his college degree from Howard University for something more profitable. But Jude loved being on the water. It was all he ever wanted to do. And he'd only gone to college because Aunt Daisy had insisted. Those winters up in DC had made him nothing but homesick.

Of course, his older brother had only two years of college. But even that was a miracle. Once upon a time, right after Momma took off, Colton had been a juvenile delinquent. But a year in juvie had straightened him out. He'd pulled his act together, gone to junior college, and turned a handyman service into a full-fledged contracting business. This rags-to-riches story made him slightly holier-than-thou.

"If it isn't Daddy, then what?" Jude asked.

"Let's get out of here."

"I was—"

"We need to talk."

The urgency in Colton's words stopped Jude cold. "What is it?"

Colton grabbed Jude by the arm and pulled him down the boardwalk, away from Rafferty's patio. "Micah's coming home," he hissed.

The two brothers stood on the boardwalk as dusk settled, looking at each other, neither able to say a word for a moment. Micah was a sore point. He'd left home at eighteen and had never come back.

"After all these years he wants to visit? Screw him," Jude said.

"It's not a visit. He's moving back."

"What does he want here?" Jude asked. "He made it plain he didn't want anything to do with us when he left."

"He probably still doesn't. But I just wanted you to know before you heard it around town. He's left the Navy Chaplain Service, and apparently the Episcopalian diocese, in its infinite wisdom, has decided to send him here to replace Reverend Ball at the Church at Heavenly Rest. The Episcopalians will be buzzing with the news by tomorrow. Micah said he'd be back on the island in a day or two and wanted to see us."

"Well, I don't really want to see him," Jude said in a hard voice.

"That might be difficult with him leading the Episcopalians."

"Yeah, well, how long you figure that will last?"

Colton shook his head. "Someone's got to tell Daddy."

"You mean me, of course."

"I'm sorry. I just can't be in the same room with him. He makes me crazy." That was true. Colton and Daddy struck sparks off each other and always had. Jude was forever running between them.

"I'll let Daddy know," Jude said, turning away from his brother and heading back toward Rafferty's and his friends.

"Jude," Colton called from behind him.

"What?" Jude turned and backpedaled, in a hurry to get away. Colton could be such an SOB.

"I'm worried about you. You gonna be okay when he comes back?"

"Why wouldn't I be? He's been gone for half my life."

"Yeah. I know. But before that, he was your hero."

"Yeah, well, I'm not twelve anymore. I'm able to take care of myself."

Chapter Four—————————

Early Thursday morning Jenna spread her yoga mat on the front porch and settled in for her morning meditation. But today she felt unequal to the task. Her mind was filled with the vivid details of a dream she'd had about sailing a boat with several tall masts. Jude St. Pierre, dressed like a cast member from *Pirates of the Caribbean*, had been prominently featured, warning her against sailing too close to the jetty and about the ship being too heavy to pass in shallow water.

Yeah. Desire was tripping her up big-time today. She tried to clear her mind, but it was impossible. So, when a small, piping voice said, "Do you have a buried treasure?" she was glad for the interruption.

She cracked an eye to find little Jackie Scott, dressed in a school uniform of blue pants and a white golf shirt, sitting on the porch railing studying her out of his sharp blue eyes.

"So, do you?" he asked.

"Do I what?"

"Have a treasure?"

"What makes you think I do?"

"Cap'n Bill says he likes the cut of your jib. He says I should treat you like a lady on account of the fact that you have a treasure."

"What?" Shock coiled in her belly.

"He's my friend. He knows a lot about sailing 'n' stuff 'cuz he used to be a pirate. He says you be a prize worth taking."

She leaned back, wondering what to do about the misogynist comment that had just come out of that innocent mouth. Who was this captain guy? Ashley Scott's boyfriend? A member of the Buccaneer fleet, who talked like pirates? And what did he know about her inheritance? That was kind of creepy. Ugh. Whoever the captain was, he sure wasn't a good role model for Jackie, teaching him to talk about women that way. "You tell your friend to mind his own business. And I do not like being called—"

"I gotta go." The boy dropped down from the railing a second before his mother appeared at the back door of her mini-mansion. It was a little eerie, as if Jackie knew he was about to be summoned before it happened.

He thumped down the porch steps and hit the footpath at a run. He got halfway across the rose garden before he skidded to a stop and turned. "Oh, I forgot. The cap'n says there's a book in the library that might help you." He spun on his sneaker and continued toward Howland House's back door.

A book that might help her do what? Figure out what she was going to do with the rest of her life? Find the answers about what happened to her father? Unlikely.

She smiled in spite of herself. How hilarious would it be to find a book that would provide all the answers when her year-long sabbatical from life had not.

She pushed that thought out of her brain and went back to deep breathing. Eventually she managed to find a kind of peace and meditated for almost an hour. But when she finished, the thoughts came back, along with her curiosity.

She didn't have much to do today. She wanted to swing by the Georgetown County Library and look at old newspapers. The town council hearing wasn't until five o'clock. Her plans, such as they were, included seeking out Jude St. Pierre and asking for another lesson. But beyond that, she had time on her hands. So why not satisfy her curiosity?

After a shower and breakfast, she crossed the rose garden and entered Howland House's back door, which opened into a butler's pantry right off the kitchen with access to the center hall.

There was a plate of oatmeal raisin cookies on the kitchen counter with a handwritten sign that said "Enjoy!" She scooped up a cookie and headed down the hallway.

Antique luxury abounded here, with high ceilings, hand-carved chair and picture rails, and ceiling moldings made of plaster. It was almost as if the house had been pressed into the pages of a book, stuck in time and unable to move forward.

Ashley Scott's house was a gem. And maybe it was a good thing that it hadn't been overly modernized. It still retained many of the original features. But those features needed restoring in one way or another. The house was like an average woman who didn't know how beautiful she was on the inside.

The library stood to the left at the end of the hallway. It was a square room with floor-to-ceiling bookshelves, a heavily curtained window with a view of the portico, and several overstuffed chairs. A round, claw-foot table stood in the middle of the room, on which stood a vase filled with roses. The commingled scent of roses and lemon-oil furniture polish hung in the air.

Jenna stopped in the middle of the room, uncertain of what precisely she was searching for. There were hundreds of books in the room, most of them hardbacked and fabric bound, although there was a section, down low, filled with paperback bestsellers, mysteries, and romances, all of them with cracked spines, suggesting they'd been read more than once.

She was an idiot for listening to a six-year-old. She was about to leave when she spied the paperback sitting on the table behind the vase: *Royce's Sailing Illustrated: The Sailor's Bible Since '56.*

She picked up the book and thumbed through it. It had diagrams of sailboats with all the rigging labeled. It also had an in-depth explanation of points of sail. And so much more. She sank into one of the big easy chairs, the mohair upholstery abrading the back of her legs.

Had her father read this book? Was this how he'd learned to sail? Or had someone taught him? The questions abounded. Always more questions than answers.

It had always been that way. But this time, instead of imagining a father, she was hunting down the real man. Collecting clues so she could understand him.

She opened the book to a diagram of a sailboat with every rope labeled with its proper name. She could do this. She could show up at Jude's door smarter than she'd been yesterday.

She settled in to read and study and lost track of time.

At four thirty on Thursday afternoon, Jude parked his pickup in the lot adjacent to Grace Methodist Church. The lot was already half full, suggesting that this evening's public hearing would be well attended.

So well attended that the town council had borrowed space from Magnolia Harbor's largest church, located on Lilac Lane, three blocks from the harbor. Like so much of the white folks' historic architecture, Grace Methodist was a Greek revival building with four columns holding up its front portico. Its facade was stucco with six-over-six double-hung windows and shiny black shutters. It proudly bore the National Register of Historic Places medallion. The very same medallion Jude had been trying to get for Old Granny's house.

But South Carolina insisted that his great-grandmother's freedman's cottage had been altered too much over the last hundred and fifty years to be worthy of the nomination. Or maybe folks still viewed the old tin-roofed houses as nothing more than shacks out in the woods.

Jude checked his tie for the umpteenth time as he crossed the parking lot. His blazer felt like a straitjacket, and his collar itched. He couldn't remember the last time he'd worn a coat and tie. Was it Annie's wedding or Uncle Josh's funeral?

Every time he had to wear a tie, he thanked the Lord that he didn't have to commute to work and sit at a desk under fluorescent lights. Barrier Island Charters, where he'd worked at one job or another for most of his life, might make only a modest living for him and his daddy, but they got to go fishing all summer long. So he had nothing really to complain about.

He headed up the church's front steps. Butterflies flitted around his gut as he strolled into the sanctuary, which had been turned into a temporary hearing room with a folding table up near the altar. The pews were already filling up with people, a few of them carrying homemade signs with slogans on them that said, GULLAH HISTORY MATTERS and SAVE GULLAH/GEECHEE CULTURE. He recognized friends. Some of them sat on his side, and many, including his own father, sat across the aisle with the pro-growth faction.

Daddy wasn't the only brown-faced person sitting on the pro-growth side of the aisle. And there were probably more white folks sitting on the side that wanted to preserve history. So this might be a hot-button issue for Magnolia Harbor, but it wasn't the usual kind that automatically divided people between black and white.

Gullah folk sat on Jude's side of the room. But there were plenty of African Americans who weren't Gullah. His own father might have had a Gullah grandmother, but Daddy had never learned the language and had never been proud of his heritage. Daddy and Momma, before she took off, had forbidden their sons from learning the Gullah language because they thought it would make their sons sound ignorant. Because the language had been stereotyped by white folks for generations.

Micah, the good child, had followed orders. Colton, the wild child, had no interest in heritage. But Jude, the abandoned one, had sought refuge with Old Granny. And Old Granny had taught him so he could carry the knowledge into a new generation.

He hoped Old Granny was sitting up in heaven nodding her head as he walked down the aisle toward the pew at the front of the room reserved for the scheduled witnesses. Dr. Greg Rushford, a short man with a shock of white hair and steel-rimmed glasses, was putting several photographs of Old Granny's house and Aunt Charlotte's house up on easels. Greg would do most of the talking tonight.

Jude got halfway down the aisle when he caught sight of Jenna, sitting on the end right behind the reserved section. Her honey hair gleamed even without sunshine to light it up, and his reaction to those golden threads was visceral and utterly unwanted.

What the hell was she doing here? She was a tourist, right?

Maybe not. Tourists didn't come to town council meetings.

His feet came to a sudden stop just as she turned her head to look over her shoulder. As their gazes met and held, her lips curved up on one side just a little bit. "Oh, you're here," she said, as if she'd been waiting for him.

He took a few more steps and looked down at her. "I am. But why are you?"

She shrugged, and red crawled up her pale cheeks. "Um, well...for one reason, I was looking for you."

"Me?"

She nodded. "I wanted to schedule another sailing lesson. I went down to your office today, but the door was locked."

"Well, the thing is, Barrier Island Charters doesn't really keep regular office hours. If you want to book a charter, you can do it online or by phone."

"I kind of figured that out. And I did go online, but there's no option for sailing lessons."

"How did you know I would be here?"

Her cheeks darkened further. "Well, everyone in town is talking about this. So..." Her voice faded out, and Jude got the distinct impression that she wasn't telling him the whole truth. Why would a tourist come to a public hearing on a zoning issue? How did she know he'd be here?

He was about to quiz her further when Dr. Rushford called his name. "I have to go," he said abruptly.

"Good luck," she said, her brown eyes lighting up.

"Uh, yeah, thanks."

"And after, I'd like to schedule another lesson."

"Um, okay. Sure." He turned away, confused and distracted.

"Who's that?" Dr. Rushford asked as Jude approached the front of the room.

"A tourist," he said. "Someone who wants sailing lessons."

"And she came here to get them?" Rushford's bushy eyebrows lowered.

"Yeah, I know. It's weird. Everything about her is weird."

Rushford took him by the arm and turned his back on Jenna and the rest of the crowd. "Listen, Jude, you need to be careful. I just heard through the grapevine that Santee Resort Group is ready to jump on that land north of town. It wouldn't be unusual for them to send people to this meeting, or even to send an advanced scouting team."

"You think she's working for Santee Resorts?"

"I don't know. All I can say is that I know every single person in this room except her. How did you meet her?"

"A couple of days ago, she stopped me on the boardwalk and asked for sailing lessons."

"She specifically sought you out?"

He nodded.

"Be careful. She could have been sent specifically to research you. Or to cozy up to members of your family."

That left a queasy feeling in his middle. If he owned Old Granny's land outright, it would have been easy to protect it, assuming he could cover rising property taxes. But even though he was living in Old Granny's house, he didn't own the land outright. The land had been in the family for generations and informally passed down for more than a hundred years without any sort of will or probate. As a result, Jude owned only a share of the land. Other shareholders included his brothers, his father, his cousin Annie, his aunts Charlotte and Daisy, and Old Uncle Jeeter.

Buying out all those family members was beyond Jude's means. And the worst part of it was that the law allowed any shareholder to sell the land. So if Colton or Daddy wanted to sell out, they could do it.

Santee Resort used this informal system of "heirs property" ownership to its advantage. They gobbled up land for their golf courses and gated communities by picking off single members of complex family-ownership stakes. And the more development that took place, the more families found themselves facing property tax bills they couldn't afford.

It was a conundrum that could be solved only by designating these lands as a historic preservation district, which would limit development, preserve the existing historic structures, and keep Santee Resorts and their like away.

"You think they sent this woman to convince me to sell out?"

"Maybe."

"That's ridiculous. I'm leading this charge."

"Maybe they sent her to find out which members of your family are the most likely to sell out."

Jude turned around to stare at the woman in the second row. Jenna didn't belong here. And worse than that, now that he thought about it, the woman had approached him by name. She hadn't taken no for an answer, and even more important, she'd agreed to his outrageous price for sailing lessons without batting an eye.

"Should I send her packing?" he asked.

Dr. Rushford shook his head. "It might be more useful to befriend her."

"Befriend her?"

"Yeah. And maybe you can make a personal pitch about what we're trying to preserve here." Greg slapped his back. "If they sent her, it means they're worried about you."

"You think?"

"I know."

* * *

Jenna hoped tonight's hearing wouldn't be as unproductive as the time she'd spent at the Georgetown County Library this afternoon. She'd found exactly two newspaper accounts of her father's accident, but they hadn't said much. Just that Jamie Bauman, son of the sunglass magnate, had drowned in the bay while sailing on a calm day. His boat had been found capsized near the place where the Black, Pee Dee, and Waccamaw Rivers entered into the bay. Jamie's body had been found about a mile downstream from the boat. The coroner had ruled the death an accidental drowning.

Now she sat in one of the hard-oak pews at the Methodist Church, studying every single man over the age of sixty. Which one was her uncle Harry? She wouldn't know until he took his seat behind the long folding table at the front of the church, where someone had put a cardboard tent sign marking his spot.

And then Jude had come in, staring at her as if she'd dropped in from Mars or something. She'd opened her mouth and said something stupid because just his presence electrified her insides and switched her brain off.

She could hardly remember their conversation now. Only that she'd blushed her way through it and left him curious about why she was here. She'd made a big mistake. She shouldn't have come early or sat up front. She should have hidden herself in the back of the room or something.

Jude St. Pierre was now super-suspicious of her motives. And she wasn't making her situation any better by staring at him. But he was hard not to look at, dressed like a corporate executive in that suit and tie.

Luckily, someone asked attendees to take their seats. Her skin prickled hot and then cold as Harry Bauman sat in the chair behind his name placard. He had thick white hair, cut short over the ears and parted on the side. His thick mustache covered his upper lip and gave him the look of a stereotypical British colonel. His face looked sunburned and leathery with a wild tracery of lines, as if he'd lived his life out in the hot sun. He wore a seersucker suit and a tie with a nautical theme, and he peered out at the assemblage from behind a pair of trifocals with square black frames.

He didn't resemble Grandfather at all, although he was her grandfather's brother. There was nothing particularly stern about Harry's face. Maybe it was wishful thinking, but he had a distinctly avuncular look. But then, looks could be deceiving.

She settled in, curious to hear what he might say and what it might reveal about him. But she was soon disappointed, because Harry said not one word. He was one of five town council members, and the other four had plenty to say. It didn't take long to realize that Uncle Harry was probably the deciding vote on the question of designating a section of land called "Gullah Town" as a historic preservation area, thereby limiting development.

A professor of art and architecture from the College of Charleston spent forty-five minutes talking about the historical and architectural significance of the buildings located in this area. The photographs he showed were of small cabins, many of them in disrepair, but all of them built in the years right after the Civil War by formerly enslaved people who had worked on the rice plantations along the Black River. The history was fascinating, but Jenna wasn't all that sure any of those small, humble buildings were worthy of being listed as historic sites.

But then Jude stood up and started to talk about his Old Granny, the daughter of a root doctor who had become a recognized artist because of the sweetgrass baskets she made and sold at the market in Charleston. He pointed to the picture of his Old Granny's house and the remnants of blue paint. He talked about how Old Granny wouldn't dream of living in a house without heaven blue shutters because blue kept the haunts away. He talked about the stories she told of growing rice and vegetables and fishing.

And then he started speaking the Gullah language. It had a lilting African rhythm, and she was astonished that she couldn't understand a word of it.

"*We bin yah. Ona kum yah,*" he said, and half a dozen folks on his side of the aisle vocalized their approval.

He stopped and continued in English. "Those of you who can still understand Gullah know what I just said. I'll bet there aren't more than ten of you in this room who can still speak it. The language is dying the way Native American languages died. Because we have all been taught to speak English, and we've been told that our own native language, the language our ancestors developed as enslaved people, is no good, that it's *broken* English. Do you know how offensive that is to many of us?" He shook his head.

"The least we can do is save the houses. If we can raise the money to restore them, we could create a site for historic tourism. Building another golf course isn't the only way to improve our economy."

Passion rang from his voice, and a shiver worked its way down Jenna's spine. This. This is what she wanted in her life. Not specifically to save a few old buildings but to know that kind of passion for something.

She envied Jude, even as she fell a little bit in love with him. He was an amazing storyteller. When he spoke about his Old Granny, everyone in the room sat still and listened. He had something important to say. And she hoped her uncle would support his petition.

A period for public comment came after Jude's presentation. A dozen people stood up and sounded off in two-minute speeches. Most of the people opposed Jude's proposal.

The majority seemed to think that the houses on Jonquil Island were of lesser historic significance than other freedmen cottages being protected on other sea islands. They trotted out the fact that the State of South Carolina had refused to nominate several of the houses for the National Register of Historic Places. And they pointed out that the buildings in question were, for the most part, beyond salvation.

Somehow, knowing that Jude St. Pierre was tilting at windmills made him even more attractive. And when the hearing adjourned, she elbowed her way through the crowd surrounding Jude and the professor. When she finally came face-to-face with him, her face heated once again. He was so damn handsome in that suit. And there was so much more to him than the swashbuckling sailor.

"I was moved by what you had to say," she said.

His mouth firmed a little, and she got the feeling she'd

stepped into a hole. Had she been condescending? Had she committed some racial faux pas? She didn't think so, so she blundered on. "Your great-grandmother sounded like an amazing woman."

"She was." It was the sort of curt answer that was designed to put her off.

"Did I do something to annoy you?" she asked.

He shook his head. "What do you want?"

She stepped back. "Um, well, I'd like to go sailing again." She paused and dug into her oversized leather satchel and pulled out the copy of Royce's sailing handbook. "And look what I found in the library. I've spent hours studying it. I'm determined to learn the name of every rope on the boat, so the next time we capsize, I'll be ready."

His stony expression softened a little. "Well, you can start by not calling any of them ropes. They are lines, sheets, or shrouds."

Her smile widened. "See? I just learned something new. So, when can I schedule my next lesson?"

He broke eye contact, and for a moment she had the panicky feeling that he was going to once again send her to the sailing school on the mainland. But then he let go of a long sigh. "Tomorrow. We don't have a Friday charter this week, so I've got time. Come by the office in the morning. There's supposed to be weather moving in tomorrow."

She nodded, but before she could say another word, Harry turned up at Jude's elbow. Her uncle grabbed Jude's arm and said something to him that she couldn't hear.

Jude turned back toward her. "I have to go. I'll see you at the office. Tomorrow morning. Let's say ten o'clock."

And then he turned his back on her to speak with Harry. Oh, if only she could hear what they were talking about, but she couldn't muscle in on the conversation. She'd been dismissed.

But now she had another reason for getting to know Jude St. Pierre. Clearly he and Harry knew each other. Very well, she'd guess, by the way Harry absently patted Jude's back as they spoke.

That touch was more than the usual business touch. There was emotion in it. And she wanted to know exactly how Harry and Jude were connected.

Chapter Five————————————

Thursday had been one of those horrible, no-good, terrible days for Ashley Scott.

It began when Colton St. Pierre stopped in to check her roof, which had sprung a leak during the last rainstorm. He went up a ladder, spent ten minutes poking around, and came down with an expression on his face that told her everything she needed to know. It would cost a small fortune to fix her roof. And she barely had enough money to get by on a day-to-day basis.

After Colton left, she went up to her bedroom and cried for ten minutes until she decided it might be better to get angry. So she hurled Adam's picture across the bedroom, breaking the frame and the glass. So stupid. She couldn't afford to replace the picture frame. And so silly to blame Adam for dying in Afghanistan while serving his country.

Then, just to make her more miserable, Mrs. Thacker, the principal at Jackie's school, called and wanted to see her right away. So off she went to the school, where she learned that Jackie had called Liam Solomons a "scurvy bilge rat." The principal frowned on that sort of thing because, regardless of the words Jackie had used, the intent had been to intimidate, and the school had zero tolerance for bullies.

Mrs. Thacker insisted that Jackie needed help and even gave her a list of counselors, none of whom turned out to be a TRICARE provider. So Ashley spent much of the afternoon looking for someone who was on the military plan. Not surprisingly, once she found a provider, she couldn't get an appointment until next month, and the doctor's office was forty-five minutes away on the mainland.

And all that searching for a doctor left her no time to bake a cake for the Piece Makers, the name her grandmother had given to the quilting club that had been meeting at Howland House for decades. Ashley loved to bake, and she hadn't minded carrying on her grandmother's tradition of baking something every Thursday for the ladies, but today the quilters were getting storebought apple pie.

Donna Cuthbert arrived first, around six thirty, and gave the dinky-looking pie the evil eye right before she said, "I thought you planned to make a German chocolate cake this week."

"Sorry. I had a conference at the school this afternoon. They think Jackie should see a psychologist."

"Oh no. Is Jackie all right?" Donna's compassion immediately made Ashley feel guilty for not baking the cake. Which was ridiculous. Really, she needed an attitude adjustment, but she didn't see the Piece Makers, a group of devout churchwomen with the average age of sixty-five, agreeing to a round of margaritas.

"He's fine. They're just concerned about Captain Bill."

Ashley repeated this explanation four more times for Sandy, Karen, Barbara, and Nancy, all of whom accepted the store-bought pie with grace, followed by hugs that made her feel worse for some reason.

And then Patsy arrived, and instead of nonspecific sympathy, the woman gave her a hug and pronounced, "You don't need a psychologist, honey. You need the Ghostbusters."

"Ha ha, very funny," Ashley said as she led the ladies into the solarium. "But I do not believe in ghosts."

"You don't have to believe. You can pretend, like Jackie and everyone else in this town does. And then you can market the heck out of your pirate ghost. I'm telling you, you're missing a bet. Everyone wants to stay at a haunted bed-and-breakfast, especially if they think they might come face-to-face with the ghost of a famous pirate."

"That's not the kind of guesthouse I want to run," Ashley said. "I know everyone in this town has turned pirates into kitschy tourist attractions. But I'm a Howland, and Grandmother would never approve of anything like that. Especially because of the family's connections to the famous buccaneer. Besides, Jackie already has an imagination that's gotten him into trouble with the principal of his school."

"Where is the child?" Patsy asked.

"He's upstairs, watching Star Wars for the umpteenth time. He'll let us know if he needs anything."

"He's a surprisingly self-sufficient child," Patsy pronounced as if that were a good thing. Patsy was particularly good at making pronouncements, and she was the only Piece Maker who didn't have any children.

The ladies sat down in a mismatched assortment of chairs around the antique quilt frame, which took up much of the solarium's floor space. They were working on a quilt designed by Karen Tighe, which she called "Gold Star Wife" because it featured eighteen large eight-point star blocks in gold calico, separated by smaller shoo-fly blocks in red, white, and blue cotton. The smaller blocks created a diagonal pattern that framed each of the stars. The quilt was a blatant homage to Ashley. But having to see those gold stars on a daily basis was a reminder of how drastically her life had changed. When Adam died, she'd refused to put a gold star in any of her windows.

She would be so happy when this quilt was finished and auctioned off at Heavenly Rest's Christmas bazaar. She sat down in one of the chairs and started threading her needle. Almost before she could knot the end of her thread, Karen started speaking. "Ladies, I know we all loved Reverend Ball, but we've got a new vicar who's supposed to be here any day, and near as I can see, no one has done one thing about cleaning the vicarage. It's been empty for the better part of nine months. All these months with a different substitute minister every week, we've all forgotten that we have an obligation to provide housing. I think we need to organize a cleaning crew."

Ashley cast her gaze around the quilt frame. There were a lot of guilty looks among the Episcopalians. The two Methodists looked down at their work.

"It's all over town, you know," Karen continued.

"About how we've got a St. Pierre as our new minister. And I think we need to take responsibility to make sure this doesn't turn into a disaster for the parish or the town. I'm glad the diocese sent Micah back to us. I remember him as a young man, worshipping with us. We don't want to make him feel unwelcome. That sort of thing could get around and cause unintended and unnecessary trouble."

"Exactly," Patsy said, nodding. "I think we should all show up on Saturday with mops and sponges."

"It's going to take more than that," Karen insisted.

"Well, then, we should think about starting a vicarage improvement fund with some of our weekly collection money," Patsy said.

"We were always trying to get Reverend Ball to take some money for improvements to that house. I think we should spend the money now," said Nancy. "And I'll clear my schedule for Saturday morning. Who has a key to the vicarage?"

"I do," said Ashley. "Grandmother was always running across the street when Reverend Ball got sick."

"Good. Now that that's settled, tell us all about Buddha girl," Patsy said.

Ashley looked up from her row of stitches. "Buddha girl?"

"The one I've seen searching for nirvana or whatever on Rose Cottage's front porch in the morning when I take my walk."

"I don't know much about her. She's from New York, and she's here for a month."

"She's from New York but she goes around town wearing a Boston Red Sox shirt? That's odd, don't you think?"

Ashley looked up. "You know, I never thought about

that, but her driver's license said New York, and her home address is in New York. I guess it's possible for a New Yorker to be a Boston fan, isn't it?"

"Not hardly likely," Patsy said. "And don't you think it's strange that she's rented the house for a month? In September?"

"Why is that such a surprise? It's nice here in September."

"True. But most people have to work. What kind of luggage did she have? Was it Louis Vuitton or Gucci?"

Patsy had an active imagination and probably could have written one of those cozy mystery books if she'd set her hand to it. Even when the truth wasn't very interesting, Patsy could embellish, sometimes spinning speculative "stories" about Ashley's tenants based on nothing more than their choice of luggage or sunglasses. Most of Ashley's guests were well-to-do, of course, so it made it easier to paint a picture, but...

Jenna Fairchild was different.

"Well, to be honest, she didn't have luggage. Just an old backpack that was—" Ashley bit off the rest of her sentence at the sound of footsteps coming through the back door into the kitchen.

Nancy giggled. "Looks like Buddha girl is making an evening cookie run."

Jenna was restless after the hearing. She walked home, made herself a salad, and sat on the porch for a while thinking about Harry and Jude talking together, until it made her itch. She wanted to *do* something, but she could almost hear the voice of her teacher in Mumbai telling her that she needed patience. Better to wait for a way to open up than to go blundering in making holes that can't be repaired.

Jenna was not a patient woman, which was why she'd embraced meditation when she was in college. Meditation was the only thing that kept her type-A personality in check, and her year-long study abroad had deepened her reliance on it. But tonight the activity at Howland House caught her attention.

The lights in the solarium drew her like a moth to a flame. Was Ashley's quilting circle meeting tonight? She couldn't remember which night of the week the group was scheduled. Maybe she could sit in and catch some local gossip.

She left the porch and headed across the garden and through the back door into the kitchen, where she scarfed another oatmeal cookie. But instead of continuing down the hall to the library, she turned right toward the solarium.

"Hi, everyone," she said in a friendly voice. "I'm Jenna Fairchild. It's nice to meet you all. And I just want to say that the quilts in the cottage are beautiful." Jenna took another step into the room, drawn by the red, white, blue, and gold calico of the quilt they were working on. "Oh. That's gorgeous. Is quilting hard to do? I'd love to learn how to—"

"Sorry, darlin'," one of the women said. "Our meetings are private."

It was like a slap in the face. Jenna took a step back. "Sorry. I didn't mean—"

Ashley stood up and headed in her direction, ushering her back into the kitchen. "I'm sorry. The Piece Makers are kind of funny about outsiders." She leaned in with another one of her smiles that didn't quite reach her eyes. "We're terrible gossips, I'm afraid."

"Sorry I intruded." Jenna backpedaled some more and pointed over her shoulder with her thumb. "I'll be in the library." She turned to go but stopped and glanced over her shoulder. "Oh, I almost forgot. Would you thank Bill for the book? It was exactly what I needed."

"Bill?" Ashley's big brown eyes widened with a look of…what? Shock? Surprise? Horror? Wow. Like maybe she didn't want people to know that she had a secret boyfriend or something.

"I'm sorry. I was talking about Captain Bill?"

Ashley's face paled. "You've met Cap'n Bill?"

Jenna turned to face Ashley once again. "Um, no, actually. But Jackie…this morning…he told me that Bill left a book about sailing for me. In the library. I found it on the table, and I just assumed…you know…that Bill was your boyfriend or something."

Ashley's mouth fell open.

"Sorry. I guess I'm not supposed to know that. You can rest assured that—"

"No," Ashley said, shaking her head, "that's not it. Jenna, there is no Captain Bill. He's a historical figure that Jackie has turned into an imaginary friend."

Before Jenna could fully process Ashley's words, one of the quilters strolled into the kitchen and said, "What did I just tell you, honey? You've got a ghost that you ought to be promoting." She patted Ashley's shoulder in a familiar way, and yet they didn't look related.

The older woman was well past sixty, with short, almost platinum hair and a pair of tortoiseshell half-glasses perched on her nose. She wore pleated khakis, a navy-blue cotton cardigan, and a white man-tailored shirt open at the collar to expose a set of pearls. A red, white, and blue nautical-themed scarf, tied in a neat square knot, completed her ensemble.

Ashley turned and gave the woman an eye roll. "I'm sure there's some other explanation. In fact, now that I think about it, our last guests were avid sailors. Mr. Taylor was always in the library reading our collection on sailboats. He probably left the book out on the table."

Ashley turned back toward Jenna with another one of her innkeeper smiles. "I'm sorry for the confusion. And please, the next time Jackie bothers you, tell him to come on home. I'm afraid he has a big imagination. And he knows good and well that he's not supposed to bother our guests."

"Big" was not the word Jenna would use to describe Jackie's imagination. She'd call it odd. Odd because it was strange for a six-year-old to tell a grown woman that she was "a prize worth taking." The kid must have heard that somewhere. And even if Mr. Taylor had left the book on the table, how had Jackie known that she wanted to learn sailing terms? It was a mystery.

She shifted her gaze back to the woman in the Hermès scarf. "I'm sorry I gate-crashed your meeting. I didn't mean to upset—"

"Oh, for goodness' sake, don't listen to Donna. She's a Methodist with a bee up her butt. If you truly want to learn how to quilt, Louella Pender down at A Stitch in Time, the local yarn and fabric store, has weekly lessons on Saturday afternoons. They're fun, and she's a good teacher. I'm Patsy Bauman, by the way. Pleased to meet you." The woman took Jenna's hand and gave it a firm shake while Jenna's heart rate zoomed into the stratosphere.

Patsy Bauman? Holy crap. Patricia Bauman was a member of Ashley's quilting club. And here Jenna had been utterly consumed with her effort to meet her uncle without even once thinking about the woman who'd married him. How blind could a person be?

"Also," Patsy said as she dropped Jenna's hand, "I'm one of the believers."

"We're all believers, Patsy," Ashley said on what could only be described as an exasperated sigh.

"Oh, I don't mean believing in the Lord. I mean ghosts. I believe this house is haunted. In fact, Miz Fairchild, you should know that the ghost prefers to spend his time haunting the cottage. And when you leave here, you might want to tell all your friends about that. Ashley can use all the word-of-mouth advertising she can get." Patsy gave Jenna a wide, genuine smile and then returned to the solarium. Out of sight.

"Please don't," Ashley said. "There's no ghost, and I'm not that desperate."

Except, for some reason, looking into Ashley's big brown eyes, Jenna got the impression of a woman who *was* desperate. And maybe hanging on by her fingertips.

Chapter Six————————

Jude sat at his small desk at Barrier Island Charters waiting for Jenna to arrive. He kept an eye on the tacky marlin with a clock in its belly, which Daddy had put up during Jude's junior year at Howard University. Jude had tried to get Daddy to take the damn thing down, but Daddy could be stubborn as a mule most of the time. One day, when Daddy wasn't looking, he was going take that fish off the wall and burn it.

It was 9:45 a.m., and Jude was feeling oddly nervous about Jenna's arrival.

Was he deceptive enough to lead her on? Last night at dinner, Greg had given him a long list of questions to ask, any one of which was likely to raise her suspicions. And Jude was a lousy liar.

He would much rather confront the woman and send her packing, but Greg didn't want him to do that. Greg wanted him to tease out her secrets. Try to figure out how she intended to co-opt him or members of his family.

It all seemed a little clandestine to Jude.

The sound of someone banging on the front door pulled him from his sour thoughts. He looked up toward the front window, and there stood Jenna Fairchild, wearing a pair of cutoffs that officially classified as Daisy Dukes and peering through the window in the gaps between the fishing photos Daddy had Scotch-taped to the window when Jude had taken a vacation three years ago.

Well, here went nothing.

He got up and opened the door onto her big smile. Gone was the enigmatic Mona Lisa curl at the corner of her mouth. This smile was like a full-frontal assault. And it knocked him back. Damn. He liked her smile. And he liked the way the morning sun lit up all that gold in her hair.

"I'm here for my lesson," she announced, her voice kind of bouncy or something.

And he suddenly didn't want to play this game. "Look," he said, stepping back into the office, giving her room to follow him, "I'm not a sailing instructor."

She cocked her head. "Oh no, are we back to that again?"

"Why did you come to me for lessons?"

Her smile faded, and she blinked a couple of times. She was one hell of a good actress because he got the feeling she was truly surprised by his attitude. "I picked you because you looked competent. And I admire competence." She cast her gaze over the office, especially the stupid clock and the photos with their curling edges.

Jude flat-out hated that judgmental look in Jenna's eyes. Like she was the high-and-mighty executive from

Santee Resorts looking down her turned-up little nose at him and his small business.

Well, that was the last straw. Tomorrow he was taking down the redneck clock and the fading photos, and he didn't give a crap whether Daddy liked it or not. It wasn't as if Daddy was running the business these days. Jude suddenly wanted to take Jenna out on the ocean on *Reel Therapy*. The Striker might be older than a lot of other boats, but she was shipshape. Jude took a lot of pride in keeping her that way.

He squared his shoulders. He was not going to let this little slip of a woman get the best of him. "So, you're a judge of sailing competence, then?" he asked, folding his arms across his chest.

Her smile returned, a little smaller this time, maybe a little slier. "Um, okay, so you have me there. What if I told you I liked the cut of your jib?"

He snorted a laugh. "I'd say that you didn't know what that meant."

"And you'd be right. I didn't at the time. But I do now."

He shook his head. "I just don't get it. What is it that you want from me?"

"Lessons?" Her eyebrows arched, and her expression was so adorably innocent.

He studied her cutoffs and worn-out flip-flops. If she was a spy from Santee Resort Group, she didn't look the part. But then, Santee Resorts wouldn't have sent a woman in a suit to mess with his head.

"I just doubled my price," he said. "I don't think you can afford five hundred dollars an hour."

"Oh." Her mouth pinched into a kissable O.

"Yeah, I thought so."

She blew out a breath and then dug in her purse, coming up with a wallet, from which she pulled an American Express platinum card. "Okay."

Damn. Should he confront her or just take her money?

In the back of his head, a small voice that sounded a lot like Greg Rushford suggested that taking her money would be appropriate, seeing as she'd come here to spy on him and she was clearly working for a corporation that had no respect for what he was trying to save. He sure didn't have to tell her anything about anything if he didn't want to. He could simply make her pay and then take her out for capsize drills.

Now, that was amusing. The idea of anyone paying a grand for two hours of being unceremoniously and repeatedly dumped overboard was downright hilarious.

"It's your money," he said. "But I told you, the sailing school in Georgetown is cheaper, and the instructors there are all certified."

She crossed her arms. "And I'm telling you that I'm not interested in certified instructors. I want you."

Had she lost her mind spending a thousand dollars for two hours with Jude in a small boat?

Probably. In her life before her grandfather dumped his money on her, she would have never done anything so outrageous. In fact, for the last year she'd hardly touched her allowance. She'd lived at the ashram for months, doing chores, scrubbing floors, cooking for others.

But she had no choice. Jude knew Harry, and she had to find some way to get him to introduce her. When you considered the personal stakes, spending a thousand dollars for two hours in a boat didn't seem like too much at all. Especially since she had the money, and by the seedy looks of Barrier Island Charters's office, Jude could probably use the income.

She gave him the American Express card that Milo had arranged for her—of course it was a platinum card; Milo wouldn't have settled for anything less. Jude ran the charge, and they headed down to the boatyard to get *Bonney Rose* ready to sail, a process that required setting up her mast, rigging her sails, and replacing the broken hiking strap.

Before they set sail, Jude bought a couple of ham sandwiches and some bottled water from Rafferty's, which he put into a big waterproof bag and stuffed into the cubby in the bow where the boat's sails and PFDs were stored.

On Wednesday they'd sailed around the harbor, but today Jude turned the boat south along Jonquil Island's western coastline, thick with salt marshes. As they sailed, they fell into an easy rhythm of tacking while Jude gave her a tour of this portion of the bay. He knew these waters, the fish that lived here, the way the landmasses affected the winds. His voice conveyed his love for this beautiful paradise.

Jude relaxed as they sailed, and his killer smile came out to shine like the sun above them. That smile triggered a deep and unwanted yearning in Jenna's core. Her life was complicated right now, and getting involved with anyone would be a mistake. And yet she could imagine herself having a little fling with this man.

Whoa, girl. Better focus on the sails and not the skipper.

They dropped anchor right in a little cove where the water was shallow and ate their sandwiches.

"So, I have a question," he said.

She smiled at him. "I know. You're wondering why I spent so much money for this lesson, right?"

His lips twitched. "Well, yeah. But that wasn't my question."

"Oh?"

"Why were you at the town hall meeting yesterday?"

Uh-oh. She should have seen that one coming. And for the life of her, she couldn't remember what she'd said when he'd first asked that question yesterday. Her face heated. "I'm interested in business," she said.

"Ah, so you're not in favor of the petition, then."

"I didn't say that."

"What kind of business are you interested in?"

"All kinds of business. I have an MBA. I think the fight between preservation and development is interesting."

"You make that sound like it's an academic question."

He had her there. For Jenna it was. For Jude it was anything but. She blew out a breath. "I was very impressed by your passion," she said.

He slipped his sunglasses down on his nose and gave her a wicked look out of those tawny eyes. "That sounds condescending."

Her face heated. "I'm sorry. I didn't mean it that way. I was truly moved by what you said and how you said it. If I had a culture that was disappearing, I'd feel the same way."

"Would you?"

"Are you angry with me for something specific, or is this just you having a chip on your shoulder?"

His eyes widened. "What's that supposed to mean?"

"It means that I can't possibly understand how you

feel. But I can admire you for the way you express yourself. In fact, you made me curious. I spent some time yesterday reading up about Gullah culture."

"Good for you," he said, crumpling up his sandwich wrapping. He didn't sound as if he was all that approving though.

But before she could press him further, he said, "Lunch is over. It's time to get wet."

"Get wet?"

"Yeah. We're doing capsize drills. Didn't I tell you?"

"Uh, no, I don't think so."

"Well, we are. It's an important part of sailing." He hauled up the anchor and got under way again while Jenna's heart rate skyrocketed. She wasn't sure she wanted to experience another capsize. But she had the feeling that protesting his plans would be futile.

A moment later, he said, "Okay, be ready. In a minute I'm going to do something stupid that's going to cause the boat to heel up and go over. When that happens—even before water spills over the leeward gunwales—you need to crawl over the windward edge and get to the centerboard. Do not let go of the jib sheet."

"Aye," she said, trying to parse out all the new vocabulary. Suddenly all her academic study went right out of her head, and her heart rate climbed even higher.

An instant later, the boat heeled up. She freaked. *Bonney Rose* rolled over on her side, dumping both of them backward into the bay.

"Well, that didn't go too well," Jude said. "But at least you're still holding the jib sheet."

She glanced at the line in her hand. How had that happened?

"I'm going to show you how to right the boat." He directed her to float alongside the cockpit while he clambered up on the centerboard and rocked the boat upright. As the boat rolled, *Bonney Rose* scooped Jenna up, and she found herself ignominiously sprawled over the centerboard cap.

"Okay," she said, climbing over the blocks and cleats that seemed hell-bent on bruising her. "How do we get the water out of the boat?" There was at least six inches inside.

He grinned at her, as if he were thoroughly enjoying this opportunity to make her feel dumb. "Not a problem," he said as he opened a couple of latches on the bottom of the boat. He took the tiller, turned the boat into a tack, and *Bonney Rose* lumbered into motion like a heavy bathtub. But as they moved, the water flowed out of the latches in the bottom of the boat, and within a couple of minutes they were sailing at speed once again. "These racing boats are built for any disaster you can imagine," he said. "So, let's try it again, shall we?"

"What, going over?" she asked.

He smiled. "Yup."

"But—"

"I'm teaching you fundamentals here. Capsize drills are super important if you want to sail fast."

Well, that shut her up. She ground her teeth and endured as he made the boat capsize two more times, all with the same result. The first time, he made her climb on the centerboard and rock the boat upright. And after the second time, she fully understood why the object of this lesson was to stay inside the boat and not get dumped overboard.

"Getting up on the centerboard is exhausting," she said, wishing there were enough room inside the small cockpit for her to stretch out and take a nap.

"Yup. And just think about how much harder it would be in deep water."

She gave him a venomous look, which bounced right off his beautifully sculpted body. He was having way too much fun, as if he was trying to teach her more than a sailing lesson. What was up with that? "Why do you hate me?"

His brow lowered. "I don't hate you."

"Okay, if you don't hate me, then why don't we find a nice beach somewhere and—"

"No. You hired me to teach you how to sail, remember? And just to be clear, I don't get involved with tourists."

"What? I didn't—"

"I know. Get ready. We're going to do this again."

"But this isn't sailing."

He pushed his sunglasses down his nose and gave her another look that made her swallow back the tart remark she'd been about to give him. Instead, she nodded and said, "Okay, let's do this thing."

Jude got the boat moving again, the self-bailers draining water from its cockpit. "Ready?" he shouted.

"Ready, aye," she responded, feeling slightly silly but determined.

The boat heeled up. Water spilled over the edge. But this time, instead of freaking out, Jenna threw one leg over the side, riding the boat like a horse. Her foot found the centerboard. She stood, throwing her weight back. The boat came back up in the water.

She knew a moment of true exhilaration. Right before the jib sheet slipped from her hand and *Bonney Rose* ignominiously dumped her overboard.

"Good work," Jude shouted from his spot in the back of the boat as *Bonney Rose* sailed away from her.

He was teaching her a lesson, but which lesson was hard to figure out. He was mad at her about something. Probably some stupid, ignorant, and insensitive thing she'd said about his culture. That's what she got for complimenting him on his passion.

"Don't worry," he shouted as the boat got farther away. "I'm executing the man-overboard drill." Just when she thought he was about to abandon her, he tacked the boat.

Wow, he was impressive, single-handedly controlling the tiller and the mainsail and the jib as he executed a figure eight and brought *Bonney Rose* right alongside her. He stood up in the back of the boat, managing to keep it flat and stable. "Grab the shroud and climb back in."

Jenna did as she was instructed, secretly thrilled that she'd understood what a shroud was. She pushed herself up on the gunwales, but even in shallow water, getting back in the boat required more upper-body strength than she possessed.

When she was about to give up, Jude grabbed her arms and hauled her back into the boat. She fell forward against him for an instant, her whole body registering the hard muscles in his chest. The boat rocked unsteadily, and an eternity passed as he took her by the shoulders and steadied her. He'd lost his sunglasses, and she lost her breath as she gazed into his amber eyes.

Hormones Jenna had forgotten she possessed flooded

through her system. She might have lost her mind and kissed him if he hadn't sent her back to snag the tiller and keep the boat from dumping them both again.

Okay, so maybe that explained his behavior. She was hot for him, and he was so not hot for her. So maybe a few more dunkings would cool down her suddenly raging libido.

She found her position in the front of the boat, inwardly scolding herself for letting her hormones take charge. She turned back to glance at him, prepared to see him scowl. But instead a slow smile blossomed on his face like a rare flower, revealing white, white teeth against his dark skin. "Next time you need to remember to climb back into the boat after it starts to flatten. Let's do it one more time."

It was a challenge now. She pointed right at him. "Let's go."

He nodded, and *Bonney Rose* took off. This time, when the boat heeled up and the water started coming over the side, she was too tired and too determined to panic. She moved up and over the edge in slow motion, her foot finding the centerboard.

Jude was right there with her this time, climbing up onto the gunwale while holding the mainsail sheet, which he'd uncleated with a flick of his wrist. The sails flapped, and the boat began to roll back to an upright position. She pushed off the centerboard and ended up in the cockpit as the boat settled back down, mast upright, in the water.

"Holy crap. I did it," she said. Then she turned toward him. "But you helped this time."

He nodded. "I know. That's what I'm supposed to do."

"What?"

"When the boat broaches like that, it's not just the crew that has to get it back under control."

"Wait a minute. Are you saying you could have helped me every time?"

He grinned. "Yup."

Damn. He didn't know what to make of Jenna Fairchild. If she'd been sent by Santee Resorts to spy on him, then they'd done a real good job of sending someone with a sense of humor.

She'd taken his abuse and then some. She'd complained a little, but she hadn't whined once. She hadn't cried. She hadn't gotten frustrated. And it bothered him a little that she thought he had a chip on his shoulder.

But how could he trust anything she said about her reasons for being here? She was obviously not a tourist in the usual sense. And she had money to burn, as evidenced by her platinum AMEX card.

He aimed *Bonney Rose* north toward Magnolia Harbor, letting the sun dry his skin as he studied the way she managed the jib. She'd learned something today. And she had a nimble grace that he admired.

And then there had been that moment when she'd stumbled into him during the man-overboard drill. Damn. His whole body had reacted in a totally adolescent manner.

Is that what Santee Resorts had sent her for?

If so, they were freaking geniuses. Despite his rules about golden-haired tourists, Jenna Fairchild turned him on in a way no other woman had in a very long time. But she stood against everything he was trying to protect. And he truly resented the fact that she'd tried to compliment him on his passion.

He could almost taste the disappointment on his tongue. A man could get used to sitting back here watching her cute ass as she ducked under the boom with every tack. He could get used to the light that glimmered in her brown eyes when she figured something out. He could get used to her.

Without a doubt, that's why the enemy sent her here.

He headed for the dock, and she managed to furl the jib and hop up onto the pier as if she'd been doing it all her life. Good God, maybe she had been doing it all her life and she'd just been playing dumb the whole time. Man, that really steamed him.

He studied her while she helped him get *Bonney Rose* onto the trailer. She was one hell of a good actress, peppering him with questions about the rigging, pretending she really didn't know the first thing about folding sails.

When the boat was put up, she turned toward him with a cocked head. "Want to get a bite to eat at Rafferty's? I'll buy."

Why was that such a temptation, when he knew damn well she was a liar? He hated liars, but for some weird reason, he liked Jenna Fairchild. Which made no sense, of course. Not logically anyway.

He shook his head. "No. Sorry. I can't. I've got a big charter coming in tomorrow, and I need to get *Reel Therapy* ready. Maybe some other time." In truth, the boat was shipshape, but that might not be true of Daddy.

"When can I get another lesson?"

Damn. "Uh, look, I—"

"I'm willing to pay whatever rate you name."

Of course she was; it wasn't coming out of her pocket. "I don't know. I need to check my schedule."

"I'll call you," she said, and then turned and walked away, the sun lighting up her windblown hair like a halo.

He watched for a long time. That glow was misleading. The woman didn't have a halo. He checked his waterproof sailing watch. It was well after one in the afternoon. He needed to intercept Daddy before he got too friendly with a bottle of Jack.

He needed Daddy sharp and sober tomorrow because it took two people to manage *Reel Therapy* on a fishing charter. One person to pilot the boat and another to schmooze the clients. Daddy was real good at the latter, but only if he wasn't recovering from one of his benders. This time of year, as the business slacked off for the season, Daddy had too much time on his hands, and that was always a problem.

If only Daddy would go to rehab and get himself sober. Jude had been pressuring him for a long, long time. Last winter, he'd thought his father had finally seen the light. Jude had checked Daddy into the rehab center in Georgetown, but Daddy had left after only three days, insisting that he didn't need to talk 24/7 about his feelings and life's disappointments. Talking about those things just made him want to get a drink.

After that fiasco, Colton told Jude he should walk away.

But it wasn't that easy. Jude could get a job working at any of the charter companies on Jonquil Island. He was respected by the other captains, and he had his master coast guard certification. He knew these waters like the back of his hand—better than many other captains. But he didn't want to work for *the man*. He wanted to work for himself. Like Daddy had. Like Granddaddy had. Hell,

Colton worked for himself. He should understand, but he didn't.

The way Jude saw it, it was time for him to take over the family business. But Daddy was hanging on to it for dear life. The boat's title was in Daddy's name. The lease on the office space was in Daddy's name. Jude couldn't just kick Daddy out, even if Daddy had no business captaining a boat anymore.

If Jude walked away, Daddy wouldn't shut down the business. He'd try to run it, and he'd take some unsuspecting tourist out on the water and get himself into trouble. Jude wasn't going to let that happen. He had a responsibility to keep people safe.

This was the definition of being caught between a rock and a hard place. But someone had to keep Daddy safe from his own worst intentions. If not Jude, then who? Not Colton, who'd given up on Daddy. Not Momma, who'd walked out on Daddy. And not Micah, who'd abandoned them all to pursue his own career.

There wasn't anyone else to do it.

These sour thoughts swirled in Jude's head as he walked up Palmetto Street to the Alibi, a dive bar on the corner of Lilac and Palmetto, which had been in business for a good forty years under the same management. This explained the garish COCKTAILS sign above the storefront windows. Advertising cocktails had once been a big deal back in the 1970s, when prohibition had finally ended in South Carolina.

The old sign had seen better days. It was missing a few letters, so it now spelled out TAIL in fading pink neon. Quite ironic, since no woman (respectable or otherwise) had set foot in the Alibi since the Clinton administration.

The place was dark inside, lit by a couple of Miller and Bud signs and a few dirty pendant lights over a long U-shaped bar. There was nothing special about the Alibi. It didn't have trendy exposed-brick walls hung with local art or a menu heavy on oysters and clams or local specialties that featured okra or grits. It had no views of the bay, and it didn't even have a television.

It was more like a cave, floored in dirty green and black checkerboard linoleum. It reeked of beer and cheap whiskey with overtones of mildew, the result of the roof leak that had watermarked the ceiling tiles. Tourists didn't come here. It was a haven for the weary who needed a place to numb themselves to life's pain. Right now, some old George Strait torch song about lost love was playing on the jukebox.

It took a moment for Jude's eyes to adjust to the gloom before he saw Daddy at the end of the bar, a longneck beer in front of him. Well, at least he wasn't drinking hard liquor.

Jude crossed the room and took the seat to Daddy's left. "Hey," he said.

His father turned a pair of dark eyes in his direction. "Where you been? I thought you'd be out washing down *Reel Therapy*."

"I was with a client."

Daddy's eyebrows rose, wrinkling his brow. "What kind of client?"

"I just earned a grand giving a sailing lesson to someone who's on your side of the fight."

"What fight?"

"The fight over our land."

"Well, it's good to know that you're not above taking

his money," Daddy grumbled, then took a long pull on his beer.

"*Her* money. The client was a woman."

"Well, that explains everything." Daddy put his beer on the bar. "You're pissing in the wind, boy. You know that. When our ship comes in, we'll be riding high on the hog."

Jonas Quick, who was anything but fast, chose that moment to notice Jude's arrival. The old man hollered down the bar, "Ya want somethin', Jude?"

"I'll have a Coke," he replied.

Jonas shook his head as if to say that Jude was wasting his time. He shuffled away, an ancient relic, like his bar.

Jude turned back toward his father. "Daddy, Santee Resorts isn't going to give us much for that land. And once you sell out, you'll need to find another place to live. You'll probably have to get a mortgage. That resort is not your ship coming in."

Daddy shrugged. "College boy. You and Colton both, always being so smart about stuff you don't even know nothing about."

That was a constant refrain. Some parents were proud of their kids' accomplishments. Daddy, not so much.

"Look, Daddy, I know how to fix what's wrong with Barrier Island Charters. All it will take is a bank loan. With a line of credit, we can beef up our advertising and get the business back in the guidebook and on the tourist map. We can also add some new tech to the boat. It wouldn't take all that much to make it the best charter on the island."

"We don't need any of that."

Jude blew out a frustrated breath and balled his fists. He loved his father, but he was at his wit's end. Between them, he and Daddy had more fishing knowledge and experience than 90 percent of the other charter captains out there. They were the best fishing guides on Jonquil Island.

They should be succeeding, especially since Jude had gotten his coast guard masters certification and even taught boat safety for the sailing club. He knew more than Daddy, really, because Daddy had never learned to sail, and sailing was harder than captaining a boat with a motor.

Jude knew the winds and the tides as well as the fishing grounds. He'd made the study of Moonlight Bay the work of a lifetime. He would put his knowledge and experience up against anyone's. He was totally confident out there on the water. But here on dry land, he was under Daddy's thumb.

Daddy was the reason their business was shrinking instead of growing. Daddy drank too much. He made stupid mistakes out on the water. And either he didn't understand the company's balance sheet or he just refused to pay attention to the numbers.

They needed a line of credit, which wasn't a bad thing. Every growing business needed access to capital. Didn't Daddy understand that? Apparently not.

It was the most frustrating thing in the world to be part of a family business but to have no control. Everything was in Daddy's name. It wasn't like Old Granny's land, where at least he owned a share and could have a say. No. He did all the work, managed the books, and kept the boat going. But Daddy's name was on everything, specifically *Reel Therapy*, their main asset.

Jude pounded his fist on the bar, the frustration mounting to the breaking point. "Dammit, Daddy," he said in a savage whisper, "if you hadn't taken out part of the pier last year, we wouldn't be struggling under the high insurance premiums, and we wouldn't have had to cut back on the advertising. Can't you see that you're driving Barrier Island Charters into the ground?"

"I am not. If we're failing, it's your fault. In my day, I didn't whine to my daddy about credit lines and borrowing money. I just worked my butt off for him. How many times I gotta tell you, we ain't borrowing any money? That's the most important thing about business that Granddaddy taught me. Never borrow a cent. And you know what? He didn't lose his business to bankers like a lot of others did."

This conversation always ended with Daddy bringing up Granddaddy's prohibition against borrowing money. Unfortunately, in Granddaddy's time, the advice had probably been good. Black folks didn't get fair loans, if they could even get a loan. But things were different today. And every other captain on the bay had a line of credit. Cash flow could be an issue with a seasonal business like theirs. But trying to get Daddy to unlearn this lesson was like sailing into the wind.

"And you know what else?" Daddy asked, pounding the bar. "You're just flat-out crazy if you think you can fix up Old Granny's house and turn it into a bed-and-breakfast. That old place is more of a shack than my place. History tourists. Lord have mercy. I heard what you said yesterday. What a load of crap." Daddy shook his head and finished his beer just as Jonas arrived with Jude's Coke.

"I'll have a Jack neat," Daddy said.

"No, he won't. Just total the tab, Jonas."

Daddy scowled at him. "Since when do you tell me what to do?"

It was an old argument. "Daddy, we have a charter tomorrow. Which means we have work to do right now. And I get to tell you what to do because I'm the only one who hasn't abandoned you."

"That's not true. I see Colton every once in a while, and you've heard that Micah is coming back."

"Every once in a while? Every time Colton comes around, you two end up arguing or worse. And Micah's been gone for half my life. So don't talk to me about my brothers. I'm here. I've always been here. And without me, Barrier Island Charters would have sunk years ago."

Daddy hung his head. "Yeah, I guess." He looked up, his eyes kind of shiny in the dim light. "I really appreciate it, Jude. You know that."

Damn. Daddy had been drinking beers for a while, hadn't he?

"Yeah. I do know it," Jude said gently. How could he walk away from this man? He couldn't. Bottom line, he still loved the bastard, and he'd promised to stick with him come hell or high water.

Chapter Seven————————

Saturday dawned clear and warm. Jenna finished her morning routine by nine and found herself at loose ends without sailing lessons to occupy her. And it was still a day away from Sunday, when she planned to attend the Church at Heavenly Rest, where she'd discovered that Patsy Bauman chaired the Altar Guild. Right now, her path to a relationship with Patsy seemed clearer than the path to her uncle.

She had no idea how to use Jude to meet Harry. And after the way he'd behaved on Friday, she wasn't sure she wanted to use him that way. In truth, she was far too attracted to him. He'd even invaded her dreams. Night after night, she dreamed about sailing, but not in a small boat. No. She dreamed of a big boat with old-fashioned square sails and a captain with a dark complexion and tawny eyes. Her dreams were like the old pirate movies featuring a stunningly handsome man with a ring in his ear, a cutlass at his hip, and a musket tucked into his waistband.

Clearly the pirate culture of Jonquil Island was invading her subconscious.

With nothing better to do, she decided to go shopping. She strolled from the cottage down to the main business district, stopped in at Bread, Butter, and Beans for coffee and a scone, and then played tourist, ducking into shops along the way.

The Treasure Chest, a seasonal souvenir shop with a clichéd pirate theme, was open, and she bought herself a new pair of flip-flops. The shop had a ridiculously large collection of pirate-themed T-shirts similar to the one Tim Meyer had worn the day he and Kyra had rescued her.

Daffy Down Dilly, a high-end gift shop selling all things daffodil, had an interesting concept, and she eyed a sundress with daffodils around its hemline but didn't buy it because it was too expensive. But the store, with all its daffodils, left Jenna thinking about her mother. Daffodils had been Mom's favorite flower. So much so that she'd insisted there be as many as possible at her funeral—not an easy task since Mom had died in December two years before Milo Stracham had darkened her door with his surprising news.

Mom had been a role model. A single mother who had doggedly worked to earn a college degree. A woman who was fiercely independent and who had taught Jenna the value of self-reliance. Jenna stood in the middle of Daffy Down Dilly and had a poignant moment. She missed her mom. And if she couldn't build a relationship with Harry and Patsy Bauman, she'd remain a family-less person. She'd always been family-less, really. But today it seemed like a heavy burden to bear.

She pushed the sudden sadness away, wiped an errant

tear from her eye, and left the gift store to continue down
Harbor Drive until she spied A Stitch in Time, the fabric
shop Patsy had mentioned.

Now, there was an idea. Maybe she could talk her way
into one of Ashley's quilting bees if she took a quilting lesson at the yarn store. At the very least, she'd have
something to say to Patsy tomorrow when she cornered
her at church.

Jenna stepped into the narrow store, which had wide-
plank wood floors and a comfy-looking couch and chair
in the front window, where several older women sat
knitting and chatting.

Cubbies of bright yarn lined the right wall of the shop,
while bolts of cloth, most of it cotton prints, lined the left.
A checkout counter stood in middle with a cutting area on
one side and a point-of-sale on the other.

Everything about the shop was bright and cheery,
starting with yellow paint and the daffodil wallpaper.
Jenna hadn't taken more than three steps into the store
before a fiftysomething woman with short hair dyed
candy-apple red approached and asked, "Can I help you
find something?"

"Um, well, I'm here for the quilting lessons. I'm staying at Rose Cottage, and the other night I met Patsy
Bauman at the quilting bee, and she suggested that this
was the place to learn quilting."

The woman chuckled. "It's not a quilting bee, dear.
That's the weekly meeting of the Piece Makers. And I'm
sure they sent you to me because they're a bunch of snobs."

"Oh."

The woman smiled, her face filled with happy expression lines. She extended her hand. "I'm Louella Pender.

My mother started this store around the same time as Mrs. Howland started the Piece Makers. That was just after Pearl Harbor, you know. My word, those ladies have bought a lot of cloth here. But you have to be someone to quilt with them."

"Someone?"

"From one of the older families in town. You have to be born a Howland or a Harrington or a Martin or a Rains. Those families were all here at the beginning, and I'm quite sure every member of the Piece Makers comes from one of those families. Ashley Scott, who was born a Howland, may be younger than the rest of them, but she's carrying on her granny's traditions like they were written in stone. I tell you what, those ladies are a tight-knit group. Now, what did you say your name was?"

"I'm Jenna...Fairchild." She tripped over the phony last name, not for the first time. "I got that impression, but they sent me here for quilting lessons. How do I sign up?"

Louella stopped and gave Jenna's worn camp pants and faded tank top the once-over as if the woman was starting to question Jenna's honesty because she didn't look like the type of person who booked a five-star B and B. She needed to reassure the woman before she clammed up. "I'm staying at Rose Cottage for a month to recover from my trip," she said. "I've been traveling all over the world this past year. Just me and my backpack. But I'm on my way home at the end of the month."

"And where is home? Boston, maybe? I'm just guessing from your accent."

She nodded. "Yes."

"And what do you do there?"

Wow, Louella was collecting information to add to her

gossip stream. Jenna needed to tread carefully but give her as much truth as possible. "I'm a businesswoman. I used to work in the business development department of a Fortune Five Hundred company. But that was before I decided to take a year off to travel."

Louella's smile returned. "Lucky you. I've been living here my entire life. I'd love to go to Italy. Did you go there?"

Jenna shook her head. "No. India, China, Tibet mostly. Then I sailed home across the Pacific, stopped off at the Galápagos Islands, and then spent a little time in South America."

"Wow. No wonder you look a little threadbare."

Jenna smiled. "So, are there quilting lessons?"

Louella frowned. "Honey, I teach people how to make a quilt top. For that you need a sewing machine. And I can't think of a time when a tourist ever came in here looking for lessons. That Patsy has a weird sense of humor sometimes."

"Oh. So you mean she sent me here just to get rid of me, huh?" So much for thinking that the path to Patsy Bauman was easier than the path to Uncle Harry.

"Honey, if you want to learn, you should do it when you get back home. And don't mind Patsy. She's kind of dictatorial at times. She was born a Harrington, and that's an old family around here. And she married very well too." Louella leaned in a little closer still. "Patsy's husband is Robert Bauman's younger brother. You know, the sunglass magnate?"

Jenna willed her body to stillness despite the sudden rush of adrenaline. "Didn't Robert Bauman pass away recently? I think I read about that in the *Wall Street Journal*."

"He sure did. And I don't mean to tell tales out of school, but I think Harry and Patsy were surprised when they didn't inherit a penny of Robert's estate. It all went to an illegitimate granddaughter no one knew anything about except Robert himself."

"Illegitimate?" Jenna asked. She hated that word. So many newspaper articles about her inheritance had taken pains to point out that Mom and Jamie Bauman had never married. And as far as Jenna knew, they'd hardly known each other.

"Well, so they say. And with billions of dollars on the table, I'm sure they did a DNA test to make sure she truly was his heir. But the thing is, I don't see Jamie Bauman as the kind of man who would father a child out of wedlock. Jamie was Robert's son, you know. And I knew him some. He spent his summers here with his aunt and uncle. I met him in vacation Bible school when I was about ten. He and I are the same age. Or would be, if he hadn't died. He was a quiet boy, and a religious one."

"He died young?" she asked, knowing the answer but hoping Louella would add more details.

"Oh, dear me, very young. Only twenty-two years old."

"Oh. What happened?" It took all of Jenna's willpower to keep her voice neutral as her heart hammered away in her chest. Louella Pender was the first person she'd ever spoken to, besides her mother, who had actually known her father. That thought humbled her. She wanted to know so much about him.

"He was out sailing in that small boat he loved so much," Louella said. "What did he call that thing? Oh, yes, I remember. *Independence.* He used to say that out there on the water was the only place he felt independent.

Anyway, he died on a clear day. No weather, no high winds, nothing. They found *Independence* near the inlet, capsized. Jamie's body turned up a few days later, way down the bay. He wasn't wearing a life vest. And you know what? To this day, there are some folks who think he might have been murdered, or worse."

"What's worse than murder?" Jenna asked, her voice shaky.

"Suicide," Louella whispered with a firm shake of her head. She stepped back with a dismissive wave. "My, but listen to me go on. Now, how about I fix you up with a learn-to-knit kit for a nice scarf? Honey, you can take knitting anywhere, but quilting requires a dedicated space."

A tropical storm had formed out in the Atlantic overnight. It wasn't close enough to threaten the coast, but it was near enough to send bands of heavy rain on shore starting in the wee hours of Sunday morning. By dawn, when Jenna left her bed for her yoga hour, the rain had let up, but the bay looked angry, roiling with whitecaps.

The weather didn't deter Jenna from her plan to corner Patsy at church. She wanted to ask her aunt so many questions about her father, and Patsy would be a much better source of information than Louella Pender. Jenna had a feeling Louella might be guilty of embellishing her stories.

Jenna didn't for one minute think her father had committed suicide. There were lots of easier ways to end a life than taking a boat out into dangerous waters and drowning yourself. And murder seemed overly dramatic and far-fetched.

More important, even though Jenna had limited sailing experience, she could see dozens of scenarios where someone might not put on their PFD or someone would take it off the way she'd done in order to escape the capsizing boat when Jude's hiking strap had broken. Jude had also demonstrated that falling out of a boat was entirely possible. And sailboats didn't have brakes. You could fall out of a boat, and it would continue sailing for a while.

All the unanswered questions remained, so she pulled out her once-new Gore-Tex rain jacket and headed off to church.

The Church at Heavenly Rest occupied a spot south of Magnolia Harbor's business district. It sat back from Ash Street in a grove of pines and live oaks, hidden from view by long trails of Spanish moss. Only a few blades of coarse grass clung to life in the sandy churchyard. The church itself was made of wood and painted white. It was, in almost every way, the antithesis of the Methodist Church, where the town council meeting had been held. And yet it too carried a medallion indicating that it was on the National Register of Historic Places.

Inside, she discovered why. Stained-glass windows in deep jewel tones colored the light. The intricately carved oak pews and altar screen had been polished to a high sheen, and two brass vases of casually arranged brown-eyed Susans sat on the altar. This was a holy place. She could almost feel the history inside the little church. People had been worshipping here for generations.

Jenna sat in the back pew, drawing a few stares from the locals as she waited for Patsy to show up. But she waited in vain. In fact, very few worshippers came out on this rainy Sunday. Maybe twenty people showed up, and the minister, a rotund man with a pink face and a bald head, gave a sermon on Christian faith that went way over Jenna's head.

Clearly this guy was not the new minister everyone in town was talking about.

She hung out for a few minutes after the service and introduced herself to the curious parishioners as a tourist. In fifteen minutes, she heard enough gossip to know that the new minister was expected sometime next week, that he was Jude's older brother, and that the Altar Guild had gone to the vicarage to clean and prepare for the new holy man only to discover that it was a bigger job than they had anticipated. There was some serious angst that the new minister would be put out by the quality of his living conditions.

As for Patsy, she was apparently under the weather today.

It was frustrating to think that she'd have to wait a whole week before trying again. After listening to Louella, she wasn't going to try to gate-crash the Piece Makers meeting a second time.

She headed back toward Rose Cottage, but as she started down Harbor Drive, another band of heavy rain moved in. Driven by a stiff wind, the rain fell sideways, right into her face. She was just thinking that maybe she should turn around and seek shelter at Bread, Butter, and Beans when a light in the window of Barrier Island Charters caught her eye. And like a lighthouse on a stormy day, it drew her closer.

Jude was working on Sunday?

Well, come to think of it, Jude probably worked most

weekends, especially when the weather was good. She followed the light to his office door. And suddenly her lonely day didn't seem so lonely anymore. Maybe she could take Jude out for lunch and find out why he was annoyed at her. And he probably didn't have much to do today either, since it was raining

She peeked between the fishing photos taped to the windows and saw Jude sitting at a computer, the blue light limning his face. She tried the door. It was locked. So maybe he was just getting paperwork done. It was raining like hell out here.

Maybe she could distract him from his chores.

She knocked as hard as she could.

He looked up, his brow furrowing the moment he saw her. Yup, he was annoyed at her for some reason. Or maybe he was just a grumpy guy who didn't like people much.

No. That wasn't right. He had friends. He ran a charter business. She'd seen him schmoozing the town council in support of his petition. He wasn't a grumpy guy.

He just didn't like her for some reason. Which was sad, because she admired him.

He came to the door and opened it. "What are you doing out in this weather?"

"Going to church."

He blinked a moment, as if the idea of her going to church was absurd, and then he ducked down and peered through the door at the rain. "You'd better come on inside before you drown."

She stepped through the door, dripping onto the linoleum floor as she slipped out of her soggy jacket. "So, you're working today?" she asked.

He shrugged. "Paying bills, and thanks to you and your sailing lessons, I can actually cover the rent this month."

He didn't say this to be funny or sarcastic, she realized. His words made her stop and look around the small storefront office. It was dusty and needed paint. The photos on the window had curled. The fish clock on the wall looked like something from a redneck decorator's dream. Nothing about this place said success. And that was odd, because everything about Jude told her he was a successful person with a lot going for him.

"Well, I'm glad I could help," she said, thinking there were other things she could help him with. Like a full rebranding of the business and an advertising strategy. She'd already noticed that Barrier Island Charters didn't advertise in the guidebook or on the Jonquil Island tourist map that every merchant on Harbor Drive handed out. But she kept her mouth shut.

"Are you really glad?" he asked, leaning back on his computer desk, eyeing the puddle on the floor that was forming as her soaked clothes dripped.

She put her hands on her hips. "Okay, I get it. You don't like me. But I don't know why. I also realize that on Friday you made the whole capsize lesson ten times harder, and more expensive, than it needed to be. But here's the thing. I'm glad you put me through it."

His mouth twitched, and his amber eyes narrowed on her, setting off a wave of reaction that was not entirely unexpected. He was beautiful to look at. "I don't dislike you," he said.

"Okay, then what?"

"I don't trust you. It's a big difference."

"You don't trust me? For heaven's sake, why?"

"Because you paid fifteen hundred dollars for four hours in a sailboat. You showed up at the town council hearing. And you specifically sought me out for these lessons. Why?"

Heat crawled up her face. He was onto her, and if she told him the truth, he'd probably run right to Harry and blab his mouth. She needed to think up a story fast.

"Maybe I just like you. A lot," she said. This had the benefit of being the truth, but saying it out loud was almost like hopping from the frying pan into the fire.

"I don't know whether to be flattered or offended." He crossed his arms over his chest. "And besides, if you think I'm about to back down on the things I believe in just because a pretty woman comes onto me, you need to think again."

"Uh... Wait. You think I'm pretty?"

He rolled his beautiful eyes. "Do not play innocent, okay? Greg wants me to play along with you, but I'm just not built that way. So, look here. I can't be bought off. And I'm going fight you every step of the way if you try to convince my brothers to sell that land out from under me. You got that?"

"Wait a sec. Who do you think I am?"

He stood up and got right in her face. "You're working for Santee Resorts. They sent you here to befriend me or befuddle me or to get me to say something about my family they can use. But here's the thing. I'm not changing my mind. And even if the town council votes down my petition, y'all are going to have a big fight getting my land away from me and my family."

His voice rang out with a righteous indignation that made her insides quiver. Here was a man who wouldn't be swayed, and it was sexy as hell.

So, she threw her arms around his neck and kissed him. Hard. Right on the lips.

Chapter Eight————

Holy crap, her lips were warm, and she smelled like honeysuckle, which made sense since her hair was the color of honey, and it took all his restraint not to run his hands up into that wet, windblown crown and fall all the way into the kiss.

Damn.

Everything he'd just avowed was probably a lie. The truth was that Jenna had gotten down into him somehow. For the last thirty-six hours, she'd been on his mind. Confusing his thoughts. Making him wonder why she hadn't complained after the sixth dunking. Why she'd been such a good sport. Why he wanted to go sailing with her again. And maybe not even charge her for the privilege.

Those bastards at Santee Resorts knew what the hell they were doing. So he took her by the shoulders and set her back. Gently. His mouth still hungry for her.

"You've got me all wrong," she said. "I'm not working for that resort company."

"Right. So that explains why you were at the town council meeting."

Her cheeks colored. "I went there because the issue sounded interesting."

"I don't believe you."

She blew out a sigh that telegraphed her frustration. "Look, here's the truth. I'm from Boston. My grandfather was a super-rich guy, and he left me a lot of money. So much money I'm never going to be able to spend it all. It's all in a trust fund, but my allowance is enough for anyone to live comfortably on. So I don't care how much you charge for lessons."

"You're a trust fund girl?" He swept his gaze over her, trying to jibe her rubber flip-flops with his preconceived notion of rich girls from Boston. "I don't believe it."

"Why? Because I don't flaunt my wealth? Except, oh yes, I did, by spending a ridiculous amount on sailing lessons. And if you want to know why I picked you, it was because you were competent, and I think competent is sexy."

Her cheeks turned a deeper shade of red as she said this.

"So, you..."

"I wanted sailing lessons from someone I found attractive."

"That doesn't explain your presence at a boring town hall meeting."

Her gaze shifted, a clear indication that she wasn't telling the truth. "Maybe I wasn't bored. Maybe I was interested in history. Maybe I—"

"Work for Santee Resorts."

She laughed. "No, that's not right. I had good reasons

for being at the hearing, Jude, but I swear on all that's sacred, I do not work for Santee Resorts. And I'm a Buddhist of sorts, so swearing an untruth is sure to unload a crap-ton of bad karma on me. So—"

"You're a Buddhist, but you went to church?" He had her dead to rights, and her cheeks flamed again.

"I went to church because the guidebook said that the stained-glass windows at Heavenly Rest were worth seeing."

Well, damn. She had him there. The guidebook did say that. And the only time you could get into the church was on Sunday since the church had been without a rector for months. Without anything else to call her on, he turned to the obvious.

"So, you kissed me because . . . ?"

"I'm here on vacation. And you are my sexy sailing instructor. Does it have to be more complicated than that? And, by the way, I'd still like to buy you lunch."

He stood there trying to decide if Jenna Fairchild was a professional liar or a flighty trust fund girl. Neither label seemed to fit.

He didn't trust her, but if she was willing to pay him five hundred dollars an hour for sailing lessons, then maybe he should go with the flow for once. If she was a tourist, she'd leave in a week or two, and he'd be able to cover a few bills he'd been worried about.

If she was working for Santee Resorts, at least he'd cleared the air. He could decide not to talk about his petition or the land. Or, what the hell, he could try to sway her. Make her see his point of view.

Not that he expected someone like her to understand it.

"I can see the wheels turning in your mind," she said.

"I promise you, I'm not trying to take your land. In fact, I'd be honored if you'd take me out to 'Gullah Town' sometime and show me around."

"See, now, that's the sort of thing that makes me mistrust you. And besides, you shouldn't call it that. 'Gullah Town' is the name the white folks gave to the place when they moved in here. Except for a few folks, like the Howlands and the Martins who built summer places here before the Civil War, this island was mostly settled by black folks. And we were left alone until they built the bridge."

"I'm sorry. I didn't know. And why does my interest in the land of your ancestors make you suspicious of me?"

"Because it's a temptation. It makes me think I can change your point of view. But that's a fallacy. If you're working for them, I'll never change your mind."

"And if I'm not?"

He shrugged.

"Okay, then. Don't take me out to there and show me around."

Why did that disappoint him? He suddenly wanted to take her there.

"But there's nothing that says I can't take you to lunch," she said before he could muster a comeback line.

Did he want to go to lunch with her? Hell yeah. After that kiss he'd like to do a lot of things with her. Decisions, decisions.

She stepped closer but didn't touch him. Just being near her seemed to make the air different. It came into his lungs charged with energy. It was hard to be rational in Jenna's presence. Would it be so wrong to have an end-of-summer fling?

Maybe. And the reality was that he'd never figure her out if he sent her packing. Funny how he suddenly wanted to figure her out. Was she an airhead or an enemy or something else entirely? If he had to bet, he'd take door number three.

Who was she? What did she want? His gut said she hadn't been totally honest with him. And he wanted her honesty for some unfathomable reason.

"I could do lunch," he said.

If it hadn't been raining, Jude would have suggested lunch at Rafferty's because it was safe, neutral ground. But with the rain coming down in sheets, sideways, he decided to take a chance and grab lunch at Aunt Annie's Kitchen, which was only a few doors down Harbor Drive from Barrier Island Charters.

Aunt Annie's was one of those places where you could get hush puppies that melted in your mouth, okra, rice, and tomatoes that tasted like manna from heaven, and fried pork chops that were the quintessential comfort food. The tourists usually missed this place because Annie saw no benefit to advertising in the usual tourist outlets. She would always say that her dining room was too small already. Jude had been urging her to move into a larger space, but his cousin was cautious. Like a lot of his people, she didn't believe in borrowing money or taking large risks.

And really, she didn't need to because everyone who lived in Magnolia Harbor ate at Annie's Kitchen all the time. She did a big business on Sundays after church, and it was only the rain that kept them from having to wait for a table. The aroma of fried food made Jude's mouth water as he walked into the narrow restaurant and headed for an open booth near the front. It had been a while since he'd had one of Annie's pork chops.

"Jude, baby. Where you been? Uncle Jeeter says you been hiding out." Annie, dressed in a sweater, jeans, and her bright red Aunt Annie's apron, intercepted him before he reached the table. She gave Jude a big hug before he sat down. Once he'd settled himself, she pinned him with a questioning look.

He pretended he didn't see and turned toward Jenna with a gesture. "Annie, meet my friend Jenna Fairchild. She's from Boston."

Annie flashed her smile in Jenna's direction. "Hey, welcome to heaven." Then she turned toward the dining room. "Y'all, we got us a Yankee here. From Boston." Dozens of eyes turned in their direction. A couple of the usuals even nodded and grinned.

"Honey, you're gonna love the fried pork chops," Annie continued, handing the blushing Jenna a menu. "You have never tasted anything like that up yonder. I can promise you that." Annie turned toward Jude. "So, how you doing, baby? Folks been burning up the grapevine about your brother coming home. I also heard you were the man at the town council hearing, telling those folks what was up. I'm so proud of you, baby."

"Thanks, and I'm fine," he said stoically. Not that Annie would pay any mind to what he said. Annie had been sticking her nose into his business since he was a little boy. She was his first cousin and had been his babysitter once.

"Uh-huh. Not sure I believe that," she replied with a lift of one eyebrow. "But you know, baby, sometimes the

Lord moves in mysterious ways. You wait and see. I got me a feeling about things. Y'all want sweet tea?" Annie gave Jenna a questioning lift of her eyebrow.

"Um, is it possible to get the tea without the sugar?" Jenna asked like a true Yankee.

Annie chuckled. "Yes, ma'am, it is. But why y'all insist on drinking tea without sugar is one of the Lord's greatest mysteries. I'll be right back." She turned and hurried off to a beverage station at the back of the house.

"You haven't lived until you've eaten one of Annie's fried chops," Jude said.

Jenna's mouth twitched seductively. "Uh, well, um. . ." She glanced away, studying the famed African prints on the wall for a moment before she said, "I'm a vegetarian."

Damn. Why was he not surprised? "You know, I should have figured that out," he muttered.

"Why?" Her gaze landed on him, and a humorous light danced in the depths of her big brown eyes. Was she laughing at him or the situation? He didn't know.

He shrugged in spite of himself. "I don't know. Because you're not from around here and you just told me you're a Buddhist. So, does that mean you're also into yoga and crystals and chakras and all that woo-woo stuff?"

She straightened her shoulders and jutted out her chin. "And what if I am?"

He closed his eyes and scrubbed his hands over his face. "You *are* into yoga and chakras and crystals, aren't you?" he muttered.

"I'm into transcendental meditation. But you can relax. I'm not into chakras or crystals." She picked up the menu and scanned. "And I'm good. There's a surprising number of vegetarian menu options. I think I'll have beans and rice, mac 'n' cheese, and a serving of collard greens... and maybe a hush puppy? I've never had a hush puppy."

"It's fried corn bread. You'll like it." He paused a moment, suddenly curious. "So, have you found enlightenment?"

She tucked a strand of hair behind her ear. Man, he wanted to touch that hair so bad. It was such a pretty color and so thick and wavy and sexy as hell. Was that why the resort company had sent her? Or was she telling the truth? It was so easy to believe her. Talking about transcendental meditation didn't seem like the sort of thing a corporate spy would do.

"Enlightenment doesn't work that way," she said.

"No?"

She shook her head but continued to avoid eye contact. "My teacher at the Indian ashram where I studied would say that the path to true enlightenment takes many lifetimes."

"Wow, and they call my people crazy for believing in root doctors."

"Root doctors? You talked about that at the hearing. So, what are they? Like wise women, or what?"

"Root doctors are part of the Gullah people's spirituality. They call it Hoodoo."

"Like Voodoo?"

"Yeah. Both are the remnants of ancient West African religions. The root doctors around here were herbalists mostly, but some of them were what we call conjurers. You could go to them and ask for luck or a curse or whatever. The root doctors are mostly gone now, like everything else. The old culture's being torn down."

"Not entirely," Jenna said.

"No?"

"Not here. Not in this restaurant."

He smiled. "No, I guess not."

"And I was listening the other night when you and the professor were talking. Didn't you say that most of the houses up north of town have blue shutters? Isn't that to ward off curses or something?"

He shook his head. "Haints."

"What?"

"In English you'd say haunts. People paint their shutters heaven blue to keep them away."

She laughed. "Maybe someone should tell Ashley Scott that."

He blinked, showing his surprise. "You know Ashley Scott?"

"I'm staying at Rose Cottage. Didn't you know that?"

He shook his head. "I thought you were camping out at the state park."

She smiled. "No. I'm staying in town, and I'm starting to think the rumors about Rose Cottage being haunted are true. Some weird things have been happening. And then there are the dreams."

"What kind of dreams?"

"About sailing mostly. There's one dream—a nightmare really—that I've had a couple of times. I'm all alone, standing on the deck of a big sailboat—you know, one with more than one mast. A storm is raging around me, and waves are coming over the sides of the ship... what do you call them?"

"Gunwales."

She nodded. "The rigging is twisting in the wind, and

I'm worried that the boat's going to come apart at the seams. It's awakened me two or three nights now."

"And you still want to learn how to sail?"

She shrugged. "Learning how to sail seems like a logical way to address my fears. Although I didn't have any fears until that moment when *Bonney Rose* turned over on me. Maybe you traumatized me." She gave him a sly smile.

Boy, she was one tough nut. He stared into her brown eyes while he tried to come up with some new way to trap her into revealing the truth. He was about to take the conversation back to Buddhism, sure she was just feeding him a line, when Harry Bauman walked into the restaurant.

Damn. Harry was the last person he wanted to talk to right now.

But the old guy saw him and immediately headed in his direction, his soaked foul-weather jacket leaving a trail of rainwater as he crossed the dining room. He stopped in front of Jude's table, his brown eyes dancing with curiosity behind his trifocals as he glanced from Jude to Jenna and back again. Did Harry know who Jenna was?

"How are you doing, son? Hope you're not letting all the gossip get you down. I swear it's all my wife's been talking about for three days solid. Take my advice: Don't ever marry a church lady."

"Yes, sir, uh...I mean no, sir. Um, are you talking about my zoning petition or something else?"

Harry snorted a laugh. "Well, the council will be voting on the petition at our next scheduled meeting. So we won't be keeping you in suspense for very long. But it would be unethical for me to talk with you about that. No, I was referencing your brother's return to the island. He has the Heavenly Rest Altar Guild up in arms over the state of the vicarage. Thought you should know."

"Uh, thanks." It was all Jude could muster. The last person he wanted to talk about was the brother who had abandoned him and the family half a lifetime ago.

Mr. Bauman gave Jenna a glance. "Are you going to introduce me?" he asked.

Jude's face heated. Damn. As much as he respected Harry, he didn't want the old guy nosing around in his personal life. Not that Jenna had anything to do with his personal life, but he had just kissed the woman. And damned if he didn't want to kiss her again.

But he couldn't afford to be rude to Mr. Bauman, seeing as they were friends and he was the deciding vote on the council. And also, he owed Mr. Bauman for a lot of things, up to and including his life.

He gestured toward Jenna. "Mr. Bauman, meet Jenna Fairchild. She's visiting from Boston. And you won't believe this, but I'm teaching her to sail." He looked Jenna in the eye. "Harry Bauman is the man who taught me everything I know about sailing a boat."

Jenna's heart slammed into her rib cage, and blood surged up into her cheeks. This is what her teacher at the ashram would call synchronicity. He was forever saying "We are all merely ripples in the fabric of the cosmos that our own intent helps to weave."

Which was his way of saying that sometimes coincidences were like signs. And then it occurred to her, with another jolt, that if her teacher was right, then somehow

Jude was a part of the fabric of her being. A thought that wormed its way deep, leaving a hot trail behind.

She smiled up at her uncle, who was dressed in all things Ralph Lauren except for the Helly Hansen rain jacket. "Hello. It's nice to meet you."

"Is he doing a good job?" Harry asked.

It took a moment for Jenna to parse the question. She'd been so busy trying to cool her reaction that she'd almost lost the thread of the conversation. Right, they were talking about sailing lessons. "He's very thorough," she said. "He took me out yesterday to practice capsizing the boat. Like, ten times."

"It was only seven. And the last time we managed to save the boat without anyone going overboard," Jude said.

Harry started taking off his coat, which was still dripping from the monsoon outside. "Good for you," he said. "When I taught Jude, that's exactly where we started."

"Hey there, Commodore. You sitting down or just visiting?" Annie asked as she came up to the table bearing plates.

This was Jenna's chance. "Why don't you join us?" she asked. "I'd love to hear stories about Jude learning the difference between a rope and a line."

The older man's face brightened. "Well, I wouldn't want to interrupt and—"

"Please," she said.

"All right."

Her uncle hung his raincoat on the hook beside the booth and slipped in beside Jenna in the space she made for him. She glanced at Jude.

Uh-oh. By the hard look on Jude's face, she'd definitely screwed up by inviting Harry to sit with them.

But then, Jude had convinced himself that she was working for the resort company. He probably thought this was some kind of lobbying effort on her part. She would have to make certain she stayed away from talking about his petition.

Meanwhile, Annie set their food orders on the table: three bowls heaped with Jenna's vegetarian options and a gigantic plate filled with a fried pork chop and heaping amounts of rice and lima beans for Jude. The food smelled heavenly, with its own unique mélange of spices. She drank in the aroma. This was what Jude considered comfort food.

"I'll have what he's having," Harry said, pointing at Jude's chop. "And don't you dare tell Patsy about it, you hear?"

"No, sir," Annie said with a smile and a head shake.

When Annie had bustled away, Jenna turned toward Harry and asked, "So, do you give lessons often?"

Harry barked a laugh and gave Jude a man-to-man glance. "Why? Are you looking to change teachers?"

"Oh, no. I'm just curious." Yeah, more curious than the proverbial cat who lost one of her lives. She had hundreds of questions, most of which she couldn't ask without revealing her true identity.

Harry shook his head. "I've taught a few people in my time. I'm not a full-time sailing instructor, though. I used to be a banker, but I retired. And since I always had this thing for politics, I somehow ended up on the town council. I saw you there. You have an interest in history?"

"I do. But I don't think it's kosher for us to talk about that, is it?"

He shook his head. "No. I suppose not."

"So, do you still sail?" she asked.

"When I can. But not dinghies anymore. You get bruised in those small boats. I've got a J/24 that I take out when I'm in the mood for cruising."

"A J/24 is a small keelboat," Jude explained. Good thing, too, because she was clueless.

"So, how'd you end up teaching Jude?" she asked.

"I caught him admiring my Lightning, which is a small boat, when he should have been trimming the hedges. He was a kid with an attitude then."

"He caught me red-handed when I was fifteen," Jude said. "I'd been hired by the yacht club to keep the weeds down and mow the lawn, but the sailboats fascinated me."

"He was a pretty curious kid."

"So, you dropped everything to teach him?" Something warm and fuzzy ignited in her chest. She could like a yacht club member who would take a moment to teach the African American lawn boy how to sail.

"I guess." The older man turned away, blinking his eyes. Maybe there was more to it. A shiver worked down her spine. There were currents and eddies in his terse reply. Something he didn't want to talk about.

"He's being polite," Jude said, jumping in to smooth the sudden halt in the conversation. "I was screwed up at that point in my life. My older brother Colton had just been picked up for smoking pot and had been sent to the juvenile detention center. Given what was going on with Colton, it's a miracle the yacht club wanted anything to do with me." Something invisible but powerful passed between the two men. There was a connection here that neither of them wanted to discuss.

"You're not your brother," Harry said with a long sigh

as he returned his gaze to Jude. "Take it from me, siblings can be a bitch."

Jenna focused on her collard greens. Being an only child, she had no concept of what it might be like to have a sibling. But it didn't take a genius to hear the emotion in Harry's voice.

"Yes, they can," Jude said as he cut a huge chunk out of his chop and popped it in his mouth.

"So, has Micah gotten in touch?" Harry asked.

Jude shook his head and chewed.

"Well, when he does, you tell him to go fly a kite."

Jude swallowed. "Go fly a kite?" His mouth tipped up at the corners.

"I would've been more explicit, but there's a lady present." Harry turned his gaze on Jenna. "So, you're from Boston, huh?" he drawled.

Uh-oh, she needed to change the conversation quick. She didn't want him putting two and two together. She nodded. "I am. But I'm an only child. So, I take it you have issues with your sister? Brother?" It was a risky question.

"My late brother. Who started out as an optometrist and became a retailer and manufacturer of high-end optics. He made a lot of money, and he was forever telling me that I was wasting my time as a banker. Like Jude here, Robert wanted me to join him in business. He was always asking me to move up north and go to work for him. But I loved Jonquil Island too much."

Annie arrived with Harry's food, and the conversation turned back to sailing, and as much as Jenna wanted to push it in other directions, she held back.

Jude and Harry had a lot of stories to tell. Most of

them about bad things happening in a sailboat. They both seemed to think their stories were hilarious, but to Jenna they seemed horrifyingly dangerous. She couldn't help but think about her father, who'd gone out in a boat and had never come back.

Jude had just finished telling Harry about their recent mishap with the hiking strap. The table was littered with empty plates and a couple of slices of pecan pie. Then Harry let out a long sigh.

"I remember that time you lost your pants," he said, and started laughing. Harry had an old man's laugh, wheezy and deep in his throat.

"You lost your pants?" Jenna asked, meeting Jude's gaze. But he wasn't laughing. His gaze was surprisingly sober, and he gave his head a little, almost imperceptible, head shake. As if to say, this story didn't happen.

"Oh yes, he lost his pants," Harry said, when his laughing fit ended.

"How did that happen?" Jenna asked, despite Jude's suddenly tense posture.

"He'd just brought the Lightning to the dock, and the boom came around unexpectedly and knocked him right into the water. He was wearing those baggy swim trunks, you know? And when he tried to climb back into the boat, the water sucked those big shorts right off his ass." He laughed again.

"And the worst thing is that they drifted off and sank. So, there he was bare-assed right in front of a bevy of girls watching from Rafferty's."

The old man blinked a few times and let go of a sigh. "She was there."

"Who?" Jenna asked.

"That girl. That Terri girl." He shook his head. "Funny how a stupid thing like losing your pants changes everything."

Oh. My. God. He wasn't talking about Jude. He was telling a story about her father.

And her mother. But her mom had never been to Jonquil Island, had she? She'd met Jamie Bauman when she was a sophomore at Boston University and he'd been a student at Harvard.

And then Jude spoke in a gentle voice that knifed right into Jenna's heart. "Harry, that wasn't me. Remember? It was Jamie who lost his pants."

Chapter Nine ———————————————

Harry eventually got tired of telling stories, grabbed his coat, and headed out the door after paying for his own lunch.

When he'd finally left, Jenna looked up from the credit card bill she was signing and asked, "Are you annoyed that I asked him to sit down with us?"

Jude shook his head. "No. I told you. Harry is a good friend."

"Who might not vote your way?"

He shrugged. "It doesn't matter. My own father and brother aren't on my side. Sometimes you gotta do what you gotta do."

"You care about Harry, don't you?"

Jenna's gaze narrowed in an avid, focused way that made Jude wonder if this was mere curiosity or something more. Some effort to get at Harry Bauman in order to influence his vote.

He hadn't thought about that before. The people at

Santee Resorts would know everything about his connection to the Baumans. And they'd be smart enough to use their mutual love of sailing to get at him, and then Harry.

Damn. Every time he started to like Jenna, something would come up out of nowhere to make him doubt.

He'd have to avoid talking about the zoning petition. He'd have to choose his words carefully. "I do care about him," he said, sending a clear message. "In fact, there are times when I feel like my life is tangled with his."

"Tangled?" She leaned in, avid. A clear indication of her ulterior motives.

"It's complicated. Our paths have crossed at key moments of my life."

"Oh. I see," she said. "My teacher in India would call that synchronicity."

"Synchronicity? Really?"

She shrugged and rolled her eyes as if to say that she didn't take herself seriously. "Okay. I know it's a pretentious word. But it means that, if you think you're tangled up with him, then you are. Put another way, if you think it's true, then it will be."

He shook his head. "Um, that makes no sense to me."

"I know. It always sounds circular. But there's some truth to it. So, when did this feeling of being tangled up with Harry start?"

She was good at prying out information, wasn't she? She threw her BS around and made you think she cared by looking serious out of those big brown eyes. But he wasn't about to delve into his complicated relationship with Harry and Patsy Bauman. He'd stay with the basics—what everyone in town already knew. What she already knew, if she was here to spy on him.

"It started when I was two years old and fell overboard without a life preserver."

"What? How did that happen?"

He shrugged. "I don't remember, and it's a story Daddy won't talk about. He swears I had a life vest on when I got on the boat, but when I toppled over the side, I didn't. And he didn't notice. He was piloting the boat, and he thought Momma was watching me, and Momma thought Micah, my oldest brother, was watching me. But it turns out no one was watching me." He paused a moment, regrouping. Why did this story always affect him down deep in some weird way? He didn't even remember the incident. But everyone else did.

"What happened?" she asked, leaning forward with a light in her eyes that suggested she'd never heard this story before.

"Jamie and Harry Bauman happened to be sailing their small boat on a port tack that took them behind the wake of my daddy's fishing boat. Jamie was crewing, in the front of the boat, and when he saw me fall, he dived in and hauled me up before I had a chance to sink or even to take on any water. When they hailed Daddy, he hadn't even realized I was missing."

As he spoke, Jenna's gaze widened, and her mouth fell open. "Oh. My. God. They saved your life."

Gooseflesh puckered along Jenna's arms, and the hairs on the back of her neck stood on end. Synchronicity, indeed. "So, it's Harry who feels the connection," she whispered.

Her teacher would say that Harry's connection to Jude had created a powerful eddy in the cosmos. An eddy that she'd unconsciously picked up that day she'd first arrived and had seen Jude out in *Bonney Rose*.

That was why she'd suddenly decided to ask him, and him alone, for sailing lessons.

She studied Jude, the too-long, coarse, curly hair, the jut of his cheekbones, and amber eyes that didn't belong in a face with skin so dark. The unmistakable thrum of sexual desire vibrated in her core. He was a magnet to her iron, his pull irresistible.

And no wonder. Her father had saved his life.

"So," he said, his sensual mouth with that plump, kissable lower lip twitching, "are you going to use this information against me?"

He wasn't going to give up thinking she was some kind of spy, was he? "No," she said firmly. "And if you want to know why I wanted sailing lessons, it's because my father, who I never knew, was a sailor."

He cocked his head. "Why didn't you say that earlier?"

She shrugged. "Because I'm a private person. So let's just say that we traded personal stories today, okay?"

"Sure. Whatever you say."

She wanted him. She wanted to invite him back to the cottage. Enjoy an afternoon. Tell him the truth—all of it.

But she didn't dare do that. He was too close to Harry. She would have to think this through before doing anything stupid or rash. Especially now, as she was starting to uncover the secrets her mother had kept from her.

She needed to play for time.

"Um," she said, losing her words like a teenager on a first date, "I should go. I have things to do."

"Of course you do. Reporting back to whoever sent you?"

She shook her head. "I'm not a corporate spy, okay? When can we schedule another lesson?"

He shook his head. "I should say no, but I'm happy to take Santee Resort's money."

She didn't argue. "When?"

"Probably not until Tuesday at the earliest. But I'll give you a call. The bay won't be fit to sail tomorrow."

They stood up. He waved good-bye to Annie, and they headed out through the restaurant's door. The rain came down in torrents, and the wind gusted, tossing their hair around their heads. "Can I drive you back to Rose Cottage?" he asked.

She shook her head. "No. It's not far. And I need to think."

He cocked his head and moved a little closer, invading her space, making it hard to be rational. "About what?"

His body heat enveloped her, and she had a deep, strong urge to fall into him, to find shelter from the storm. But she resisted.

"I need to think about you," she murmured.

One of his eyebrows arched. "Of course you do. You think I'm going to be easy to sway or compromise or whatever," he said on a puff of air right before he moved in.

He came at her slowly, just as a wind gust swept in, sending cold mist at them. She could have avoided him. She could have put her hands on his chest and pushed back.

But she didn't. She waited for his arrival, anticipation blossoming like one of Ashley's roses. His kiss was gentle. A brush of warm lips like an invitation. Her core melted, and she might even have given up a small, breathy moan. She took a step closer, brought her right hand up around his neck, her cold fingers on his hot nape. She opened her mouth.

And he plundered like a pirate. The polite kiss disappeared, and suddenly she got the full, knee-buckling force of Jude St. Pierre. He ravished her mouth. There was no other word for what he did.

And damned if she didn't want to arch her back and let him ravish the rest of her. A tide of longing swept through her, washing away all caution and all sense.

It lasted until he moved back, like a retreating wave. She expected him to come at her again, but he didn't. "There," he whispered right before he turned and walked away. "Why don't you think about that?"

Chapter Ten————————————

Jenna was soaked to the bone by the time she reached Rose Cottage. She drew herself a hot bath and spent a long time in the soaking tub, thinking.

Thinking was not the same as meditating. When she meditated, she worked—sometimes too hard—to let her thoughts go and live in the moment. Meditating was often exhausting, probably because she was better at thinking than meditating.

But this time, thinking was enough to make her feel crazy inside. When she wasn't thinking about that scorching kiss Jude St. Pierre had laid on her, she was thinking about how he mistrusted her. And overarching all of that was her family problem. She didn't know how to handle family problems. For most of her life it had just been Mom and her. And until today, Jenna had always thought that her mother had been honest with her.

Now everything Mom had said about Jenna's father was thrown into question. As Jenna thought about it,

Mom had said very little about him over the years. Her mother had been happy to let Jenna draw her own conclusions. Once Jenna had gotten over her fantasies of Dad as superhero, she'd come to accept that her father, whoever the bastard was, just didn't care. And she'd built a solid shell around that empty place inside of her.

Mom had never done one thing to stop her from that heart-hardening exercise. In fact, by word and deed, her mother had taught her the value of being self-reliant and having a heart made of tempered steel.

She'd thought she understood her own life story. But now, suddenly, she felt as if she'd missed half of it.

Mom had been here on Jonquil Island the day she'd met her father, on the day he'd lost his pants. What had Harry called her mother? *That Terri girl.* As if Mom was the villain of the story.

How could she be a villain if she'd only hooked up with her father for a few nights? It seemed unlikely. Did Harry's comments mean there had been something more between her parents?

More troubling was the fact that Jamie Bauman had perished at the age of twenty-two under mysterious circumstances. Louella had even suggested suicide. Why would he commit suicide? Had Mom broken his heart? Or was there something else she didn't know?

Jenna got out of the tub, feeling exhausted and jumpy as she dressed in a pair of well-worn sweats. The occasional rumble of thunder over the bay put her on edge as she picked up her phone and called Milo on his private line. Milo was always available, even on Sunday afternoons.

"Jenna, it's good to hear from you. Are the arrangements I made for your stay on Jonquil Island acceptable?"

"Yes."

"And how's it going?"

Milo's English accent never failed to intimidate her. He'd come to America as a young man, but the accent had stuck. And now he sounded faintly imperial or something.

She liked Milo, really. He was mostly harmless and kind of sweet and old-fashioned. But the man was also like a bulldog, focused and relentless when it came to guarding her well-being.

"Things are not going all that well," she said on a long sigh.

"Oh? Did Harry and Patricia slam the door in your face?"

"No. They don't know who I am yet. That's not the problem."

"Oh?" There was a world of censure in that one word. Milo had made it clear that he was not fully on board with her plan to visit Jonquil Island incognito. And he had a point. Lying had a karmic consequence, but in this instance, she was willing to incur the debt. Milo, on the other hand, had urged her to approach her uncle in an "aboveboard" manner. Milo had a quaint way of putting things sometimes. But, she had insisted on doing this her way, and he'd capitulated after a lot of grumbling and grumping.

In the end, though, he'd not only booked her into Rose Cottage, but he'd secured a fake driver's license and credit card in her assumed name. When Milo put his mind to something, he always took care of every small detail. It was astonishing what money and Milo's expertise could buy.

"My plan is working," she said, somewhat defensively. "But I've learned some troubling things."

"About Harry and Patricia?"

"Patsy. They call her Patsy."

"Patsy?"

"That's what Patricia goes by. She's a member of a quilting club that meets weekly at the B and B. She's also a devout church lady. She's pretty impressive, actually."

"She quilts? Really?" The incredulity in his voice underscored the fact that Milo had never lived anywhere except London and New York.

"Yes, and she's also a little bit of a snob. So it's a good thing she doesn't know who I am."

"So, what disturbing things are troubling you?"

"Do you know anything about how my father died?"

"You've asked me this before. All I can tell you is that he perished in a sailing accident on Moonlight Bay. Beyond that I have no details. As you know, your father died well before I became your grandfather's attorney. I never knew your father, and aside from the pride your grandfather took in displaying your father's sailing trophies, your grandfather rarely spoke about his son. I fear he never quite got over Jamie's death."

"I talked to someone who suggested that his death might be suspicious."

"Suspicious how?"

"A murder? A suicide?" She said the words, and her chest tightened. She didn't believe Louella Pender.

"Really? That is disturbing. Jenna, did you go to Jonquil Island to discover the truth about your father or to meet your aunt and uncle?"

"Maybe a little of both," she said. "And that's just it.

Today I found out that Mom met Jamie here on Jonquil Island. I didn't know that. Mom always let me believe that they met in Boston when she was going to BU and he was at Harvard. And now, suddenly..." Her voice wavered and faded out.

"What is it, dear?" Milo's voice sounded deeply concerned.

"I don't know. Mom always loved daffodils, you know? She wanted them at her funeral. And now I'm wondering why. Was it because she met him here on Jonquil Island, where the daffodils are a tourist attraction? Was it because Jamie meant more to her than just a one-night stand? I mean, she always gave me the impression that my father was not in the picture because she chose to live that way. Or maybe because he didn't care. But..."

"I can't help you. I never spoke with Jamie or your mother. But, if you'd like, I can check the firm's files and correspondence for you. My predecessor, Brian Hughes, kept copious notes about everything he did for your father. Let me see what I can find out."

"Thank you, Milo. I would appreciate that."

"Of course. But, Jenna dear, you should keep your focus on the living, not the dead. Remember that you're there to connect with your aunt and uncle, not to dig up your parents' sordid past."

Was it sordid? God, she hoped not. Especially after learning today that her father had saved a life. It was funny, really, now that she thought about it. She'd always wanted a father who was a hero, and it looked as if Jamie Bauman fit that bill, regardless of how he might have died.

And just like that, the little girl inside her wanted more

than that. She wanted to discover that Mom and Dad had loved each other.

Later in the day, Jude was beginning to regret his decision to kiss Jenna Fairchild. That kiss had only made him want her, and until he knew what kind of game she was playing, he needed to stay as far away from her as possible. And yet she was on his mind as he padded down the sandy path between Old Granny's cabin, where he'd been living for the last five years, and Daddy's place, a one-story house with a cinder-block foundation and indoor plumbing that had been built on the St. Pierre family land back in the 1920s. At one time, the St. Pierre house had been one of the finer homes in the area.

But today Jude's home place resembled the much older cabins that surrounded it. The siding had gone so long without paint that it had weathered to gray. The windows needed reglazing, rust had attacked the screens on the porch, and the foundation leaned a little to the left. Jude took the porch steps two at a time, carrying several grocery sacks. The rain had slacked off, and the wind had changed direction. The tropical depression was moving on up north, but its winds would be with them all day tomorrow, making sailing or fishing out of the question.

He let himself into the house and found Daddy sitting at the old enameled kitchen table with a half-full bottle of Wild Turkey at his elbow. Jude dropped his groceries on the table. "I'm going to start some coffee and fry up some steaks. I don't want to hear that you're not hungry. And then, after supper, we need to talk."

"About what?"

"About your drinking, to start with. Then we need to

talk about Barrier Island Charters and how I'm a grown man and it's about time that you hand the business off to me."

"I ain't got nothing to say to you on either account. I'm tired of those conversations."

Jude snatched the bottle from the table.

"Hey, that's mine," Daddy said, standing up on unsteady legs and making a sad attempt to stop Jude from pouring the contents down the kitchen drain.

"Wha'd'ya do that for?" Daddy asked.

"Because I'm tired of seeing you drunk. You need to go to rehab."

Daddy shook his head and collapsed back into his chair. "No way you're getting me back there again. All they do is talk, talk, talk. And I got nothing I want to say. Besides, what do you expect me to do on a rainy Sunday with no charters?"

Jude might have told him to go to church, but that would have been like the pot calling the kettle black. Jude had given up on God the winter Micah had left them. Daddy had given up on God around the same time.

So Jude said nothing. He turned his back and started putting groceries away. The only reason Daddy had groceries was because Jude went shopping for him every few days. The old man lived on hot dogs and frozen dinners mostly. But even when Jude brought steak or a covered dinner from Annie's Kitchen, Daddy wouldn't eat much of it.

Especially when he'd been drinking.

Daddy said not one word to him the whole time Jude put away food and prepared to fry up the steaks. Jude fully expected his father to give him the silent treatment right through supper, so when someone knocked on Daddy's door, it was a relief.

Daddy, maybe a little more sober now after a cup of strong coffee, pushed up from the table and weaved his way to the door. "It's probably Old Jeeter wanting to go fishing," he said.

But it wasn't Old Jeeter at all. Standing on the other side of the rusty screen stood a large man, easily six foot three, dressed in dark-blue khakis and a light-blue, short-sleeved clerical shirt. He stood there with that military-erect bearing as his dark eyes swept past Daddy and landed on Jude where he stood in the kitchen, which was open to the cabin's main room.

Micah.

Emotions Jude couldn't name, and didn't want to show, tumbled through him, turning his insides to ice. He took a deep breath, but it hurt down deep in his chest, as if he'd bruised a rib. Right at that moment he wanted to tell his brother to get lost and never get found again.

Damn. It had been half a lifetime since his brother had abandoned the family. Micah's gaze returned to the man hanging on to the door and listing like a sinking ship.

"Daddy," Micah said, taking the old man's arm and guiding him back to the table. Beyond the still-open door, Jude saw a navy-blue duffel bag sitting on the weathered porch.

What the hell? Did Micah intend to stay here tonight?

Resentment or some other toxic emotion he couldn't quite name burned in his chest. He had to swallow down a rancid metallic taste. He was not happy to see his brother or that expression on Micah's face as he realized just how drunk Daddy was.

"Well, I'm glad to see you, son," Daddy said, tears in his eyes as she slapped Micah's back.

"I guess you heard that I've been sent as the new vicar for Heavenly Rest."

"Yeah, we heard that," Jude said in a flat voice as he turned back toward the steaks, which were starting to sizzle in the pan.

"You've grown up," Micah said.

Jude's head suddenly throbbed, as if he'd been the one drinking Wild Turkey all afternoon. Yeah, he'd grown up, but so had Micah. And it irked him on some deep level that his big brother was still bigger than him. Well, it didn't matter. The boy who'd idolized Micah was dead and gone now. Micah was a deserter in Jude's book. And what the hell right did he have to come back here all dressed like some conquering hero, or some champion of God, when he'd abandoned the family?

"Yeah, well, that happens. You hungry? We probably have enough steak for three." He didn't add that Daddy wouldn't eat much.

"Uh, well, I was wondering if I could stay here for a couple of days. I heard from the Heavenly Rest Altar Guild that the vicarage in town isn't ready for me. I guess they were expecting me later in the week. They've got volunteers coming in to paint the place tomorrow."

"Sure, son. I got plenty of room. It's just me here."

"Just you? Where does—"

"I'm living in Old Granny's house," Jude said. "But I bring groceries every Sunday and cook him a good meal." Why the hell was he so defensive?

Oh yeah, it was that promise he'd made as a little boy, right before Micah had gone away to college. He'd promised to look after Daddy, which he'd been doing most of his life. More than either of his brothers, in any case.

He finished frying up the steaks, slapped them onto a couple of dishes, and threw the prepackaged salad into a bowl. He slammed everything onto the table.

"Enjoy your meal. I'm going home," he announced, and marched out of Daddy's house. He'd gotten as far as the sandy track that led to Old Granny's house when Micah caught up to him.

"Don't go. Please."

He stopped and turned. "I have nothing to say to you."

Micah nodded. "I know. But for what it's worth, it's good to see you. You may not believe this, but I've prayed for you."

"Yeah, well, thanks. It might have been better if you'd stayed for me. But since you didn't, don't think you can come in here and judge us all. You got that?"

"I didn't come to judge. I'm here to help. Please, let me help you."

"I don't need your damned help now. I'm a grown man, not that boy you left. He needed your help, but I don't. Go on back and eat your steak. Daddy's totally lit. You'll need to put him to bed tonight. And just so you know, that happens every Sunday. And every Sunday I have this talk with him about rehab. There's a bed open at the center in Georgetown. All I need to do is to get him to realize that he needs it. But he won't. He's stubborn as a mule."

He turned around and stalked into the scrub pine.

The brother he'd once loved above all others didn't come after him. And he was okay with that. More than okay. That was the way he wanted it.

But since when did Jude ever get what he wanted?

The next morning Colton came knocking on Jude's front door. He knocked and hollered until Jude rolled out of bed, stepped into some boxers, and opened the door.

"Get dressed," Colton said. "Micah needs our help."

"So?"

Colton jutted his chin. "Don't be that way, Jude. He's back, and he's our brother, and that house the Episcopalians want him to live in is in disrepair. The ladies of the Altar Guild have planned a volunteer paint party for today. I can just imagine what those old biddies are about to do to that house. We need to go make sure things are done right."

"*We* need to? Since when? Look, I don't feel like I need to do a thing for Micah."

Colton blew out a sigh. "Come on. Don't be that way."

"What way?"

"Bitter. You'll be way happier if you let the past go, you know? I mean, not just about Micah, but everything." He gestured to Old Granny's house, which Jude had been renovating bit by bit, as his resources allowed. "This old place. It isn't worth it, Jude. It's time to move on."

"Yeah, well, you and Daddy and Micah can move on. I'm staying here. And I'm going back to bed." He shut the door in Colton's face and did go back to bed.

But damned if he got any sleep at all.

Chapter Eleven ————————

Monday dawned cloudy and breezy. Jenna stayed inside for her morning yoga and meditation. Jude had been right about the bay today. A heavy wind whipped at the water, churning up whitecaps. There would be no sailing even though the rain had stopped.

Now that she knew Jamie Bauman had saved Jude's life, it was hard not to connect the dots or to want to spend more time with him. Maybe some people would say that it was mere coincidence that she'd seen Jude on her very first day on Jonquil Island. But no one would ever convince Jenna of that. No. She'd come here looking for answers about the father she'd never known, and within a few hours she'd met Jude St. Pierre, a man who owed his life to her father.

Which Jamie was he?

Would she ever find out?

Feeling restless, she went seeking refuge in the library but not before stealing several chocolate chip cookies and a glass of sickeningly sweet iced tea from the kitchen. She settled into the big mohair wing chair with a well-thumbed Sue Grafton mystery.

She had just started chapter two when someone asked, "Whatcha reading?"

She peeked over the top of the paperback. Jackie Scott, resembling a freckled elf, sat cross-legged on the thread-bare Persian rug at her feet. How the hell had the kid entered the library without her noticing? Six-year-old boys were not usually so quiet. And why wasn't this child in school?

But instead of giving him the third degree about his truancy, she played along with him. After all, he'd directed her to a very useful book on sailing.

"It's a mystery," she said.

He flashed her a grin. "Like you?"

Odd. The boy was odd, and his big blue eyes seemed older than they should be. "Why do you think I'm a mystery?" she asked.

He lifted one shoulder in an almost-there shrug. "I heard Ms. Tighe say that to Ms. Jernigan. She said you're a mystery 'cuz you don't dress well enough to be staying at the cottage."

Thank God. Or maybe not. It was a bit discomforting to know that she was the subject of local gossip. "Are Ms. Tighe and Ms. Jernigan members of the Piece Makers?" she asked.

The boy nodded.

"What else do they talk about?"

"Lots of stuff."

"Like what?"

"Like the new preacher."

Well, no surprise there. Everyone was talking about the new minister. "What else?" she asked.

"The woman with the booty."

Jenna worked to keep her mouth from dropping open. Wow. The Piece Makers might be a bunch of sixty- and seventysomethings, but they obviously talked some serious smack while they stitched away on patriotic quilts.

"Why do they talk about her?" Jenna asked, her curiosity getting the better of her.

"Because they're mad about her booty. Especially Ms. Bauman."

What? Ugh. Her gut tightened. Was Aunt Patsy more than merely a snob, as Louella Pender had suggested? Was she Magnolia Harbor's slut shamer in chief, as well?

"Why would she be mad about someone's...?" Jenna couldn't say the word *booty* out loud to a child Jackie's age. It seemed wrong somehow. She also shouldn't be encouraging him to gossip. That was wrong too.

"'Cuz it was ill gotten," Jackie said, apparently understanding her question even though she hadn't said the word.

An ill-gotten booty? What?

"Cap'n Bill says that ill-gotten booty is a curse," Jackie added, just as the proverbial lightbulb went off in Jenna's head. The little boy wasn't talking about the size of some woman's backside. He was talking about pirate treasure. Loot. Money.

My money. Or, to be more precise, her grandfather's money.

She was the woman with the booty. Which, given the puny size of her butt, was almost hilarious.

She wanted more information about her aunt, but

before she could ask her next question, Ashley called Jackie's name from down the hallway, and the little boy hopped up.

"Gotta go," he said.

Ashley tied the bandanna around her head and studied her face in the mirror above the powder room's sink. She looked tired. Probably because she hadn't been sleeping well. And somehow, she always seemed to be frowning these days. The fold at the bridge of her nose had become permanent.

Her life had taken a bad left turn onto a rocky road. When she'd married Adam, she'd accepted the risks. After all, she was an army brat; she knew the drill. She knew about the long deployments and the moving around. She was self-reliant. She could cope.

But she wasn't ready when the worst happened. She hadn't expected to become a widow at the age of thirty-three. And three years ago, right after Adam died, she hadn't come to stay with Grandmother to become an innkeeper. Life had unfolded on her in a relentless fashion that had left her stranded, alone, and in financial difficulties. She leaned on the sink.

Maybe it was time to call it quits and go back to Kansas, where Mom and Dad would gladly take her in. She could sell the house and the cottage and be debt free.

But she'd lose her independence and disappoint her grandmother, who might be watching from up there in heaven.

She blew out a sigh. How could she sell the house and land that had been in the Howland family for generations?

Short answer: if she got desperate enough. And right

now, with yesterday's rain soaking through the roof in several places, she was desperate enough.

But first she had to help paint the vicarage. How she'd been volunteered to coordinate this project remained a mystery. It had started as a simple cleaning operation but had escalated at every turn. And with the minister already here in town and staying out at his father's place, which was nothing but a falling-down cabin in the woods, the heat was on. Volunteers had ended up missing services yesterday, as they'd started work patching holes in the walls.

She should have said no. She should have known it was more than she could handle. And, of course, she hadn't planned to be still mired in this project on Monday, which was one of those teacher work days where the kids got a three-day weekend. So Jackie would be underfoot again. All day.

She turned off the light and stepped into the hallway. Where was Jackie? She'd left him in the kitchen with a cookie and had told him to stay put.

"Jackie, where have you gone off to now?" she hollered, inwardly cringing at the exhaustion ringing in her voice.

"Gotta go." Jackie's voice sounded from the library, where Ms. Fairchild was last seen reading a paperback novel.

A knot of anger and helplessness caught in her throat. How many times did she have to tell her son not to bother the guests? She pulled in a breath. She would not cry. She was an army brat, an army wife, and an army widow. She was stronger than this.

She stalked down the hall to the library's doorway and

put her hands on her hips when she found Jackie. "I've told you five times today that we needed to go over to the vicarage to help with the painting. And why are you in here talking to Ms. Fairchild?"

"It's all right. He was—" Ms. Fairchild began.

"No, ma'am, it's not all right. Come on, let's go." Ashley gave Jackie her no-nonsense glare. The one she'd learned from Mom. He hopped up from the pitifully threadbare carpet, jammed his grubby hands in the pockets of his too-small jeans, and slowly headed in her direction, head down. A wave of love, wide and deep, washed over Ashley and almost buckled her knees.

Jackie was the spitting image of Adam. And even though he tried her patience, she'd never loved anyone as much as she loved that little boy of hers. When he got close, she grabbed him and pulled him into a hug he clearly didn't want.

"I'm sorry," Ashley said to Ms. Fairchild. "He won't bother you again. We're off across the street to help paint the vicarage."

The right corner of Ms. Fairchild's mouth tipped up, and her eyes took on a mischievous twinkle. "Ah, the new minister," she said.

"How'd you know about that?"

Ms. Fairchild shrugged. "Everyone's talking about it. In town."

Yes, they were. And Ms. Fairchild was listening and taking notes. Maybe Patsy, who called her *Buddha girl*, was right about Jenna Fairchild. Patsy had convinced herself that Ms. Fairchild was working for one of the resort companies that had been scoping out the land north of town for a new development. Because the woman was not only pretending to be poor, but she'd also showed up at the town council hearing last week on Jude St. Pierre's petition to rezone that land north of town.

Now, what tourist goes to town hall meetings?

But as much as she wanted to cross-examine Ms. Fairchild, Ashley also couldn't afford to rock any boats. She needed the rental income. "Well," Ashley said, "maybe people need to find something else to gossip about."

Ms. Fairchild sat forward in her chair, her gaze suddenly avid. "Is it because Jude St. Pierre is his brother?" she asked. "Or is there some other reason people are so upset?"

Interesting. In a week, Jenna Fairchild had learned a lot about the locals, hadn't she? And mentioning Jude St. Pierre, the man behind the efforts to designate the land north of town as off-limits to the resort developers, was also revealing. "The St. Pierres live in 'Gullah Town,'" she said, "and I guess there are one or two parishioners who have a problem with that. But not everyone. Not by a long shot. The truth is, Micah St. Pierre used to worship at Heavenly Rest when he was teenager, so I think a lot of folks are pleased that a Jonquil Islander is coming home to be our minister."

Ms. Fairchild nodded, clearly understanding the subtext. "I see."

Ashley's face flamed. "I'm afraid we have some people who haven't yet realized we're living in the twenty-first century. But you know what? I don't care about people like that. Which is why I'm off to help paint the vicarage for our new preacher."

Ashley turned to go, swallowing back her annoyance.

Sometimes the people living in this town were small-minded. But that was none of Jenna Fairchild's concern.

"Can I help?" Ms. Fairchild asked.

Ashley stopped and turned to gaze at her guest, who was dressed in ancient flip-flops, a pair of old camp pants, and a dingy T-shirt that said, ALL THAT WE ARE IS THE RESULT OF WHAT WE HAVE THOUGHT. A quote from the Buddha, apparently, which seemed oddly apt given the topic of their conversation.

Ms. Fairchild's threadbare pants and faded shirt suggested that she'd planned to come help with the painting all along. Had she known about the painting day? Was she here to spy on the St. Pierres because of Jude's efforts to designate "Gullah Town" off-limits to developers?

"Why would you want to help?" Ashley asked.

Jenna smiled. "Because you need help."

Well, Ashley hadn't expected that answer. She'd expected a response that sounded like a lie. But when Ms. Fairchild looked her right in the eye and said, "you need help," it was nothing but the God's honest truth.

She did need help.

And she was oddly grateful for Ms. Fairchild's offer. So she gave her guest a wide smile and said, "We can use all the help we can get."

Jenna followed Ashley and Jackie across the street to an unremarkable brick, ranch-style home that looked as if it had been built in the 1960s. It sat surrounded by several older, historic homes, which made it an architectural sore thumb with zero curb appeal. Add in the overgrown landscape and the patchy grass and the home looked sad.

Hardly the kind of place where a congregation wanted their minister to live.

But then again, the crowd at yesterday's services had been tiny, so maybe this was the best the congregation could afford.

The door was already open, and they headed inside, where they found Patsy Bauman sitting in the middle of the empty living room in a folding chair. Aunt Patsy had come to paint the vicarage in a pair of white linen slacks, a pale-blue-striped man-tailored shirt, and a summer-weight, cream-colored cardigan. The woman was a septuagenarian fashion plate. Clearly she intended to direct volunteers and not get her hands, or her clothes, dirty.

Patsy took one look at Ashley Scott and said, "My word, Ashley, where have you been? I've been waiting on you for half an hour." She followed this rude comment with an intimidating stare that shifted from Ashley to Jackie to Jenna and back again.

Jenna was not intimidated in the least. In fact, she wanted to walk right up to her great-aunt, get up in her face, and tell Patsy to give Ashley a break. Her landlord was giving off stress in hot waves like one of those oscillating electric heaters.

But when Ashley started apologizing, Jenna almost got right up in her landlady's face to give her a pep talk on assertiveness.

"Sorry, Patsy," Ashley said in a small voice, "it's been a tough few days. I didn't anticipate this project being so big. And the school has a teacher workday and I couldn't find babysitting and..." Ashley's explanations trailed off when a tall, handsome man came striding through the front door, put his hands on his hips, and said, "Where can I find Ashley Scott?"

"Oh, my word, Micah St. Pierre, you've grown up, son." Patsy got out of her chair, crossed the room, and shook the man's hand.

"Miz Bauman?"

"It's me. I don't reckon I've changed as much as you have." She gave him a smile. "I'm so sorry about the mess. We weren't expecting you until later in the week. So sorry you had to find other accommodations last night."

"It's no problem. I needed to catch up with my family. And to that end, a few reinforcements should be here any moment."

His gaze shifted toward Jenna. "Miz Scott?"

She shook her head. "No. I'm Jenna Fairchild. This is Ashley." She gestured toward her landlady, who was staring at Micah with an odd look in her eye.

Jenna didn't blame her. The Reverend St. Pierre didn't look like a holy man. He was an older, bigger, slightly paler version of Jude. But his eyes were much darker. Where Jude was a bronzed statue with tiger eyes, Micah's skin was more tan than brown. His eyes had fine lines at their corners, and a hint of gray shone at the temples of his military-short haircut.

Dressed in a black T-shirt with a hole at one shoulder seam and a pair of jeans with ragged knees, he didn't look one bit like Jenna's notion of a minister.

"I understand you're the chair of the painting committee?" he said to Ashley.

"I...um...yes. And we haven't really done any painting yet. We had so many holes to patch, and..." Her voice faded out.

"No problem. Reverend Ball lived here for a long, long time. There were bound to be a few holes."

He shifted his gaze toward the little boy still standing beside his mother. He hunkered down to be on the same level as Jackie. "Well, hello. Are you Jackie?" he asked.

Wow. Obviously, the new minister had done some homework on his flock.

The little boy nodded, his eyes round.

"It's nice to meet you. I've heard that you are a good friend of Captain Bill's."

The boy's eyes grew wide. "I am," he said.

"Well, he's a good man to be friends with." The minister gave the boy a shoulder squeeze and stood up again, facing Ashley.

Who was now frowning. "How did you—"

"I spoke with several of the substitute ministers who've been filling in the last nine months."

"Oh. I didn't think—"

He interrupted with a smile. "Jackie made quite an impression on most of them."

Ashley tensed, if that was even possible. The woman was already wound tighter than an overwound clock. She put her hands on her hips and was about to say something she might have regretted when another large man wearing an impressive tool belt strolled through the front door.

"So, this is the vicarage?" he drawled as he stepped up to Reverend St. Pierre and gave him a fist bump to the shoulder. The resemblance between the two men was startling. This newcomer wore a maroon golf shirt with ST. PIERRE CONSTRUCTION embroidered on the chest, and like Micah, his eyes were dark.

The other brother? She couldn't remember his name. In any event, two St. Pierres in this tiny living room didn't leave much space for anything else.

"Colton, so glad you could come," Patsy said.

"Did you call Colton?" Ashley asked.

"Of course I did. After all the problems we discovered yesterday? You didn't think I expected the Altar Guild to single-handedly repair everything that's wrong with this house when our minister has a contractor for a brother?" A slow smile turned Patsy's mouth up at the corners, and her judgmental expression disappeared. Clearly the old woman had done this to surprise Ashley and ease her worries.

Right then Jenna decided Patsy was a good person. And for some reason that warmed her heart a little. Could she be friends with Patsy? Could they one day regard each other as family?

"Don't you worry about a thing, Miz Scott," Colton drawled. "I brought help."

Three more guys in tool belts, work boots, and St. Pierre Construction golf shirts strolled through the front door as if Colton's words had conjured them from out of thin air.

"Oh, thank you," Ashley said. "We could use a few experts."

Colton smiled. "That reminds me. How's your roof holding up with all this rain?"

Ashley's shoulders sagged a little. "It's okay," she said in a voice that conveyed the opposite.

The exchange confirmed what Jenna already knew. Ashley Scott was in financial trouble.

"Well, you give me a call, and we'll get it fixed, okay?"

Colton said, and then he turned his gaze on Jenna. "Hello. I don't think we've met."

"Jenna Fairchild. I'm a guest. At the cottage. I came by to help because I had nothing better to do."

"Well, y'all don't need to bother. I got this taken care of." He turned to his guys and issued a few commands. The men spread out like an invading army. One of them headed into the kitchen, and the rest headed down the hallway to the back of the house.

Colton turned toward Patsy. "We'll have that bathroom leak you called me about fixed in no time at all. And I got some leftover subway tile. It should be enough for the bathroom and the kitchen. Come on, Micah. Let's get that stuff hauled in here."

As the two men turned toward the front door, Jackie piped up. "Can I help?" he asked, tagging after them like a puppy.

"Sure you can, matey," the minister said, stopping for the little boy to catch up and then taking his hand as they walked out the front door.

"I'll go see if they need any help," Ashley muttered, following after them, her shoulders tight and her expression still worried.

"Well, that was interesting," Patsy said as she watched Ashley disappear out the front door.

Jenna turned toward the door herself, suddenly concerned about her landlord.

"Don't go," Patsy said, calling her back. "Those boxes of tile probably weigh more than you do. Let the men handle it. Besides, this gives me a chance to figure out what you're up to."

Jenna's stomach dropped a couple of inches as the

adrenaline hit her system. Had Patsy figured out her ruse? She turned and met the older woman's stare, trying to maintain the outward appearance of calm surprise. "What do you mean?" she asked.

"Well, you have to admit you're a mystery. You don't fit the mold of Ashley's usual guests. You're not obnoxious. You don't throw your money around. You don't name-drop. You even offer to help at times. You seem interested in everything. And you attended a town council hearing on development, which is odd. And I'm told that you showed up at church yesterday in the middle of a tropical storm. And you piqued the interest of my husband, who's sure your intentions toward Jude St. Pierre are not honorable."

"I'm paying Jude to give me sailing lessons."

"So I've heard. But I've also heard other things about you. So, tell me the truth. Are you working for Santee Resorts?"

"No."

Patsy studied her out of a pair of sharp blue eyes. "I believe you, but you're not telling the whole truth, are you?"

"I can assure you that I'm not here to spy on Jude, or to compromise him, or to lobby your husband in favor of development. I have nothing to do with any of that."

"But you went to the hearing."

"I did. It's a free country. I was interested in the topic."

"Why?"

Wow. Patsy was far more direct than her husband. And Jenna had two choices. Make up a lie or tell Patsy the truth.

She ought to tell the truth, but she couldn't. Not now. There were still secrets she needed to uncover about her father. Besides, she needed to tell Jude the truth before she announced it to the world. She didn't want him to find out about her through the local grapevine. Not after the way she'd brazenly kissed him and the way he'd answered that kiss.

"The truth is I'm interested in history," she said. "That's the reason I went to that hearing. And I'm hoping your husband supports Jude's petition on that land."

A little smile twitched on Patsy's lips. "So, maybe you're not working for Santee Resorts. To be honest, I would expect one of their people to dress better. Maybe we've gotten you all wrong, Miz Fairchild. Maybe you're one of those Yankee do-gooders, come down here to see if Jude is onto something."

"Maybe I am," Jenna said, looking Patsy right in the eye. If she had to choose a lie to live, let it be a lie where she supported Jude instead of working against him.

Chapter Twelve————————

*H*unnuh wake? E dun pass dayclean ya kno."

The sound of Old Jeeter's voice out on the porch pulled Jude out of his funk. He opened the door to find his great-uncle standing there in a pair of tattered pants and a golf shirt that had probably come right out of the Salvation Army bin.

Old Jeeter was Granny's older brother. He was about ninety, although no one really knew for sure. He'd worked as a shrimper for most of his life, but now he lived with Aunt Charlotte, who looked after him. He would still come by from time to time with a cane pole and a basket of crickets or night crawlers, looking for someone to go fishing with him.

Old Jeeter loved to fish, but today he wasn't carrying his pole or his bait basket.

"Hey," Jude said.

"Wha hunnuh da do ya ef Colton dey dey?"

Damn. Had Colton sent Jeeter to be his conscience?

Come to think of it, Old Jeeter would make a perfect Jiminy Cricket, except the old man spoke Gullah most of the time, so not many folks would understand what he had to say.

Jude shrugged in answer to Jeeter's question.

"Da ting ain no good!," Jeeter said. *"Ebeedbodee gwine memba dah."*

"Yeah."

"Go." The old man pointed a finger at him and then turned and headed down the porch steps, surprisingly spry for his age. When he'd disappeared into the woods, Jude sank down onto the single rocker on his porch.

Damn.

Micah was the last man on earth Jude wanted to help. He was still so angry with his brother for going away seventeen years ago. But Old Jeeter had a way of cutting through the BS and getting right to the heart of things. People would remember that he didn't help. Colton would never let him forget it.

And Colton was so good at telling him how to live his life. How he was wasting his time trying to get Daddy into rehab. How he should get another job and stop trying to get Daddy to sign over the title to *Reel Therapy* and give him the reins of the family business. And how misguided his attempts were to save this land from the bulldozers that were surely coming.

Yes. For sure people would remember how he didn't help his brother. The inevitable tide had turned. Micah was back, probably for good, and Jude would have to learn to live with that.

So he went looking for his tool belt and headed on into town. Fifteen minutes later, he pulled into the vicarage's driveway and parked behind one of the St. Pierre Construction diesel trucks where Colton and Micah were working unloading supplies.

"I see Old Jeeter changed your mind," Colton said, giving his shoulder a brotherly slap and a big smile.

"That was unfair," Jude said.

"No, it wasn't."

"I'm glad you're here," Micah said, his expression wide open and kind of vulnerable.

Damn. He didn't want to forgive Micah. Ever. But staying angry with him wasn't going to work either. "Yeah, well..." he said because he didn't know what else to say.

"Thank you. The house needs a lot of work, and I don't think the church ladies are up to the job." Micah rolled his eyes. "I have to tell you guys, I'm a little out of my element here. In the navy, I didn't have a permanent church. And I certainly didn't have a bunch of little old ladies sticking their noses into everything and giving me endless and contradictory opinions. I only had to help people in crisis, you know?"

Jude shook his head. "No. I don't know." He cast his gaze over the ugly ranch house. "So, this is the house they gave you?" he asked, unable to stop being angry.

"Don't judge," Colton said. "It's nicer than the one you're living in right at the moment. But then..."

"Don't," Jude said, shaking his head and giving Colton his super x-ray stare, which tended to bounce off Colton, and always had. Older brothers were a nuisance. "Let's not argue about Old Granny's house, okay?"

"We could cash in big, if you would—"

"Come on, Jude. We could use your help carrying this

tile," Micah interrupted, as he reached into the truck's bed and handed him a cardboard box that turned out to be heavier than it appeared. "This goes in the kitchen," he said, and gave Jude a push toward the front door.

Behind him, he heard Micah tell Colton to lay off. And for some reason, a little chink formed in the wall he kept around his heart. He'd forgotten how Micah had always stepped in when Colton got dictatorial and bossy.

Jude lugged the box to the open front door, wiped his feet on the big mat that had been placed in the foyer for that purpose, and made his way into the living room. Where he got the surprise of a lifetime.

There sat Patsy Bauman, presiding over everything like the Queen of Sheba. And who was there with her? None other than Jenna Fairchild, wearing a T-shirt with a tiny Buddha on it and one of those hippy-dippy sayings that made no sense at all. Something about how people's thoughts created reality. Yeah, right.

Why the hell was she there? What was she up to now? How had this stranger posing as a tourist managed to worm her way into the fabric of daily life in Magnolia Harbor?

He stood there holding the heavy box of tile, staring at her.

"Jude," Patsy said, breaking through his toxic thoughts, "I'm so glad you came too. I was worried that you're still angry at Micah."

Damn that woman. She knew too much about him, and the last thing he wanted was her running her mouth with Jenna standing right there taking it all in and making mental notes. "Ma'am," he said, ducking his head to be polite. "Where's the kitchen?" he asked.

"Over yonder." Patsy pointed him in the right direction. He put his head down and didn't look back.

For the next hour and a half, he was too busy following Colton's, Micah's, and Miz Bauman's sometimes-conflicting orders to confront Jenna about this latest invasion of his privacy. The idea of a big-ass resort company coming in here and cozying up to the members of his family and digging into his personal problems with his older brothers was just wrong.

He was not changing his mind. They needed to get that through their thick skulls.

At midday, Annie showed up with enough food to feed an army. There was gumbo, rice and lima beans, okra and tomatoes, and some German chocolate cake brought in by a couple of Micah's new parishioners. The sun was beginning to peek through the clouds, and almost everyone adjourned to the back patio to eat.

But not Jenna.

She hung back in the kitchen, her old pants spattered with the off-white paint they were slapping onto every wall in the house. She looked as if she'd been working hard, but that didn't deter him from cornering her and giving her hell.

"I don't appreciate what you're doing," he said, putting his paper plate down on the counter and folding his arms across his chest.

Her forehead rumpled. "What do you mean? Don't you like my painting technique?" She was trying to sound innocent, but there was a little vibration in her voice that suggested something else. She continued to play with the rice and beans on her plate.

"You know what I mean. Coming in here and getting

all friendly with my family and my friends. The way you and Patsy Bauman have been chatting all morning, you'd think you were long-lost relatives or something. I don't appreciate it. It's not fair. If Santee Resorts wants to have a conversation about the land north of town, they can just come in here and talk to me." He folded his arms.

She put her plate down next to his. "I'm not working for anyone, Jude. I told you that. Why won't you believe me?"

"Because you're not telling the truth. I can feel it in my bones. And I'm tired of it. I want you to leave Jonquil Island. Right away. And never come back. Is that clear? You mess with my family and it's over. Understand?"

She stood there for the longest moment as several unreadable expressions crossed her face. "I'm not messing with your family."

"Then what are you up to? And please don't give me another lie. I want the truth. I deserve the truth."

Yes, Jude did deserve the truth, but did Jenna want to tell him?

Karma slapped her in the face. She was responsible for his worry. And it didn't matter that he'd made the mistake or that the gossips in town had made up a likely story without any evidence to support it. All of that was on her because of her choice to use a false identity. Never had the connection between emotion, intention, and action been clearer. It was exactly as her T-shirt said.

"We need to talk," she said. "Not here." She picked up her lunch and headed through the front door and across the street to the rose garden's rear gate. Jude followed her, carrying his own lunch.

The sun chose that moment to peep from behind a cloud. Ashley's garden was beautiful, even this late in the season. The roses were mostly finished, but the brown-eyed Susans were lush. Color abounded here, reminding Jenna that the divine could be found anywhere. You just had to look for it.

Even now the divine was lighting up a pathway, steering Jenna toward the porch and a decision.

She stopped and dropped into one of the rocking chairs. Out beyond the hanging plants, the bay still churned in the wind, its choppy water topped with foam.

"Okay," Jude said, perching on the porch rail, balancing a plate full of ham and okra in one hand and an undersized plastic fork in the other. "I'm ready. Who are you, and why are you here?"

She took a bite of her beans and rice and chewed them thoroughly before she spoke. "I'm going to tell you the truth. But I need you to please keep it to yourself. I—"

"I can't make that promise." A muscle bunched along his jawline.

"Okay. I understand that. But when you learn the truth, I'm hoping you won't run off to tell Harry and Patsy, okay?"

He frowned. "What do they have to do with anything?"

She put her plate down on the porch floor and leaned back in the rocker, closing her eyes. "They have everything to do with why I'm here and why I attended that town council hearing. My name isn't Jenna Fairchild. It's Jenna Fossey."

She opened an eye when the silence stretched out for an eternity. "You don't recognize that name?"

He shook his head.

She sat up in her rocker and leaned her elbows on her knees. "If I said my name was Jenna Bauman, would that tip you off?"

"What?"

"If my father had married my mother, that would be my name. But my father didn't. He died before I was born." She took another long breath. "He died not even knowing that I existed." Her voice wobbled. And here she thought she was so strong.

She studied Jude as her throat closed down. He was still frowning as if he didn't quite get the joke, or maybe because he'd gotten it and was semi-horrified.

"I'm Harry and Patsy's niece. The one they never knew about. The one who got all of Robert Bauman's money." She laughed. "Patsy talks about me in her sewing circle. Did you know that? She must have really wanted that money."

She shook her head. "Jackie hears a lot of stuff, you know? Like how they all think my inheritance is undeserved. And how I'm illegitimate. I hate that word. It's makes me feel like I don't deserve to be alive."

"Holy crap," he said, his gaze sharpening into shock. Story of her life. But, then, it didn't matter. She was self-reliant. She didn't need these people. Much.

"I came here to see if there was any hope of having a relationship with Harry and Patsy," she continued. "Because my conscience demanded it. Because of bad karma, you know?"

He shook his head. "I've never understood karma," he said, his amber eyes locked on her.

"Yeah, well. I couldn't just knock on their door and

introduce myself, could I? I'd be told to leave and never come back. So, I pretended to be someone else. But you know, the funny thing is..." Suddenly, getting words out became a struggle. "I thought I didn't care. I was prepared to fail, you know. But..." She wiped the tears that filled her eyes.

Oh, crap. She was crying. She never cried. "I thought... you know, that my...father was a loser. Only that's all wrong, because he was a hero. He saved your life. And that means something. It changed the course of things. Jude, don't you see? Neither one of us would be alive today were it not for Jamie Bauman."

She sank her head into her hands as a huge bubble of emotion rose up in her, battering its way into the light. She sobbed, and it seemed so stupid. So after the fact. So unhelpful. But she couldn't stop once she started.

And then she wasn't alone anymore. He was there, kneeling in front of her rocker, taking her into his arms, giving her a place to rest her head. He was her sanctuary in that single moment, a haven against the howling wind of her emotions. In his arms she felt a deep connection she'd never expected, almost as if he carried a flame that was big enough and strong enough to keep her warm and safe through even the worst storm.

She should have seen this coming. She should have realized there would be pain caused by coming here looking for answers about the man who had abandoned her.

When at last she'd drained the giant well of emotion inside her, he pushed her away a little, his warm hands still on her shoulders. "We should go inside, just in case Ashley or Patsy come searching for you," he said, his tawny eyes so serious.

She wanted to tell him that his logic was flawed, but she didn't have the energy to argue. Sooner or later someone *would* come. But for him only.

She would never be missed.

Chapter Thirteen————

Jude had to push Jenna through the front door. She didn't seem to care about being discovered out on the porch crying on his shoulder. So he would care for her. And care about her.

She was the daughter of the woman Patsy and Harry hated. And she was right about one thing: If she'd knocked on their door and introduced herself, they would have sent her packing. Patsy and Harry blamed Jenna's mother for Jamie's death. Jude didn't know exactly why. He'd just heard enough to know it.

Should he tell her? Or should he let her discover the truth for herself?

He left her standing in the open foyer while he went back to retrieve their plates. He closed and locked the door behind him. "If anyone knocks, don't make a sound," he said to her back.

She turned, her face tear-ravaged, her nose blotchy and red. And yet her beauty shone through. His heart unfolded. She wasn't a spy at all.

Damn.

In a weird way, Jenna belonged on this island, the way he belonged here. As if the land had claimed them in some elemental way. He couldn't articulate this, but it resonated down in his gut. Maybe he would keep what he knew to himself. Maybe if Patsy and Harry got to know her first, they would change their minds.

"Are we hiding?" she asked, her voice low, husky, and sore.

He nodded. "Yes. And I promise to keep this secret until you're ready to tell everyone." He held out her plate. "Hungry?"

She shook her head.

"Neither am I." He stepped around her and moved across the sitting room to the small kitchenette. He put the food on the counter and turned. She hadn't moved.

"What you said a minute ago about Jamie. It's kind of freaky."

She took a deep breath and rolled her shoulders as if trying to let go of the tension. She took a step in his direction. He stayed put. "You mean the part about us both owing our lives to the same man?"

He nodded. "Someone neither of us knew."

She took another step. "Remember the other day, when I told you about synchronicity? This is an example of it."

"Yeah, I remember. And I don't really get all that woo-woo stuff."

She nodded, her mouth twitching a little. "It's okay. I don't always believe it myself, to tell you the truth."

"You don't?"

She shook her head. "A year ago, I ran away because inheriting a fortune cost me everything. My job, my self-esteem, my—" She stopped and shook her head before beginning again. "I thought, if I went to India and China and really worked at becoming a Buddhist, I would find some balance in my life. So I went off searching for something different to believe in, and I came back more confused than ever. There. I've said it out loud." She blew out a long breath. "I need to wash my face," she announced, and headed off into the bedroom.

He ought to go. He needed to get back to the vicarage before he was missed. But he stood there as if his feet were superglued to the floor.

She emerged from the bedroom after a few minutes, her nose still swollen and her eyes still red. But she'd taken her hair out of the ponytail and brushed it.

His fingers itched to touch all that honey-gold glory. But he said nothing. The ball was in her court, and he wasn't even sure what game they were playing now. Maybe they weren't playing games, which was even more sobering.

"So, um, anyway," she said, "I went to the town council hearing because I found out that Harry was a council member. I went there just to get a look at him. I didn't know you had anything to do with the hearing. And then afterward, Harry came over to you and patted you on the back as if you were old friends. That was an example of synchronicity, or if you prefer you can call it a coincidence or a sign from heaven. I realized that I had to continue with sailing lessons because you knew Harry and would lead me to him eventually. And you did."

"So that's why you agreed to the outrageous fees for those lessons?"

She nodded. "But you should know that it didn't start that way. On the first day I arrived, I saw you sailing out on the bay, and I knew I needed to learn what it felt like to be in a small boat. Because when I first arrived, that was all I knew about my father. That he was a sailor. And not just any kind of sailor. He raced small boats, the way you do."

She took another step closer. If he wanted, he could reach out and touch that golden hair of hers. "So, this thing you said. This synchronicity?" His words came out as a whisper.

The corner of her mouth twitched upward, revealing the laugh line that was almost a dimple. Man, that little expression was so damn kissable. Desire, hot and liquid, flowed through him.

"According to Eastern philosophies," she said, "we make our own universe. There's no such thing as coincidence. Coincidences are signs that pop up because of the paths we've taken. Our path creates the connections in front of us. I came here. I made this connection. You are the big surprise..." She paused a moment before continuing, "You and my father, whom I never knew. But in any event, these connections aren't random. They were created by my father's actions before he died. He conceived me; he saved you. We're here because of him. And I came to make a connection, and you were the first person I connected with."

He stepped closer and brought his hand up to caress her cheek. "Kind of freaky," he murmured.

She leaned into his touch, sending sweet, hot sparks up his arm. He tugged at her, and she came to him willingly. When their lips met, the reaction was instantaneous and deep.

Jude. His lips. His tongue. His scent, like an exotic spice from some far-off land. The bite of his beard against her cheek. And his taste...so sweet and so carnal.

She spiked her fingers up into his hair, reveling in its slightly coarse texture. She pulled him deeper into the kiss, her whole body melting. She opened him like a cosmic present, as if he were her heart's unspoken and unknown desire.

He tangled his big hands in her hair, unleashing sensation down to the tip of each split end. His kiss breathed life into her.

Where there was fear, he brought strength. Where there was uncertainty, he brought clarity. Where there was disquiet, he brought peace.

Whoa, wait. Scary.

The inner alarms began to sound right on cue. Why was it that she could never quite get out of her own way? A whole raft of what-ifs lined up and flooded her head. What if she let herself go? What if she allowed this connection to blossom? What if Harry and Patsy never accepted her? What if Jude's family hated her? What if...?

The possibilities were endless, and they all ended in disaster.

This. This had always been her problem. Being unable to accept the impermanence of everything. Wanting to hold on too hard to whatever she wanted or desired. Buddhists called this suffering. They had a point.

She put her hands on his shoulders and pushed him away a little. "Wait," she whispered out of her kiss-swollen lips.

He backed up like a gentleman, and when she gazed up into his amazing amber eyes, made dark by passion, she felt a tug deep in her belly. Yes, they were connected in some strange way.

"What?" he murmured.

"I..." She didn't know where to begin.

"Look," he said. "I get it. You're a Bauman, and I'm a St. Pierre. That's going to cause problems."

"I don't care about your last name," she said, instead of telling him the real reason she hesitated. It was one thing to fall in love, whatever that was, but this need she felt for him...It was frightening.

"Then you're a remarkable woman. But I knew that already. But if you're not sure..."

She shook her head, deciding to ignore the doubts. She could stand there thinking about this for a thousand years and be no closer to understanding herself. Maybe it was better to go with the lust that had seized every cell in her body.

So she lied. "No doubts. Just insecurities. The truth is, I've never been any good at sex." Well, that last part was true. She hadn't had a lot of practice at sex.

This half-truth earned her the sweetest smile. "I find that hard to believe," he said, right before he moved in again. His lips met hers, and her body exploded with the same deep need that had so frightened her.

But he was strong and unafraid. She could shelter in his arms, and maybe that was enough. Besides, they were connected. They had synchronicity, whatever that truly meant.

She let go and fell into his kiss, and his touch, and the wonders of his beautiful body.

Much later, when he'd undressed her and laid her out on the handmade quilt in the bedroom, she allowed herself to experience the true wonder of the strange and unexpected connection between them. A connection she'd felt from the first moment she'd seen him, out in *Bonney Rose*, the sun on his brown skin, the wind in his dark, curly hair.

Jenna's caress was like the bay on a warm summer day. It flowed over his skin, touching the guarded place deep within. And when he lost it, when, at the moment of climax his eyes filled with tears, it knocked him for a loop.

He knew something had changed when they were coming down from the high, when she spotted the water in his eyes and seemed to see right into him.

Damn.

The sex had been great, but…it didn't explain why they were tangled up. Like that word she used—synchro-whatever.

That connection made this more than a casual hook-up. And no matter what he might have told himself, he'd known it before he'd come into this room. He opened his eyes, her golden hair a tangled mess across the pillow.

Damn.

Was he making the same mistake his father had made? It frightened him. The idea that one day he might end up like Daddy scared the crap out of him. He'd never seen himself settling down with a golden-haired Boston Yankee. His dream had been so much simpler. A nice island girl from a good family, maybe with some connection to the Gullah culture.

Jenna lifted her hand and gave him a wide-eyed stare as she ran her fingers over his brow and down the side of his face. "You're beautiful," she whispered.

Not really. But he didn't argue. Instead, he rolled away

and headed to the bathroom. He needed a moment to re-gain perspective.

She was Harry's niece. She was a Bauman, whether she used that name or not. She belonged to the people on this side of the divide. And even if he and Harry had a friendship of sorts, the fact remained that Jude was not a member of the yacht club. Although he could probably join now if he wanted to. Twenty years ago, when he'd worked there mowing the lawn and trimming the hedges, the club had been "private." A code word for segregated.

And even if she was blind to the racial divide, there was the money. He leaned against the sink as a strange, uncanny tremor rippled down his back, sending goose-flesh prickling along his skin. For an instant it felt as if someone were watching him. Judging him.

He straightened and glanced over his shoulder. He was alone.

Maybe those stories about Rose Cottage were true. In which case, the spirit of Captain Teel was checking him out. An ironic thought, given the island's myths and the role his ancestor Henri St. Pierre played in that story of love gained and lost. Captain Teel was either an idiot or so blind in love that he'd tried to sail a ship over-loaded with stolen gold through the inlet in the middle of a hurricane.

Yeah. Sometimes treasure was a big problem. And Jenna...Bauman was a woman who'd inherited treasure in dispute. Never a good thing.

He should go. He straightened his shoulders and men-tally prepared himself for a difficult scene before he opened the door. But the laugh was on him. The bed was empty. She hadn't been waiting for him.

He found his clothes, dressed, and then strolled out onto the porch, where she sat on her yoga mat in the classic Buddha pose. "I have to go," he said.

"I know."

He wanted to confront her, but for what reason? She could do the relationship math as well as he could.

"I want you to know that I'll keep your secret."

She blew out a long breath and broke her pose, drawing her legs up to her chest and hugging her knees. The posture was defensive. He understood why. Like her, he was an abandoned child. Trusting was difficult. And in this case, she was wise not to trust, not to fall. And so was he.

Chapter Fourteen————————

Jude was avoiding her, and Jenna could understand why. The sex had been amazing. So amazing that they'd both retreated into their separate corners. But she missed him almost as soon as he walked through the garden gate. So she texted him a couple of times on Tuesday, trying to schedule the sailing lesson they'd discussed. But he didn't reply.

Not having anything else to do, she ended up sitting on the porch, finishing the Sue Grafton novel. Later in the afternoon, she went downtown and bought the dress at Daffy Down Dilly and then went to Rafferty's, hoping to see Jude sailing out on the bay with the rest of the Buccaneers. He wasn't there, and *Bonney Rose* remained in the parking lot while Jude's friends headed out for practice races.

On Wednesday morning, she drove onto the mainland and visited a couple of the historic plantations. It was interesting, but she wasn't making any headway in con-

necting with Patsy or Harry, and all she could think about
was Jude St. Pierre.

By the afternoon, sitting on Rafferty's deck drinking
a glass of chardonnay, she felt exactly like a sailboat in
calm waters. Just sitting there bobbing on the water while
the sun beat down on her. Stuck. Unable to move.

And then she remembered what Harry had said the
other day. She fired up her cell phone, went onto the Magnolia Harbor town web page, and confirmed that the
council was holding a meeting this afternoon. Since the
zoning petition was up for discussion, Jenna was pretty
sure Jude would be there. She could kill two birds with
one stone.

An hour later, she entered Magnolia Harbor's town
council chamber. The room was tiny, which explained
why they'd borrowed space from the Methodists for their
hearing last week. The place was standing-room only for
today's meeting. She squeezed into a spot in the corner of
the room and had to stand on tiptoes and crane her neck
in an awkward way to see anything.

Jude had a seat in the first row, and he looked awe-
somely handsome in his gray suit and red tie. Jenna's heart
took off at a wild gallop the moment she spied him. No
question about it, she wanted to make love with him another time. But it was more than just that. She cared about
him. She wanted him to win this fight, and the idea that
her own uncle might deny him made her queasy.

The meeting of the council began right on time, but it
took a good thirty minutes to get through the approval of
the last meeting's minutes and a list of old business items
dealing with garbage disposal and a new car for the small
police force.

And then, finally, the issue was called and the council members each made a speech about the proposal. Two board members spoke against it and two spoke for it before Harry took the microphone.

He cast his gaze out over the assemblage, stopping for a long moment as he made eye contact with Jude. Jenna's heart began to sink. She knew even before he opened his mouth that Harry Bauman was going to vote against Jude.

"I appreciate the culture of the folks living in 'Gullah Town,'" Harry began. "And I think the town council should give some thought to a museum or some other interpretive site to commemorate those people. My staff and I are working on a proposal to create a museum someplace downtown, where cultural artifacts can be preserved and history can be presented."

He looked right at Jude. "Including the language, Jude. I envision making Gullah storytellers available for live presentations. And I'd like to raise funds to record the language before it disappears. I think Magnolia Harbor needs to acknowledge this part of its history, and I will do everything I can to make sure that happens."

He shook his head. "But in the end, I can't support this petition to radically change the town's master plan. I'm swayed by the opinion of the South Carolina Historic Preservation Office, which has declined to nominate any of the structures included in this proposed zoning amendment for inclusion in the National Register of Historic Places. All of these structures have been significantly altered over the years, reducing their historic value. And I truly believe there is a better way to interpret and save the Gullah culture that is so important to our island.

"And so I reluctantly vote no on this proposed amendment to our master plan."

A roar of triumph and despair filled the tiny room, forcing the chairwoman to bang her gavel and demand order. Jude slumped back in his chair and scrubbed his hands over his head, a portrait of frustration and disappointment. Her heart ached for him, and her opinion of Harry Bauman took a nosedive.

How could he have done such a thing to a man he purported to like?

Maybe she didn't want to know Harry. Maybe she was better off never letting him know who she was.

But then it occurred to her that if she chose that path, she'd have to leave Jonquil Island and never come back. And that wasn't what she wanted either.

Was it?

No. It was not. And that thought was nothing short of a revelation.

"Well," Greg said with a shrug of his shoulders, "it was worth a try."

The chairwoman had just gaveled the meeting to a close, and folks were streaming out of the small, stuffy room. Jude tried to feel something, but he was numb. Greg had never really held out much hope for this gambit. Not when South Carolina had decided that the structures were too damaged or altered to merit protection.

They had a point. Most of the original freeman cottages had been one or two rooms, and folks with families had added on. To protect those houses, they'd have to be taken back to their smaller state. And at this point, most of those places had been abandoned. People were ready to sell off the land and cash in.

And that would spell disaster for everything he cared about.

"We'll have to see if we can get private help, although so much of the money is going to other sea islands with more historic structures. We're a little late to the party," Greg said as he buckled up his old-fashioned briefcase. Greg gave Jude's shoulder squeeze. "I'll be in touch," he said, and then headed out the door with everyone else.

Except Harry, who came over to sit down next to him. "I'm sorry," he said.

Jude tried to be angry at his old friend. But it was hard. Harry had always been on the side of development. Jude had never expected to win his vote. But he didn't fully accept Harry's apology. He just nodded his head.

"Look, I know this is hard. But without the seal of approval from the state's historic preservation office we just couldn't move forward the way you wanted us to. But look here. There's another way. I've been telling you this for months. Are you ready to listen?"

Jude shook his head. "Where are we going to find the private money for a museum? And I know a museum is a good thing, but there's this part of me, down deep, that just hates the idea of shoving my great-grandmother's culture into a museum. Is that what we're down to, becoming something extinct that people have to go to a museum to see?"

"Look, I know you're angry at me right now, but think about it. I want to even up the score. We need to include Gullah as part of our history. And it's long past time."

Harry also gave his shoulder a squeeze before he left. Jude stayed put, letting everyone leave before he got up. He really didn't have the energy to deal with people's disappointment, or regret, or pity, or whatever emotion they wanted to pin on him.

He was about to get up when the hairs on the back of his neck stood on end. He turned, as gooseflesh puckered his back. She was there, walking down the aisle in a sundress with daffodils all over it.

She had nice legs, and she'd upgraded her sandals and lost the rubber flip-flops. "Hi," she said as she dropped into the seat next to him. "I'm sorry about what happened. I wish there was something I could do to help. For what it's worth, I don't think I like my uncle very much. And I know the museum doesn't solve your problems. It's really about the land, isn't it?"

Damn. It was like she understood. How did that happen? A warm, liquid feeling swamped his chest. "Hey," was all he managed to say.

"I looked for you last night, sailing with the Buccaneers."

"Oh, I didn't make it. Greg and I were doing last-minute meetings with the council members. Not that it did much good."

"I'm sorry. You know, I'd love to see your ancestor's land," she said.

He let go of a hoarse laugh. "So you want to see the place before it gets divided up and paved over, huh?"

"Isn't there some way you could raise private funds to save the structures?"

He shook his head. "It's not just the buildings."

"No? What, then?"

She didn't fully understand, which was predictable since she was a white woman from Boston with more money than God. "It's everything. A way of life. And all the money in the world can't save it."

She reached out and squeezed his hand, and comfort flowed through the connection. He didn't want to feel that. He didn't want her to understand.

Damn.

"Would you show me? Please?"

He turned to look her in the eye. "When? Now?"

She shrugged. "I was thinking of buying you dinner now. At Annie's Kitchen. I love her beans and rice. But maybe you could take me on a tour tomorrow if you don't have a charter."

He shook his head. "I don't know."

"Are you trying to avoid me?" she asked.

Well, she had him there. He had been trying to avoid her because she looked like a big mess of trouble. If he didn't watch out, he'd end up exactly like Daddy, strung out on some blond woman who didn't belong here. And what the hell would Harry say if he knew Jude had gone to bed with his niece?

Harry was a good man, but he was still commodore of the yacht club, which had yet to accept an African American as a member. And hadn't Harry just chosen development over saving Jude's culture?

"Look, Jenna, I think maybe we should—"

"Don't. Don't push me away just because Harry did something asinine. He may be related to me, but I don't know him from Adam, remember?"

He looked up into her warm brown eyes. "You really want to go see what the fuss is about?"

"I do."

"Okay. I'll pick you up at the cottage around ten tomorrow."

"And dinner?"

He shook his head. "I'm sorry. I have to get home," he said, using Daddy as an excuse. He didn't trust his heart around this woman. He couldn't afford to fall in love with Jenna Bauman. There was no scenario where a relationship between them could ever work. Tomorrow he'd show her why.

Chapter Fifteen————

Jude was early, but he strolled through the back garden gate off of Lilac Lane and found Jenna on the porch wearing a pair of yoga pants and a sports bra. She was lying on her mat, her body flexed upward. The pose gave him a killer view of her breasts, which were just the right size. Enough to fit in the palms of his hands.

Damn. He was supposed to be here trying to discourage her. And himself. This was not a good omen. He didn't say a word though. Instead he stood there admiring the way she could flex her body, until she became aware of him. Funny how her loose and supple muscles tightened right up the moment she laid eyes on him. Yeah, there was a lot of chemistry here. Strong chemistry that could blow up if he didn't watch himself.

She scrambled up from the porch. "Oh my God, did I lose track of time? I'm so sorry. I—"

"Chill. I'm early. I was enjoying the view," he said, unable to help himself.

Her cheeks colored. "Um, I'll just go in. You know...
and change." She cocked her head and studied him. He got
the feeling she was about to say something else, but she
held her tongue. Good.

He didn't think she needed to change at all. She was
perfect exactly as she was, with a glow on her pale
cheeks, her lithe body hugged by the spandex, and that
light in her big brown eyes.

He wished to heaven he didn't like her so much. He
dropped into one of the rockers and waited for her. She
didn't take long to change—another thing to admire
about her. When she reappeared, she was wearing a pair
of faded blue jeans and a Boston Red Sox T-shirt, both of
them a little oversized. He found himself wishing she'd
left her yoga clothes on.

"So," she said with a bright smile, "tell me about everything."

"Everything?" He couldn't help but smile at her enthusiasm.

She nodded.

"I think showing might be better than telling."

Jude took her to a beautiful place way back in a forest
filled with live oak, scrub pine, and palmettos. It was
shady here under the twisted branches of ancient trees,
and everywhere, the long trailing beards of silver Spanish
moss draped from branch to branch.

He parked his truck in a sandy spot in front of an old
house sitting under the biggest live oak Jenna had ever
seen in her life. Chickens ranged free in the sandy front
yard, and a neat vegetable garden grew along the side of
the house in a patch of sunlight.

The house had a rusty tin roof and looked in need of painting. The siding was uneven, as if it had been hand hewn. A couple of women sat in straight-back chairs on the porch weaving baskets.

"Come meet my aunts," he said.

"Are you bringing me home to meet the folks'?"

He turned and gave her a sober stare out of those amber eyes of his. "Yes. But not for the reason you think."

"Oh, you mean you're trying to scare me off?"

He blinked.

"I wasn't born yesterday. I realize that my being Harry Bauman's niece is a big problem for you. But hey, I don't know Harry, and he really doesn't know me. So it's not like we're a real family. And furthermore, I don't have a family at all. Just my mother, and she passed away three years ago. So scaring me is going to be hard. Just sayin'."

"Noted," he said with a little smirk as he opened the truck door.

She hopped down from the pickup and followed Jude across the yard, studying his aunts as she walked. One of them was a thin, ancient-looking woman with white cotton hair and a sinewy look to her. She wore an Atlanta Braves sweatshirt and a pair of white cutoff jeans that showed her sticklike legs. She hadn't looked up from her work, not even when Jude pulled the truck into the dirt driveway. The woman sitting beside her was much younger and stouter and wore a straw hat, a jean skirt, and a flowered blouse in pink and purple. She looked up and gave Jude a broad smile that flashed a gold filling.

"Hey," she said. "How you doing, Jude? Heard about the town council. It's a shame. A sad, sad shame."

"Yes, it is. Aunt Charlotte, come meet my friend Jenna. She wanted to come out here to see what the fuss was all about. As you can see from her shirt, she's from Boston."

Charlotte got up from her seat and came down the porch steps. "Nice to meet you. Are you a baseball fan, or are you just wearing that shirt?"

Jenna grinned. "Been a BoSox fan all my life."

Charlotte glanced toward Jude. "I like her already."

Jenna's face heated, and Jude rolled his beautiful eyes before he said, "Aunt Charlotte is Annie's momma."

"That's right. And I taught her everything she knows about cooking."

"Well, that's a lot," Jenna said. "I especially like her rice and beans."

"Come on up and sit for a while," Charlotte said with a wave of her hand.

They followed her up onto the porch, and Jenna soon found herself sitting next to Jude on an old, slightly rusted metal glider.

"Hey, Aunt Daisy," Jude said once they sat down.

The old woman finally lifted her gaze from the gorgeous basket she was weaving, studied Jude for a moment from behind her metal-rimmed trifocals, and said, "*Me glade fa see oona.*"

Jenna thought she heard the words "me" and "glad," but the rest of it sounded like some other language.

"I'm glad too," Jude said, confirming at least one of the words the old woman had spoken. He turned toward Jenna. "That's Gullah," he said. "It sounds pretty foreign, but if you listen carefully, it's got a lot of English and African words all jumbled together."

A moment later, Charlotte returned with some sweet tea. "Aunt Daisy, tell Jenna about your basket," Jude said in English.

The old woman nodded, clearly capable of understanding, but then she started talking in a rusty voice in a language Jenna couldn't follow but which had a beautiful, syncopated rhythm to it that sounded African.

Daisy did more than lull Jenna with the way she talked. Her old bent fingers working, stitching together a basket made of grass and palmetto fronds, was nothing short of mesmerizing. This old woman was a master craftsman. The basket she was making was a thing of beauty and utility.

"You want to start one?" Charlotte asked, looking right at Jude.

"Sure," he said, picking up a handful of grass and bundling it together. He wrapped the palmetto around the grass and began working. His young fingers were as skilled and nimble as the old woman's.

After he'd been weaving for a few minutes, he looked up at Jenna. "My old granny—that would be my great-grandmother, Aunt Daisy's momma, was a basket maker. And it's a tradition that basket makers teach their children from an early age. Old Granny taught my grandmother, who was Aunt Charlotte's mother. And Charlotte taught Annie, although Annie always had a knack for cooking. But my daddy never learned, and my momma was a white woman from Chicago."

"Yes, well," Charlotte said, "my momma, Jude's granny, married a St. Pierre. And our daddy wasn't part of Gullah culture. So that's where the handing off got lost."

"*Ain so wid hunnuh*," Daisy said, giving Jude a smile.

"No, not with me. Because I ended up staying with Old Granny a lot of the time when I was little."

"'Cause your momma was a party girl," Charlotte said, looking up at Jenna, sending a message. Okay, she got it. He'd brought her out here to make a point. They came from different worlds. So what?

"Can you teach me to do that?" she asked.

Silence. Both Charlotte and Daisy looked up at her. And then Daisy said, "*Ona kum yah. We bin yah.*" She gave a nod and returned to her work.

Uh-oh. She'd clearly stepped on a land mine. "I guess that means no," she said.

"Well, roughly translated it means that you just came here, but we've all been here," Jude said.

So she was an outsider. Clearly. Or maybe the old woman was trying to say that she was white and they were black.

Jude put down the basket he'd started. "I want to show you something." He stood up and offered her his hand. She took it and let him pull her out of the old glider. The warm, rough texture of his palm unleashed a torrent of chemicals in her bloodstream. He was handsome, and strong, and stubborn, but he could still sit down with a couple of old ladies and make a basket.

She admired that about him.

"Come on," he said as he pulled her down the porch and around the house. Along the way, he pointed out the hand-hewn siding and the handmade bricks in the old chimney. "That's the kind of thing I wanted to save, you know? But this house was added on to, back in the 1940s, so it's not historic enough." He shook his head as he guided her down a sandy track at the back of the yard that led down to the edge of a marshland bordering the bay.

"See that?" He pointed to the tall grass growing at the end of the marsh. "That's the sweetgrass my aunts use to make those baskets up there. It takes a day to make a simple basket, and as much as a month to finish something like what Aunt Daisy is working on. But that's okay because each of those baskets fetches a lot of money when Charlotte takes them down to the market in Charleston. Charlotte and Daisy and Old Jeeter, my uncle, depend on that income. And if Santee Resorts comes in here and forces these folks off this land, that stand of sweetgrass will be uprooted and destroyed to make way for yet another resort golf course."

Jenna turned to stare at him. "You don't care about the houses, do you? It's all about that." She pointed at the grass.

He nodded. "It's way more important than preserving the buildings. But no one gives a crap about the grass. This is where it grows. And if Charlotte and Daisy have to sell out, their livelihood will be gone."

"They don't have to sell out, do they?"

He shook his head. "Once the development starts, the property values around here will get so high that they'll have no way to cover the taxes on the land. Plus, it's complicated because this land is something called 'heirs property.' It's been passed down informally from generation to generation without legal paperwork. So there are at least thirty people who own shares in this land. Any one of them could sell out."

"That's not fair."

"No, it's not. But it's reality. And the sad part is that

there aren't many places you can get sweetgrass anymore. Either it's been bulldozed into oblivion or it's inaccessible, growing behind the gates of new communities.

"When it's all gone, not even shoving my aunts into a museum will save the culture."

"Oh, Jude, I'm so sorry," Jenna said, turning toward him with what looked like real understanding in her eyes.

Damn. He kept trying to make this difficult for her, and she kept seeing right through him.

"There must be some way we can stop it from happening."

He laughed because he didn't know what else to do. "So says the trust fund girl."

"I wish you wouldn't call me that. I didn't ask for the money, you know. And now that I have it, it's a huge responsibility."

"I'll bet," he said, turning his back on her.

"Look, I get your resentment. I do. But I'm trying to be helpful."

"Right."

"Stop!" She grabbed him by the arm and turned him around to face her. Overhead a seabird cried.

"What?"

"I know what you're thinking. I'm a white girl from a white-bread world with a ton of money, and here I am swooping in to provide advice. Yeah, I get it. But if we could just leave the stereotypes aside for one minute, that would be helpful."

"Okay."

"What I was about to say was that I have often found

that it's faster, easier, cheaper, and more effective to find private solutions to problems like this, instead of waiting around fighting the government."

His lips twitched. "You sound Republican too."

"I am a card-carrying independent. But that doesn't matter. What you need here is a nonprofit corporation. You know, like the Nature Conservancy, only for culture."

"What?"

"The Nature Conservancy. It's a private group that buys up environmentally significant land to ensure it never gets developed. Have you ever tried that route?"

He shook his head.

"Well, you should. And if that doesn't work, I'll bet you could put together a nonprofit of your own, composed of family members, and raise money to pay the taxes and keep the land out of the developers' hands."

"Okay. I admit I never thought of that. But hell, we all own shares anyway. Why not turn it into a corporation?" He stared down at this remarkable woman. "You are very smart, aren't you?"

"Don't sell yourself short. I've never owned my own business. I've always worked for someone else. So I envy you, Jude St. Pierre. I envy your passion. And your cause. And your experience. You may have brought me out here to scare me, but you've failed."

"I don't really own my own business. It belongs to Daddy."

"BS. Maybe his name is on the papers, but you're the guy paying the bills."

"It's hardly successful."

"Doesn't matter. We don't learn by our successes,

Jude. To get far in life you have to fail. Numerous times."

He laughed at that. "Is that another wise saying from Buddha?"

"No. It's something I got from my professors. You have to fall down before you can learn to walk."

"Yeah, well, I think I'm good at falling down."

"Which means you've got loads of experience that I don't have." She rose up on tiptoes and kissed his chin. "You don't scare me, Jude."

"That's funny because you scare the hell out of me."

She cocked her head, and her big brown eyes grew wide. "Why?"

"Because of your optimism. And because you have the ability to hurt me. You're not what I've been looking for. And yet, when you talk, it's like I can see a future I never thought could possibly exist. Believing in that future is frightening as crap."

"'All that we are is the result of what we have thought,'" she said. "Now, that's Buddha." She poked him in the middle of his chest. "So stop thinking about yourself in the negative."

He couldn't contain a smile. "Why is it that all your woo-woo stuff is starting to make sense to me?"

"Because Buddha was a wise man. And you are a smart, capable, passionate, and stubborn man. I find all those traits enormously appealing."

He should have known it would be impossible to scare Jenna away. So they stayed for supper. Laughed around the table. Taught Jenna a few words of Gullah. And even managed to get Aunt Daisy to finally admit that she could speak English as well as—or maybe better than—anyone. Daisy had been a schoolteacher for years before she retired at the age of seventy.

By the time they finally waved good-bye to his aunts, it had started to rain again, but Jude still broke a couple of speed limits driving back to the cottage by way of the convenience store on Harbor Drive, where he purchased a box of condoms.

And then they dodged the raindrops from the cottage's parking lot to the porch while simultaneously kissing. Once the door closed, they lost their clothes in a big hurry. Limbs became entangled with T-shirts, toes got stubbed on furniture, and Jude's nose got bumped inadvertently when Jenna straightened up after shucking her jeans.

Luckily, no blood was shed by the time they made it to the bed.

Where her kisses ignited something inside him that unfolded into more than five senses. She smelled like heaven. Her skin was like silk under his hands. The glow from the gas fireplace haloed her hair. She tasted like heaven. And when he touched her most sensitive places, she sighed and gasped in delight. But for all that, he felt something more. Something without a name and yet just as palpable.

And when they came back down, they lay together, wrapped in each other's arms as the afternoon slipped away, the rain beating at the metal roof. Jenna drifted off into sleep, but Jude remained awake, her deep breathing whispering against his ear, the firelight flickering across the ceiling.

The hand of fate had brought her into his life. He could

see that now. They were tangled up together in some odd way. He twisted a lock of her hair around his finger. It shimmered a hundred different colors in the firelight. Maybe he'd resisted her so hard because he'd known all along that he'd end up here, falling in love.

She moved a little, snuggling deeper against his body. He studied her skin, so tan in the sun-exposed places and so milky white in all the spots where the sun couldn't go.

She wasn't his ideal woman. And yet…

Would this connection last? Their bodies might fit together perfectly, but it was more than sex. He'd taken her out there to Aunt Charlotte's place expecting her to have second thoughts, and she'd simply enjoyed herself and asked questions and tried to understand Aunt Daisy's Gullah, which was just Daisy's way of testing her.

Maybe she wasn't like his mother. Maybe she could see herself staying.

He swallowed back the hurt. He was repeating Daddy's mistakes. And no matter how he tried to convince himself otherwise, the truth was right there in the color of her hair.

He squeezed his eyes closed. Damn. Damn. Damn. Moments ago he'd let himself get lost in Jenna's wide, strange, wonderfully optimistic but ultimately privileged world. He didn't want to lose her. He didn't want to come down from the high. He didn't want to think about the inevitable bad stuff.

But the bad stuff always found him, no matter what.

He took a deep breath and listened to the rain and tried to empty his mind. He dozed on and off, waking once from a dream where he'd been sailing a beautiful schooner across a vast ocean. The rain gradually tapered off, and the night grew quiet.

He awoke hours later to the sound of his cell phone. Damn. This early in the morning it could only be Daddy.

"Where are you?" Daddy asked when Jude connected.

"None of your business."

"Yeah, well, it is my business when you don't show up for a charter."

"What?"

"Have you got your head up your butt? It's Friday morning. We have a charter to take the Weiss family out for some deep-sea fishing. They'll be arriving here in about twenty minutes."

"Damn. I forgot."

"Yeah, well, that happens when you start messing around with blond tourists who have money to spare. But trust me, it ain't gonna work out. Get your ass over here, you hear?"

"I heard that," Jenna mumbled as she rolled over in bed, giving him a delicious view of the pale skin of her breasts. "Guess you have to go."

"Yeah. And I'm going to be busy the next few days."

"Of course you are."

He hated the tone in her voice. "I'm sorry. I work weekends mostly."

"Yeah, I know. Day and night. And I'm sure you wouldn't want to be seen letting me buy you dinner at Rafferty's."

"I gotta go." He rolled out of bed and started looking for his clothes.

She followed him out into the sitting room, beautifully naked and utterly distracting.

"Look, I get it. This is just going to be one of those is-land flings or whatever. But I have a favor to ask."

"Okay." He wasn't sure he wanted to do her any favors. He wanted to grab her by the shoulders and tell her to be careful with his heart, because he'd fallen for her. And he knew she would leave him one day.

"One day next week, can you sail me out to the inlet?"

"What? Are you out of your mind?"

She shook her head. "I want to go out there to where my father died."

"If you want to pay your respects, you can visit his grave at Heavenly Rest."

"He's buried here?"

Jude nodded.

"I didn't know that." She looked away for a moment. "Okay, but it doesn't change my mind. I want to go out to that place. I need to go there, and I'll pay you whatever rate you name."

He shook his head. "I don't want to be paid." He blew out an angry sigh before speaking again. "Look, taking a small boat out to the inlet is crazy. You don't want to do it. I can take you out there on *Reel Therapy*. Having an engine can be a lifesaver if things get hinky."

"No. I want to go in a small boat. Like *Bonney Rose*. Was my father sailing a Bucc?"

He shook his head. "No. He had an old Albacore that he'd rescued from someone's backyard as a teenager. They found that old boat after the accident and towed it back. Harry put it up on blocks in his yard. It's been there for decades. The dry rot has ruined it, but Harry refuses to let it go."

She nodded. "Yeah, I saw it there. When I first came

to the island. I stood on the sidewalk and decided not to knock on their door."

"You should tell them the truth, Jenna."

"I know. And I will. When I'm ready. But—"

He pulled on his T-shirt. "Sorry. I understand what you want. But I'm not taking you out there." He blew out a breath. "I had a good time last night. I did. But I gotta go now."

Chapter Sixteen

Having mind-bending sex with a guy who didn't want to fall in love was not really a problem, was it?

She didn't want to fall in love either. Love was messy. Especially since she was falling for Jude St. Pierre, who was a friend of her long-lost uncle, whom she'd been lying to and who probably hated her anyway.

Oh yeah, and he was skittish about the whole race thing. And who wouldn't be?

So it didn't surprise her when he didn't call or text on Friday night and didn't offer to take her out for dinner on Saturday. The sex had been beautiful and mind-altering and scary for two people who were dealing with abandonment issues.

She embraced her solitude. Being alone had never much bothered her. And she finally acknowledged that her year-long vacation from her life was almost at its end. Sooner or later, she'd have to return to Boston or New York and figure out what to do about the rest of her life.

She already knew that she wasn't cut out for the idle life. She may not have worked at a job this last year, but she'd worked on herself. And during the time she'd spent at the ashram, she'd been busy with more than meditation.

So she started to polish up her résumé, but the more she worked at it, the more dissatisfied she became with the idea of returning to some Fortune 500 corporation, working for someone other than herself. What was she afraid of anyway? Failing?

Yes. Back when she'd gone for her MBA, she was always the one person in the group who wasn't hell-bent to become an entrepreneur. She'd been happy working for someone else because she craved the security of it.

Ha. The laugh was on her. There was no security in life. It was ever changing, and bad stuff happened all the time. You had to learn how to go with the flow. If she'd learned anything this past year, it was that happiness was found when you stopped resisting it.

Maybe she could learn something from Jude. He'd never worked for anyone but his father, which was a way of saying that he'd been working for himself, even though he might not see it that way. There was a one hell of a difference between working for some faceless corporation and working in a family business.

So she abandoned her résumé almost as soon as she started working on it. And she allowed the familiar restlessness in. She needed a passion. She needed a purpose. She needed one good business idea that she could develop for herself instead of handing it off to someone else. But good business ideas were hard to come by. They could be elusive if you pursued them directly.

Sometimes it was best to just be aware and not to force the issue.

So she was glad when Sunday finally rolled around, providing a distraction from one problem and an opportunity to work on another. She dressed in her new sundress and headed off to Heavenly Rest. Jenna had a feeling Patsy and Harry would be there this time since it was Micah St. Pierre's first Sunday on the job.

And what a difference a week made. It was a glorious September day filled with bright sky and sunlight, and it looked as if the entire congregation had turned out. Almost every seat was filled. She slipped into one of the back pews and settled in for the worship service she didn't quite comprehend. But when Micah St. Pierre stepped up onto the historic wooden pulpit, wearing a black cassock, a white robe, and a green stole, her boredom disappeared. His presence was commanding, and when he began to speak in a resonant baritone, it was hard not to listen.

He read a passage from the Bible that told a story about a man entrusting large sums of money into his servants' care. In the story, two of the servants invest the money and make big profits, while the third hides the money because he's afraid of losing it.

Jenna found herself suddenly consumed with the simple parable and then riveted when Micah St. Pierre started to draw a lesson from this story. On the face of it, the story seemed to be about investment strategy, but somehow Micah St. Pierre drew a line from riches to love, creating a grand metaphor.

"God wants us to invest our love, not hide it away," he said. "He gave us a choice. We can love or not. But the thing is, to truly love, we must risk it all. Our hearts might get broken. In fact, it's quite likely that every one of us will suffer a broken heart at one time or another because we chose to love.

"And yet if we risk nothing, what can we possibly gain? In this story about the rich man and his servants, God is telling us that he wants us to risk everything and not to hide our most precious treasure in fear."

A strange shock worked its way through Jenna as she listened. It almost seemed as if Jude's brother were speaking directly to her, using her own thoughts as a conduit to open up a vista she'd never seen before.

And suddenly the plan she'd been looking for emerged. A way to move forward in the world. She hadn't expected to find it here, in a Christian church. But the universe had a sense of humor sometimes. It could send a person searching in circles when the answer was right at hand. Sometimes it wasn't the answer but the search that was important.

The Sunday school building, clearly built in the twentieth century, sat behind the church and had none of the main sanctuary's charm or history. But it had plenty of space for the fellowship hour.

Jenna had blown off this social gathering last week because of Patsy's absence. But today she strolled into the room, ready to be treated as a tourist or an outsider. But that didn't happen.

Karen, one of the volunteers on Monday and also a member of the Piece Makers, intercepted her at the door with a welcoming smile and directed her to the coffee and doughnuts.

As she headed in that direction, Jenna was greeted again and again by people who had been at the vicarage on Monday as well as a few others who stopped to introduce themselves and thank her for her help.

Wow. She'd earned some good karma helping to paint the vicarage, in addition to possibly losing her heart to Jude St. Pierre. It didn't take long before she found herself face-to-face with the woman she'd come to see this morning.

"You're a foul-weather painter," Patsy said as she approached, a surprisingly welcome smile on her face. "Once the sun came out, you disappeared."

"I guess I am," Jenna said, her face heating. "I'm sorry. I should have—"

Patsy waved her hand in dismissal. "Honey, you're here to enjoy the sun and the beach, not to help paint the vicarage." Her gaze narrowed. "You are here as a tourist, aren't you?"

"I told you. I'm not working for any developer."

"Yes, you did. But you are a mystery, Jenna Fairchild. You helped paint the vicarage, and everyone wants to know why. And you've been seen twice now at town hall meetings."

"I helped because I was bored," she said, "and the paperback I was reading didn't hold my interest. And I told you before, I'm interested in history."

"Well, I guess those are reasons. Kind of flimsy though."

Jenna sipped her coffee before speaking again. "The thing is, I've been so busy this last year, it's hard to stay still."

"I heard from Louella Pender that you went on a tour around the world or something."

Jenna realized her aunt was deeply connected to everything that happened in Magnolia Harbor. What Jenna said to one person would get repeated over and over again until it reached Patsy. Jude would keep her secret, but she needed to be careful.

Jenna gave Patsy her best smile. "I suppose I did go around the world, technically speaking. But mostly I went off in search of myself."

Patsy's blue eyes widened. "Really?"

Jenna nodded. "Yes. I started in China, spent time in India, and came back by way of Australia and South America. But I spent most of my time in China and India. I spent months learning more about the Eightfold Way. I also walked all the way up Mount Emei."

"What's that?"

She took a moment to describe the temple at the top of one of China's four sacred Buddhist mountains. And then she hurried on to talk about the months she'd spent in Mumbai at the ashram. "I've been busy," she said. "Even when I was spending up to five hours a day in meditation. That takes a lot of work. And, of course, at the ashram we were required to do chores like cooking and cleaning. So..."

"Oh, honey," Patsy said in a sympathetic tone, "all that work and here you are at church?" Her eyebrow arched.

Jenna laughed in spite of herself. She hadn't come here for spiritual guidance. She'd come for this conversation and later to sneak off for a visit to her father's grave. And yet...

Funny how the universe worked sometimes.

"I know," Jenna said. "I could have saved myself a year of searching."

Patsy laughed. "I don't believe for one moment that's true."

"Well, maybe not. But I liked Reverend St. Pierre's sermon today."

Just then two of the women came over, coffee cups in hand. "Well, that's the first time in ages we've finished before eleven o'clock. You think that's the way it's always going to be?" one of them said.

"And it was refreshing to have a sermon about love. I can't remember the last time one of our substitute ministers preached about that," the second woman said.

"Ladies," Patsy said, "I'd like you to meet Jenna Fairchild. Jenna, meet Sandra Jernigan and Nancy Jacobs. They're longtime members of the Piece Makers." Patsy gestured toward each of the women as she introduced them. Sandra's hair was a beauty-parlor red and cut into a short, curly bob. She had smiling blue eyes and wore way too much makeup. Nancy Jacobs was a tall, thin woman, easily five foot ten. She towered over the rest of them and wore her graying brown hair in a Dutch-boy cut with a fringe of bangs across her brow.

"It's nice to meet you. I was so impressed by the quilt you were making the other day," Jenna said.

"I'm sure y'all heard how Jenna helped out at the vicarage on Monday."

"That was nice of you," Nancy said in a voice so soft it was almost hard to hear her in the noisy fellowship hall.

"Are you really interested in learning how to quilt?" Sandra asked. "I was there the other night when you dropped in on us. I heard you wanted to learn how."

"Ladies," Patsy said, "Louella told me that Jenna went

down to A Stitch in Time asking about quilting lessons." The older woman smiled like the cat who had swallowed the canary as she pierced Jenna with a sharp, blue-eyed stare. "Reckon you didn't realize that her lessons were about piecing the quilt top and not about the actual hand quilting itself."

Jenna shook her head. "No, I didn't. But that's okay. Louella fixed me up with a learn-to-knit package. I think she may have turned me into a knitter. It's very Zen, isn't it?"

"Not as much as quilting," Patsy said. "So, are you still interested in learning?"

Was she? Yes. More than she'd been before Louella had introduced her to knitting. And, of course, she'd love to spend a Thursday night with the Piece Makers, especially Patsy. "I am still interested," she said.

"What do you say, ladies?" Patsy asked. "Shall we let her sit in on Thursday?"

They nodded their heads, and Patsy turned with a smile. "Come on by, and we'll give you a lesson. It's the least we can do for someone trying to find themselves by climbing up Chinese mountains."

Jenna chatted with Patsy and the other members of the Piece Makers for about ten minutes before people started drifting away, one by one. Now was the time for her to escape before she wore out her welcome.

She excused herself and headed out under the live oaks and pines in the churchyard, where an old, much-painted chain-link fence ringed a cemetery adjacent to the church. Like the churchyard, the hallowed ground was so sandy that only scrub grass grew here. At the center of the graveyard stood a collection of crooked headstones with writing that had been washed away by the ages. Clearly, the people of Jonquil Island had been burying their dead here for generations.

There were a lot of Howlands buried in this earth and a fair number of Martins too. But only one Bauman, set off in a corner. A fresh bouquet of out-of-season daffodils had been laid against the grave marker, no doubt by Patsy herself.

She stood for a long, solemn moment staring at the name: James Arthur Bauman. His birth and death dates were marked in granite, and she waited for the urge to speak to him, but it never came. He wasn't here. Maybe his bones were, but not his spirit. She almost laughed. Her Hindu friends would be happy about the absence of a spirit here. It meant Jamie had moved on to another life. Spirits who stayed around were usually bound by terrible karma that made it difficult for them to move into the next life. She hoped her father's next life was better than this one had been.

She was about to leave when Micah St. Pierre showed up. He'd ditched the priestly robes and wore a pair of relaxed-fit jeans and a dark T-shirt. "It's a pretty place," he said in his low baritone.

She let go of the breath she'd been holding for ages. "It is."

"I heard from someone who heard from someone that you visited Mount Emei."

She turned away from her father's grave. "I did."

"It's beautiful, isn't it? With the clouds above and below. Did you see the sun rise?"

She smiled. "I did. It was unearthly."

He nodded, his eyes flicking to the grave and back.

Had Jude told him the truth? She didn't think so. Jude was the kind of man who took his promises seriously. It was one of his admirable qualities.

"So, I was wondering," she started, "if I could ask a favor."

"It depends on the favor."

"This one has to do with investing in love. Of putting a treasure to good use to reap rewards that might not be entirely monetary but perhaps more in line with good karma."

A slow smile curled his mouth. "Then I'd be happy to help in any way I can."

On Monday morning, as Ashley was walking back from Jackie's bus stop, two St. Pierre Construction vans pulled into her home's circular drive. She stood there for a moment, panicking.

Had Colton St. Pierre misunderstood her? She hadn't confirmed that she was ready to have the roof repaired. Had she?

No. She hadn't. She'd told him that she would give him a call. Which, of course, she had no intention of doing. Instead, she'd planned to call Bobby Don Ayers down at Berkshire Hathaway and start the process of putting Howland House and Rose Cottage up for sale. Mom and Dad were foursquare behind this decision. And if all went well, she'd be in Kansas by Christmas.

She walked up the drive just as Colton arrived in his big silver Dodge Ram pickup. He hopped out of the truck, wearing his usual uniform of work pants, a maroon St. Pierre Construction golf shirt, and steel-toed boots. With his dark hair, dark eyes, and dark skin, he was like an HGTV casting director's dream.

He was handsome, all right. Heck, all the St. Pierres were handsome. But Ashley's heart belonged elsewhere.

She walked up to him. "Um, Colton...uh, why—"

"It's taken care of," he said.

"What? I—"

"Micah called yesterday and told me to fix your roof as soon as possible. We had a day available to do the work. So here we are."

Ashley hadn't been born yesterday. Colton didn't have any available days. He was scheduled out until December probably. If he was here fixing her roof, then he'd dropped some other job for someone else, and all because Micah had asked. She shook her head. "No. You can't—"

"Oh yes, I can. And by the way, as far as I'm concerned, this is not charity. I've been paid in full. No discounts. And I get a bonus if I get it done in the next two days. So that's what I'm going to do, Ms. Scott." He bobbed his head and turned away, issuing orders to his crew.

What the heck? She didn't know whether to be angry or relieved. She needed the roof repaired, but she didn't want to be anyone's charity case. She could almost hear Adam's voice in her head, telling her that this had to be stopped. That she would be bound to the church forever if she allowed the minister to swoop in and start fixing things.

She marched around the side yard and through the rose garden. Jenna Fairchild was on the porch, eyes closed, meditating, so Ashley kept her anger in check. No swearing out loud within the hearing of guests. It was an iron-fast rule.

But when she hit the sidewalk, she let the expletives fly. If the other Piece Makers had been in range, they might have all fainted dead away or even kicked her out of the club. Now, there was an idea.

But she reined herself in. For Adam's and Jackie's sake, if not for her own. She knocked on the vicarage door and waited. And waited. And waited some more.

Crap. He wasn't home.

She knocked again, folding her arms across her chest to keep from shaking.

The door finally opened to reveal Reverend St. Pierre, wearing a white T-shirt and a pair of red plaid flannel pj bottoms. His face looked as if he'd had a boxing match with his pillow.

He'd been asleep? She checked her watch. It was eight o'clock. She'd been up for hours already.

She stood there hugging herself, trying to decide if she should let him have it or apologize.

"Good morning," he said in a sleep-roughened voice that awakened something deep inside her. Say what? No. She hugged herself harder and let fly. "Where the hell do you get off meddling in my life?"

"What?"

"You heard me. Your brother and six other big guys are across the street putting a new roof on my house. I know how much that costs. And I can't afford it. Even more important, I can't afford for you to pay for it. Can you imagine the gossip? I mean, you know how this town is. You can't be doing that. And besides, I don't want your pity or your... whatever."

She waved her hands and continued to vent at him for several minutes, while he leaned against the doorframe, yawning and stretching.

"Are you done?" he asked calmly when she finally ran out of steam.

She nodded as unwanted heat crawled up her face.

"First of all, I didn't pay for your roof."

"But Colton said—"

"I *am* the one who called Colton to find out how much it cost. And I *am* the one who delivered the check to pay for it. But the check wasn't drawn on my pitiful checking account. Are you kidding? You sit on the church board. You know my salary." He smiled. It was a nice smile.

"But...then who?"

"I'm not at liberty to say."

"But..."

His smile broadened. "All I can say is that someone was moved by my sermon yesterday."

"You're joking."

He shook his head. "I know. Kind of amazing for a guy who hasn't sermonized in a long while." He seemed pleased with himself.

"Really? Why is that?"

"Because I didn't officiate at services at my last duty station. I spent most of my time holding hands."

"Holding...what?"

He pushed away from the doorframe, his gaze as sobering as black coffee. "I was stationed with the First Marines Division in San Diego. I was on notification duty. So you can imagine how pleased I am that my first sermon in a long while moved someone to undertake a selfless act of love."

"What? No. Who did this?"

"That's the point, Ashley. Your benefactor does not wish to be named. In fact, the person told me the money is an investment. Like in the parable we studied yesterday."

Chapter Seventeen

After the crap storm that had hit his life last week, something had changed for Jude. If he believed in luck, he'd say that his luck had changed.

Daddy had been sober for four solid days. And thank goodness for that because on Friday Jude had gotten so tangled up in a combination of fear and lust that he'd completely forgotten about their morning charter. And they'd had charters on Saturday, Sunday, and Monday as well. And then on Tuesday they got a call for another Friday charter and two more requests they couldn't fill for Saturday because they were already booked.

It was like a sudden breath of fresh air and totally unexpected in September, when business should be winding down.

The weekend fishing trips went off without any mishap or boat issues. Daddy charmed the clients with his salty fishing tales and his knowledge of the fishing spots around the bay and out in the Atlantic. The clients left with smiles and photos of their catches.

The charters also kept Jude away from Jenna during the day. The need to keep an eye on Daddy's sobriety, along with a good old-fashioned dose of fear, kept him away from her during the evenings. Of course, staying away didn't stop him from thinking about her naked every five minutes. But thinking wasn't the same as doing.

But then Wednesday rolled around. And they almost never had charters on Wednesdays except in the high season or during spring break. So he planned to sleep in on Wednesday.

But Jenna, clearly a woman on a mission, wasn't about to let him off the hook that easy. She called him in the early hours of the morning, awakening him from a sexy dream about her. He groped for his phone and hit the talk button before he was fully awake; otherwise he would have probably let it go to voice mail. "Yeah?" he muttered.

"Wake up, sleepyhead. It's going to be a nice day, according to the weatherman." Her voice was as sweet as honey. Or maybe as sweet as hidden poison. He didn't know which. But just the sound of her made him wake up . . . all the way.

"Have you any idea how early it is?" he asked, reaching for annoyance and discovering that he was happy she'd called. Damn.

"Uh. Um. Sorry. I get up before dawn. I forget sometimes that others don't. But still, it's a nice day."

"And?"

"Perfect for a sail out to the inlet."

He let go of a breath. She wasn't going to give up on this crazy idea, was she? "I told you I didn't—"

"I know. But I'm determined to talk you into it." Her

voice was so sultry he had no doubt that she would talk him into it eventually.

"I'd offer money," she continued, "but you'd refuse it and call me trust fund girl, which I hate. So I'm going to appeal to your vanity as a sailor. I'm sure you can get us there and back in one piece."

It was futile to argue. She was like a siren singing him to his doom. And at least one part of him was happy to go there to die.

"Hang on. Let me check the tides." He brought up the tides and the weather forecast on his iPhone. Damn. She was right. It was a nice day. With light winds and tides that would be perfect for a sail out to the inlet. He checked the extended forecast. That was a little more iffy. If they were going to do this, they needed to do it in the morning.

He returned to his phone app. "Look, Jenna, sailing out there is risky."

"I know. But sometimes you have to take risks."

It was like she was talking to him in code. Was she talking about the manageable risk of sailing out to the inlet, or the unpredictable risk of allowing himself to fall in love with her and try to build a relationship? Yeah, that was risky all right.

"You know," he said, "you aren't going to learn anything by going out there."

"No?"

"No. I can tell you what happened to your father. It's not hard to guess. *Independence* got knocked over by a gust or swamped by a rogue wave. Or maybe he just fell out of the boat like I did, but he wasn't wearing a PFD. There's no point in—"

"I'm not going out there to discover what happened, Jude. I'm going out there to connect with him."

"What?"

"I know it sounds crazy. But I have this feeling his spirit is out there. Restless. Like he's been unable to move on to his next life."

"Wow. You really are into all that woo-woo stuff."

"It's no stranger than Christianity and the whole Communion thing. And I'll bet your root doctors have some interesting beliefs too."

"Okay, okay. I guess I just showed my cultural bias."

"You did. But I won't hold it against you. So, will you take me?"

"Why do you think your father is out there?"

"You'd laugh if I told you."

"I promise I won't laugh."

"I've been having dreams about the inlet. Every night the same one. About a boat breaking up. And I don't know if I'm dreaming about Captain Bill's ill-fated pirate ship or my father's little sailing dinghy. I need to go out there."

His Old Granny, who had deeply believed in root doctors and Hoodoo, would have said that Jenna was messing with a powerful haunt, and he should do what she asks because it might help the spirit cross over. He didn't believe in ghosts, but his Old Granny had. And he felt her presence at that moment.

"Okay. I give up. Meet me at the dry dock in half an hour."

Before they left the dock, Jude wrote out a message on a piece of notepaper outlining their planned sailing route and tucked it under the windshield wiper on the driver's side of his old F-150. It chilled Jenna to the bone when he locked gazes with her and said, "If Jamie had done this, it might have saved his life. No one realized he was missing for almost twenty-four hours."

"You think he went to the inlet on purpose?" she asked, her heart thumping in her chest.

Jude shook his head. "I don't know why anyone would do something like that in a small sailboat. I don't even know why we're doing it. I personally think we should ditch the inlet idea and practice sailing with a spinnaker. The winds this morning are light but steady. Perfect for teaching you how to manage the big sail."

"I told you. I need to go."

He nodded and didn't argue any further.

They put *Bonney Rose* in the water and sailed past the marina. As they passed by, Jude pointed out a large fishing boat. "That's *Reel Therapy*, in case you're interested."

She studied the boat. It was more than twice as long as *Bonney Rose*, and its flying bridge made it seem impossibly tall in the water. It sparkled in the sunlight, and like *Bonney Rose*, it was in pristine condition.

But even someone as ignorant about boats as Jenna could see that *Reel Therapy* was older than most of the boats around her. And there were so many other fishing boats.

"How many of those boats are charters?" she asked.

"Most of them."

"Wow. You have a lot of competition."

"Yup."

They sailed on for several minutes, lazily tacking as they sailed under the bridge that connected Jonquil

Island to the mainland. "I have an impertinent question," she said after a long moment.

"I usually don't answer impertinent questions," he said, "but go ahead."

"Why a fishing charter, when you're a sailor?" she asked.

He laughed. "I was a fisherman before I was a sailor. And I come from a long line of fishermen. Barrier Island Charters was started by my granddaddy back when there weren't as many tourists or as much competition. My ancestors have been fishing this bay for hundreds of years."

She nodded. "Yes, and you hold that history sacred. I can see that about you. But..."

"But what?" he snapped.

"But near as I can see, there aren't any sailing charters on Jonquil Island. What if you bought a big sailboat—you know, with more than one mast—and took people out to where Captain Bill ran aground or whatever happened to him."

A stony silence wafted from the back of the boat, and she looked over her shoulder. The winds were so light this morning that neither of them hiked out, and the sailboat moved on a flat bottom. "Did I say something wrong?" she asked.

"No. I'm just annoyed at you for suggesting that I buy into the prevailing myth, that's all."

"You mean Captain Bill is a myth?"

"No. He was real. But he was an idiot. He brought his sloop through the inlet right before a hurricane hit. The *Bonney Rose* was overloaded with pirate treasure and should have stayed out to sea until the hurricane moved northeast. The sloop was so heavy it was riding low in the water, and that's why it ran aground near where the jetty is today. And I bet you don't know that the only survivor of the wreck was Henri St. Pierre, my six-times-great-grandfather or something like that. So no, I don't have any desire to take tourists out to see the jetty."

She blinked at him. "Your ancestors were pirates?"

"One of them. He was also a runaway slave. But unlike the rest of the guys on that ship, he could swim."

"Did he end up back in captivity?" she asked.

Jude shook his head. "No. He teamed up with Rose Howland and helped her plant the jonquils."

Jenna sat there for a long moment, stunned. She'd read the chamber-of-commerce booklet about Rose Howland and her love for the dashing pirate Bill Teel. That unrequited love affair had produced a bastard, John Howland, who was Ashley's six-times-great-grandfather or whatever. John Howland had gone on to become a wealthy rice planter whose plantation was now a museum up on the Black River. But nowhere had she heard the story of Henri St. Pierre or the fact that someone had helped the grief-stricken Rose to plant the daffodils. It was as if the man had been written out of history altogether.

"I'm sorry about that. But isn't that what Harry was talking about the other day? The fact that Magnolia Harbor needs to tell the entire history, not just one side?"

"Sure. He was talking about Henri St. Pierre. But that's different from preserving the African roots of Gullah culture. A museum would be a positive step for correcting the island's biggest myths, but it won't preserve the sweetgrass."

"No. But aside from the museum, it might still be fun to run sailing charters and set everyone straight on the foolishness of Bill Teel and the bravery and wisdom of Henri St. Pierre. And you'd have a business with almost no competition. Not to mention that you're a descendant of the man in question. In business school, we'd call that an intangible asset."

"Are you telling me how to run my business now? Weren't you the one who said that I have more experience than you do?"

She laughed. "You're right. I'm not telling you anything. I'm just in one of my looking-for-a-good-business-idea modes."

"Well, just to be clear, there is a sailboat for sale like the one you're talking about down in Hilton Head. It's a 1981 LaFitte. That's pretty old for a boat, but she's in good shape and she's almost affordable. She'd require some refitting."

"So you've been looking, huh?" she said with a grin.

He nodded. "Yeah, and they just dropped the price. The truth is I've dreamed of owning a sailboat big enough to charter. And I could probably find financing, but that would require leaving the family business. And that's complicated."

"You couldn't add sailing charters to your services?"

He shrugged. "Maybe. If Barrier Island Charters were my company. But it's not. It's my father's, and he's not a sailor. He's also got views about debt financing."

"Oh." She turned her attention to the jib and adjusted it. She should shut up now. She might have an MBA, but she didn't have a family. She had no idea how complicated it might be for Jude to walk away from his father's business. Or to convince his father to expand into sailing charters.

She had no idea at all. And in a weird way, she envied him for his connections. Sure, they might constrain his decisions, but in the end he had all those connections in his life. She had none, and wasn't that why she'd come out here in the first place—searching for connections that had never been and would never be?

They continued to tack in a northerly direction, and when they reached the channel markers, Jude dropped anchor, directed Jenna to furl the jib, and allowed *Bonney Rose* to go nose to wind. The current and tides tugged at the small boat, but she wasn't going anywhere.

"So this is it?" she asked in a hushed tone.

"The spot's up there." He pointed toward the mouth of the inlet. "See the lighthouse?"

She nodded.

"They found the boat capsized there. But we'll never know if that's where the problem occurred. He could have broached in a wind shift, or gotten swamped by a rogue wave, and the currents and tides could have taken the boat to that spot. His body was found way down by the mouth of the inlet, almost a mile from the boat.

"The weather that day was calm, like today. There were no storms or chop. So it's a mystery. The accident that put him in the water could have happened anywhere."

Jenna stared at the spot where her father's boat had been found, mast down in the water. Her iWear polarizing sunglasses cut the glare and showed the ripples and swirls that disturbed the water's seemingly placid surface.

"So now you know. There's nothing to see here. We should go before the wind fills in," Jude said.

She shook her head. "No. Give me a moment more." She closed her eyes and started the deep-breathing regimen she'd learned years ago as an anxious college freshman looking for ways to deal with her angst. When she'd centered her being, she asked the silent question: *Where are you?*

Something tugged at her heart like the tide, and the current tugged the boat. She opened her eyes and searched the shoreline. The tops of the pine trees, live oaks, and cypress waved in the breeze, the motion revealing divine beauty and something more. She could almost hear it in the quiet, punctuated by the sound of the water against the hull and the distant cry of an egret. There was a message here.

She thought about the bright bunch of out-of-season daffodils on her father's grave. They memorialized the wrong thing. He was gone in body, but a part of him was still here, like the current and the wind and the silence. Her father had invested in love, and she was the treasure he'd reaped.

Without even knowing it.

And for that she owed him more than anger and more than resistance. She had to let his unsaid and unknown love in. She had to welcome him into her life, across all these years and all these miles.

Her eyes teared up. "I love you," she whispered. His love raced through her with the wind.

"What?" Jude asked from the back of the boat. She almost repeated the words but thought better of it. They might be true in more ways than one.

Instead, she wiped the tears from her cheeks before she turned to look over her shoulder. She managed a smile as the pieces of her broken heart finally knit themselves back together. "I'm ready now," she said.

He cocked his head. "Are you okay?"

She nodded. "Better than ever. Thank you so much for bringing me here."

They weighed anchor and headed south, back toward Magnolia Harbor on a run, with the wind behind them the whole way. When they'd left the currents of the river delta behind, they furled the jib, and Jude launched the big spinnaker.

It was Home Depot orange with a big black skull and crossbones on it. It billowed out in front of *Bonney Rose* like a giant pirate flag.

"Oh yeah, I can see that you're too proud to play the pirate card," she said, giving him a glance.

"I didn't say I was too proud. I said that I was committed to the family business. And, of course, I can't afford a sailboat that big."

"But if you could?"

He gave her a sober stare from behind his sunglasses. "Don't even think about it, trust fund girl. I have no desire to become a kept man."

She snorted a laugh. "No? I've heard the gigolo life has merit."

"And you want a gigolo?"

"If he looked like you it wouldn't be all bad." She gave him her best come-hither smile.

He shook his head. "No. I'd love to have a sailboat big enough to take charters all the way to the Caribbean in the winter, and maybe even pirate tours during the summers, but the family business comes first."

Of course that's the way he thought. He was, first and foremost, a preservationist. He wanted to save things. The business, the seagrass, the buildings, the culture.

He had so much to preserve. He was knitted into his community and his family and his way of life. God. She envied him. He wasn't independent, but he wasn't alone either.

"Okay, Harvard girl, it's time for you to learn how to jibe a spinnaker," Jude said from the back of the boat, pulling her away from her thoughts.

She glanced over her shoulder at him. He was grinning at her like he was enjoying every moment of this sail now that they'd left dangerous waters behind them.

But had they? She wanted him. But even more startling was the fact that she wanted to become like him—connected, interdependent. And she wanted to be in his life and, yes, to make him happy.

If only that last part wasn't so complicated.

Jenna was a natural when it came to trimming the spinnaker, and when the breeze filled in on the way back, she was utterly fearless as she jibed the big sail from one side to the other. They had so much fun out on the water that they stayed out for almost three hours, just sailing around the bay practicing various sail sets.

So they were both ravenous by the time they got *Bonney Rose* back on her trailer with her mast stepped, sails dried and folded, lines coiled, and canvas cover buttoned up tight.

"I could go for some spinach queso and a glass of wine," she said once they'd tied the cover down with bungee cords.

"I think maybe a burger and a Coke for me," Jude said, watching the twinkle in her big brown eyes. No question about it. If he followed this breeze, he'd end up back at

Rose Cottage with her, spending an afternoon wrapped in her arms.

Did he want that?

Hell yes. But there were complications. Always complications. He was a little uneasy about the way she'd asked him about sailboat charters. As if she were ready to swoop in and buy him the world. And that comment about being a gigolo. She must know that he wasn't that kind of guy.

Had it been a joke, or...?

Damn. She was so confusing.

"We need to get our stuff out of the truck," he said, turning his back on her as he crossed the parking lot. As he approached the vehicle, he realized that someone had put a second slip of paper under his wiper blade.

"What the hell?" he asked as he pulled the note away from the windshield.

"What is it?" Jenna asked.

He shook his head. "It's Daddy."

"What about him?"

"He took *Reel Therapy* out on a last-minute charter late this morning."

"Isn't that good?"

He turned around. "No. Not single-handed. And look out there." He nodded toward the bay, and she followed his gaze. "Wind's picking up. It's probably going to rain this afternoon."

"So he should have said no?"

Jude nodded, trying to hide his misgivings. If Daddy went out alone, he might do something stupid, like take a cooler full of beer with him. He crumpled the paper. "I should be out there with him. Two is better than one." Guilt sounded in his voice like an alarm bell.

Jenna cocked her head, her eyes soft with under-standing. "I'm sorry. I shouldn't have—"

"No. It's not your fault." He yanked open the truck's door and started hunting for his wallet and her purse. "It's just this crazy season. It's like all of a sudden we've got more business than we can reasonably handle. I mean, Wednesday charters are practically unheard of this time of year."

"You're worried about him, aren't you?" she asked.

"Yeah."

"Can we call the Coast Guard or something?"

He pulled her purse from the front seat and handed it to her. Her face had paled with worry. Wow. She really cared. "Unfortunately, no. He has to screw up before the Coast Guard gets involved."

"So, can we hire a boat and go looking for them?"

He shook his head. "We don't know where they went. It would be like searching for a needle in a haystack." Which was true. With the weather setting in, Daddy was probably on his way back by now.

And when he got back, Daddy would probably give him a big load of crap for being out in the sailboat this morning, sailing out to the inlet in a small boat. So it wasn't as if either one of them had been responsible today.

Chapter Eighteen —————

Jenna clamped her mouth shut as guilt swamped her. What would Jude say when he found out that she'd taken out an ad for Barrier Island Charters in the *Harbor Times'* Last Gasp of Summer edition? She'd called the local paper on Monday morning, the same day Colton St. Pierre showed up to fix Ashley's roof. She'd asked about advertising opportunities only to discover that, if she moved fast, she could get a spot in the special supplement that would be available all over town for the next couple of weeks.

Her stomach roiled a little with the uncomfortable thought that one of her acts of kindness might backfire. It was supposed to be good karma to do something nice for someone without seeking any personal benefit or credit for the good deed.

And yet this situation had trouble written all over it.

Jude reached out then, sending her thoughts in another direction entirely as his hand curled around her neck and shoulder. He reeled her in as if for a hot, salty kiss. "Don't look so worried. It will be okay," he said in a manly way that made her want to believe it.

She rested her head on his shoulder for a moment. He was so sturdy. And he smelled so good, like salt spray and suntan lotion and something else utterly delicious. She could rest here forever.

But he didn't stay still. He pulled her alongside, and they headed, arm in arm, down the boardwalk toward Rafferty's. Her insides hummed as they walked.

Had they reached a new point in this on-again, off-again relationship where public displays of affection were allowed?

They took a table inside, out of the wind and sun. After they ordered food, the conversation didn't turn personal. Instead, Jude used the salt and pepper shakers to explain the right-of-way rules during sailboat races, but all that stuff about port and starboard tacks, boat overlap, and lay lines confused her.

"So, does this mean you'll let me crew for you in a sailboat race?" she finally asked.

"Well, Tim is my usual crew. But I'm sure we can find you someone to crew with during next Saturday's regatta. It's the Last Gasp of Summer regatta. We get boats from all over the state."

"I'm not sure I want to sail with anyone but you."

That got her a smoky look out of his tawny eyes. "Um, why don't I get the check?" he asked in a gruff voice.

She had just finished off the last drop of her wine when Harry came through the restaurant's front doors, a heavy frown riding his brow like a thundercloud. He set a course toward them and stopped to give her only the most cursory of greetings before he turned toward Jude.

"We gotta go, son."

"What?"

"I just heard it on the Georgetown Coast Guard working channel. The *Reel Therapy*'s run aground on the jetty past the Howland Bridge. Your daddy put in a distress call on channel sixteen. Said they're taking on water fast. I've got the yacht club's Boston Whaler ready at the dock. Come on. Let's go."

Jenna stood up, her heart pounding. She was to blame for this. "I'm coming too," she said.

Jude took her by the shoulders, staring her right in the eye, and shook his head. "You've had a glass of wine, and you've got no business out there during a rescue. I'll call you when I know more." He leaned in and kissed her on the cheek. "Thanks for offering though."

Jenna stood in the middle of Rafferty's dining room, her whole body trembling as Harry and Jude disappeared through the restaurant's front door.

Now what? Should she go down to Barrier Island Charters and camp out? Should she go back to the cottage? Should she stay here?

She'd set this disaster in motion, proving that no act of kindness goes unpunished. The only thing was, she hadn't reaped the punishment directly. Her throat closed up. What if she started investing in the people living here only to have every dollar turn into a disaster?

She picked up her purse and headed to Harbor Drive. She walked, head down against the wind, which tossed her hair, turning it into tiny whips that stung her face. She stopped and savagely gathered it all back in a ponytail before she continued, trying to breathe through the lump in her throat and the pressure in her chest.

When she reached the corner of Harbor Drive and Tulip Lane, she had to stop and study Harry and Patsy's house. The wind hissed through the palmettos, giving testament to the forces in the universe that sometimes went unseen. She couldn't move, despite the push of the wind as she studied *Independence*, moldering away on its cinder blocks.

Why had her father named his boat *Independence*?

She would never know. Although the name suggested so many possible reasons.

She ought to tell Harry and Patsy the truth.

And then she should go.

She crossed the street and was about to walk up the path when the door opened and Patsy stepped out onto the porch, wearing a pair of white cropped pants and a boat-necked blue-and-white-striped sweater. Her helmet of blond-gray hair seemed impervious to the wind.

She waved. "Hey," she said. "I know all about Jude's daddy. I've got some sweet tea and cookies. You can wait with me."

Jenna set her feet on the path, and a moment later, she stood on Patsy's porch gazing into a pair of sympathetic blue eyes. "It's always hard when the men go out to rescue someone and leave us behind."

"How do you know that I—"

"Honey, Harry and I can see the harbor from this porch. We watched you and Jude out there this morning, practicing with the spinnaker. Jude's orange Jolly Roger makes *Bonney Rose* easy to spot. Y'all were doing really nice out there for a while, given the way the wind filled in during the morning. Harry told me that you never sailed before Jude started teaching you."

She shook her head, and Patsy's smile widened. "Come on in." She opened the door.

Jenna didn't know what she had expected out of Patsy's house. Something formal. And dark. And heavy. Like the interiors of her grandfather's mansion on the Hudson.

No, check that. The Big Monstrosity, as she liked to call it, belonged to her now. And Milo even expected her to live there. He was dreaming. The first chance she got, that mausoleum was going on the market at a rock-bottom price.

But Patsy's house wasn't anything like Robert Bauman's home. Sailors lived in this house. It was floor-to-ceiling nautical, with lots of stripes and anchors and ropes and a model sailboat on the mantel in the living room. It had a cozy-cottage vibe with photos on the end tables in silver frames. She wanted to stop and pick them up to see if any were of her father, but Patsy ushered her back to the kitchen.

"Have a seat." Patsy waved toward a banquet breakfast nook with an old-fashioned red Formica tabletop. "I'm afraid my chocolate chip cookies come from the bakery. I don't have any skills in the kitchen like Ashley does." She set a plate of cookies in front of Jenna along with a pitcher of tea. "It's sweet. I'm warning you. If you want some without sugar, I can get some instant."

"No. It's fine." Jenna had given up trying to drink iced tea without sugar. Besides, her year-long travels had taught her the inherent wisdom of doing as the Romans do.

She poured herself a glass of tea and wondered what to do next. The urge to confess came over her. But when she opened her mouth, fear took hold, and she didn't say one word about herself. Instead she said, "Harry cares about Jude, doesn't he?"

"He does." Patsy refreshed her own glass of tea and cast her gaze out the back window, where the wind seemed to have worked itself into a fever pitch. "Jude became a stand-in for someone we lost a long time ago."

Jenna dropped her gaze to study the ice in her glass. She didn't dare look up at Patsy. She might give too much away. "Oh?" she asked as neutrally as possible.

Patsy sighed. "Unfortunately, my husband and I were never able to have children. So we poured our affections onto our nephew, Jamie. He was a beautiful boy. That's him right there."

Patsy pointed to a group of black-and-white photos in simple black frames hung on the wall near the window.

"May I look?"

"Of course."

With her heart pounding, Jenna stood up and studied the photos on the wall. They were all of the same boy at different ages. Jamie in a bathing suit. Jamie asleep in a hammock. Jamie sailing a small boat, the wind in his hair. It was funny. All of Jamie's trophies sat in a bookcase in the foyer of the Big Monstrosity on the Hudson. But there wasn't one photo of Jamie to be found in the house. She knew, because she'd searched for them.

She had to swallow back the tears. "He's quite handsome. Where is he now?"

Patsy shook her head. "He died when he was only twenty-two."

"Oh." Jenna sat down again.

"I'm sorry. I'm being maudlin. I guess this emergency with Charlie St. Pierre has brought back a few bad memories. Jamie died out on the bay."

Patsy's choice of words sent something shivering down Jenna's backbone. Had Louella Pender gotten her suicide theory from Patsy?

Patsy continued. "The Coast Guard called it an accident."

"And you think it was something else?" Jenna asked, her heart slamming against her ribs.

Patsy shook her head. "I don't know. I just can't shake this feeling that it wasn't an accident. That he..." She let go of a long breath. "He was a beautiful soul, my Jamie. But he was not strong enough for this world."

The hairs on the back of Jenna's neck rose.

Patsy took a drink of her tea and continued unprompted. "He got himself involved with a tourist girl who was all wrong for him. He needed someone who understood his ups and downs. And believe me, his ups could be way up, and his downs could be deep. He was on meds, of course. But this girl...she convinced him that the medications were wrong for him. We were all so afraid that she was trying to trap him into a marriage. I'm sure you've heard the gossip by now. My nephew was Robert Bauman's son. You know, the iWear Inc. CEO. So Jamie was wealthy, or he would have been wealthy once he came into his trust fund—"

Jenna stopped breathing. This picture Patsy painted of her mother was all wrong. Mom would never have told anyone to stop taking their meds. She'd worked so hard to earn a master's degree in social work and had spent her time working with children in need of special services. Mom would move heaven and earth to help families get the medications they needed for their loved ones.

And Mom would never try to trap anyone into a marriage. Mom wasn't a huge fan of marriage; she felt that every woman needed to be self-reliant. That independence for women could come only when women quit tying themselves down to unfaithful men. This explained why Mom had never married and had never been terribly interested in dating.

Jenna's eyes filled with tears. She wanted to get right into Patsy's face and defend her mother. But she didn't dare.

Patsy leaned forward and patted Jenna's hand. "Honey, don't cry. It all happened such a long time ago. Sometimes I let my sorrow get the best of me. The important thing is that in a special way, Jude took Jamie's place. For Harry, at least.

"And anyone can see that you and Jude have made friends. Still, you know, Harry and I worry about him. He's got a sensitive streak like our Jamie did. And people come and go on this island, but Jude belongs here."

"I know that," Jenna said a little defensively. "I just found out that he's descended from one of Captain Teel's crew."

Patsy nodded. "Henri St. Pierre. And, of course, you know about that petition of his to have the master zoning plan revised since you attended the town council meetings. A man that tied to the land isn't about to move someplace else."

What the heck? Was Patsy trying to tell her to leave Jude alone? Was she suggesting that Jenna would never fit in here? Or worse yet, was she drawing some comparison between Jenna and her mother, the woman Patsy clearly blamed for Jamie's death?

She wiped the tears from her cheeks, more angry now than sad.

Patsy hopped up from her seat, crossed the room, and ducked into a doorway leading who knew where. She returned a moment later with a tissue in hand.

"Here, honey. You look as if you need this."

Jenna wiped the tears from her eyes, feeling more confused than ever. Patsy seemed like a nice woman, but she hated Mom. And she *was* warning Jenna to stay away from Jude. Maybe the idea of revealing herself to this woman was a bad one. Maybe she didn't have a place here and never would.

Just before she got up to go, Patsy's cell phone rang.

"Oh, thank goodness, it's Harry." She accepted the call and let him know that Jenna was there waiting with her. Then she put the call on speaker.

"No one got hurt, thank goodness," Harry said, "but they were all pretty much in the drink with their PFDs when we got there. *Reel Therapy* is lying on her side in about six feet of water. That fool Charlie forgot to top off the gas when he left, and they ended up being pushed onto the jetty when the engine died."

"I'm so glad everyone is safe," Patsy said.

"It's going to take a while before we get back." Harry's voice stalled for a moment before he continued. "Jude is pretty upset, Jenna. I'm not entirely sure he wants to see you right at the moment. It might be best if you go on back to the cottage."

Okay. Message received. The universe had come to her

rescue before she'd told the truth. Clearly this was not the moment to tell Patsy and Harry that Theresa Fossey was her mother. And maybe this karmic explosion was a message telling her to leave Jonquil Island and never come back.

Patsy ended the call. "Looks like it's going to be a long evening. You can stay if you—"

"No," Jenna interrupted. She could see the writing on the wall, and she needed to get out of this house before she said something she could never take back. She stood up. "It's fine. I understand. Thank you for the cookies and iced tea. And the company while we waited for news. It's about to storm again. I should get going."

She retraced her footsteps through the house, her heart pounding and her head aching. She turned around once she reached the door. "Please tell Jude I'm sorry about the boat."

Chapter Nineteen————————

Jenna stripped off her soaked clothes and took a long, hot bath in the cottage's free-standing tub while she fought tumbling emotions that ranged between sadness and fury. Had Mom lied to her? Or had Patsy? Or was this an example of the Rashomon effect, where every witness to an event had a different story, all of them equally true?

Had Mom convinced Dad to go off his medications? That didn't sound like Mom.

Had Mom tried to trap Dad into a marriage? No way Jenna believed that.

Jenna had no reason to believe Patsy about those things, but she couldn't imagine Patsy lying about them either. Maybe there was no right and wrong here, just differences in perception, or maybe a misunderstanding that never got discussed because Jamie Bauman died unexpectedly.

The thought made her chest tighten until it became

impossible to take any deep, calming breaths. She needed more than deep breathing. She needed—no, she wanted—the truth.

Fighting tears, she climbed out of the tub and dressed in her soft, warm sweats, and then she called Milo.

"Jenna, what a coincidence. I was about to call you. I just noticed that you wrote a sizable check on your account. What are you up to?"

Milo was dependable and predictable. He complained when she didn't spend her allowance, and he noticed every time she wrote a larger-than-normal check. In short, he was nosy. But it was still a comfort to hear his British accent over the phone. If anyone could suss out the truth, it was Milo.

"If you must know, I'm making ill-advised investments in love," she said. "And so far one of them has backfired spectacularly."

"Good heavens. Love? Have you fallen in love?"

Had she? Maybe. But she wasn't about to admit that to Milo. "I was using 'love' in the 'love thy neighbor' context," she replied.

"Oh. You gave money away to charity, didn't you? I've told you before that charitable giving needs to be carefully managed. There are tax implications and—"

"Yes. I know. And repercussions. I got it, Milo. The repercussions of one of my acts of kindness—a few hundred dollars in advertising for a friend's business—has resulted in significant damage. I basically sank a fishing boat."

"You didn't."

"I did. And I need to make amends for that blunder, and quite frankly, I don't care about my taxes."

Silence hissed on the telephone line for a moment before he said, "So, I take it you were calling for advice on how to clean up this unintended consequence of your ill-advised investments in brotherly love?"

"No, actually not. But we'll have to talk about that sometime, I guess."

"Oh? Then I'm assuming you're calling about that request you made the other day, for more information about your father's death."

Jenna curled up in the king-sized bed and pulled the quilt over her. She stared through the Bahama shutters at the rain, which was coming down in buckets. She should be with Jude right now, making sure he was safe and dry, not obsessing about how her father died or whether her mother contributed to a suicide. But somehow she needed to settle the past before she could move into the future. "Have you found something?" she asked.

"Well, I haven't discovered anything new about his death. But I have run across a cache of letters Jamie wrote to his father during his years at Harvard. These letters were quite painful for your grandfather, evidently. After Jamie died, Robert asked Brian, my predecessor, to have the letters shredded. But Brian felt that your grandfather might regret that decision. So he wrote a memo to the file and then purposefully misfiled the letters as general correspondence. They turned up when I asked my associate to look at everything Brian handled for your grandfather.

"I'm having him scan them right now, and he'll be sending you an e-mail with a PDF. You'll want to read all of them."

"Oh." Her voice came out in a whisper. Now, after

all these years, her father's voice was within her grasp. "Thank you, Milo. You have no idea how much—"

"Well, before you thank me, I should tell you that the letters are mostly about your father's health. He was not well. I'm afraid he was—"

"Clinically depressed?"

"Bipolar, actually. But how did you learn that?"

"I had a long conversation with Patsy today. She told me that my mother was the one who convinced Jamie to go off his medications. She blames Mom for Jamie's death."

"Oh. Interesting. But not true. I'm fairly certain he went off his medications entirely on his own."

"He did?"

"Read the letters, my dear. They will shed light on that issue. Now, tell me about this good deed that has gone wrong. How expensive is this going to be?"

"Not very, I suspect. The cost of towing and refitting a fishing boat." She blew out a long, mournful sigh. "You know, Milo, I've been thinking about my future."

"Always a good thing to do."

"And it occurred to me that I've always worked for someone else. And that's why I lost my job a year ago. I thought I was secure, but my life was really in someone else's hands."

"Not now."

"That's not true. My life is in your hands, Milo. The only difference is that you can't fire me, and I can't fire you."

"That is true. The situation creates a certain amount of security for both of us, doesn't it?"

She snorted a laugh. "True. But you have things to do.

I have nothing to do. And I need something in my life. And the other day I was working on my résumé and I realized I didn't want to work for anyone else but myself. I want to put all that stuff I learned at Harvard into practice. I want to fail a few times."

"You want to fail? For heaven's sake, why?"

"Because failure is the best teacher. And unlike almost everyone else in the world, I have a cushion for all of my failures. But, you know, Jude doesn't have a cushion like that."

"Jude?" Milo's tone changed audibly. He was curious.

"I sank Jude's boat. And I'm pretty sure he can't afford to have it salvaged."

"Oh, I see."

Did he? Really? "Anyway, so I have this idea."

"Do tell." His voice sounded amused.

"I made a mistake doing a good deed for Jude because I thought it would improve my karma. Obviously that was wrong, especially because I did it to improve my karma. That's like daring the universe to screw it up, you know?"

"Um, not really. Karma is a concept I have difficulty with."

"That's okay. After this disaster, it's occurred to me that it would have been better to simply invest in the man's business instead of doing a kindness for him. And you know what? If I could have just a tiny part of Grandfather's capital to work with, I could use it to create an equity capital firm specializing in small businesses. And I could do a lot of good even though I wouldn't be giving my capital away. I'd just be investing it. You know, like that Bible story."

"Bible story? Good Lord, have you actually gone to church?"

She chuckled, her chest easing. "I have. But only to meet Patsy and Harry. On Sunday, the minister gave this sermon about investing. It made an impression."

"Obviously. But you are aware that the return on small-business investments will be insignificant."

She rolled her neck, easing the tension away. "I don't need to strike it rich, Milo," she said in her calmest voice. "I'm already richer than anyone has any right to be. And this would be a way to avoid the tax and karmic consequences of simply giving the money away."

He laughed.

"And you might be surprised. I might make money. And if I do, I'm going to invest all the profits into a worthy nonprofit or something."

"So, is this what you want to do for the rest of your life?"

She closed her eyes. Was it? For the last two weeks she'd been seeing the signs everywhere. Like coincidence or synchronicity. Annie's Kitchen, which needed a bigger dining room. Daffy Down Dilly, which needed a better merchandise assortment and reduced price points. Charlotte and Daisy's baskets, which required the endangered sweetgrass. Ashley's historic house, which needed a restoration. And, of course, Jude, who needed financing for that sailboat he'd been talking about. But Jude had bigger problems than that now. *Reel Therapy* had been sunk.

"Yes," she whispered, and then cleared her throat. "Yes," she said in a stronger voice as she opened her eyes onto the rainy day. "Milo, for the first time in months

I've found something worthwhile. I want to invest in this island, and not to build resorts. But to save it from the resorts."

"You want to move there permanently?"

Wow. That was a heavy question. She'd never seen herself living in a place like this. But earlier today, as she sat in the boat watching the wind in the live oaks along the shoreline, she'd felt as if she was already part of this place.

"Yes?" she said, aware of the uncertain inflection she'd given the word. "I mean, for now. I mean, I'm excited about this. I can do some good. If you'll let me." She cringed.

Another one of Milo's oppressive silences followed. "Jenna, if this is what you want, then you have to make peace with Harry and Patricia...Patsy."

No truer words had ever been spoken. He was right, of course. Milo was always right. It was mildly infuriating and probably the reason Grandfather had put him in charge of her trust fund.

"I know."

"Do you want them in your life?" Milo asked.

Her throat tightened with sudden, unexpected emotion. Yes, she did. A family would be so nice to have. All her life she'd wanted a family bigger than just herself and Mom. "I'd like to try," she said.

He was silent again for a long time before he said gently, "Well, then, I suggest a couple of things. First, you should read the letters I'm going to send you. And feel free to share them with Harry and Patsy. I think they will help shed light on your father's illness. And as for your equity capital venture, I'll consider it, but to convince me,

I need a business plan from you indicating just how much initial capital you will need and why. And I expect a plan worthy of a Harvard business school graduate."

It was all gone. All of it. All of the sweat. All of the investment. Three generations of his family business, all of it sunk in six goddamn feet of bay water. He'd lost his boat and his petition with the county, and he was going to lose Jenna too. It was all tumbling down after he'd spent a few days living on optimism.

How could his luck have turned in the blink of an eye?

Easy. He'd overestimated his luck in the first place. And Daddy had taken care of the rest.

His father had taken the last-minute charter out, along with a cooler of Heineken, to the inland fishing ground south of the harbor. But the clients were unhappy when they didn't find any fish. So Daddy, who'd had a few beers by then, had decided to take *Reel Therapy* north toward the inlet even as the wind built and the tide changed. Had he checked the gas tank before he left the marina? No. Had he checked the weather forecast? No.

And when they ran out of gas, he'd consumed just enough alcohol so that his judgment was impaired. He failed to get the anchor out fast enough, and the river currents did what they often did to the idiots who didn't take that part of the bay seriously. They pushed *Reel Therapy* up onto the jetty, where the rocks tore the hull apart.

Thank God no one was seriously hurt. Although the Coast Guard was pretty damn quick to administer a Breathalyzer test to Daddy, which he failed. The incident report would include that important fact. The customers would probably sue. And Barrier Island Charters's insurance company would probably not pay.

Gary down at Boat-Tow was ready to refloat *Reel Therapy*, for a price. He was pretty sure the hull was reparable. But what the hell was the use? Jude couldn't afford it, even if he took out that loan he'd been talking about. He was dead in the water of his life.

It was getting near eight o'clock. They'd returned hours ago, and Jude had been so furious with his father that he'd walked away from him on the pier. God only knew where Daddy was now. Jude had been sitting right here at the Alibi's scarred bar, drinking beers for the last hour and half.

Jonas Quick had been providing a steady stream of them, and Jude had forgotten just how many. Enough so that they were beginning to taste better. Not great, but better. He mostly hated the taste of beer. But at least the alcohol dulled the pain a little.

Which made him exactly like his father, didn't it? Sitting here at the end-of-the-world bar feeling sorry for himself.

He couldn't enjoy the irony. In fact, he hated himself. But he took another sip of the bitter brew and hung his head. What a fool he'd been to think that things were looking up in his life. What on earth made him think Barrier Island Charters had any hope of making it through another winter? What on earth made him think Daddy would stay sober for more than a week? What on earth made him think Jenna Bauman was the kind of woman for a man like him? And why the hell had he let her optimistic words about nonprofit associations and sailing ships get into his brain?

He stared down at the foam on his beer. He was toasted, wasn't he? That's why the room was spinning a little. Just then someone put a hand on his shoulder, and the spinning stopped. It was almost as if someone had anchored him to dry land.

He looked up, immediately disappointed that it was Micah. For an instant his heart had soared with the stupid idea that maybe Jenna had come looking for him. He was such an idiot. Harry had already told him that Jenna had gone back to the cottage. Apparently, she'd ended up using the disaster to chat with Patsy. But then she'd bailed and gone home. Yeah, he should have seen it coming. He shouldn't be surprised.

Jenna was using him to spy on her aunt and uncle. To reconnect with a father she'd never known. He was a means to an end. Not anything more. Except maybe a gigolo. Hell, with her money, she could buy anyone she wanted.

But not him. He was not for sale. Much.

He gave his brother a hard stare, wishing him away, even though his hand clamped to Jude's shoulder was the only thing keeping the room from spinning out of control.

Micah was going incognito today, having ditched his clerical collar for a plain white golf shirt and a pair of blue jeans. "I thought I might find you here," Jude's brother said, his gaze dropping to Jude's beer.

Whoa, was that some kind of reprimand? Like Micah had expected Jude to become a chip off the old drunken block? "Don't judge me," he said out of oddly numb lips.

Micah said nothing in reply, which was annoying as hell. Instead he sat down on the adjacent barstool. "I heard about what happened. Is Daddy at home?"

Jude shrugged. "I don't give a good goddamn where he is." The words burned his throat as he said them. Probably because they were a lie.

"I don't believe that," Micah said, calling him on his idiocy.

"Okay, I do give a goddamn, but I wish to hell I didn't."

"Now you're telling the truth," Micah said, waving Jonas away.

Jude laid his forehead on the cool surface of the bar. His stomach seemed to be spinning just like the room.

"Come on," Micah said in a gentle voice, as he ran a hand down Jude's back.

The touch was comforting in its way, but Jude resisted. "Leave me alone."

"No." Micah removed his hand, but he didn't go. He was like the proverbial rock in a hard place and just as stubborn.

Jude closed his eyes, the room spinning once again as a strange thought wormed itself into his brain. Once, a long time ago, when he'd been a kid who still thought there was a God, he'd prayed for Micah to come back home. Hell, he'd done more than pray. He'd made bargains with God. He'd promised to be good. He'd promised to look after Daddy. He'd promised to stay in school and earn good grades. Because he didn't want to burden Micah when he came home.

All his good behavior hadn't done the trick. It hadn't brought his brother or his mother back. It hadn't kept Daddy sober. How could someone believe in a God who didn't listen?

Damn. He was going to be sick. He lurched up off the

stool and ran all the way out to the sidewalk in the cold September rain and puked his guts out.

But he was not alone. Micah was right there beside him. And when he'd hurled up all the booze he'd foolishly consumed, Micah turned him around, gave him a big warm hug, and then walked him slowly to his car parked right up the street.

The sun sneaking in through the thin drapes in the vicarage's spare bedroom found Jude's eyes. He jolted awake, disoriented as he sat up and glanced at the still-unpainted pink walls and the ridiculous girl's white bed that he'd crashed in last night.

He blinked a couple of times as reality crashed into his head with the force of a swinging boom. He flopped back and curled up into a tight ball, eyes closed.

When that didn't keep the light out, he buried his head under the pillow. But the morning sun was relentless.

He would never drink another beer. So help him...

He pulled in a deep breath, and the smell of coffee and bacon made his abused stomach clutch. If only he could go back to sleep and forget about his disastrous life.

But Micah had other plans. Jude's older brother banged on the door and hollered, "Time to get up, sleepyhead."

The words hurt. Physically, they pierced his bruised gray matter like pins and needles. Emotionally, they took him back to another time and place and wrenched his gut.

After Old Granny died, Micah had started banging on the bedroom door in the mornings. Every school day, he'd gotten Jude and Colton up in time for the bus. He'd made peanut butter sandwiches and put them in brown paper sacks. And he'd been there every night to help with homework. Until he left for college.

"You awake in there?" Micah rattled the door again. He wasn't going to leave until Jude made some kind of response.

"Yeah."

"Breakfast in ten. Be there or be square."

More memories.

Especially the promise he made to Micah that day seventeen years ago, when his big brother had packed up his old Ford truck and gone away.

"Take care of yourself," Micah had said.

"I will."

"And Daddy. You need to take care of Daddy. You know how he can be."

Jude had nodded. And he'd done what Micah had asked of him.

"Jude!" Micah called again. The urgency in his brother's voice said it all. Micah wasn't going to let him hide out in this room with its bright Pepto-Bismol walls.

He got out of bed and pulled on the clothes he'd been wearing yesterday. Once dressed, Jude ventured out into the hallway and headed toward the kitchen, where he found Micah banging around with pots and pans.

"I need to go home," Jude said. "I need to check on Daddy. I should have—"

"Daddy's fine. He's with Colton."

"He's with Colton?"

"He's fine. Colton's taking him to the rehab center in Georgetown. The one you reserved for him."

"He agreed?"

"Yes. Sit down," Micah directed.

Jude sat.

"You should know that one of the requirements of becoming a full-fledged navy chaplain is making good coffee." Micah put a steaming mug in front of Jude.

"I'm not sure I could drink or eat anything right now."

"You got no choice," Micah said, gesturing to the glass of water and the bottle of aspirin on the table. "Don't be brave. The aspirin will help, trust me." His tone was a little autocratic. As a child, Jude had never hated the fact that Micah was so good at issuing orders. Micah's orders made the chaos go away.

Now he wanted to rebel, but it was hard to when Micah was just trying to make him feel better. A little bit of the concrete and steel wall around Jude's heart crumbled.

After he'd taken the aspirin and drained the water, Jude ventured a sip of the coffee. It *was* good. He drank some more while Micah went back to puttering around the kitchen.

A few minutes later, Micah put two plates of eggs and bacon on the table. Micah took a seat and started eating without talking, which brought back more memories. No one ever talked at the dinner table when he'd been a boy. None of the St. Pierre men were real good communicators back then. Funny how Micah had turned into a minister. He was supposed to be a good communicator now. But he wasn't saying a word.

Jude studied his eggs, his stomach roiling at the thought of eating anything.

"You need to eat," Micah said.

"Not hungry."

"Okay." Micah leaned back in his chair, took a sip of

coffee, and said, "Come unto me, all you that labor and are heavy laden, and I will give you rest."

Jude had known that Micah wasn't planning to remain silent forever. But he sure didn't want a sermon from his brother.

"That's from Matthew, by the way," Micah said. "It was one of Old Granny's favorites. Did you know that she's the one who sent me to Reverend Ball?"

Jude looked up from his eggs. "No way. Old Granny would never have sent you to the white church."

"She did. She told me that the Lord came to her and instructed her to do that. Have you any idea what a burden that was?"

No, not really, but he could imagine a young Micah walking into the Church at Heavenly Rest, where there was nothing but white folks. Why had Old Granny done that to Micah, when she'd done nothing but the opposite with Jude, teaching him the Gullah language from the time he was a little-bitty boy and taking him to the AME church, where they sang more than prayed? "I don't understand," Jude said.

"Neither did I until Reverend Ball repeated that verse to me right after I got that full scholarship to Clemson. I was ready to turn that offer down, but Reverend Ball convinced me not to. He and Old Granny both thought I had a calling. He told me that I should give my burdens to the Lord and that he would take care of them."

Jude closed his eyes. They burned behind the lids. "I'm sorry," he said for no reason at all.

"You got nothing to be sorry for. You've been doing the best you know how. But here's the thing. I thought I put my burden on the Lord, but what I really did was put it on you. I made you promise something that you weren't ready for. And I need to pay a penance for that."

"No, you don't. I mean, you had a full scholarship to Clemson. You didn't have to give that up."

"True, but I never came back home, did I?"

"No. And I hated you for it."

"I didn't come home because I couldn't deal with Daddy. He made me so angry, and I was afraid I might not let the Lord take care of him, you know?"

Jude shook his head.

"Of course you don't understand. Because you stayed. And you took care of him. And I've never seen a better example of God's grace in my life. You humble me and inspire me, Jude. The Lord used you to ease my burden. But here's the thing. I never wanted you to sacrifice yourself."

Jude stared down at his uneaten eggs. Had he done that? No. "It wasn't a sacrifice. Daddy needed help. And then there came a time when I had to make sure he didn't hurt anyone. I fell down on that one yesterday."

"But you stayed with it and did what had to be done even at your own expense."

He looked up. "Are you going to lecture me the way Colton always does? He's forever telling me to walk away from Daddy and go to work for someone else, like I want to leave the family business."

Micah let go of a long breath. "I don't think Colton's been lecturing you. I think he's just concerned is all. Jude, it's time for you to stop thinking about everyone else and start thinking about your own self."

"But—"

"Wait." Micah cut off his argument and then pushed up

from the table. A moment later he returned with a thick manila folder, which he pushed across the table.

"What's this?" Jude asked as he picked up the folder and opened it to find several legal documents inside, including *Reel Therapy*'s title with the change-of-ownership section filled out in Daddy's chicken-scratch handwriting. There were other documents as well, all of which amounted to the fact that Daddy had just given him ownership of Barrier Island Charters.

It was everything Jude had been asking for, but it had probably come too late.

"When did he do this?"

"Colton went looking for Daddy after we heard about the accident. He found him at home, sitting at his table, sober, with all these documents signed. No one forced him to sign them. He told Colton he'd been waiting for you to come home so he could give this to you. He said a lot of other things, which you should have heard."

"Except I was off getting drunk."

"Well, don't beat yourself up too hard. From what I've heard, that was possibly the first time you ever got drunk in your life. Unless you binged when you were at college."

Jude shook his head. "I hate the taste of beer. And most other alcohol."

"So Colton tells me." Micah paused for a moment, giving Jude time to stare at the documents he'd been hassling Daddy to hand over for years. What now?

He sat there thinking, his head pounding. Maybe it wasn't too late. Maybe he could get a loan and salvage *Reel Therapy*. And then maybe, after a few years, he could save up enough for a down payment on the sailboat he wanted. Something like that forty-four-foot, 1981 LaFitte that was up for sale in Hilton Head. And then, out of nowhere, he flashed on Jenna telling him that the road to success was paved with failure. Somehow that made him feel so much better about everything.

"So, what are you going to do?" Micah asked.

"I guess I'm going to pick myself up and go talk to Boat-Tow and see about getting *Reel Therapy* salvaged. I reckon I'll need to talk to a banker before that though."

"And running Barrier Island Charters is what you want?"

He didn't have to think about that. "I love being on the water. And I can make something of that business without Daddy's interference. And maybe, if I work hard enough, I can finally turn it into the sailboat charter I want." He paused a moment. "But what happens after Daddy gets out of rehab? I mean, I'm not optimistic that he'll even stay."

"It's not your problem anymore. Daddy's my problem now."

Jude shook his head. "No. He's my daddy, and I love him even though he's a pain in the ass most of the time. I want him to get sober. I want him to be well. And I'm not walking away from him. Not ever. So I guess that makes him *our* problem."

Micah's mouth twitched. "Why am I not surprised? Old Granny used to say you were like a dog with a bone. You just don't give up, do you?"

"I guess not," Jude said, feeling a weight lifting from his shoulders. "Maybe that's my most valuable intangible asset."

Micah laughed out loud. "Maybe it is. But here's the

thing. You're going to have to get used to having help. Colton's going to try to do better too. And he agrees with me. You need to get out from under Daddy's thumb. It's okay to love the old guy, but it's time for you to do what you want to do."

Micah paused for a moment and sipped his coffee. "Which brings up the other thing I wanted to talk to you about."

"What other thing?"

"Colton and I talked about this the other night when we heard about the town council's decision on that zoning proposal you were behind. And we're both agreed. We don't want to sell Old Granny's land either. There are about fifteen of us in the family who agree on that. We all own shares in that old place. So maybe we can figure out a way to get it fixed up and rent it out as a B and B or something. Maybe after we restore it, the state will rethink and agree to nominate it for the National Register of Historic Places."

Jude didn't know what to say. His brothers' hearts were in the right place, but neither one of them had ever understood about the seagrass and the baskets. In fact, as kids, both of them had teased him for spending so much time with Old Granny working on learning that skill. But it was a start. And maybe there was a way to turn this into something more than just a family agreement about Old Granny's place. Maybe they could turn this into a solution for everyone living north of Magnolia Harbor.

He looked up at his brother. He'd missed him so much over the years. If he could forgive Daddy, he should be able to forgive Micah too. "Um, I may not have said this before, but welcome home."

Chapter Twenty—————

Jenna woke early on Thursday, spent extra time meditating, and then called the boat salvage people at the marina and got a price for refloating and refitting *Reel Therapy*. A quick text exchange with Milo and the consequences of her act of kindness were taken care of.

She did this without Jude's blessing because the man had gone silent on her again. She'd left him half a dozen voice mail messages and had texted him like a stalker. And nothing.

Well, he'd find out what she'd done soon enough, and then he'd come storming in, complaining that he didn't want to be rescued. And she would explain that this wasn't a rescue but a restitution. A vain attempt to make sure she didn't spend her next lifetime as a slug or something.

The e-mail from Milo's associate arrived midmorning with a PDF file attached that contained almost a hundred pages of correspondence from Jamie Bauman to his father. She settled in to read them. Her father's hand-writing was bold and slanted backward, suggesting that he was left-handed. He wrote on lined paper with holes punched on one side and a ragged edge where he'd torn the page from a spiral notebook.

He had a beautiful way with words, his writing rich with metaphors and vivid descriptions of the Harvard campus and his very lonely life. He was not happy, but neither was he sad. At one point, he wrote to his father that the medications took his colorful world and turned it into black-and-white.

As she progressed through the letters, it became clear that Jamie's father didn't truly understand him. Jamie was desperately seeking a connection with Robert but evidently found Robert's responses to his letters wanting in some way. Was it love he wanted, or attention, or just someone who could sympathize? Jamie's mother had died in a private plane accident when he was only six. And her death may have left a mark on him. He seemed like a very lonely person.

Jenna also didn't have Robert's responses, of course. She was reading a one-sided conversation, which made it easy to paint Robert as the villain. But then, in the spring of his senior year, Jamie's letters changed. The complaints about his medications disappeared, and the letters became manic, as if he'd finally decided not to listen to his father. As if he'd finally chosen to go off his meds.

And there was one other thing in the last line of the last letter home. *I met a girl on Jonquil Island*, he wrote to his father. *She's beautiful and fun. I took her to see the daffodils. She says they are her favorite flower. I know she's just a tourist, Dad, but she's from Boston and our apartments aren't all that far away from each other. Her name is Theresa*, he wrote to his father, *and she's changed everything*.

On Thursday afternoon, Jude left the vicarage once his headache had receded. His first stop was Barrier Island Charters, where he got to work trying to salvage his boat, his business, and his future. But first he called Wayne Hubble Jr., Colton's friend and lawyer. He told Junior he needed to talk about a way to organize the family's shares in Old Granny's land. Junior suggested that he come by the office later in the day.

After that Jude called all his customers, letting them know that charters were canceled for the foreseeable future. Then he printed out the company's year-to-date financials before heading home, where he took a long shower and dressed up in his one business suit.

His temples were pounding again when he got to the Citibank office on Harbor Drive. Damn. He'd been hounding Daddy about having this conversation with their banker for years, so he was doubly aware of the stakes. And his position wasn't nearly as strong as it might have been a week ago, when their main asset wasn't sitting at the bottom of the bay. So maybe this was going to be one of those times when he failed.

And what had Jenna said about failure? That it was the best teacher around.

Bull. He didn't want to fail. He couldn't fail. He was not going to fail. He squared his shoulders and walked into the bank. He was ready for this.

But he wasn't ready to find Onyeka Ochoa sitting

behind the desk in the small office reserved for the commercial accounts manager.

"Jude, it's so good to see you," she said, standing and shaking his hand. "It's been a while."

Damn. He'd taken Onyeka to senior prom when he was seventeen. At one time, she'd been that girl who'd reminded him of Phylicia Rashad, his ideal of feminine beauty. Her name had been Onyeka Vargas then, and her Mexican daddy had been super intimidating on prom night when Jude had shown up with a corsage.

But her momma was one of Aunt Charlotte's friends, and Charlotte had been trying all through high school to match them up. He'd thought Onyeka was beautiful, but he'd never truly loved her, which explained why they'd lost touch during college.

By the time they'd both returned, she'd gotten engaged to Ricky Ochoa. Charlotte sometimes talked about her as if she were the woman who got away. Onyeka had a bunch of kids now, if he remembered right.

"Hey," he said, "I didn't know you worked here. So, um, you're the new commercial account manager?"

"I am," she said, her smile widening.

Damn. He had to make his pitch to an old girlfriend? Life was truly unfair sometimes. On the other hand, Granddaddy's head would have exploded if anyone had ever told him that one day the commercial accounts manager at the Citibank would be a female of Gullah and Mexican descent.

So maybe it wasn't unfair at all.

He took a seat in her office cubby and started talking about his business. The numbers in his financial statements weren't as good as they could be. But he explained all that. He also made a point to sell himself by talking about his intangible assets, such as his experience and knowledge of local conditions and fishing areas, and the fact that he had certifications in both motorized boats and sailboats. And then, because Onyeka seemed really interested, he started talking about the sailboat for sale in Hilton Head and his ideas for a sailing charter, and he might even have thrown in Jenna's suggestion for pirate adventure sails.

Onyeka stopped him right there. "Oh, that sounds like fun. And educational. And you wouldn't have much competition." She parroted all of Jenna's thoughts back to him, and something in his chest expanded.

"And I'm related to Henri St. Pierre."

"You are."

After that they got down to business. She pulled out a bunch of sales brochures outlining various financing options, for both the boat and a business line of credit. With *Reel Therapy* damaged, he opted to take out a personal line of credit because the interest rate was lower. He'd had to use his share of Old Granny's place as collateral, which just might tick off a few family members.

But he had a plan for that. So he did what he had to do to save the family business first. He wasn't going to let Citibank get ahold of the family land. He had every intention of paying back the money he borrowed.

With his business at the bank concluded, he headed down to Boat-Tow. He was a little surprised when Gary, the head man there, seemed to think he'd already called for an estimate and approved the work. In fact, the Boat-Tow salvage team had gone out to refloat the boat earlier in the morning, and *Reel Therapy* was on her way back to the harbor.

Thank goodness he'd gotten that line of credit; otherwise he'd be red-faced trying to figure out how to pay for the salvage he hadn't ordered.

He had time to kill before his meeting with Junior, so he hung around the Boat-Tow office until they brought the fishing boat in. And then, as if today were truly his lucky day, Gary gave him an estimate for the hull repair that was a whole lot less than he'd been anticipating.

Jenna spent most of the afternoon working on a business plan for her equity capital firm, her mind distracted by the things she'd read in her father's letters. Should she show them to Patsy and Harry?

Maybe not. Maybe they would read them differently. Maybe they'd still blame Mom for Jamie's death. Would they blame her too? Could she ever bridge the divide created by the tragedy of her father's death?

She wasn't even sure she knew where to begin. And yet the stakes were now impossibly high because she wanted to stay here. She wanted to make Jonquil Island her home. But would it be home if her family shunned her? Would it be home if Jude wanted nothing to do with her? Would it be home if Milo said no to her equity capital fund idea?

These thoughts filled her mind as she headed across the rose garden for the Piece Makers meeting that Patsy had invited her to attend at church on Sunday. Jenna didn't plan to "come out" to Patsy tonight. But she hoped to lay some more groundwork for the moment when she did reveal her true identity. Maybe if she and Patsy could connect in a deeper way, a relationship with her and Harry could be built.

So high were the stakes that her heart thumped in her chest as she entered Howland House and made her way into the solarium. She was a little late, so the members of the quilting club had already assembled around the big quilting frame.

She stood in the threshold for a moment, waiting for someone to scold her, but instead, Patsy jumped up from her chair. "Oh, there you are. I thought, with all of yesterday's excitement, you might have forgotten."

"No. I've been looking forward to this. Have you heard from Jude? Is he okay? I texted him a couple of times, but..." She stopped speaking as the ladies around the quilt frame looked up at her in avid interest. Yikes. Was she a subject of gossip? Had anyone noticed that she and Jude had left the vicarage together last Monday? And, for goodness' sake, they'd been seen sailing together in the harbor.

Wow.

"No, honey, I haven't. But Harry said he saw the salvage crew from Boat-Tow hauling *Reel Therapy* in. So I'm sure he's just really busy dealing with the boat repairs and insurance and whatnot."

Jenna's face heated as she stepped down into the room. Of course they assumed Jude had arranged for the salvage. But he hadn't. So what was he doing? Had he gone off fishing with his old uncle, the one she'd met a few days ago? Or was he dealing with a lot of family drama? Or maybe it was a little of both. Whatever it was, he wasn't interested in sharing it with Jenna—a fact that made her feel small and guilty.

She pushed those thoughts from her mind as she

nodded to Sandra and Nancy, whom she'd met at church on Sunday. She also greeted Karen, who had been at the painting party at the vicarage. Karen and Sandra were sisters and looked it, despite the fact that one had allowed her hair to gray and the other had not.

Patsy also introduced Donna Cuthbert and Barbara Blackwood, another pair of aging sisters who, it was pointed out, were Methodists.

Once the introductions were made, Ashley hopped up from her place. "There's hummingbird cake in the kitchen. Let me cut you a piece."

Jenna had no idea what hummingbird cake was, but her stomach was so jumpy she couldn't possibly eat anything. "It's no bother, Ashley. I'm not hungry."

"Really?" the stout woman wearing the tent-like shirt asked. Was that Donna or Barbara? Crap. Jenna couldn't remember which was which. "Ashley's hummingbird cake is divine. It's exactly like the cake her grandmother used to bake."

Ashley rolled her eyes as if she'd had enough of being compared to her grandmother. Jenna gave her a smile. "I'm sure it's wonderful. Maybe later."

"Come, sit by me," Patsy said, patting an empty chair beside her. "So, you've never quilted before?"

Jenna shook her head. "To be honest, I'm not the most coordinated person when it comes to stuff like this."

"So why did you want to learn?" This came from Karen, the blunt-speaking woman Jenna had met at the vicarage. Karen gave her a thunderous stare from under a pair of bushy gray eyebrows.

"Because I think what you do is beautiful," Jenna said, hoping to disarm the grumpy woman.

Nancy, a woman with a soft voice, said, "It doesn't take much coordination, honey."

Patsy set to work giving Jenna the basics. It was straightforward, except for threading the needle. Quilting needles were incredibly tiny with even smaller eyes. Thankfully no one laughed at Jenna's lame attempts to get the thread through the eye. It took her a good two minutes before she managed it.

"The main thing is to keep your stitches as even as you can. And shoot for six stitches to the inch if you can," Patsy said, and then demonstrated.

Within minutes, Jenna was leaning forward over the pieced fabric, loading her needle up with stitches and pulling the thread through. "Well," Patsy said, "you're not as clumsy as you say you are."

Jenna's face heated. Patsy's compliment meant a lot—more than she would have been willing to admit two weeks ago. But then, quilting was kind of Zen, like knitting or deep breathing. The repetitive motions cleared the mind or might have, if she hadn't been sitting next to her great-aunt, longing to tell the truth.

Sandra broke the silence by asking, "Are y'all at all worried that Reverend St. Pierre's sermons are too short?"

Beside her Patsy stopped quilting. "No," she said in an authoritative voice, daring anyone to disagree with her. Patsy could be kind and gracious at times, but she had a dictatorial streak. No one challenged her.

Instead, soft-spoken Nancy at the end of the quilt frame changed the subject and said, "I see that you had the roof repaired, Ashley."

"Replaced," Ashley said.

Jenna looked up in time to see Ashley flush. Big mistake because she pricked her finger. "Ow."

"You'll get used to that," Patsy remarked.

"Just don't bleed on the quilt, please," Barbara (or was it Donna?) said.

She studied her finger. No blood. Good.

"I'm so glad you've started renovating Howland House," Nancy continued.

"Amen to that. And we're sure it's going to come out beautifully. None of us believed you could fix up that old shack out back and turn it into a cottage," Karen said.

Ashley's blush deepened, but she concentrated on her needle work.

"So, what's next?" Nancy asked.

A muscle ticked along Ashley's jaw, and she dropped her needle and leaned back. "Ladies, I'm sorry, but I'm not renovating Howland House. I'm selling it."

"What?" The Piece Makers spoke in near unison while Jenna's chest tightened and her pulse soared. No, not again. But what had she expected? You couldn't buy good karma. It just didn't work that way. Maybe if she'd invested in Ashley, instead of simply giving her a new roof, it might have turned out better.

"You can't move away," Karen said. "Where would we—"

"I can. And I must. I can't afford the house," Ashley said in a shaky voice. "And honestly, whoever gave the money to Colton for the roof needs to tell me now. Because just as soon as I sell the house and pay off the mortgage, I will return your money." She stared at Patsy when she said this.

"What are you talking about?" Patsy asked.

"I'm talking about the person sitting in this room who listened to Micah's sermon on Sunday and got the crazy idea that I was some kind of act of selfless charity." Her voice wavered, and tears filled her eyes. She pushed up from the quilt frame and hurried from the room.

Jenna sat there, her spirit sinking right into the pit of her uneasy stomach. Karma could be a bitch, but not always in the way people thought.

"Oh, for goodness' sake," Patsy said, standing up and following Ashley. Patsy might have chased her up the stairs if Nancy hadn't gotten up and blocked her way.

"Let her go," Nancy said in that quiet way of hers.

"But—"

"Really, Patsy. We all know you like to control things, but tell us you didn't pay for that roof repair." This came from Karen in her blunt way. "You know how proud Ashley is."

Patsy turned her gaze on the ladies of the Piece Makers. "I don't know where y'all get the idea that I can afford something like a roof repair. If I had the money for something like that, believe me, I'd be fixing my own roof, not Ashley Scott's."

The other ladies stared at her. "You've always given the appearance of being quite wealthy," Karen said.

"Appearances can be deceiving." Patsy sank down into a chair with a deep, mournful sigh. "Ya'll know how much we were counting on some money from Robert's estate. Even a little would have helped. The economic downturn did a number on our savings because Harry decided that we could do better with an aggressive portfolio.

The truth is he lost a lot of it on poor investments, and we've had to tighten our belts.

"So no, I didn't pay for Ashley's roof. I couldn't afford it." She leaned back in the chair.

"You should write to your niece," Karen said.

Patsy's back snapped straight. "I will not talk to that woman. Period. I don't want or need her charity. I don't ever want to see her face. Is that clear?"

A cold shiver started at Jenna's shoulders and worked its way down her spine to the tips of her toes. It was almost as if someone had breathed icy-cold air on her neck. Why on earth was Patsy so angry? What had she done besides being born?

Easy answer: She'd inherited Robert Bauman's billions. And Patsy and Harry needed the money.

Proving once again that her inheritance came with a boatload of issues attached to it. Money could do so much good in the world. It was also the root of all evil. How could she have a place here on Jonquil Island or make a family with Patsy and Harry when there was so much anger and so much grief to surmount?

Her throat closed up. It was so unfair. She'd come so close and now...

"Ladies," Patsy said, putting her hands on her hips and pulling Jenna out of her own despair. "We can't let Ashley sell this house."

"Why not?" Karen asked. "She just told us that she can't afford to keep it. And you just told us that you don't have enough money to help her keep it. So what can we do?"

"We could help her write a business plan to turn the entire house into a B and B, not just the cottage," Jenna said. "I'll bet she could find someone willing to give her a line of credit."

Everyone turned in Jenna's direction, evidently astonished that an outsider had the temerity to speak. If she invested in Ashley Scott, would that be the same as buying good karma with Patsy? She didn't know. But obviously she needed to fix this mess too. But with Ashley, it wasn't as easy as calling up a salvage service and paying for them to refloat a boat.

"That's a great idea, Jenna, but have you seen the rooms upstairs?" Karen asked, folding her arms across her Clemson sweatshirt.

"No. But I've been staying at the cottage. And you yourself said you couldn't wait to see what Ashley did with the rest of the house."

"She mortgaged the place to the nines to fix up the cottage," Barbara (or was it Donna?) said. "I doubt she could get a line of credit."

"Don't be so negative," Patsy said. "We need ideas. Including some that might sound crazy or outside the box." She turned toward Jenna with a genuine smile. "That's good thinking, Jenna, but I'm not sure she's creditworthy. Maybe we can find her a business partner or someone who could cosign a loan." Patsy turned her gaze on the rest of the Piece Makers. "Any ideas?"

The rest of the ladies shook their heads. But a germ of an idea sprouted in Jenna's mind. She could easily cosign a loan. And maybe Milo would let her put a few bucks into Howland House as a means of cleaning up another one of her acts of kindness.

"Well, I don't know what. But we need to figure something out quick. We can't let her sell Howland House.

There's been a Howland living on this land since before the Revolution."

"Well, that's about to change," Karen said. "And Ashley would be the first one to tell you it's none of our business."

"But don't you see? It *is* our business."

"How do you figure that?" Nancy asked.

"Use your imagination. The Howland House ghost is going to be very upset if the last Howland sells this house. And really, can the town afford that? I mean, we need our ghosts to be friendly, not vengeful."

Karen laughed. "You're not serious. You don't really believe...Oh my goodness, you do believe in the ghost."

"Well," Nancy said in a voice hardly above a whisper. "I don't have any ideas on how to keep Ashley from selling the house, but I will pray for her. And the ghost too. If you want my opinion, it's well past time for him to cross over to the other side. I mean, I'm sure Rose is waiting for him."

Karen shook her head. "Y'all, there is no such thing as ghosts. And I think we should quit meddling in Ashley's life. She's had a rough time. If she wants to go back to Kansas, we shouldn't be standing in her way."

Jude arrived at the law offices of Hubble & Hubble at six o'clock and was ushered into Junior's modest office with its view of tree-lined Lilac Street. The law office was located far away from Magnolia Harbor's downtown area, in an older, historic section of town.

"It's nice to see you," Junior said, shaking Jude's hand. "I want you to know that I was following your battle to protect our ancestors' land."

"I guess a lot of us were disappointed," Jude said.

"So, you said you had a land issue. I'm not really a real estate attorney. If this is about heirs' property, you should see—"

"It's not about heirs' property exactly," Jude said.

"No?"

Jude shook his head. "Junior, I want to form a nonprofit corporation to help our people protect their land from gentrification."

Junior lifted an eyebrow. "That's an interesting idea," he said.

"Yeah, isn't it? I'd like to tell you that I came up with it myself. But to be honest, I didn't. Just recently someone told me that it's faster and more effective to accomplish things privately than to rely on the government. And since the government's decided that we need a museum instead of protection, I need to figure out a new way of fighting this battle."

Junior smiled. "Excellent idea. What exactly did you have in mind?"

Jude leaned forward in his chair and started to talk. "I'd like to create an organization that could raise money either to help folks cover the taxes on land they've held for generations, or alternatively, to buy up historically significant sites and ensure that they will be protected from development. And I'd also like to figure out a way to fund legal help for families dealing with the complexities of heirs' property. Or something like that. And, what the hell, maybe we could even support that museum Harry Bauman thinks we need. But bottom line, we need a way to raise money from rich people for all of these things. And I'm hoping that we can raise enough money to keep companies like Santee Resorts off this island."

Junior nodded. "I like it. We could get this up and running faster than you think."

Jude noticed the pronoun Junior had used, as if he'd adopted the idea. And something warm and exciting rushed through him. He could do this. Not alone, but with some help from his family and his friends in the community. They didn't have to sit back and wait for the resort company to come destroy everything.

"So, how the hell do we get something like that started?" he asked.

And Junior had a lot to say on the subject. Including the fact that Hubble & Hubble would be happy to provide pro bono legal services for the creation of articles of incorporation and the filings necessary to obtain nonprofit status from the federal and state government. That still meant that Jude had to find some startup money, but Junior suggested that it wouldn't take much before they could go into fundraising mode.

It was after seven o'clock when they finished talking and Junior stood up and offered his hand. "Jude, I'm honored to help you do this."

Pride coursed up Jude's spine as he shook Junior's hand. "Thank you," Jude said.

"So, let me put some of this down on paper and shoot you an e-mail tomorrow or the next day. You'll need to think about who you want on your initial board of directors, and we'll need to hammer out a mission statement and a list of programs the group intends to undertake."

"Okay," Jude said, a little stunned.

He left the office filled with the possibilities of success. Funny how all the failures had kind of turned themselves around. How had that happened?

He had a short answer: Jenna. She was full of a lot of woo-woo Buddhist ideas, but that one about making your own reality was kind of true, wasn't it?

Once Daddy had freed him.

He wanted to share his enthusiasm with someone. No, not someone. Jenna.

She'd been texting him all day, and he'd been trying to figure out how to respond. He was glad he'd waited until now. But as his fingers began typing out a message, he decided it would be better to tell her the news in person, and maybe to thank her for the things she'd said to him the other day. All that stuff about being optimistic, about taking charge, about not being afraid to fail. He'd needed to hear those words.

He drove his pickup across town and parked it in the lot at Howland House, and then he let himself into the rose garden by the back gate. But as he approached Rose Cottage, he was disappointed to see that all the windows were dark.

He stepped up onto the porch and knocked. No answer. He knocked again and waited a good five minutes. Jenna was not there.

Damn.

Jude considered waiting on her porch but opted against it. He was hungry...finally. Maybe he should go on home and get a good night's rest. He swallowed his disappointment and headed back toward his truck.

Fifteen minutes later, when he pulled up to Old Granny's place, he was surprised to find a whole mess of family waiting for him. Charlotte and Daisy, Annie, Jeeter, Colton, and Micah, and a half dozen cousins. Every single one of them had a key to Old Granny's house, because they all owned a share in it.

The family was sitting around the table with the remnants of a meal that Annie had probably cooked. There was fried chicken, rice, okra, lima beans, and stewed tomatoes. His stomach rumbled.

"Where you been, baby?" Annie asked. "We got hungry and ate while we were waiting. But I made you a plate."

"What are y'all doing here?" he asked as he sat down and let Annie put a huge plate of food in front of him.

"Micah called us," Charlotte said. "He thought we should talk about how to save this old place."

A pit opened in his stomach. "Um, I got something I need to tell y'all. Something I don't think you're going to like much."

"What is it, baby?" Annie patted his back.

"I went down to the bank today, and I took out a line of credit in order to salvage *Reel Therapy*. I had to use my share in this place as collateral. I'm really sorry. I—"

"Oh, darling, you don't need to explain about that," Annie said, giving him a big hug. "How do you think I started up my kitchen?"

"You used your share?"

"I did. And I paid back that loan. We all have faith in you, Jude. I reckon that's why we're here. Just to let you know that."

He swallowed down a big knot in his throat. "Thanks."

"Eat," Annie directed.

But he didn't eat. Not yet. "I need to tell y'all something else."

"Boy, you have been busy today," Micah said with a little grin on his face.

"I guess I have," Jude said. "And we're all going to be busy for a while, I think. We're going to form a corporation." Jude finally picked up a chicken leg and took a bite. Man, he really was hungry, and Annie knew how to fry chicken just right.

"Lawd have mercy," Daisy said, shaking her head. "I don't want to be part of no corporation."

"A corporation to do what?" Charlotte asked.

"We're going to form a nonprofit corporation to raise money from rich folks to help our people pay their taxes and keep the resort people away."

"How are we going to do that, Jude?" Charlotte asked, her eyes lighting up.

"Well, Junior Hubble's going to help us. But the very first thing we need to do is to name a board of directors and come up with a mission statement."

"Oh, I like that," Annie said. "We'll be like David kicking Goliath's butt."

"Amen to that," Micah said with a wink and a nod.

Chapter Twenty-One————

On Friday morning, after another night disturbed by the same dreams she'd hoped to lay to rest, Jenna decided that today was the day to clear up all the problems she'd created over the last couple of weeks.

First thing on the agenda was to talk to Patsy and Harry. Second thing was to come clean with Jude and explain why she'd paid for *Reel Therapy*'s salvage. And third, she needed to have a long chat with Ashley Scott.

It was a gigantic agenda for a person who hadn't slept well in several days. But Milo was right. If she wanted to start this business and make a difference in this town, she had to come clean with Harry and Patsy first. Without that, nothing was possible.

She bypassed her yoga, took a long, hot shower, and put on some clean clothes without paying too much attention to what she pulled out of her backpack. She restrained her hair in a ponytail, stepped into her new flip-flops, and headed out down Harbor Drive.

The wind had diminished and had shifted direction,

coming out of the southeast and bringing heat and sunshine. By the time Jenna arrived at Harry and Patsy's house, her hands were sweaty and her heart was bumping against her chest wall with such force that it shook her whole body.

She squared her shoulders and took a couple of cleansing breaths, redolent with pine needles, boxwood, and sea air. She would remain calm.

If they hated her because of the money, she'd lay out the terms of her grandfather's will, making it clear that she wouldn't have control of the money until she turned forty-five. A term in her grandfather's will that would probably enrage the Baumans because it looked as if it was specifically designed to keep her from sharing her wealth. With them or with anyone.

And if they hated her because of Mom, she'd offer to send them the PDF file of her father's letters, which seemed to suggest that Jamie went off his meds before he met Mom. It was quite possible that Jenna's mother knew nothing at all about his medications. Although Mom might have realized that Jamie was bipolar.

And if they still didn't want anything to do with her, she would...

No. She shook her head. She wouldn't be negative. This was going to work out. They had met her. They knew her. It wasn't as if she was some stranger knocking on their door.

She ground her back teeth on that thought because, for all intents and purposes, she *was* a stranger. A stranger who had *lied* to them.

Time froze. Only the relentless throbbing of her heart marked the moments until Patsy opened the door.

"Jenna. What a surprise." She opened the door wide.

"Is Harry here?"

"He is. What did you—"

"I need to talk to both of you. It's important."

"Come in, dear. You look as if you've seen a ghost. Oh my goodness, have you?"

Jenna shook her head even though she'd felt haunted by her father these last few days. "No."

Patsy's blue eyes turn up a little at the corners. Patsy could be dictatorial and bossy, but she was also kind-hearted. "What is it, dear? Is this about Jude?"

"No," she said, even though, in a way, it was all about Jude. Until this moment she hadn't fully understood the stakes. If Patsy and Harry rejected her, they could turn her into a social pariah in this town. They could make it impossible for her to stay, and she wanted to stay... because she wanted to build something with Jude.

In that moment, staring into Patsy's eyes, she realized that she'd fallen in love with Jude. Not just in lust or infatuation, but love. True love. The kind of love that helps two souls find each other because, perhaps, they had loved in other lifetimes. Had that happened to Mom and Dad? Was that why Jamie's letters had turned manic?

Just then, as her chest felt as if it might explode, Harry came out of the kitchen carrying a coffee mug. "Who is it, dear?" he asked, and then stopped in his tracks and gave Jenna a scowl. "What do you want?"

"Harry, really." Patsy turned, shooting her husband a disapproving look. Boy, Jenna didn't want to be on the receiving end of a look like that. But she had a feeling she was going to be before the morning was out.

"Look," she said in a breathless voice, "can we sit down? I have something important I need to tell you."

"Of course, dear. Can I get you some coffee? Tea?"

Jenna shook her head. "No. I'm good."

Patsy gestured to the couch in the front room, and Jenna sank down into its soft cushions. Everything about this room was comfortable and homey. She glanced over at the photographs sitting on the end table, and there, smiling from behind a silver frame, was her father. He was older in this photo. He must have looked like that when he died. He was very handsome.

"What do you want?" Harry said again in a gruff voice as he dropped into one of the side chairs.

Jenna laced her fingers together and gulped down air in nothing like the controlled fashion she practiced every day. Suddenly, her plan to deceive her aunt and uncle seemed impossibly foolish. She should have followed Milo's advice. Milo was always right. About everything.

"This is about Jude, isn't it?" Harry said. "You've been stalking that boy, and I'm telling you that if you don't quit, I'm going to call the law on you. So whatever it is you want to say, say it quick but know that we aren't a couple of senile old fools."

"Harry. For goodness' sake," Patsy said.

A frisson of anger curled around Jenna's core. Where did Harry get off treating her like that? Yes, she'd been dishonest with him, but her dishonesty hadn't hurt either of them. Her decision to help Jude had definitely hurt him, but she would make full restitution.

Jude was the last person she wanted to hurt. She'd been honest with him. Maybe not from the start, but early on. Clearly something else was happening here. Like maybe

Harry saw the past repeating itself. Like he had Jamie and Theresa tangled up with Jude and herself.

She tried to swallow back her frustration, but a little of it entered her voice as she finally spoke. "I have lied to both of you. And I apologize, but it was necessary because I doubt that either one of you would have given me the time of day if I'd been honest. Each of you, in your own way, has told me as much."

"What are you talking about?" Harry demanded, his face getting red.

"My name isn't Jenna Fairchild. It's Jenna Fossey. I'm your niece. I'm the daughter of *that woman*, as you put it the other day. The woman you both seem to blame for Jamie's death. But you know what? She was my mother, and she did a good job of raising me, except that she never told me anything about my father. So I came here looking for him. But I knew I wouldn't get the information I wanted if I just showed up on your doorstep one day."

She turned toward Patsy, whose face had gone as white as *Bonney Rose*'s mainsail. "At last night's meeting, you made it clear that you had nothing to say to me. Imagine if I had knocked on your door two weeks ago and told you the truth right then. I would never have seen those photos of Jamie in the kitchen. And up until that moment, I had never seen a photograph of my father in my life. Can you imagine that?"

"You spied on us? Oh my God, have you been using Jude to get to us?" Harry stood up and pointed a finger at her. "Does he know this?"

"Of course he does. I told him a week ago, maybe more, when he thought I was working for Santee Resorts. The truth is, I went to the public hearing to get a look at you since I didn't have any photographs of you either. And you're part of a family that I'd like to have.

"And I just discovered something important. Something you both should know. My lawyer found a cache of letters that my father wrote to—"

"Jamie Bauman was not your father," Patsy said, standing up and glaring at her, her blue eyes sharp as knives.

Sitting on the sofa, Jenna suddenly felt small and vulnerable. "But my mother and father—"

Patsy put up a hand, palm out, to stop Jenna. "Your own mother told us years ago that you are not Jamie's child. How can you even think that we wouldn't want a relationship with his baby? If I thought for one moment that you were Jamie's daughter..." Her voice got wobbly. "But you're not."

"And Robert," Harry said with a snarl, "was so determined to keep his money out of our hands that he decided to give it to a total stranger and then make doubly certain by limiting your access to it until we were sure to be in our graves."

"You know about the trust?"

"Of course I do. Robert made sure I knew about it when he changed his will just months before he died. He was practically gleeful."

"I don't—"

"You're just a pawn in one of Robert's schemes. The truth is, Robert could have given the money to charity or some worthy cause, but no. My brother was a miserly bastard who blamed me for Jamie's death. He never forgave me for teaching Jamie how to sail. And this is how he ground my nose in it." He pointed to the door. "Get out of my house. I swear if you try to buy Jude off or steal him away from this island, I will hunt you down and make your life a living hell."

Jude stood on Lilac Lane by the back gate to the Howland House rose garden. It was later than he'd planned because the family had kept him up last night, all of them talking about the new corporation. They'd even started a mission statement, and the family had agreed that the initial board of directors should be made up of people with business experience, which was how Jude ended up as president with Colton as vice president and Annie as treasurer. Cousin Emory, a schoolteacher, got nominated as secretary when he offered to write down everyone's ideas for the mission statement.

So it had been a very late night, and Jude was more than a little worried because Jenna hadn't answered his texts this morning. Maybe she was annoyed because he'd ignored her texts for a couple of days. But really, he'd needed that time to get his head straight.

Jude blew out a sigh and told himself that failure wasn't an option as he opened the gate and strolled into Ashley Scott's beautiful garden. He filled his lungs with the sweet, subtle scent of brown-eyed Susans and crape myrtle as he strolled up to the cottage's door and knocked.

No answer.

His heart lurched in his chest. She hadn't been here last night. Had Jenna left the island? Had she gone away?

No. Maybe she'd gone for a walk. Or down to Bread, Butter, and Beans for breakfast. He sat down in one of the rockers ready to wait as long as it took.

He knew a moment of supreme relief when Jenna arrived twenty minutes later wearing a pair of blue jeans with holey knees and a bright green Boston Celtics T-shirt. But his relief at seeing her evaporated in an instant when he saw the tears streaming down her face.

Damn. She'd done it. She'd gone to tell Harry and Patsy the truth, and it hadn't gone well. Maybe this wasn't a good time to talk about what had happened yesterday, about the decisions he'd come to. Not just about Barrier Island Charters or the new nonprofit, but about *her* too.

Because without her, he might never have had the courage to do what he'd done yesterday. He might never have tried to make a new reality for himself. And the more he thought about the future, the more he saw Jenna being a part of it.

But this was a very bad omen.

He stood up and met her on the crushed-shell footpath and pulled her into his arms. "You told Harry and Patsy the truth, didn't you?" he asked.

She nodded against his shoulder, gathered the fabric of his T-shirt in her fist, and started to bawl. This was unlike that moment on the day they'd painted the vicarage. Her sobs seemed to come from right down in the depths of her soul.

While he was standing there, holding Jenna up, Ashley came out of her house and stared at them from across the flower beds for a long moment. Then she nodded her head, turned around, and returned to her house.

"We should go inside," he said. "Ashley is watching."

Jenna pushed away from him, wiping tears and snot

from her cheeks. "It doesn't matter. By now she's probably heard from Patsy."

"What happened? I thought you—"

"I'm not Jamie Bauman's daughter, apparently. I'm probably the daughter of some random guy Mom picked up, which is why she never talked about my father. And you know what? It doesn't matter if Jamie loved her if she didn't love him back. Maybe she is responsible for Jamie's death. Maybe she dumped him for someone else and he was heartbroken." Her voice grew shaky and thin.

She jogged up the porch steps and unlocked the cottage. He followed her.

"Look, give it time. It will—"

She turned on him. "No. It's not going to work out. They hate me. Worse than that, really. Harry sees me as an evil person intent on hurting you. And I don't know . . . Maybe he's right. Maybe I'm just bad karma all the way around. And I'm going to have to pay the price in this lifetime for something I did in a previous one."

She stalked into the bedroom and picked up a battered backpack, threw it on the bed, and then headed into the bathroom. She returned a moment later with a small toiletry kit that she stuffed into the pack.

"Are you leaving?" he asked, his heart crumbling like brittle concrete. She was going away. Damn.

He loved her. He'd come here to say that out loud. To tell her that she'd changed everything, maybe from the first moment he'd seen her on the dock. But she was going away.

"I can't stay," she said, yanking open one of the bureau drawers, scooping up clothes and jamming them into the backpack.

"But why?"

"I can't, okay? I just can't. I don't belong here."

"But—"

"I don't, Jude." She turned around, tears streaming from her eyes. "You know, I thought I did. I fooled myself into thinking I did. I believed in synchronicity and interdependence and a whole lot of other BS. But there aren't any coincidences. Life is just random. And I'm not Jamie's daughter. There isn't any great cosmic connection between us. And I don't want to hurt you. Hell, I probably already have."

"But—"

"Look, I'm like walking bad juju, or whatever your root doctors would call it. I have a huge karma cloud hanging over me. I'm like a reverse Midas. Even my acts of kindness blow up on me."

"What are you talking about?"

"I'm the reason *Reel Therapy* ended up underwater. I thought I would do something nice for you, so I paid for an ad in the Last Gasp of Summer edition of the *Harbor Times* that's been distributed to every merchant and B and B on the island. That's why your business has been picking up."

"But—"

"Don't you see? You would never have gotten that midweek charter without the advertising. And look what happened because of that. And, you know, it's worse than that. I paid for Ashley's roof repair, and she hates the fact that someone gave her charity, so she's moving away when everyone wants to find a way to help her stay.

"I'm a disaster, Jude. Like the *Flying Dutchman* or whatever." She continued to throw clothes into her backpack. "But it's okay, because I fixed it with the towing service."

"You fixed what with the towing service?"

"I paid for *Reel Therapy*'s salvage. Yesterday morning. It's all taken care of. It was the least I could do."

"You did what?"

"I told you. I had to. It was my fault."

"No, it was my daddy's fault. What is it with you? Are you so rich you think the rest of us can't manage? And what's this about advertising?" he asked.

She stopped throwing things and turned to face him. "I paid for some advertising for you."

"But...why?"

"Because I wanted to invest in you."

"Invest? Is that all?" Disappointment precipitated like lead in his gut. She just wanted to invest in him? Damn. He wanted so much more from her.

She wiped more tears away from her cheeks. "No. Yes. It's complicated. Maybe you should ask your brother. It was because of something he said, and I should have known better than to listen to a Christian sermon. I'm not Christian, so what do I know? Anyway, I'm profoundly sorry for messing up your life. For meddling. For thinking I had any capacity to do any good for anyone."

She turned back toward her pack and started zipping it up. "You know," she said, "it's almost ironic. Little Jackie Scott told me that my riches were ill gotten, and that ill-gotten riches were a curse. I think that little boy and his ghost are right."

She hoisted the pack onto her shoulders and brushed past Jude. He followed her all the way to the parking lot, where she tossed her pack into her rental car, a nondescript Hyundai. "I'm sorry," she said as she slammed the trunk and then yanked open the driver's door. "I need to leave. It's better this way." She got into the car and shut the door.

He wanted to stop her, but he was pissed off. And besides, it all became clear like mist lifting from the bay on a summer's morning. Jenna Bauman or Fairchild, or whatever her damn name was, would never be anything more than a tourist.

Milo called about the time Jenna hit Route 17 South heading for Charleston. She thought about letting his call go to voice mail but decided that, one way or another, she needed to talk to him. So she pressed the phone button on the Hyundai's steering wheel.

"Hello, Jenna," Milo said in his infernally calm British tones. "I just saw the e-mail you sent last night about the B and B. I thought you wanted to start an investment equity firm. What's this about the B and B?"

"Nothing. Forget it, okay? I'm finished trying to do good in the world."

"Oh dear, what's happened?"

"Why did Robert Bauman make me his heir?" she asked.

"That's an odd question coming from his granddaughter."

"How do you know I'm his granddaughter?"

"Because he told me you were."

"But you never did a DNA test, did you?"

"What on earth has gotten into you, Jenna?"

"The truth. I don't think I'm Jamie Bauman's daughter."

Silence. Milo was so good at it. It hung between them

for a long moment as traffic slowed to a creep. "I'm assuming Patsy or Harry told you this," he said.

"Good guess. Did you know they would tell me the truth? Is that why you sent me to Jonquil Island?"

More silence before he said, "I have always operated on the belief that you are Robert Bauman's sole heir. I have no reason to doubt his assertion. If you like, I can do some more research on this issue."

"Don't bother. I don't care. I've never cared. And I want to give all my money to Harry and Patsy. Can you make that happen?"

Another long silence.

"Can you?" she almost screamed at Robert Bauman's lawyer.

He cleared his throat. "No. I can't. As a matter of fact, your grandfather anticipated this. You can't give away any of your inheritance. I'm explicitly required to make sure of that."

"You're kidding, right?" Something inside her deflated. "Is that why you're always lecturing me about charity?"

"Yes and no. You can give away as much of your allowance as you'd like. But the capital can't be given away. And for the record, your charitable giving does have important tax consequences that you regularly fail to consider."

"Would the equity capital firm I talked about yesterday qualify as charity?"

Milo Stracham actually laughed. "I'm sure your grandfather would call it charity, but no. That would be a business venture in my definition, since you'd be charging interest or, more likely, asking for a share of each business you invest in."

"Robert Bauman isn't my grandfather."

Milo gave a long sigh. "Well, if you like I could cut off your monthly allowance."

"What happens to the money if I walk away from it?"

"The firm will invest it wisely. And when you're forty-five, you'll have to make a decision about it."

"And what if I die before I'm forty-five?"

"Then it goes to your heirs. And if you have none, then all of it gets rolled over to the Bauman Foundation for the Study of Blindness, which, as you know, was originally endowed by your grandfather. So you'll either have to wait until you're forty-five or die. I hope you don't die, Jenna. I've become rather fond of you."

"I can't give it to the foundation now?"

"No, you cannot. As I said, your grandfather anticipated your antipathy."

"I don't understand why he did this to me."

"I believe he thought he was giving you something of value. And giving you enough time to come to terms with it."

"It's a curse. It's never going to bring me happiness."

"Jenna, in my experience, money rarely does. Perhaps that's why he put it in trust for you."

"Ha. Good try, Milo. But I don't believe you. If Robert understood that, why didn't he reach out to me when he was alive? He knew I existed. Why did he deny a relationship with me? He must have known that I'm not Jamie's child. He did it to hurt Harry and Patsy, didn't he?"

"There was a rift between Robert and his brother, no question about it. But I don't think that motivated him when it came to you and the money. Jenna, what happened?"

"It's not important. I'm on my way to Charleston. I'm going to get on the first plane back to Boston."

"Boston? Not New York?"

"Boston is my home," she said, her throat thickening. "Was my home."

"Is it still?" Milo asked as if he could read her mind. Knowing Milo, he probably could.

"It's where I was born."

"Why not come to New York? You can stay at the house on the Hudson, and we can talk through this equity capital firm you were thinking about."

The idea of spending an evening at some stodgy restaurant with Milo appealed to her even if the idea of staying at her grandfather's monstrous house did not. When she thought about it, Milo was the only family she had. And he wasn't even family. He was paid to look after her.

There wasn't anyone in Jenna's life like Jude's aunts Charlotte and Daisy or his cousin Annie. Or even a group of friends like Ashley's Piece Makers. Or Jude's Buccaneer sailors. She was alone. How had she let that happen?

"Jenna, my dear," Milo said in a gentle voice, "it's clear that I should never have insisted that you go to Jonquil Island. This is my fault. I thought perhaps if you went there and met your aunt and uncle, the family rift could be healed. I'm a stupid romantic, I suppose. I truly hoped that you would find some connections there."

"Well, I haven't. They hate me. They hate my mother, whom they blame for Jamie's death. And who knows. They might be justified in that. What if Mom cheated on him and broke his heart and he went out in that boat, intent on...?" She couldn't say the words.

"I'm sorry," Milo said. "Won't you think about coming to New York?"

"No. And I'm no longer interested in that equity capital idea. In fact, I might just go back to India."

"Oh, that's a shame. I liked that idea. I was looking forward to seeing your business plan."

"Well, too bad. I'll call you when I get to Charleston and decide whether I'm going back to Boston or heading to India. Oh, and you know what? Stop the allowance. I don't want any of this money. Captain Bill was right. It's cursed."

Chapter Twenty-Two ─────

Ashley had watched the lover's quarrel unfolding in her rose garden and driveway. Jenna, with tears in her eyes, and Jude St. Pierre looking like he'd just been kicked in the head by a mule.

So something had happened between them when they'd disappeared that day everyone showed up to paint the vicarage. Looking at Jude's face as Jenna pulled out of the drive, Ashley couldn't help but feel for him. He looked as if his heart was breaking.

She sure knew what it felt like to have a broken heart.

Like Jude, she wasn't all that happy that Jenna had checked out early. Even though Ashley was selling the house, every dollar in rental income was precious.

She opened the front door. "Has she gone for good?" she asked.

He turned, blinking at her. "I guess so." He looked shell-shocked.

"Can I get you something. Some iced tea? A cookie?"

Not that tea and cookies would mend what was wrong with him.

He shook his head.

Ashley was about to close the door to give the poor man a moment to pull himself together when Patsy Bauman pulled her old Lincoln Town Car into the drive. She hopped out, looking a little frantic, which was kind of amazing for Patsy. Her gaze landed on Jude as she said, "Oh my goodness, she's gone, isn't she?"

Jude turned toward Patsy, and his expression changed. His brows lowered, and his gaze narrowed. "What did you say to her? How could you have thrown her out? You know she came here hoping to connect with you and Harry. She's your family."

"I didn't... Well, it was mostly... Oh, dear..." Patsy stumbled a little, and Ashley shot out of the doorway to steady the older woman.

"What happened?" Ashley asked.

"Well," Patsy said on a long breath, "I think I may know who paid for your roof."

"Who?"

"Jenna."

"Why?"

"Maybe for the same reason she bought advertising for Barrier Island Charters," Jude said, his voice low, a sheen in his eyes conveying his emotions.

"What?" Ashley asked.

"She told me she wanted to invest in us. I guess that's what happens when you're as rich as she is," Jude said.

"She's rich?"

"She's Robert Bauman's heir," Patsy said. "The bastard I wanted nothing to do with."

"You know, I liked her. A lot," Jude said. "But I don't know what the hell she meant when she told me she wanted to invest in me. That sounds like banking, not..." His voice trailed off.

"Oh dear," Patsy said in a frail, angst-filled voice.

Jude sprang into action. "Let's get her inside," he said as he took Patsy's arm and helped guide her into the library, where they settled her into the big mohair chair.

"Are you sure she said the word 'invest'?" Patsy asked.

"Yes. I am sure, because to be honest, I wanted more from her than that."

Just like that the lightbulb flicked on in Ashley's brain. She knew exactly who might be able to untangle this situation. "Wait right there," she said to both of them.

"I have no plans to move," Patsy said in her drama-queen voice as she laid her head back against the chair.

Ashley turned and dashed through the door and across Lilac Lane to the vicarage. It was midmorning on a Friday, and she hoped Reverend St. Pierre was in his office working on Sunday's sermon. And hopefully this week's sermon wouldn't cause as many problems as last week's.

She knocked on the door and waited. And waited.

She was about to leave when the door opened, and there he was, dressed like a proper preacher for once in a black shirt and a Roman collar. He gave her a smile that did something untoward to her middle. "Ashley, what can I do for you?"

"Not me. You said the other day that you were used to being a chaplain, ministering to people in crisis? Well, I've got two people across the street who are definitely in crisis, and one of them is your little brother."

"What? Is Colton in trouble?"

"Not Colton. Jude. He wants to know why the woman he's fallen in love with thinks he's an investment and not something bigger than that." She folded her arms across her chest and tried to give him one of Jackie's pretend x-ray stares. He, like Superman, was impervious.

But at least he sprang into action, following her back across the street and into the library. Where he got up in Jude's face and tried to explain last week's sermon, which Jude hadn't heard until this moment.

And after that, he turned toward Patsy and said, "Last week's sermon was all about taking a chance on a broken heart and investing in love. I think this week's sermon is going to be about kindness." He got down on one knee and looked right into Patsy's eyes. "Tell me the truth. Wouldn't you love to have a granddaughter who would go to Piece Maker meetings with you every week, who would help out when there was a need, who would undertake kind gestures without being asked, and who would love you? Does she have to have the right DNA for that to happen? I guarantee you, if you open your heart you'll discover that Jude isn't the only one who's fallen in love with Jenna these last few weeks. I think maybe you have too."

He stood up and came face-to-face with his brother. "You did fall in love with her, didn't you?"

Jude looked away, avoiding eye contact.

"Okay, so I get it. You're scared about being like Daddy. But you are nothing like him, Jude. And Jenna is nothing like Momma. Momma was a party girl who led Daddy down a treacherous path. All Jenna wants to do is invest in you."

"Yeah. That's not enough. And that's not what you were saying in your sermon anyway."

"No? Be honest with me. She's the one who convinced you to go see Junior and start this whole discussion about a nonprofit, isn't she? And if you stopped to think for a minute, she'd probably be one of those rich folks we were all talking about last night who'd be willing to contribute to the cause. Or do we want to exclude her money for some reason?"

"Um." Jude blew out a long breath. "She paid to have *Reel Therapy* salvaged. And that pissed me off for some reason. Like she was saying I couldn't afford it."

"Well, that was true. You used your share in Old Granny's place as collateral for the loan to pay for it, right?"

"I guess. But I'm capable of running Barrier Island Charters. And—"

"I know. We're here to encourage you. Jenna especially. When someone gives you encouragement, it's a blessing and a gift."

His gaze snapped back toward his brother. "I guess."

Micah shook his head. "You know, I talked with her the day she gave me the check for Ashley's roof. She said something interesting you both should hear."

"What?" Jude asked.

"She said that she admired Ashley because she'd taken the risk of working for herself instead of relying on the security of a steady job. I got the feeling that Jenna is a little in awe of both of you because you have firsthand experience in running a business, and all she has is a pile of money she inherited from a man she doesn't know. A pile of money that she's worried about, not because she fears losing it, but because she is compelled by her beliefs to find some way to use it for good. It's a requirement of her religion.

"So I want you both to think about the fact that maybe she came here because she needs to invest in people. Maybe that's why God handed her all that money and sent her here." Micah turned around and gazed at Ashley out of his deep brown eyes.

Once again something stirred inside her. Something she didn't want.

"What Jenna did wasn't charity, Ashley," Micah said. "It truly was an investment, but the kind where she's not looking for a monetary return. It's a deep thing with her, a part of her belief system. She does something kind for you, and you are able to pass it on to someone else. Somewhere, sometime. And that gives her good karma. When you turn your back on an investment like that, it makes her feel as if she's made the world a darker place. And for Jenna, that's a disaster."

"But why me?"

"Because you needed help, and she admires you. It's as simple as that. And it's not a sin to need help, Ashley. We all need help. And the Lord provides. In this case, the Lord sent you Jenna Fossey. I'm certain of that."

He turned back toward his brother. "Are you going to chase after her, or what?"

"Um…" Jude continued to study his shoes.

"Oh, for goodness' sake, when Momma left, didn't you want Daddy to chase after her?"

"Yeah."

"And weren't you furious when he didn't?"

"Yeah."

"Okay. So? You don't want to be like Daddy, do you?"

Jude looked up into his brother's eyes. "No, sir," he said.

"All right, you get in your truck and you follow her."

"I don't know where she went."

"She's probably driving to Charleston to get a plane back to Boston or New York," Patsy said. "I'm sorry, Jude. I think this is all my fault. And I feel so bad about it. She didn't know. She was trying her best. She came to us because she wanted a connection, and we..." Her voice hollowed out and tears cascaded over her cheeks. In that moment, Patsy truly looked her age.

"Don't worry," Ashley said, giving her friend a quick hug. "Jude will bring her back. Won't you?" She looked up at Jude.

"There you go," Micah said, giving his brother a little man-hug. "It's not just you with a stake in this. I think all of Magnolia Harbor is rooting for you to go get that woman and bring her home where she belongs."

Her gas gauge was reading almost empty, and her bladder was reading almost full. She hadn't made much progress, less than forty miles, and it had taken her the better part of an hour and a half because of an accident on Route 17 that was all but cleaned up by the time she passed the spot.

It was confirmation of something that, even out here in middle-of-nowhere South Carolina, there could be traffic jams.

She pulled off the highway and into a Citgo station with a mini-mart in McClellanville, which didn't look like it was much of a place.

She filled up and used the restroom and then pulled to one side of the parking lot to check flight times and availabilities to New York. She'd decided to have a conversation with Milo because there wasn't any other place to go.

The thought left her hollowed out. She'd definitely left in a huff, and now that an hour and a half had passed, she was no longer running on sheer emotion.

And there was no need to rush to Charleston if she couldn't get a flight anytime soon. She took the phone out of airplane mode and was mildly surprised to discover she had several bars of service, even out here in the boonies.

And then the phone went into text alert mode, beeping at her as one text message after another came rolling in, along with at least a dozen voice mails.

She checked. All but one of them were from Jude.

She sat in her car, the sounds of the highway coming through her open window like white noise or static in her head as she read one message after another, all with a similar terse message:

Don't go.
Come back.
Patsy regrets what she said.
Call me.
Please.

And then her phone beeped again and a message came in from Milo:

Jenna, would you be so kind as to get in touch at your earliest convenience? I have some information about your father.

Good old Milo, he even texted in British English. And this particular text was time stamped forty minutes ago—not long after they'd ended their phone conversation.

She blew out a long breath. Did she want to talk to Milo now? She'd decided to go back to New York. They could chat then. On the other hand, hadn't she asked him for information about her father?

Back when she'd thought her father was Jamie Bauman. Good grief, was she about to go on another journey of discovery? She wasn't sure she wanted to know.

"Much," she muttered out loud.

She took a few deep breaths and felt a little calmer before she punched the call button and Milo's voice came over the line. "I'm so glad you returned my call," Milo said. "Not ten minutes after we concluded our conversation, my associate came into my office with some information that's relevant."

"Relevant to what?"

"To the question of your parentage. I have in my hand a report from the man who used to be your grandfather's head of security. It's dated nineteen months ago, shortly after Aviation Engineering had a meeting at iWear's corporate headquarters about the possibility of a joint venture in the area of advanced automotive optics. I believe you are familiar with this meeting because you were there and were briefly introduced to Robert."

A shiver worked down her back. "I was. He stopped in for about a minute and a half. Just long enough to shake some hands. He hadn't been expected."

"No. He hadn't been. But he'd seen you walking in with the group. And the moment he saw you, he wanted to meet you."

"Ew. That's disgusting. You—"

"Robert was not that kind of man, Jenna. He wanted to meet you because he thought you looked like his son. So much so that he insisted on interrupting that meeting. And when he heard your last name, he knew. He detailed his security team to secure a sample of your DNA, which they did by going through your trash. A DNA analysis was done a year before Robert died. You are most definitely Robert Bauman's granddaughter."

"They went through my trash?"

"Robert was a bulldog when he wanted something. And he wanted you, my dear. As his heir."

"But I don't understand. If he wanted me as his heir, why wasn't he interested in me before he died?"

"Well, he died suddenly, before he had a chance to get to know you. And, by the way, his prior will provided for his money to go to the foundation. Patsy and Harry were never going to get any of it. Robert and Harry had irreconcilable differences."

"I'm not talking about after he went through my trash and violated my privacy. I'm talking about when I was a little kid. Why wasn't he interested then?"

Milo said nothing for a very long time, and since Milo excelled at the pregnant pause, Jenna braced herself. "Well, I don't think he knew about you."

"What?"

"I don't think your mother ever told him about you."

"Patsy said that they found out about me when I was a baby, and Mom told them I wasn't Jamie's child. Why would she do that?"

"I don't know. But I have a guess."

"Okay. Guess, then."

"I think she must have known that they both blamed her for Jamie's death. She must have lived in fear that a rich man like Robert Bauman could swoop in and take you away forever. I'm guessing that's why she lied to Harry and Patsy. And I have no record of any meeting between Robert and your mother, but I wouldn't be surprised if there had been one.

"In fact, I think it's curious that your mother moved to Connecticut before you were born. You spent your first four years there before she returned to Boston. I think she was hiding you."

The traffic on Route 17 was a bitch. There'd been an accident just north of the bridge across the Santee River that backed things up for miles. Jude didn't know whether the backup was a gift or a curse.

Once the traffic cleared, he drove like a madman, bobbing and weaving through traffic until he spotted a nondescript Hyundai parked right under the sign at the Citgo station this side of McClellanville. There were probably a million steel-gray Hyundais out there, but when the wind lifted a few strands of Jenna's honey-colored hair through the open driver's window, he knew he'd found her.

It was almost as if the wind wanted him to find her.

Lucky. Lucky. He pulled alongside the rental, but she barely noticed. She was looking down. Reading his texts or ignoring them? His heart lurched in his chest.

Suddenly the fire that Micah had lit under him faltered. Okay, so he'd come after Jenna. What happened if he couldn't convince her to come back?

Damn.

He hopped down from the truck and circled around it. He approached Jenna's open window from the back of her car like a traffic cop. She was still looking down when he leaned into the window. "Hey," he said.

She started and looked up. And Jude lost himself in those wide spaced, big brown eyes with their red, puffy lids. It looked like she'd done a whole mess of crying. Not just the abbreviated jag in the rose garden but maybe all the way down the road.

And then it occurred to him that she didn't resemble a woman who was happy to be running away. And now that he thought about it, on the day Momma left, she'd been happier than a jay on a spring day. He remembered the way she stared down Daddy and told him she was looking forward to her independence.

"You need to come back," he said.

She blinked. "Why?"

"Because I need you to invest in the nonprofit my family is creating to save the seagrass."

"That's it? You just want my investment?" The corner of her mouth twitched when she said this, and he heard his own words come out of her mouth.

"I'm sorry. I didn't understand what you meant. And here's the thing. I don't know where you were last night, but I came by the cottage. I was on fire, Jenna, just so excited to tell you that I'd spent a couple of hours talking to a Gullah lawyer I know who's ready to help us with all the legal work needed to start a nonprofit to save the seagrass. And I never would have done that without you. I took you to meet my aunts as a way to discourage you, and instead you turned it all around and ended up giving me a life-saving idea. And I guess my pride got in the way when I found out that you'd paid for *Reel Therapy*'s salvage. You didn't have to do that, you know?"

"So you chased me down because you want me to invest in your nonprofit?"

She wasn't going easy on him, was she? And he probably deserved it. He tried to remember the stuff Micah said, and then he leaned a little closer. "No. I want you to invest in love," he said.

Her eyes filled up. "What's that supposed to mean?"

He opened the car door and pulled her out so that they stood chest to breast. He ran his palm down over her wayward hair. It was so soft. As soft as the look in her eyes. "Micah explained about his sermon. And you know what? I don't, for one minute, blame you for what happened to *Reel Therapy*. You are not responsible for the bone-headed actions of my father. He's been an accident waiting to happen, and I couldn't stop it no matter how hard I tried. I guess he had to screw up royally before he hit bottom and realized he needed help. He's in rehab now."

"But I—"

He put his fingers over her mouth. "You. Are. Not. Responsible. That's something I just learned myself. And Micah is the one who helped me see it. He learned some real useful stuff in the navy, apparently."

He leaned in and kissed her forehead. "I was mad about you paying for the salvage, but I've gotten over it. It was just your way of trying to make the world right again."

"I'm sorry," she said.

"You have nothing to be sorry about. To be honest, I'm

blown away by the fact that you wanted to do a kindness for me and for Ashley. Who does a thing like that?"

"You know about the roof?"

He nodded. "But that's not all of it, Jenna. I'm blown away by the fact that you actually understand why I don't want my people shoved into a museum. And I'm blown away by the fact that you understand about the seagrass. And I'm sorry I judged you."

"You judged me?"

He nodded. "I put you in a box and labeled it 'white woman' and 'tourist.' And while you are a white woman and nothing's going to change that, you are not a tourist. I get this feeling that you've been crying all the way down the highway because you don't want to leave Jonquil Island."

She rested her head on his shoulder, and it felt good to hold her up. "I don't," she said. "But when I sat down with Patsy and Harry this morning, they made me feel like the biggest outsider. Like I had no business even visiting. And they have issues with me and you being together."

"Well, they can keep their racist views to themselves."

She backed away. "No, no. Not because we're from different races. Jude, don't you realize how much they love you? I mean, it's like you're their adopted nephew or something."

"Well, if that's the case, Harry could have helped me out with that vote."

"Okay. So maybe not. But they warned me off because they think I'm bad for you. They're confusing me with my mother. They're afraid history will repeat itself or something. And it's not logical, of course, because there's so much hurt and sorrow and loss..." Her voice cracked.

"They think I'm not Jamie's daughter. And I let them convince me of that. But I just talked to Milo, my lawyer, and..." Tears overflowed her eyes, and her chin began to tremble.

"Of course you're Jamie's daughter," he said as he pulled her into his arms. "I've seen pictures of him, you know, in Patsy's kitchen and living room. He's all over that house, really. And you have his eyes."

She looked up at him, her cheeks streaming with tears. "I do?"

"Yeah. Harry has the same eyes. Anyone who was looking hard enough would see how much you and Harry resemble each other." He tucked a strand of hair behind her cheek. "Forget about Harry and Patsy, Jenna. They'll come around or they won't. The important thing is, I don't want you to leave. I want you to stay. And I want to build a relationship with you. I've been looking for someone like you for a long, long time. I always thought she'd look different, but you can't fight fate, you know?"

"Fate?"

He shrugged. "What's that word you use? Synchronicity?"

"Woo-woo stuff, in other words."

"Or maybe just love at first sight?" He leaned in and nuzzled her neck and then whispered in her ear, "And I have fallen for you, Jenna Bauman. Hard. I wouldn't have come chasing after you if I hadn't. And I probably broke nineteen different traffic laws doing it, which is risky behavior for a black guy."

She backed away. "I don't want you doing anything

like that ever again, okay? Because, the thing is, there's a good chance my mother kept me a secret from my grandfather and from Patsy and Harry. So the only family I ever had was her. And when she died, I was left completely alone.

"Jude, I love you, and I love your aunts and your cousin, and your brothers too. I'd also like to meet your friends and become a regular member of your sailing club and invest in Jonquil Island in ways that will keep Santee Resorts from ruining what's good about the place. I want to be connected."

"I think we can make that happen," he said, right before he leaned down and kissed her like a man in love. And she kissed him right back like a woman who had finally found the place where she belonged.

Epilogue

It was springtime, mid-March, and the tourists were flocking to Jonquil Island to enjoy the sight of thousands of naturalized daffodils blooming in wild abandon. It was an annual festival, without a specific date. The flowers bloomed when it got warm enough.

This particular Saturday, another festival was happening in the clearing where Old Granny's house stood. Over the winter, Jude and Colton, with occasional help from Micah, Daddy, Old Uncle Jeeter, and Annie's big sons, had demolished the newer portion of the house, revealing the old cabin that stood in the center of the structure, which had been built in 1867. The tumbling-down chimney had been rebuilt, the porch now rested on a solid foundation, and the shutters had been re-created and painted heaven blue—the right color to keep the *haints* away.

Today the porch railing was bedecked with flowers and streamers. Off toward the back, Annie and Aunt Charlotte had set up a big drum barbecue, and the smell of their pulled pork hung on the air. Folks wearing bright African colors and headcloths and neutral yacht club navy blue mingled in the yard.

And in the middle of it all stood the love of Jude's life, the newly minted Mrs. Jenna St. Pierre, wearing a slim, ethereal white dress that she'd made herself, with a little help from Louella Pender and Ashley Scott.

Jenna wore flowers in her hair. Not daffodils, but buttercups, which she explained were from the same narcissus family as jonquils and daffodils.

She wasn't the woman he'd expected, but she was the woman he loved. She belonged to him. And he belonged to her. And once they had stopped fighting the messages the universe had sent them, the truth had revealed itself.

Not just to the two of them, but to their families and friends as well. Micah had performed the ceremony today. Jenna's business partner, Ashley Scott, had been the maid of honor. Colton had been his best man. Little Jackie had been the ring bearer. And Harry Bauman had given the bride away.

And now, there she was, laughing with Patsy Bauman as if they'd been friends all their lives. Who would ever have thought that a St. Pierre would marry a Bauman?

Jenna. That's who.

She turned and smiled at him, her eyebrow lifting just so. It was an invitation. *Are you ready?* it seemed to say.

Hell yeah. He was ready. Annie's food had been heavenly. The music by his second cousin's garage band had been loud and almost good. The company had been fun.

But it was time to go.

She walked toward him, the rest of the people fading to gray as he got lost in the lusty gaze of his wife. When she reached him, she put her arm around his neck and pulled him close. "Let's go christen the boat," she whispered.

He took her by the arm, and they left the party. No one stopped them.

They reached the pier, where the new sailboat, the forty-four-foot, 1981 LaFitte Jude had purchased and refitted with a business loan from Citibank, was anchored. He'd insisted on financing his charter business on his own. And Jenna had agreed. She had plenty of other local businesses to invest in.

"You ready for this?" he asked.

She nodded, and he climbed down into the cabin and came back with a bottle of champagne.

"Why do women christen boats?" she asked as he unwired the cork and popped the bottle without spilling a drop of wine.

"I have no idea. But it's tradition. And we sailors are a superstitious lot."

"Should I break the bottle?"

He rolled his beautiful tawny eyes. "It's not a steel battleship. It's made of fiberglass. We'll pour the champagne, okay?"

He handed her the bottle, and she headed toward the sailboat's bow. "I christen thee ... *Synchronicity*," she said right before she poured the wine over the boat's bow. "Now what?" she asked.

"Now we go belowdecks and christen the new bed in the captain's quarters."

"And then?"

"And then tomorrow we take her on a shakedown cruise." He held out his hand. "You coming?"

"I will be," she said with an impish grin.

And, hand in hand, they went belowdecks.

You can enjoy more of Hope Ramsay
and her Southern charm
in her Last Chance series.

Please turn the page for an excerpt from
Welcome to Last Chance.

Available now.

One ticket to Last Chance," the agent said as he took Jane's money. "The bus leaves in five minutes."

Jane picked up the flimsy slip of paper and hurried through the Atlanta, Georgia, Greyhound terminal. She found the gate, climbed aboard the motor coach, and sank into one of the plush seats.

She tried to think positive thoughts.

It was hard. She had five dollars left in her pocketbook, a zero balance in her checking account, and bad guys in her recent past. Her dreams of making it big in Nashville had just taken a dive over the cliff called reality.

Thank you, Woody West, you peanut-brained weasel.

The diesel engines roared to life, and the bus glided out of the parking lot heading toward South Carolina, which was not where Jane really wanted to go.

She took three deep breaths and tried to visualize her future the way Dr. Goodbody advised in his self-help recordings. If she could just unleash her inner consciousness through positive thinking, the Universe would give her a road map for success.

That seemed like a good plan. She needed a road map to a better future in the worst way. And where better to seek a new start than a place called Last Chance? She had never been to Last Chance, but the name sounded hopeful.

She sank back into her seat and tried to see the place in her mind's eye. She imagined it like Pleasantville, where the streets were picturesque, the people friendly, and the job opportunities plentiful.

Eight hours later, reality intruded.

The Greyhound left her standing on a deserted sidewalk right in front of a place called Bill's Grease Pit. Fortunately, this establishment was not a fast-food joint but an auto-repair service that doubled as a bus terminal. Both the garage and the terminal were closed for the night.

She looked down the street and knew herself for a fool. Last Chance had exactly one traffic light. The only sign of life was the glow of neon shining like a beacon from a building two blocks down the main drag.

Okay, so Last Chance wasn't Bedford Falls, from the movie *It's a Wonderful Life*. She could deal.

She told herself that where there was Budweiser and neon there was hope of finding some dinner. Although how she was going to pay for it remained a mystery. She fought against the panic that gripped her insides. She hugged herself as she walked up the street, running through her usual list of positive affirmations.

She would get herself out of this mess. She had done it before. And the truth was, she should have read the warning signs when Woody walked into the Shrimp Shack six months ago. If she had read those signs, she wouldn't be standing here today. Well, every mistake was an opportunity to learn, according to Dr. Goodbody.

The bar bore the name Dot's Spot in bright blue neon. It sported a dark wood exterior and small windows festooned with half a dozen beer signs. Jane stood in the garish light cast by the signs, thinking it would be truly awesome if she could walk through that doorway and find Sir Galahad waiting for her. But wishing for Sir Galahad was not positive thinking. Heroes didn't magically appear in southern honky-tonks on a Wednesday night.

Besides, this particular fantasy of a knightly rescue had gotten her into trouble every time she allowed herself to believe it. So she pushed it out of her mind. She needed to focus on manifesting a hot meal and a place to spend the night. Period. She fixed that positive plan of action in her mind and pushed through the front door.

Hoo boy, the place was like something right out of a bad country-and-western tune. Smoke hung over the place and a five-piece country band occupied a raised stage at one end of the barroom. They played a twangy Garth Brooks tune in waltz time. No one was dancing.

The men in the band were, by and large, a bunch of middle-aged geezers, with beer bellies and wedding rings and receding hairlines.

Except for the fiddler.

Jane stared at him for a moment, recognition washing through her. No question about it—there stood another peanut-brained weasel in the flesh. She could tell this because he was a big, powerfully built man with a ponytail and facial hair. He also wore a black Stetson, and a black shirt, and black jeans that hugged his butt and thighs, and a gem that sparkled from his earlobe like a black diamond.

What was that thing? A sapphire?

He was the real-deal, bad-for-any-females-who-came-within-range package. Someone should hang a big yellow warning sign on his neck that said "danger."

Guys like him didn't rescue girls. They rode around on Harleys, and were mean and tough and bad, and got into lots of trouble with the local law. They also had really big shoulders that a girl could lean on, and in a moment of confusion, a girl could confuse one of these bad boys with Sir Galahad, only on a motorcycle.

Good thing Jane planned on rescuing herself, because this guy was like some walking embodiment of Murphy's Law. The spit dried up in her mouth, and her heart rate kicked up. The Universe had just thrown her another curveball.

So she looked away, sweeping the room with her gaze. The rest of the pickings were slim and ran to old men and floozies, and a few obviously married guys in John Deere hats. She might be about to do some serious flirting in order to get a drink and some food, but she would not hit on any married men. That ran counter to her moral code.

She scanned the bar. Bingo. Two prospects, twelve o'clock.

Prospect One wore a dirty Houston Astros hat, his chin propped up on his left fist as he watched the World Series game on the big-screen television. He was devilishly handsome, but the words "hard drinking" scrolled through her mind.

Jane turned her attention to prospect Number Two.

He turned on the stool, and she got a good look at him. He was a smaller-than-average guy, with sandy hair, a widow's peak, and regular features. He wore a blue work shirt with his name—Ray—embroidered above the right pocket. Unlike the other two hunks in the room, this guy wore work boots. He wasn't a cowboy, and he didn't look dangerous at all.

He looked up from his drink.

Okay, he would do. Kindness shone from his eyes. She concentrated on holding his gaze...counted to three...then dazzled him with a smile.

He blinked two or three times like a deer caught in a hunter's sight. But she wasn't a hunter, not really. She was vulnerable, and scared, and hunted herself. And that explained why she was about to do something not very nice—something she would most likely regret in the morning.

The bodacious brunette hit Dot's Spot like the hurricane expected to arrive tomorrow. She wore high-heel boots and a little tank top that barely constrained her assets. Clay Rhodes had never seen her before, which had to mean she'd just gotten off the nine-thirty bus from Atlanta.

She waltzed her butt through the door and captured the attention of every male in the place, except maybe Dash Randall, who was concentrating on the World Series. She stopped just inside the door and gave the place a once-over.

It took all of three seconds for her to look Clay's way, and about fifteen for her to catalog him and move on. But that was all it took for Clay Rhodes to feel the unmistakable pull of lust centering right behind his belly button.

Yeah, he could go for some of that, if it wasn't for the fact that he was a responsible, almost middle-aged grown-up, and she looked like trouble on high heels.

He pulled the fiddle down and tried to put some feeling into his harmony line on "Night Rider's Lament," but since he had played this song about five thousand times, it was hard to do.

The little gal distracted him as she scanned the room. It didn't surprise him one bit when her sharp gaze lingered on Dash. The ex-jock was unaware of it, though. He sat at the end of the bar wallowing in self-pity and doing battle with God-only-knew-how-many demons as he watched the baseball game.

The girl was interested, of course. Dash was a fine-looking man, but a woman would have to be nuts to tangle with a guy like that. Clay gave her points when her gaze shifted and moved on.

He pulled the fiddle up to his chin and played the bridge, while Kyle tried his hardest to sound like Garth Brooks. Kyle failed, like he did every night, which was no surprise to anyone.

What happened next, though, surprised the heck out of just about everyone in Dot's Spot.

That girl aimed her laser-beam look at the back of Ray's head and darned if the boy didn't jump like he was some kind of marionette with a nervous puppeteer. He jerked his head around, and disaster struck about twelve hours earlier than expected.

The woman aimed a smile at Ray that had all the subtlety of a Stinger missile, and poor Ray didn't have any defenses for something like that.

Uh-oh.

The song ended, and Clay turned toward Kyle. "Let's cut it short and go to break," he said.

"But—"

Clay jerked his head toward Ray and rolled his eyes.

"Not again," Kyle said under his breath, as he took in the unfolding scene.

"Looks like."

Kyle leaned into the mic and told the crowd they'd be back in ten, while Clay put his fiddle into the hard-shell case that sat atop the upright piano. Then Clay stepped down from the stage and headed toward the bar.

"Clay," Ray said as he approached. "Look, it's April. What do you figure the odds are on that? A million to one?" Ray rocked a little on the bar stool and gave Clay his goofy smile. Eighteen years ago, that grin, combined with Ray's uncanny ability to do math, had made the boy semipopular with the girls at Davis High who wanted to adopt him, or befriend him, or otherwise allow him to do their homework. But that had changed three weeks before graduation.

Clay came to a halt and turned toward the little gal in the white tank top. Man-oh-man, she was something else. Tawny skin and dark eyes with a pair of killer cheekbones and pouty lips that said kiss me quick. She was pure sex on three-inch stiletto heels.

A man didn't get within five feet of this and not lose his perspective on things. Even a half-dead man like himself. The little tingle in his private parts was kind of reassuring, though. It confirmed that he was still alive. Sometimes living in Last Chance, South Carolina, it was hard to tell.

Her pink nail polish was chipped, the neck of her tank

top sported a little stain, and the cuffs of her jean jacket were frayed. Her gaze seemed a little guileless, which surprised the heck out of him. He had taken her for trash, but up close she didn't look trashy at all—just a little rumpled and forlorn.

And utterly irresistible.

"So your name's April?" he asked, knowing darn well her name wasn't April. She did look like April, though, which made her hotter than a chili pepper. Hot and forlorn. A deadly combination if there ever was one.

She shook her head. "No...uh...my name's...um... Mary."

Clay went on guard. She was lying. "How old are you, Mary?" he asked.

Her square chin inched up. "Why? Do I look like jailbait?"

Yeah. But he didn't say it out loud. He studied her for a long moment, trying to ignore the sexual rush. She had incredible skin. It looked silky soft, firm and warm. He wanted to touch it.

He forced himself to look into her wide brown eyes. No, she wasn't a teenager. But she was still trouble. He needed to rescue Ray from this woman. Ray could get himself into a heap of trouble if someone didn't do something quick.

Clay turned away. "Hey, Ray, you got a minute?"

Ray ducked his head in that funny little tic that had been there ever since the accident senior year. "Sure. Whatever you want."

Clay jerked his head. "In private."

Ray turned toward the little gal. "You stay right here, April. I'll be back. Don't go anywhere, okay?"

The girl nodded, and Clay got the feeling that she was happy to be rescued. Like she had maybe figured out Ray was playing a few cards short of a full deck.

Clay pulled Ray down to the end of the bar and put his arm around his shoulder. "Listen, Ray, I'm your oldest friend, right?"

Ray nodded.

"Got you fixed up with my uncle Pete at the hardware store, didn't I?"

"Yeah, Clay."

"Bailed you out with my brother Stony that time when you busted up the place?"

Ray kept on nodding.

"Helped you out with Mr. Polk down at the bank when your momma got sick."

"Yeah, Clay, I know all that."

"So you know I wouldn't lie to you."

"No, Clay, you wouldn't ever lie to me."

"Look, Ray, that little gal isn't April."

Ray rolled away, then turned and squared up his body. "She is, too. Look at her."

"April is a photograph of a girl. This isn't her. This is a girl named Mary, who's new to town. I'll bet she came on the nine-thirty bus from Atlanta."

Ray wet his lips. His fists curled up. "Don't you say that, Clay. She's April. *Look* at her."

Clay shook his head. The last person in the world he wanted to fight was Ray Betts. He hated fighting in general, since it messed up his hands. But fighting Ray would be like fighting with one of his brothers.

"Look—" Clay started to say.

"Hey, Ray," Dash called from his place by the bar.

Ray turned and relaxed his hands a fraction. "Yeah?"

"You wanna go down to the high school and shag some balls?"

"Really?" A slow smile filled Ray's face, and Clay breathed a sigh of relief.

In Ray's injured brain, this invitation from Dash Randall was like being asked if he wanted to go hang out with God. Ray loved baseball, and since Dash had once played it professionally, Dash had become one of Ray's personal heroes.

Dash gave Clay a meaningful and surprisingly sober glance. Maybe the rumors were true, and Dash was on the wagon these days. Although why a man on the wagon would spend time in a bar was kind of a mystery. Well, even if it wasn't true, he owed Dash a favor for this.

Dash leaned over and collected an aluminum cane. He stood up, favoring his bad leg. "Yeah, Ray, I mean it. But you'll have to do all the running since my knee isn't up to it, yet. C'mon, I'll even put the top down, and we can cruise over to the Tastee Freeze afterward."

"Gee, Dash, that sounds like fun," Ray said.

Dash winked at Clay as he led Ray out of the bar. Disaster had been averted.

But when Clay turned back toward the little gal, his gut tightened up like a warning. Was she desperate or just looking for some action? He had a feeling it might be a little of both.

And he'd just sent his competition packing.

Two hours later, Jane picked up the little slip of paper and read her bar tab: Six dollars for three Cokes. It might as well have been a hundred dollars. She didn't have the cash to pay it—unless she dug deep in her purse and found a dollar in change and added it to the five-dollar bill in her wallet. Then she would be officially broke.

She should have nursed a single Coke all night. She should have taken steps to get a credit card, years ago. But she hadn't done either of these things. The first because it had been years since she had been this poor. The second because getting a credit card was risky, given her background.

She swallowed the lump in her throat and told herself she wasn't going to cry. Her attempt to find someone semi-nice to buy her dinner had flopped. There was just the fiddler who had run all the semi-nice guys off like some kind of reverse bouncer.

That man had spent the last two hours boring a hole in her back with his silver-eyed stare. About an hour ago, she had given up trying not to look back.

Jane could parlay this into something, if she wanted to. But she had to remember that he was not going to rescue her from her current situation. She needed to fix her own life. And, right now, staying away from a bad boy seemed like a good first step.

But then all her other choices were worse. She couldn't sleep in the public park tonight—assuming, of course, that Last Chance had a public park. But even if it did have one, the weather report on the television above the bar said a hurricane was bearing down on the South Carolina coast. It wasn't a big hurricane by Katrina standards, but even so, everyone in the bar was talking about torrential rains starting sometime after two in the morning.

Jane had hoped they might have a hurricane shelter open where she could blend right in, like a refugee or something. But there wasn't any kind of evacuation going on—no doubt because the hurricane was making landfall a hundred miles away near Hilton Head Island. She didn't have many other options in a small town like Last Chance.

Jane stole a glance up at the fiddler, and heat sizzled through her. The Cosmos and her own hormones were against her. She shouldn't do this. This was a mistake.

She turned away and stared down at her bar tab. Behind her, the lead singer signed off for the night. Someone punched up a bunch of songs on the jukebox.

Well, first things first. She needed to pay the bill. She dug deep into her purse, drawing out a handful of pennies and nickels, and started counting. In the background, the jukebox played Tumbleweed's new country single...

> *Feel the rush of my breath*
> *Feel the heat of my hand...*

Heat crawled up her backside as the words of the song suddenly made themselves manifest. The fiddler had snuck up on her. He put one of his ginormous hands on the bar, leaned his big body in, and slapped a ten-dollar bill down on top of her tab like he'd been counting the number of Cokes she'd drunk.

He turned toward her, his unreadable wolf eyes shaded by the brim of his Stetson. "You want to take this somewhere else?" he asked in a blurred drawl. Her insides clutched and burned.

She was close enough to see a network of lines at the corner of his eyes, and little threads of silver in his goatee. He wasn't young. That scared her a little. He was more man than she was used to handling—older and bigger and more dangerous than anyone else in her past.

"Maybe I was mistaken," he drawled in response to her slight hesitation. "I got the idea you might be interested."

Jane looked up into his eyes. A hot, blue flame flickered there. An answering heat resonated deep down inside her. Was this wishful thinking, desperation, or real desire made manifest by her own weakness for guys like this? It was kind of hard to tell.

Her head screamed that going with this guy would be like repeating the mistakes of the past. Getting soaked on a park bench would be better than this. But her body wasn't listening. Instead she gave the fiddler a smile and said, "Cowboy, take me away."

"You drive a minivan?" The girl—Mary, he reminded himself—stood beyond the service entrance to Dot's Spot with her hands fisted on her hips and a semisurprised look on her face.

"Yeah, well, it's practical for hauling around sound equipment and guitars. Disappointed?" Clay said, as he opened the side-panel door of his ancient Windstar and hoisted his fiddle, mandolin, and guitar cases into the cargo space.

The question was rhetorical. She *was* disappointed. Women had a habit of mistaking him for someone else—usually some bad-boy jerk with a Harley who would do them wrong sooner or later. Ironically, most women wasted no time in doing *him* wrong, as if he were the punching bag for their collective disappointments with males in general and bad boys in particular.

He turned around and faced the girl. She had the

wrong idea about him. And he wasn't going to disabuse her of it. He was going to take her to the Peach Blossom Motor Court and become that bad boy she was looking for. He wasn't going to apologize to anyone for it either.

He was tired of being a good man.

He was tired of living his life along the straight and narrow.

But most of all, he was weary of being alone.

The girl stepped forward, her body swaying in the lamplight, the gusty wind lifting her hair and whipping it across her face. She tucked the hair behind her ear and gave him a simple smile that curled up the dimples in her cheek. Desire, sweet and warm, flooded through him.

He opened the van's door for her, and she stepped close enough for him to catch the blended scents of cigarette smoke and something spicy like sandalwood or jasmine. Awareness jolted him to full arousal. He felt like a sixteen-year-old with a killer hard-on—the kind that blinded a boy and made him do stupid things. He had to admit he liked that mindless feeling.

She turned in the corner of the door and glanced up at him. She stopped moving, her lips quirking in a clear show of interest. He leaned in, slanting his mouth over hers, pulling her lower lip into his mouth. He tasted cinnamon and the hopefulness of youth.

He fell hard into that kiss and knew he was a goner the minute she responded to him. He put his hand on the flare of her hip and pulled her hard against him.

He was headed straight to hell, with only a short layover at a no-tell motel before the Devil took him.

* * *

The sign said "Peach Blossom Motor Court" in flaming pink neon. Jane had hit rock bottom in her life. The fiddler had checked them in, and she watched through the windshield of his van as he returned with the key in his hand.

He was something, all right. A big man striding across the parking lot on a pair of the pointiest cowboy boots she had ever seen. Yessir, she would probably forget about this low-rent scenario the minute he put his mouth on hers again.

He opened the van door for her and looked up at her out of a pair of eyes that were as pale as a winter day on Meadow Mountain. The fire in those icy eyes burned so hot she felt the flame in the middle of her chest.

He gave her his hand, and she laid her fingers on him. His hand was huge, and warm, and rough, and male.

He helped her down and then shut the door behind her. He leaned his big-boned body against her, pushing her up against the van, his hand sliding down her rib cage and coming to rest on her hip. He was sturdy and hard, and so large that his body shielded her and made her feel safe in some inappropriate way.

How could she feel safe with a man intent on taking her without even giving her his name or asking for hers? But there it was. She knew the fiddler wasn't going to hurt her. The Universe kind of whispered in her ear and told her this would be okay.

She found herself inside the shadow of his Stetson, caught up in the heat of his mouth. He lost his hat, then she lost her mind.

About the Author

Hope Ramsay is a *USA Today* bestselling author of heartwarming contemporary romances. Her books have won critical acclaim and publishing awards. She has two grown children, granddaughters she dotes on, a demanding lap cap, and a dog named Miss Daisy. She lives in Virginia, where, when she's not writing, she's knitting or playing her forty-year-old Martin guitar.

You can learn more at:
   HopeRamsay.com
   Twitter, @HopeRamsay
   Facebook.com/Hope.Ramsay

Event planner Claire Donovan needs a venue for a wedding—fast. She knows the perfect place for the bride and groom to exchange their vows under a canopy of stars. But the owner of that house on the hilltop is serious and seriously sexy architect Bo Matthews. And Claire and Bo have a past history that might prevent them from building a future together.

For a bonus story from another author that we think you will love, please turn the page to read "A Wedding on Lavender Hill" by Annie Rains.

Chapter One

Claire Donovan had a bit of a reputation in Sweetwater Springs. She loved to shop.

As an event planner, she was always looking for a special item to make the *big day* just a touch more special. Last week she'd found a clown costume for a purse-sized Chihuahua to wear to its owner's eightieth birthday bash. It was a huge hit with the crowd; not so much with the little dog, who yapped, ran in circles, and tore at the shiny fabric.

The only shopping Claire would be doing this morning, however, was glancing in storefront windows on her way to meet with her newest client, Pearson Matthews. Claire's reputation extended beyond shopping. In Sweetwater Springs, she was also known for being professional and punctual, and for putting on the best parties in town.

She passed Sophie's Boutique and admired the window display, wishing she had more time to pop inside and say hello to the store owner—and try on one of those dresses that she absolutely didn't need. Then she opened the neighboring door to the Sweetwater Café and stepped inside to a cool blast of air on her face. She was instantly accosted by the heavy scent of coffee brewing. *Best aroma in the world!*

"Good morning," Emma St. James said from behind the counter. She had the smile of someone who'd been sniffing coffee and sugary treats since five a.m.

"Morning." Claire glanced around the room, looking for Pearson. The only people seated in the coffee shop though were two twentysomething-year-old women and a man with his back toward her. Judging by his build, he was in his twenties or thirties and liked to work out. He wore a ball cap that shielded his face. Not that Claire needed to get a good look at him. If his face matched his body, then he was yummier than Emma's honeybuns in the display case. Claire would do better to have one of those instead.

Pulling her gaze away from him, she walked up to the counter.

"Your usual?" Emma asked.

"You know me so well."

Emma turned and started preparing a tall café latte with heavy cream and two raw sugars. "Your mom was here the other day," she said a moment later as she slid the cup of coffee toward Claire.

Claire's good mood immediately took a dive. She loved her mom, but she didn't exactly *like* her. "Oh?" she said, her tone heavy with disinterest. "That's nice."

Emma tilted her head. "She asked about you."

"Well, I hope you told her that I'm fine as long as she stays far away."

"She said she's going to AA now," Emma told her as she rang up Claire's items at the register.

Drinking had always been Claire's father's problem though. Nancy Donovan had so many other, more pressing issues to deal with, none of which Claire wanted to concern herself with right now. She paid Emma in cash, took her coffee and bagged honeybun, then turned and looked around the shop once more.

"Are you meeting someone here?" Emma asked.

"Pearson Matthews. I guess he's running late," Claire said, turning back.

Emma shrugged. "Not sure, but his son is over there." She pointed at the man in the ball cap, and Claire nearly dropped her coffee.

What is Bo Matthews doing here? She didn't have anything against his father, but the youngest Matthews son ranked as one of her least favorite people in Sweetwater Springs. Or he would have if he hadn't left town last April.

Bo glanced over and offered a small wave.

"Maybe he knows where his father is," Emma suggested.

A new customer walked in so Claire had no choice but to step away from the counter. She could either walk back out of the Sweetwater Café and text Pearson on the sidewalk or she could ask his son.

You hate him, she reminded herself as attraction stormed in her belly. She forced her feet to walk forward until she was standing at his table.

Hate him, double-hate him, triple-hate him.

But *wow*, she loved those blue-gray eyes of his, the color of a faded pair of blue jeans. The kind you wanted to shimmy inside of and never take off.

"What are you doing back in town?" she asked, pleased with the controlled level of irritation lining her voice.

He looked up. "I live in Sweetwater Springs, in case you've forgotten."

"You left." And good riddance.

"I had a job to do in Wild Blossom Bluffs. But now I'm home."

Like two sides of a football stadium during a touchdown, half of her cheered while the other side booed and hissed. She was not on Team Bo anymore and never would be again. "Where is your father?"

"I'm afraid he couldn't make it. He asked me to meet with you instead."

Claire's gaze flitted to the exit. Pearson Matthews was her biggest client right now. He was a businessman with money and influence, and she'd promised to do a good job for him and his fiancée, Rebecca Long. Claire also had her reputation to maintain. She took her responsibilities seriously and prided herself on going above and beyond the call of duty. Every time for every client.

And right now, her duty was to sit down and make nice with Bo Matthews.

* * *

Bo reached for his cup of black coffee and took a long sip as he listened to Claire do her best to be civil. If he had to guess, the conversation she really wanted to be having with him right now was anything but.

"The wedding is two months away," she said, avoiding eye contact with him. "We're on a time crunch, yes, but your father could've called and rescheduled the initial planning session." Her gaze flicked to meet his. "It's not really something you can do."

Bo reached for his cup of coffee and took another sip, taking his time in responding. He could tell by the twitch of her cheek that it irritated her. She couldn't wait to get out of that chair and create as much distance between them as possible. Regret festered up inside him. He couldn't blame her for being upset. He'd handled things with her all wrong last year. "There's a problem with the wedding."

Claire's stiff facial features twisted. "What? Pearson and Rebecca called the wedding off?"

"No, unfortunately," he said, although that would've made him happy. Bo had been certain his dad would eventually come to his senses about marrying a woman half his age. Then, a few months ago, the lovebirds had announced they were pregnant.

"If the wedding is still a go, then what's the problem?" Claire lifted her cup of coffee and took a sip.

Naturally that brought his focus to her heart-shaped lips. He'd kissed those lips once—okay, more than once—and he wouldn't mind doing it again. Clearing his throat, he looked down at the table. "Rebecca is in preterm labor. The doctor put her on hospital bed rest over the weekend. She's not leaving there until the baby is born. Not for long at least."

From his peripheral vision, he saw Claire lift her hand to cover that pretty pink mouth. "That's awful."

He nodded and looked back up. "She wants to be married before little Junior arrives, which could be a couple days to a couple of weeks from now, if we're lucky."

Women weren't supposed to be beautiful when they frowned, but Claire wore it well. "So the wedding is postponed?" she asked. "Is that why Pearson sent you here to talk to me?"

"Not exactly. Dad and Rebecca want to speed things up a bit. Rebecca can get approval to leave the hospital, but only for a couple hours."

"Speed things up how much?"

Bo grimaced. This was a lot to ask, but his dad was used to getting things done his way. Pearson Matthews demanded excellence, which was one of the reasons Bo guessed he'd hired Claire in the first place. "They want the wedding to happen this weekend."

"What?" Claire nearly shouted.

"No expense spared. Dad's words, not mine."

She shook her head and started rattling off rapid-fire thoughts. "I don't even know what they like or what they want. I haven't met with Rebecca for planning yet. She's the bride; it's her wedding. Today is Thursday. That only gives me—"

"—three days," he said, cutting her off. "They want to marry on Saturday evening."

Claire's face was flushed against her strawberry locks. Her green eyes were wide like a woman going into complete panic mode. He'd seen her in this mode when she'd woken up beside him in bed last spring, and that had been his fault as well.

She pulled a small notebook and pen out of her purse and started writing. "I guess I could meet with Rebecca in her hospital room to discuss colors and themes."

Bo cleared his throat, signaling for Claire to look up. "About that. Dad doesn't want Rebecca involved. No stress, per doctor's orders. Dad wants you and me to plan it."

Claire's mouth pinched shut.

Yeah, he wasn't exactly thrilled with the idea either. He had other things to do than plan a shotgun wedding that he didn't even want to happen. For one, he had architectural plans to finish by Friday for a potential client. Having just returned to town, it was important to reestablish his place as the preferred architect in Sweetwater Springs.

"You and me?" She folded her arms across her chest. "I don't think so."

He shrugged. "Dad said he'd double your fee for the trouble."

That pretty, heart-shaped mouth fell open. After a moment, she narrowed her eyes. "What's in it for you? Aren't you busy?"

"Very. But despite his poor sense in the love arena, Dad has always been there for me. He even bailed me out of jail once."

Her gaze flicked away for a moment. Claire had told him about her family history during their night together last spring. Not that he hadn't already heard the rumors. Her dad was a drunk, now serving time for a DWI. Claire's mom couldn't hold down a job and had a bad habit of sleeping with other women's husbands. Most notably was her mom's affair with the previous mayor of Sweetwater Springs. That had ensured that the Donovan family's dirty laundry was aired for everyone to talk about.

Claire was cut from a different cloth though, and she did her best to make sure everyone saw that.

"Why am I not surprised that you would've spent the night in jail?" she asked with a shake of her head. The subtle movement made her red hair scrape along her bare shoulders.

"I guess because you have low expectations for me."

She pinned him with a look that spoke volumes. "How about *no* expectations?"

Maybe that was another reason Bo had agreed to help with this farce of a wedding. Claire might never forgive him, but maybe she'd stop being angry at him one day. For a reason he didn't want to explore too deeply, he hoped that was true.

* * *

Saying yes to this request would be insane.

Claire lifted her coffee to her mouth, wishing it had a splash of something stronger in it right now. "Okay, I'll do it." She'd never bailed on a job, and she wasn't about to start now.

Even if the wedding was in three days. And she had to plan it with Bo Matthews. And... "Oh no."

"What?" he asked.

"There aren't going to be any venues available. You can't book a place three days out. Everywhere in town will be taken. I wouldn't even be able to empty out a McDonald's for them to get married in with this short a notice."

Claire's hands were shaking. *The best and nothing less* was her personal motto. But she wasn't going to be able to deliver this time. There was no way. Her eyes stung with the realization.

"What about the Mayflower?" Bo asked.

That was a popular restaurant that she sometimes reserved for less formal events. "It'll be booked."

"The community center?"

Claire rolled her eyes. "Such a male thing to say. No woman dreams of getting married at the local community center." Claire dropped her head into her hands. *Think, think, think.*

She listened as Bo rattled off some more options, and shot them all down without even looking up.

"A wedding should be about the people, not the place," he said a moment later.

She looked up now. "I wouldn't have pegged you as a romantic."

He smiled, and it went straight through her chest like a poisonous barb. "It's true. If two people are in love, it shouldn't matter where they are. Saying vows under the stars should be enough."

She swooned against her will, immediately imagining herself in his arms under said stars. She'd danced with him at Liz and Mike's wedding reception last year. And he'd smelled of evergreens and mint. She remembered that when he'd held her in his arms, she'd thought he was the perfect size for her. Men who were too large put her head level at their chests. Too small put them face-to-face, which was just awkward.

But in Bo's arms, her head was at the perfect height to rest on his shoulder. Close enough to where she had to tip her face back to look into those faded denim eyes behind the Clark Kent glasses.

Bo reached for his coffee. "I couldn't care less where they get married. They'll be divorced within the year if my dad maintains his track record."

Right. Rebecca would be the third Mrs. Matthews.

"Maybe Rebecca is *the one*," Claire said, feeling a wee bit of empathy for the man sitting across from her.

"Nah. But I am going to have a new brother. *That* I'm excited about."

"You'll lose your spot as the spoiled youngest," she pointed out.

"Trust me, I was never spoiled." He tipped his coffee cup against his lips and took a sip. "I started working at the family business as a teenager after school. Dad made me save every penny to put myself through college."

Claire already knew the history of Peak Designs Architectural Firm and how it had grown from a one-man show to employing all three of Pearson's sons. Bo was the architect of the group. The middle son, Mark, was in construction management with the company. Cade did landscape design. The project he'd done that Claire liked best was Bo's own yard on Lavender Hill. The landscape, covered with purple wildflowers, was open and elevated over the water, with Bo's home—one of his own designs—seeming to touch the sky. She'd often looked out on that home while canoeing downriver and thought to herself that it was one of the most romantic places on earth.

"I've got it." She bolted upright. "Your place on Lavender Hill is the perfect place for a wedding!"

"My place?"

"I'm assuming your yard isn't taken for the weekend."

"It is. It's taken by me. No."

His expression was stiff, but she wasn't going to be deterred.

"Yes," she countered, leaning forward at the table. As she did, she caught a whiff of his evergreen scent, and her heart kicked at the memories it brought with it. Him and her, kissing and laughing. "It's your dad, your stepmom."

He groaned at the mention of Rebecca.

"And you owe me."

His eyes narrowed behind his glasses.

Yes, she knew she'd gone into his hotel room on her own volition last year. But he'd never called the following day, and she'd hoped he would. Instead, he'd taken a job in Wild Blossom Bluffs and promptly left town. She'd pined for his call even after the rumors had started popping up about them. Some people, more accurately, had compared her to her wanderlust mother. In reality, only a handful of people had talked, but even one comparison to Nancy Donovan stung. Claire wasn't like her mom and never would be.

Bo stared at her for a long moment behind those sexy glasses of his and then cursed under his breath. "Fine," he muttered. "You can have the wedding at my place."

Chapter Two ————————————

B o was in over his head, and he'd barely waded into the water.

Helping Claire pick out colors or themes for his dad's wedding was harmless enough. Inviting her into his home on Lavender Hill, letting her rearrange things and set up for a wedding was another.

And even though he was convincing himself of how awful this new turn of events was, there was some part of him that was excited to spend time with her. The night they'd shared last spring had been amazing. Being best man at the wedding of his childhood buddy and the woman who'd left Bo at the altar a year earlier had promised to be akin to having his appendix removed sans anesthesia. Instead, as the night was ending, Bo found himself kissing Claire, who'd tasted like some exotic, forbidden fruit. They'd both been too drunk to drive home and had gone up to the hotel room he'd booked. Best night of his life without question, even with hindsight and the events that followed tainting it.

In the morning when he'd woken, he'd watched Claire climb out of bed, looking sexy as anything he'd ever laid eyes on. She'd had that sleepy, rumpled look he found so attractive. She'd smiled stiffly and had made some excuse about needing to go. Then he'd promised to call later, knowing good and well he wouldn't.

That was his main regret. What was he supposed to say though? *That was fun* or *Have a nice life*? Claire was the kind of woman who men fell in love with, and he wasn't a glutton for punishment. He'd gone that route once and had been publicly rejected by Liz. He didn't fancy doing it again.

He also hadn't looked forward to seeing Liz and Mike be newlyweds around town. So he'd taken a job opportunity outside of Sweetwater Springs to clear his head. Putting the lovely Claire out of his mind, however, hadn't proved as easy.

His cell phone buzzed in the center console of his car. He connected the call and put it on speakerphone. "Hello."

"Our new stepmom is in the hospital?" his older brother Cade asked.

"That's right. She's at Mount Pleasant Memorial on bed rest. And she's not our stepmom yet... not until Saturday," Bo corrected.

"So I hear. You're planning the wedding with the event planner? Isn't she the one you disappeared with after Liz and Mike's wedding?"

"Yes and yes," Bo said briskly. "I plan to give her free rein over all the details. Dad said money was no object, and I trust Claire's taste. I just hope she doesn't mess up my house in the process."

"Your house? That's where you're having it?"

"Outside." But guests had a way of finding themselves inside at events, either to use the bathroom or to lie down when they weren't feeling well. Bo wasn't naive enough to think that wouldn't happen. His cousins would likely want to put their small children to sleep in one of his guest rooms.

"Well, I'd say 'Let me know if I can help,' but..." Cade's voice trailed off.

"But you'd be lying."

"And I'm an honest guy," Cade said with a chuckle. "No, seriously. I'm designing some gardens behind the Sweetwater Bed and Breakfast right now. It's a big job, and Kaitlyn Russo wants it done before the Spring Festival and the influx of guests she has coming in for the event."

"It's okay. Claire will do most of the work. She's top-notch."

"You speaking from experience there, brother?" Cade teased.

Bo ground his back teeth. "I already told you what happened." And he took offense at people jumping to the worst conclusions about Claire just because of who her parents were. "Listen, I have to go," he said as he pulled into the driveway of his home. He'd taken years to design this house himself, working nights while creating the plan. He loved every curve and angle of the structure. He loved the rooms with their high ceilings. His bedroom even had a skylight that allowed him to stare up into the sky while lying in his bed at night. Set on a hill, the house overlooked the river and the mountains beyond. *This* was his idea of heaven. He'd missed it while he'd been licking his wounds in Wild Blossom Bluffs. But now that he was back, he didn't plan on leaving again.

He walked inside, went straight to the kitchen, and grabbed an apple. Taking it to his office, he started working on the proposal designs for Ken Martin. Landing this contract would be good for business.

An hour later, he let out a frustrated sigh. He couldn't concentrate. All he'd been able to think about was that night he'd shared with Claire last spring. And the next three days he'd get to spend with her.

* * *

Claire had briefly considered going to school to become a nurse. Then her grandmother had fallen sick during her senior year of high school, and Claire had spent quite a few months visiting her at Mount Pleasant Memorial. That experience had ended any nursing dreams. She didn't like hospitals. Didn't like the sounds, the smells, or the dull looks in the eyes of the people she passed.

Making her way down the second-floor hall, Claire avoided meeting anyone's gaze. She liked being an event planner because most of the time people were happy. They were excited and looking forward to the future.

Just like the patient she was here to see.

Stopping in front of the door to room 201, Claire adjusted the cheerful arrangement of daffodils she'd picked up at the Little Shop of Flowers on the way here and knocked.

"Come in," a woman's voice called.

Claire cracked the door and peered inside the dimly lit room. Rebecca was lying in bed wearing a diamond-print hospital gown. The TV was blasting a soap opera, and she had a magazine in her lap. "Hi. How are you feeling?" Claire asked, stepping inside.

"Like a beached whale," Rebecca said with a small smile. She was practically glowing with happiness.

"Well, you definitely don't look like one. Pregnancy looks great on you," Claire said. "I know you're not supposed to be doing work of any kind right now so I'm only here as a friend. I brought you flowers."

"Oh, they're so beautiful!... And that rule about no work of any kind is Pearson's," Rebecca added in a whisper, even though no one else was in the room. "He's so protective toward me. It's adorable, really."

Rebecca also had that look of love about her. Her brown eyes were lit up and dreamy. Bo might not think what his father and Rebecca had was real, but Claire always got a good feeling for her clients. She could tell who was legit and who was getting married for all the wrong reasons. Maybe the baby was speeding things along, but Rebecca loved Pearson. It was as clear as her creamy white skin.

"I agree with Mr. Matthews. You should be taking it easy. We don't want that baby of yours coming any sooner than he needs to."

Rebecca sighed. "It's just, I've been dreaming about getting married since I was a little girl," she confided. "I wanted more time to plan this out and do it right."

"Relax. If you and Pearson are there, it will be perfect," Claire said, remembering how Bo had told her something similar this morning. "All you'll remember by the time it's over is the look in his eyes when he says "I do." Assuming you can see through the blur of your own tears."

Rebecca's lips parted. "Wow. You're good."

"Thanks. And don't worry—your wedding day is going to be everything you ever dreamed."

"I hope so. The main thing I want now is to have it before the baby gets here."

"We'll make sure that happens," Claire promised. "Do you have any favorite colors?"

Rebecca drew her shoulders up to her ears excitedly. "I was thinking that soft purple and white would be pretty."

"That's a nice springtime combo." Claire pulled a little notebook out of her purse along with a pen and wrote down Rebecca's color preference. "I'll see if Halona at Little Shop of Flowers can do some arrangements in those colors. Maybe with a splash of yellows and pinks as well for the bouquets."

Rebecca's eyes sparkled under the bed's overhead light. "Perfect."

"What about food? Since it's such short notice, I was thinking we'd skip a full dinner and just have light hors d'oeuvres at the reception. And drinks too, of course, for everyone except you." Claire winked at the bride-to-be.

They sat and chatted for another ten minutes while Claire wrote down a few ideas. Then she stood up and shoved her little notebook back into her purse. "I promised I wouldn't stress you out so I better go. You need your rest. But I'm so glad we got a chance to talk. I'm clearing my schedule for the rest of the week to focus solely on your big day."

And not on Bo Matthews. Which would be easier said

than done, since she would be spending the next several days at his house.

"Thank you so much," Rebecca said, bringing a hand to her swollen stomach.

"You're very welcome." With a final wave goodbye, Claire headed back down the hospital halls, keeping her gaze on the floor and not on passersby. She resisted a total body shudder as the smells and sounds accosted her. Once she was outside again, she sucked in a deep breath of fresh air. She walked to her car, got in, and then drove in the direction of Bo Matthews's home on Lavender Hill.

Butterflies fluttered up into her chest at the anticipation of seeing him again. But this was just business, nothing more, she reminded herself. And that was the way it needed to stay.

* * *

After a walk to clear his head, Bo settled back at his desk and worked steadily, making good progress on his proposal. Somehow, he put Claire out of his mind until the doorbell rang. Just when he'd gotten into the zone. With a groan, he headed to the door and opened it to find Claire staring back at him for the second time today.

She looked away shyly and then pulled the strap of her handbag higher on her shoulder as if she needed something to do with her hands. Did he make her nervous?

What would've happened had he called her the morning after they'd spent the night together? Would they be a couple right now? Would she be stepping into his arms to greet him instead of looking anxious and agitated? Would she be pressing her lips to his in a kiss that promised to turn into more later?

Bo cleared his throat and then gestured for her to come inside.

"I thought I'd go ahead and get started," she said. "I want to walk around the yard and get a good feel for the size and layout so I know where we can set up chairs and a gazebo."

"Okay." He was working hard to keep his eyes level with hers and not to admire the pretty floral dress she was wearing and the curves that filled it out so nicely. She had shiny sandals strapped to her feet that glinted in the light of the room.

"I stopped by to see Rebecca on the way here and brought her flowers." Claire held up her hand. "Don't worry. I didn't cause any stress. But she did give me her color preferences though."

"That's good," Bo said.

"I was thinking we should keep things simple. Even though your father said no expense spared, less is more depending on the venue. Your yard is the absolute perfect place for a wedding. The view is amazing, and as long as there's good music and food, it'll be as nice as some of the bigger events I plan in pricier spots."

Bo wasn't going to argue with her about saving money. Especially since his father was likely to have another wedding sometime in the next five years if history repeated itself.

"Feel free to walk around and do whatever you need to do," he said. As long as she kept her distance from him. He needed to work, and he had a feeling his brief streak of productivity was now broken for the rest of the afternoon. "There's a spare key on the kitchen counter for you to use over the weekend. You can come and go as you need." He gestured toward the back door. "That'll take you to the gardens. Let me know if you have any questions."

"Thanks." She turned and headed in the direction he pointed. His gaze unwillingly dropped as he watched her walk away. With a resigned sigh, he returned to his office to work.

This is going to be a very long three days.

An hour and a half later, he lifted his head to a soft knock on his open door. Then the door opened, and there was Claire, her cheeks rosy from her walk outside. The wind off the river was sometimes cool this time of year, and the humidity had left her hair with a slight wave to it. "Sorry to disturb you."

She'd been polite and civil toward him since their new arrangement. Whatever resentment she harbored toward him, she'd locked it away for the time being. The same way he was doing his best to keep his attraction toward her under wraps. "What do you think?" he asked. "Will Lavender Hill work?"

She nodded. "You have quite a few acres of land. We'll need to set up a few Porta Potties somewhere out of sight so that guests don't come in and out of your house all night. I think three will be enough, and I know a company that can arrange that on short notice. I'll also be having wooden fold-out chairs delivered. We rent them, and the company typically picks them back up on the day after the ceremony. The ground is nice and firm, and I checked the weather for Saturday. Sweetwater Springs isn't expecting rain again until later next week."

"Sounds like everything is falling into place."

"There's still more to do, of course. There are so many things to consider when you're planning an event for nearly a hundred people. But first I was thinking about having some food delivered. I'm starving, and I can't think when my stomach is growling. Are there any pizza places around here that deliver?"

He thought for a moment. "Jessie's Pizza delivers. It's my favorite." Just thinking about it made his mouth water. "The number is on my fridge."

She gave him a strange look as if she was debating whether to say something else. With a soft eye roll that he suspected was at herself rather than him, she folded her arms across her chest and met his gaze. "Are you hungry? I certainly can't eat a whole pie."

This was where he should practice self-control and say no. "I haven't eaten all day, actually. But if we're sharing, I'm buying. It's the least I can do considering the pinch my dad has put you in."

"Great. What do you like on your pizza?"

"I like it all," he said, not intending for the sexual tone in his voice.

Claire's skin flushed. "Okay, well, um...I'll let you work until it gets here," she called over her shoulder as she headed back out of his office.

Work. Yeah, right. With the anticipation of eating his favorite pizza with Claire, his brain had no intention of focusing on architectural plans right now. The only curves he was envisioning were those underneath that floral sundress she was wearing.

Chapter Three

While Claire waited for the pizza to arrive, she sat at Bo's kitchen counter and made a to-do list. Priority number one was lining up all the services for Saturday's wedding. Years of planning events meant she had close contacts for everything. Most would drop whatever they were doing and work extended hours to meet her needs. She'd already spoken to Halona about the floral arrangements, and that was a go. *Thank goodness.* She jotted down several people she planned to call after lunch, and then she found her mind wandering while she drew little hearts on the side of her paper and thought about Bo.

Whoa! She wasn't going down that path again. It'd been a long hike back the last time. Being seen coming out of Bo's hotel room had been mortifying enough. Even worse, she'd left that morning so smitten with him that she couldn't see straight. He was charming and funny, and undeniably gorgeous. She'd always thought so. He had this Clark Kent sexy nerd look about him that just *did it* for her.

Bo also had muscles plastered in all the right places. Not too bulky. No, his were long and lean. They'd run their hands all over each other's bodies last spring. That night had been hotter than anything she'd ever experienced, even though their clothes had stayed on—mostly. She was drunk, and he'd said he didn't want to take advantage of her. So they'd spent the night driving each other crazy with their roaming hands. They'd also spent it talking and laughing. Then, after Claire had left the next morning, it was out of sight, out of mind for Bo. But not for her.

The doorbell rang. As she walked down the hall, she turned at the sound of heavy footsteps behind her.

"I told you I'd pay." Bo caught up to her and reached to open the door ahead of her.

A young, lanky, twentysomething guy held a box in his hand. "Someone ordered an extra-large pizza and chicken wings?"

Bo glanced over his shoulder. "Wings, huh?"

Her cheeks burned. "I'm going to be here a while tonight so I thought it'd be a good idea to have plenty of fuel on hand." And pizza and wings were her biggest weaknesses, right after the clearance racks at Sophie's Boutique. And Bo, once upon a time.

Bo chuckled as he pulled out his wallet and paid the guy at the door. Taking the food, he closed the door with his foot and walked past her into the kitchen. "I'll get the plates. There's sweet tea and soda in the fridge. Help yourself."

She opened the fridge and peered inside. A man's

fridge said a lot about him. If there was more alcohol than food, that might be a problem. Bo appeared to have only one bottle of brew, and a healthy selection of fresh fruit and vegetables was visible in the drawers. She reached for the pitcher of tea and brought it back to the counter, where Bo had put out two plates. The open box of pizza was at the center of the kitchen counter.

He placed a slice of pizza on each plate and carried them to the table. "I have two glasses over here," he said. "You can bring the pitcher over."

Apparently, they were eating together. She'd just assumed that he would take his food back to his office and work.

He glanced at her for a moment. "Everything okay?"

She softly bit the inside of her cheek. She'd already had breakfast with the man. Lunch too? Her stomach growled. "Yep. Just fine." She moved to the table and took a seat, where the delicious smell of Italian sauce and spices wafted under her nose. "Mmm. If that tastes as good as it smells, I'm going to be having seconds."

Bo laughed. It was a deep rumble that echoed through her. "It tastes even better than it smells," he promised. "Jessie's is the best."

Her eyes slid over as he brought the slice to his mouth and took a bite. A thin string of cheese connected his mouth to the pizza for a moment, reminding her of all the pizza commercials on TV. Bo could be the guy in those commercials. Watching him bite into a slice of pizza would have her craving it every time. Craving *him* every time.

She lifted a slice herself and took a bite, closing her eyes as her taste buds exploded with pleasure. "You're not kidding," she moaned. When she looked over, he was watching her.

She swallowed. "It's very good."

For the rest of the meal, she kept her eyes and moans to herself as she filled Bo in on Rebecca's thoughts for the wedding. "She's really excited. She has the bride-to-be and the mother-to-be glows combined."

Bo grunted.

"I've known Rebecca ever since she moved to town two years ago. I don't think she's the type to marry someone for anything other than love."

Bo finished off his third slice and reached for his glass of tea. "It's just hard to fathom that a twenty-eight-year-old woman would want to marry a fifty-year-old man."

Claire laughed. "Love is crazy that way. It doesn't let you choose who you fall for."

"True enough. Maybe if you did, it would turn out a whole lot better."

She knew the whole ugly story about his ex-fiancée, who'd fallen in love with his best friend. Even after their betrayal, Bo had stood in as best man for the wedding that had led to him and Claire spending the night together.

"Have you ever been in love?" he asked, surprising her. They'd talked about a lot that night last spring, but that topic hadn't come up.

She nearly choked on her bite of pizza.

"Sorry. You know my history. It's only fair."

She reached for her glass of tea and washed down her bite. "I've been in what I thought was love in college. It was really just infatuation though."

"How do you know the difference?"

"Well," she said, chewing on her thoughts, "infatuation

fades. Love survives even after you know about all the other person's faults. Sometimes knowing the faults makes you like them more... This is not personal experience talking, of course. I'm talking as an event planner who has worked with countless couples in love. I've seen couples crumble under the pressure of big events, and I've seen others come out stronger."

He wore an unreadable expression on his face. "I guess I could say I've seen the same in my line of work. Making plans for the house you want to grow old in can be as stressful as it is exciting. Couples have torn into each other in the process, right in front of me. At those times, I'm almost glad that my ex walked away from me." He sat back in his chair. "That just meant I got to plan the home of my dreams all by myself. No drama involved."

Claire shook her head. "Well, you did a great job. This could very well be my dream house," she said. "I haven't seen the upstairs, but I'm sure it's just as perfect as the downstairs."

"I'll have to give you a tour at some point."

She shifted restlessly. Was his bedroom upstairs? She didn't think stepping inside alone with him would be wise. Probably asking him the question that sat right at the tip of her tongue wasn't wise either. She asked anyway. "Why didn't you call?"

Bo shifted his body and his gaze uncomfortably. She needed to know though. Yes, he'd left town, but he hadn't gone far and not for good. "I needed some space from everything. It had nothing to do with you. It wasn't personal."

But it was to her. She hadn't felt so connected to anyone in a long time. They'd had such a great time, and he'd promised to call. Only he never did. He must have been hurt watching his ex marry his best friend, and he'd used her as a crutch to get through the night. That was all.

"I see," she said briskly. Then she started cleaning up her lunch, even though she could stomach another slice of pizza or a chicken wing. What she couldn't stomach was continuing to sit with Bo right now.

"I had a good time that night," Bo said, as if backtracking from his response. "A *very* good time."

"So good that you never spoke to me again."

"We didn't sleep together, Claire. Why are you so mad at me?"

She slammed her paper plate and napkin in the trash and then whipped around to look at him. "Is that what defines whether a guy calls the next morning? Sex? You know, forget I asked the question. Forget everything. I have work to do and so do you."

* * *

It was well after eight p.m. when Claire arrived home. Her slice of pizza and sweet tea had worn off midafternoon, and she'd been running on adrenaline and fury since then.

It wasn't personal.

Those three little words had burrowed under her skin and had been festering for the last several hours. How dare he? She'd shared intimate details of her life with him that night. Hopes and dreams. She'd told him about her dysfunctional childhood that she never spoke of with anyone. It was *very* personal to her.

Stepping into her bedroom, she shed her clothes and

traded them for something comfy. Then she turned off the lights, climbed into bed, and reached for the book on her nightstand. She kept rereading the same line because her brain was still trained on Bo. It'd only been one night, but that night could've filled several years' worth for some couples. She always left a wedding feeling romantic and hopeful for her own happily ever after. Like a fool, she'd felt there was a potential for that with Bo.

A few days later, she swung by his house on Lavender Hill. Instead of finding Bo, she'd run into his brother Cade, who'd informed her that Bo had taken a job out of town. He didn't know when Bo was coming back, but it wasn't anytime soon. With him, Bo had taken a little bit of her pride and a big piece of her foolish heart.

Well, not this time. In fact, she wasn't even going to waste any more energy being mad at him. Bo was right. This wasn't personal; it was work.

* * *

Bo startled at the sound of his front door opening and closing early the next morning. He jolted upright, realizing he'd fallen asleep at his desk, which wasn't uncommon. His muscles cried out as he moved. Even though he was only thirty years old, he was too old to be grabbing shut-eye in an upright office chair.

"Bo?" Claire's voice called out from the front entrance hall.

How had she even gotten in? Oh, right. He'd given her a key.

"Bo?"

He stood and met her in the hallway. Unlike him, she

appeared to be well rested. Her hair was soft and shiny—perfect for running his fingers through. Today she was wearing pink cropped pants along with a short-sleeved top featuring a neckline that gave him ample view of her breastbone—the sexiest nonprivate part of a woman, if you asked him. Claire's was delicate with a splash of freckles over her fair skin. He'd spent time sprinkling kisses there once.

And if he didn't stop thinking about it, he was going to have a problem springing up real soon.

"I brought you a cappuccino and a cream cheese bagel." She lifted a cup holder tray and a bag from the Sweetwater Café. "And you look like you could use it." She laughed softly. She'd been royally ticked off the last time he'd seen her. What had changed since then?

"I fell asleep working on my latest design," he told her.

"And you have the facial creases to prove it." She smiled and breezed past him, leaving a delicious floral scent in her wake. He followed her into the kitchen and lifted the coffee from its tray.

"To what do I owe this act of mercy?" he asked suspiciously.

Claire lifted her own cup of coffee. "I'm calling a truce. What happened last spring is done and over. We won't think or talk about it ever again."

He sipped the bittersweet brew. The only problem with that suggestion was that he'd been thinking about that night for the past twelve months.

"I can put it behind me. It wasn't personal for you so I'm assuming you can as well." She notched up her chin, projecting confidence and strength even though something wavered in her eyes as she waited for him to reply.

"I can do the same," he lied.

"Great." She smiled stiffly. "Then I need your assistance this morning. If you're available."

"I got a lot done workwise last night so I guess I have some time. What do you need?"

"I brought some fairy lights to hang outside. You have some great gardens. Your brother Cade is so talented." She shifted her gaze, almost as if looking at him directly made her uncomfortable. "Since the ceremony will be at night," she continued, her voice becoming brisk, "I thought fairy lights in your garden beyond the arbor will add to the romantic feel. Do you have a ladder?"

"Of course."

"Great. I'm just going to take a walk around out there while you finish your cappuccino and bagel. I usually walk in the mornings down my street, but when I woke this morning, I just couldn't wait to go for a stroll behind your house. If that's okay?"

"Sure. I need to shower. I'll meet you out there with a ladder in about twenty minutes." Showers and coffee were his usual morning ritual. Perhaps he should start adding in a morning walk as well. Especially if it included a gorgeous redhead with dazzling green eyes.

He grabbed his cappuccino and went upstairs to prepare for the day ahead. It was Friday. Last night, he'd made a lot of progress on the Martin proposal. Tonight, he was meeting the couple over dinner to discuss his plans. He hated the social aspect of his job. Going to the Tipsy Tavern downtown with his buddies was fine, but having a nice dinner and wooing potential clients made his skin itch. It was a necessary evil though. He'd just have to suffer through it and hopefully come out of the night with a contract.

* * *

The gardens were a feast for Claire's eyes, but watching Bo string those fairy lights over the last hour was even yummier. His arms flexed and stretched while he hammered nails into the wooden posts that weaved in and around his garden. And the tool belt he'd looped around his waist was a visual aphrodisiac.

"You okay back there?" Bo asked, glancing over his shoulder.

She jolted as if she'd been caught with her hand in the proverbial cookie jar. Nope, she'd just been checking out the way he filled out the backside of those jeans. Her gaze flicked to his eyes, which were now twinkling with humor. *Yeah*, he knew exactly what she'd been doing. "Fine."

"Fine, huh? A woman who says she's fine never is. Am I hanging these things to your satisfaction?"

"You are. I might have to contract you for all my jobs."

"As much as I'd love to be at your beck and call, I'm afraid I already have a job that keeps me pretty busy." He climbed down the ladder and folded it, then carried it out of the garden and toward the arbor that had been delivered yesterday evening. He set the ladder back up and climbed to the top.

Claire handed him another string of fairy lights. "I'm meeting with the caterer in an hour and then swinging by the Little Shop of Flowers after that. Since your father asked you to help, I thought you might be interested in coming along."

Bo looped the lights around the arbor with an eye for spacing them out perfectly. "I'm not sure I'm the best person to ask for opinions on catering or flowers. Can't you get one of the women in that ladies group you go to?"

The group in question was a dozen or so Sweetwater Springs residents who regularly made a habit of having a Ladies Day (or Night) Out. They went to movies, had dinner, volunteered for community functions, anything and everything. It was girl power at its finest.

"I spoke to Rebecca, but you know your dad's tastes. I always like to represent the groom as much as the bride. Going to a wedding or anniversary function that is one-sided is a pet peeve of mine."

She watched him shove his hammer into the loop on his tool belt. Part of her physical attraction to Bo was his intellectual look, complete with glasses and a ready ballpoint pen always in his pocket. He had those thoughtful eyes too, always seeming to be thinking about something.

But this handyman look was really appealing as well. She'd created an online dating profile on one of those popular websites a couple of months back with the ladies group, but she hadn't activated it. She was a bit chicken, and the spring and summer were her busy months for planning events. Maybe she'd make it active in the fall and expand her search for bookish professionals to include muscle-clad guys who did hard labor. Bo was a perfect blend of both, except he wasn't available. After the way his ex betrayed him with his best friend, he might never be again.

He climbed back down the ladder and faced her. "I've got a proposition for you. I'll go with you to meet the caterer and look at flowers if you have dinner with me tonight."

She blinked him into focus. "You mean a date?"

"No."

She swallowed and looked up at the work he'd done with the lights, pretending to assess the job. Why had her mind immediately jumped to the conclusion that he was asking her on a date? If he was going to do that, he would have last spring. "Why do you want me to have dinner with you?"

"I'm meeting a potential client and his wife. It's social as much as it is business, and I hate doing these things alone. So yes, I guess they'd see you as my date, but—"

"It isn't personal," she said with a nod. "Fair enough." She jutted out her hand.

As his hand slid against hers, her body betrayed her iron-clad decision not to want him. Those hands were magic, she recalled. The stuff that her fantasies would forever be made of.

She quickly yanked her hand away. "Deal."

* * *

Two hours later, Claire was standing beside Bo and sampling finger foods and hors d'oeuvres at Taste of Heaven Catering. Claire usually came to her friend Brenna Myer's business with the prospective brides and grooms. It was usually them sampling the cheese, crackers, and little finger sandwiches.

"This is divine," Claire said with a sigh. She turned to Bo. "What do you think?"

"It's good," he said with a nod.

Claire punched him softly. "It's better than good. Are you kidding me?"

He chuckled softly. "Okay, it's the best thing I've put into my mouth in a long time."

Those words sliced right through her like a knife on that soft cheese spread in front of them. *Get it together, Claire.*

Brenna was watching them the way she usually did with the clients that Claire brought in. Claire guessed that her friend, who was also a member of the Ladies Day Out group, was scrutinizing every facial reaction and weighing whether her potential clients were satisfied.

Speaking of clients… "Do you think Pearson would like it?" Claire asked Bo.

"My dad is a carnivore. Put any meat in front of him, and he's a happy man."

"Especially with Rebecca at his side," Claire said, throwing in two cents for her currently bedridden client. If Rebecca made Pearson happy, then Bo should be happy too.

"Great. We'll definitely have a spread of various meats then," Brenna said, pulling a pen from behind her ear and writing something down on her clipboard.

"And the cheese," Claire said. "What pregnant woman doesn't love cheese?"

"I don't know any," Brenna said on a laugh. "You'll probably want something sweet as well."

"That's what I'm looking forward to sampling." Bo rubbed his hands together as a sexy smile curved his mouth.

"You have a sweet tooth, huh?" Claire asked.

"I do."

"Me too," she confessed. "Brenna's cheesecake squares are my favorite. I swear that's what she named this business after. They are the epitome of what heaven would taste like if it was food."

Brenna laugh-snorted.

Bo was also grinning. "Then we need to add them to the menu," he said, turning to Brenna.

"Oh no. This event is not about me and what I like," Claire protested. "It's about your dad and future stepmom."

The word *stepmom* drew a grunt from him. "We're the ones planning this wedding, and if cheesecake squares are your favorite, then cheesecake squares it will be."

Claire melted just a little bit at his insistence. "Let's add some chocolate macarons and white-chocolate-dipped strawberries as well," Claire said, with a decisive nod in Brenna's direction. Those were also one of her favorites, but Rebecca had also mentioned how much she enjoyed those.

By the time they left Taste of Heaven, their bellies were full, and there was no need for lunch.

"That was actually a lot of fun." Bo walked on the traffic side of the sidewalk as they strolled down Main Street to their cars. They'd driven there separately so that she could go home and prepare for tonight.

"It was. Thanks for coming."

"Well, as you pointed out, it's my dad and his soon-to-be wife. Coming along with you is the least I can do. Plus, now I get you tonight." He raised his brows as he looked at her.

It wasn't a date. He'd said so himself. But her heart hadn't received that message, because it stopped for a brief second every time he looked at her.

He opened her driver's side door and then stared at her for a long, breathless second.

There went her heart skipping like a rock over Silver Lake. He leaned forward, and she forgot to breathe as his face lowered to hers and kissed the side of her cheek. Part of her had thought maybe he was targeting her mouth. Would she have turned away? Probably not.

"See you tonight." He straightened, holding her captive with his gaze.

Maybe she should've held on to her anger at him. At least that would have buffered this bone-deep attraction that she couldn't seem to kick.

"Yes. Tonight." She offered a wave, got into her car, and watched him head to his own vehicle. She could still feel the weight of his kiss on her cheek. His skin on hers. She touched the area softly and closed her eyes for a moment. When she opened her eyes again, she saw a familiar face crossing the parking lot.

Everything inside her contracted in an attempt to hide. Luckily, her mom didn't seem to notice her as she walked to her minivan and got in. Seeing Nancy Donovan was just a reminder of everything Claire wanted and didn't want.

She wanted respect, success, and a man who wanted her as much as she wanted him.

She didn't want to lose her heart or her pride to an unavailable man. No, Bo wasn't married, which was the kind of guy her mom preferred. But he was no more on the market. Being with him tonight would have to be more like window shopping. Claire could look, but there was no way she was taking him home.

Chapter Four ─────────────

Bo wasn't sure if he was more nervous about meeting with the Martins tonight or about spending the evening with Claire.

He pulled up to her house, parked, and headed up the steps. As he rang the doorbell, he felt empty-handed somehow. Maybe he should've stopped and gotten flowers. That would've been stupid though. This wasn't a real date. But the tight, hard-to-breathe feeling in his chest begged to differ. It was a blend of anticipation and nerves with a healthy dose of desire for this woman.

The door opened, and Claire smiled back at him. She had on just a touch of makeup that brought out the green of her eyes. She'd swiped some blush across her cheeks as well, or maybe she really was flushed. With her strawberry tones and fair skin, she seemed to do that a lot.

There was something between them. There always had been. Their chemistry was off the charts, but it was more than that. Claire was funny and smart, and he admired the heck out of her. She would've had a right to view the world with bitterness and skepticism as much as anyone. Instead, she seemed to have unlimited optimism, and she romanticized everything. Bo could learn a lot from this woman, if he chose to spend more than three days with her.

"You're staring at me," Claire said. She looked at what she was wearing and back up at him with a frown. "Do I look okay? I wasn't sure what to wear for a business dinner, and there was no time to go shopping for something new. I can go back upstairs and change if you think this isn't good enough."

"It's perfect. You look beautiful." And heaven help him, it was all he could do not to move closer and taste those sweet lips of hers.

"Great," she said. "Let me just grab my purse. You can come on in."

Bo stepped inside her living room and looked around. It had been her granddad's place before he'd moved south to Florida and left it to her. Bo had never renovated a historic home before, but his mind was already swimming with ideas on how to modernize it just a touch by adding more windows for natural lighting.

As he waited for her to return, he walked over to the mantel and looked at the pictures encased in a variety of frames. There was a photo of Claire with her grandparents, who'd done a good bit of raising her while her parents shirked their duties. He thought he remembered that her grandmother had died several years back. There was one of Claire and her brother, Peter, whom Bo hadn't seen in quite some time. He wasn't even sure what Peter had been up to in the last decade since high school graduation.

Claire breezed back into the room. "Okay, got my purse, and I'm ready to go."

Bo turned to face her, and his breath caught. He wasn't dreading tonight's dinner like he had been this morning before inviting her along. On the contrary, now he was starting to look forward to it.

When they got to the restaurant, Ken and Evelyn Martin were already seated and waiting for them.

"Oh, you brought a date," Evelyn said, looking between them with a delighted smile. "This is such a nice surprise."

Bo wondered if he should clarify that Claire was just a friend. Evelyn didn't give him time to say anything, though, before launching into friendly chitchat.

"I'm Evelyn, and this is my husband, Ken," she said, reaching for Claire's hand.

Bo pulled out a chair for Claire and sat down while they all made their acquaintances. Then he made the mistake of looking around the restaurant. On the other side of the room, his vision snagged on Liz and Mike. They were expecting their first child if the rumors were true, which in Sweetwater Springs was fifty-fifty. A mix of emotions passed through him.

"I'm so glad you could meet us tonight," Ken said, pulling Bo back to his own dinner party.

Bo nodded. "Me too."

Liz had never been *the one* for him. He had come to terms with that during his time in Wild Blossom Bluffs. Perhaps he should walk over and thank them for that invitation to their wedding last year, because it'd led to an amazing night with the woman beside him. The *only* woman he had eyes for in the room tonight.

* * *

Claire had thought since this was a business dinner, that it would be tense or maybe a little stuffy. The Martins were probably twenty years older than her, but even so, Claire was having the best time. The older couple picked on each other in the most endearing way. And since Bo was paying, Claire helped herself to a steak with two sides of vegetables and a glass of wine. She didn't feel bad about it either. This was payback for last spring. They might have called a truce this morning, but she hadn't forgotten.

"It must be so rewarding to plan so many life events for others," Evelyn said, stabbing at a piece of shrimp on her plate and looking up at Claire.

"Oh, it is. I couldn't imagine myself doing anything else."

"I was a schoolteacher for thirty-one years," Evelyn said proudly, "and I loved every moment. If you love what you do and who you're with, life is always a party."

Claire was midway through lifting her glass of wine to her lips, but she paused to process that statement. "I love that philosophy."

"Well, it's true. I fell in love with Ken thirty-three years ago, and we haven't stopped partying since."

Ken Martin reached for her hand.

After that, the conversation turned to Bo's architectural proposal. The Martins loved all his ideas, and they seemed to love him too. Why wouldn't they? She hadn't been lying when she'd told him earlier that he was talented. He was. He was the architect behind the designs for so many of Sweetwater Springs' big businesses and houses. He was amazing.

By the time they left the restaurant, Bo and the Martins seemed like old friends. And Claire was totally and completely smitten with her date. Exactly like she'd promised herself she wouldn't be. But being with him was so easy.

He walked her out to the parking lot and, like a good gentleman, opened the passenger door for her.

"Thank you," he said, once he was behind the wheel. He pulled out of the parking lot and started to drive her home.

"It was no problem. I had a good time, and I had to eat anyway, right? Thanks for buying me dinner. Usually, the night before a wedding, we'd be doing a dress rehearsal. But nothing is the norm about tomorrow's ceremony." She was chattering away for some reason.

"Looks like we make a good team."

There was a smolder in his blue eyes when he looked over. Was she imagining that?

"Yes, I guess so."

"Maybe you could call me for all your catering and flower needs, and I could ask you to be my date for all my client meetings."

She knew he was only teasing. "I daresay, you'd grow tired of sampling food and picking out flowers." She cleared her throat. "I saw Liz and Mike. You were fixated over there for a moment at dinner."

She saw the muscles along his jaw tighten. "They didn't stay long, thankfully."

"Is it hard to see them together?"

"A little," he admitted. "Not because I still love her. Just knowing that they did things behind my back. Trust isn't an easy thing to repair." He sucked in a deep breath. "All for the greater good, I guess. They have a baby on the way, from what I hear."

Claire had heard the same. She reached a hand across the car and touched his shoulder, wanting to offer comfort. The touch zinged through her body. She hadn't touched this man since last spring. She'd made a point not to. Now she felt his hard muscles at her fingertips, and her body answered.

She yanked her hand away and turned to look out the window. "Not every woman would do that to you, you know."

"I never thought Liz would do that to me. Or Mike. So no, I don't know." There was an edge to his voice, making her sorry she'd even brought it up. He was obviously bitter about relationships now. No doubt that spilled over into his view on his dad and Rebecca's nuptials tomorrow.

They rode in silence for a few minutes, and then Bo turned on the radio.

Claire looked at him with interest. "Jazz? I would've pegged you for classical."

To her relief, the hardness of his face softened.

"I've always thought classical was boring. I played the saxophone in high school band."

"I remember. Do you still play?"

"I have the sax, but all the neighborhood dogs start howling when I put my lips to the mouthpiece."

Claire laughed. "I play piano. I had six years of lessons."

"Really? I thought we spilled all our secrets the night we spent together." His gaze slid over. There was a definite smolder there, contained only by thick-rimmed glasses.

He pulled into her driveway and cut off the engine. "I'll walk you to your door."

"How about a nightcap? I have wine. Or beer if you'd

rather." What was she doing? She'd resolved earlier this afternoon not to take him home with her.

"I'm not sure you can trust me not to kiss you if you invite me in," he admitted.

Gulp.

Without thinking, she ran her tongue along her bottom lip, wetting it. Which was just silly because she absolutely was not going to kiss this man. While her mind was starting to make a rational argument for saying good night, her body was warming up for first base, maybe second.

Bo leaned just slightly and tucked a strand of her hair behind her ear. Then his fingers slid across her skin as he took his time with the simple gesture. Her heart pattered excitedly. Then she leaned as well, almost against her will. One kiss wouldn't hurt anything, right? One tiny, little...

His mouth covered hers in an instant, pulling the plug on her mind. Her thoughts disappeared along with everything else, except Bo. It was just him and her and this scorching-hot kiss. His hand curled behind her neck, holding her captive. Not that she wanted to pull away. Nope. She was close to climbing across the seat and straddling him at this moment.

He tasted like white wine from the restaurant. Smelled like a walk through Evergreen Park. Kissed like a man who wanted her every bit as much as she wanted him.

She heard herself moan as their tongues tangled with one another. She remembered this. How good he kissed. It was like a starter match lighting a fire that burned in her belly. He broke away and started trailing soft kisses down her cheek and then her neck. There was a slight scruff of a five o'clock shadow on his jawline. It felt sinfully delicious.

She tilted her head to one side, giving him access. Eventually, his mouth traveled to her ear and nibbled softly. That fire in her belly raged to a full-on hungry blaze.

"That nightcap sounds good," he whispered, tickling the sensitive skin there. "And I don't want to think about Liz and Mike anymore tonight."

Claire's brain buzzed back to life. That was exactly why he'd invited her back to his hotel room last spring. She was a distraction, nothing more.

She opened her eyes and pulled away just enough to look at him. This was a mistake. There was no denying that she had it bad for this guy, but he wasn't emotionally available and she wasn't going to be used.

"Actually, I'm really tired." She averted her gaze because looking in his eyes, heavy lidded with lust, might sway her sudden resolve. "I'll see you in the morning. There are a few last-minute touches to do before the wedding. Thanks for dinner. Good night." She pushed her car door open, slammed it shut, and hurried up the porch steps as if running for her life.

But she was really running for her heart.

* * *

What happened tonight?

Bo sat out on his back deck and looked out to the garden. He'd turned on the fairy lights they'd strung earlier, giving the yard an ambient glow. Claire was right. It was a romantic touch.

He still couldn't decide if he was glad or disappointed that she'd slammed on the brakes to their make-out session. Going inside with her would have almost definitely led to her bed, and he didn't think Claire was the kind to have sex casually.

He'd been in a different place in his life last year. Liz and Mike's affair had plunged a knife through his heart, and he wasn't sure he'd ever be able to pull it out. It'd been hard to breathe for a long time after that. He'd dated casually, hooked up a few times, but he had no interest in anyone.

Until Claire. She'd sparked something deep inside him that was terrifying to him back then. The thought of allowing himself to have actual feelings for a woman felt like marching himself right up to Skye Point and preparing to jump off without a parachute. It was nuts.

But now...

He liked her. She evoked feelings he'd never experienced before. Not even with Liz, whom he'd planned to spend his life with.

Damn. He wasn't sure what exactly had happened tonight; all he knew was he needed to fix it. After tomorrow's wedding, there'd be no need to see Claire anymore. Not unless he climbed that proverbial mountain and forced himself to look off the ledge and jump. Getting into another relationship was a risk. Claire could hurt him even more than Liz had. But would she?

An hour later, he dragged himself to bed and flopped around restlessly until he drifted off. After what seemed like just a few minutes, he awoke with the chirping of springtime birds nesting by his window. A slant of sunlight hit his face, prompting him to sit up and shuffle down the hall. He made coffee, enough for two, and then showered.

Claire still hadn't arrived by the time he'd dressed and started preparing breakfast—also enough for two. A little worry elbowed its way to the forefront of his mind. Had he scared her off last night? He knew that she'd be here to finish the job no matter what. He trusted that she wouldn't let his dad and Rebecca down.

He trusted *her*.

That one thought stopped him momentarily in his tracks. His heart was more easily won than his trust, but it appeared that Claire had captured them both.

He continued walking to his office and opened his computer to scan his email. There was already a message waiting for him from Ken Martin:

Loved having dinner with you and Claire last night. Evelyn and I both love your plans for the mother-in-law suite we want to add on. We were unanimous in our agreement that you are the right man for the job. We'd love to work with you. We'd also love to have you and Claire over for dinner at our place again sometime soon. She's a keeper. A wise man wouldn't let her slip away.

Ken

Bo pumped a fist into the air. The deal was done. Success! He reread those last two lines.

It was good advice, and he planned on taking it.

Chapter Five

Claire was taking her time getting ready to go to Lavender Hill this morning. When she'd agreed to this business arrangement, she'd resolved not to let herself fall for Bo again. And who fell for a guy after only a few days anyway?

Apparently, she did. She wasn't in love with him, no. But she was long past lust.

Claire gave herself one last glance in the mirror. She hadn't put on the beautiful dress she'd purchased at Sophie's Boutique a few weeks back just yet. She still had work to do at Bo's house. Speaking of which, she guessed it was time to go.

She headed to her car, got in, and then, continuing to procrastinate, veered off toward the Sweetwater Café for a strong cup of coffee.

A few minutes later, Emma smiled up from the counter as a little jingle bell rang over Claire's head.

"Good morning, Claire," Emma said with all the warmth of one of her delicious hot cocoas. "You have a big event this afternoon."

"I do." Claire gave a nod. On the morning of a special event, she was usually buzzing with so much energy that she didn't even need to stop by the Sweetwater Café, even though she always did anyway. "Are you going to be there?" Claire asked.

"I wouldn't miss it. Rebecca is one of my favorite customers. I'm so happy for her."

"So you're not against the marriage because of the age gap?"

"No way. Not if she's happy, and I wholeheartedly believe she is." Emma was already preparing a cup of coffee for Claire per her usual specifications.

Claire fished her debit card out of her purse as she waited.

Turning back to her, Emma narrowed her eyes. "And you've been holed up for the last couple of days with Bo Matthews, I hear."

"Because the wedding is at his house," Claire clarified, handing her card over. "Not for any other reason."

Emma swiped the card and handed it back. "I wouldn't blame you if there was. He's hotter than that cup of brew you're holding. Don't tell him I said so though. He's not really my type."

Claire grabbed her cup of coffee and took a sip. Bo was *her* type. "No? What is your type?"

Emma shrugged. "I dunno. Chris Hemsworth, maybe."

"You do realize that he's a world-famous movie star, and that it's very unlikely he'll walk into your coffee shop, right?"

"Yeah, yeah. Just a technicality. It could happen," Emma said with a soft giggle.

Yeah, and Bo could realize he was falling for Claire too. Which would never happen.

Claire started to turn and leave, but Emma grabbed her forearm.

"I have to warn you," she said, biting down on her lower lip. "Your mom is here."

"What?" Claire looked over her shoulder, and sure enough, there was Nancy Donovan. How had she missed seeing her when she'd walked in? And why hadn't Emma warned her sooner? Not that it would've helped. There was only one way out and it was past her mom.

Claire turned back to her friend. "Thanks for the heads-up. I'll see you tonight." She took her cup of coffee and turned to leave. As she headed toward the exit, her mom's gaze flicked up and stayed on her. Her mouth curved just slightly in a sheepish smile. Then she lifted her hand and waved.

Crap. If Claire kept walking, she'd be the bad guy here, and that wasn't fair. Claire was always the one trying to help her parents growing up. She was the one victimized by their lack of attention and their shaming of her family's name.

Forcing her feet forward, Claire walked over to her mom's table and slid into the booth across from her. "I can only stay a few minutes," she prefaced.

Her mom nodded. Soft lines formed at the corners of her eyes and mouth as her smile wobbled. "I'm just happy to get to talk to you. How are you?"

Claire swallowed, wondering if she should answer that question truthfully. And if so, what was the honest answer? Work was great, but her personal life was all screwed up because she'd once more allowed herself to have feelings for Bo. "Swell. And you?"

"Better these days." Her mom molded her hands around her own cup. "I'm working on things I wish I'd worked on a long time ago."

"Hindsight and everything," Claire said, hating how sarcastic she sounded. She blew out a breath as she looked around the shop and shook her head. Then she turned back to her mom. "Look, I'm sorry. I don't mean to be so rude."

"It's okay," her mother said. "I deserve it. I was hoping that we could work toward having some sort of relationship again though. Even if it's only five minutes every now and then over coffee."

Claire stared at the woman in front of her. Time hadn't been kind, mostly because of the way Nancy had chosen to live her life. "How's Dad?"

"Jail has helped him sober up. He's going to stay dry once he gets out next month," she told Claire with a hopeful lilt to her voice. "We're going to get a second chance to do right by each other. That's what we both want."

Claire sucked in a deep breath and let it go. It was hypocritical of her to expect Bo to believe his dad could change and settle down with Rebecca when she couldn't do the same with her own parents. It was easier said than done though. "I hope that happens, Mom."

They spoke for a few minutes more, and then Claire pushed back from the table and stood. "I really do have to go...But maybe we can do this again."

Her mom's brows lifted. "Really?"

"I'm usually here on Saturday mornings"—Claire shrugged a shoulder—"so maybe I'll see you next weekend."

"Yes. Maybe you will." Her mom reached for Claire's hand and gave it a quick squeeze, the closest to a hug that either of them were ready to give. "Thank you."

As Claire walked out of the coffee shop, she felt lighter. Maybe her mom would let her down again. But there was also the possibility that she wouldn't this time. Claire had always been an optimist. She never wanted to lose hope that things could change for the better.

There was no hope for Bo changing his mind about love and romance though. No matter how much her heart protested that maybe, just maybe, there was.

* * *

Claire had drained her cup of coffee by the time she pulled into Bo's driveway. She was surprised to find him outside setting up the chairs.

"Wow. You've been busy," she said, walking toward him. She kept her shoulders squared. Kissing him last night didn't change anything. She wasn't going to let it affect the task at hand.

Straightening, he looked at her. He was all hot and sweaty, with the same ball cap on that he'd been wearing at the coffee shop a few days before. "I promised to help, so I am. Ken Martin emailed this morning and offered me the contract, by the way."

Claire's smile was now sincere. "That's great, Bo. I thought he would. Last night went really well." Except for that last part.

Judging by the look in his eyes, he was thinking about that too.

"I'm, um, just going to call Halona and Brenna and make sure everything's on track. I'll use your kitchen for that, if you don't mind."

"I don't. There's coffee, eggs, and bacon in there too. I made plenty this morning."

It was official. Emma could have Chris Hemsworth, because he had nothing on Bo Matthews.

* * *

Claire was obviously ignoring him. Bo wasn't sure how to make things right, but he knew he wanted to. He wanted a lot more than that, and he was ready. Seeing Liz and Mike together last night at the restaurant had barely stung. In fact, he almost felt happy for the two of them. Yeah, they'd hurt him, but he knew they hadn't meant to.

Love didn't let you choose. He understood what Claire had meant by that now, because he was falling hard and fast for the sweet, smart, gorgeous event planner. *How the hell am I going to fix things with her?*

A delivery truck pulled into his driveway with SOUTH-ERN PORTA-JOHN written in large black letters on the side. Bo guided the guys toward the back of his house, where the porta-johns would be available to guests but not readily seen during the ceremony. After that, Halona Locklear showed up in a navy SUV with all the flower arrangements in the back. Claire came out of the back door to help her set things up.

It wasn't a good time to talk to her right now. Not

when she had so many things to get done before tonight's wedding.

The next few hours were a blur of activity going on in and around his house. Brenna showed up with trays full of food. He helped her set up tables to display it all. A DJ showed up and set up a place to play music for the reception. The entire Ladies Day Out group showed up after that and helped Claire with a host of other things that he never would've considered. They set out tablecloths and large baskets full of party mementos for the guests. Pearson's and Rebecca's names and the date were written on little paper hearts attached to each favor.

"Aren't these the cutest?" Lula Locklear asked as she walked up to peek inside one of the baskets. "The ladies and I were up all night making these." Lula was Halona's mom. She was often involved in the community, increasing awareness about her Cherokee Indian culture.

"They are," Bo agreed, unable to resist lifting his head and looking around to see where Claire was. He spotted her laughing with Kaitlyn Russo, the owner of the Sweetwater B&B. The sight of Claire happy and enjoying herself made his heart skip a beat. He longed to be the kind of guy who put that smile on her face.

"You are a man with the look of love," Lula said with a knowing nod. She followed his gaze to where Claire was standing. "She's such a nice girl. She needs someone who will treat her well." She gave him an assessing look as if trying to decipher if he was capable of being that kind of guy. *Was he?* "Maybe there'll be more weddings on Lavender Hill in the future," she said.

* * *

As the sun started to creep toward the mountains, the sky darkened, and guests started to arrive. Claire slipped on the beautiful satin dress she'd purchased from Sophie's Boutique and then headed outside to turn on the lights. The aroma of the food wafted in the air along with laughter and casual conversation.

Pearson and Rebecca would be on their way at any moment. Rebecca's obstetrician had okayed her to leave for two hours. That was enough time to greet guests, walk down the aisle, say their vows, and maybe even have a dance under the stars.

Claire sighed dreamily, imagining Rebecca getting the wedding of her dreams tonight.

Bo stepped up beside her, scrambling those happy thoughts and feelings. "I need to talk to you. There's a problem."

She whipped her head around to face him. "What kind of problem?"

"Rebecca is in labor. The wedding has been called off."

"What?" Claire's lungs contracted as if the wind had been knocked out of her. "But she wants to be married by the time the baby comes. She needs to get here."

Bo frowned. "I just spoke to Dad. Rebecca's water broke when she was putting on her wedding dress." He grimaced. "It's not going to happen tonight. They can do it after the baby is born. She can buy a new dress and have it anywhere or any way she wants."

Claire shook her head. "The only thing she really wanted was to exchange vows before she gave birth."

Claire looked around at all the guests, seated in wooden fold-out chairs. The scenery was perfect. There were even hundreds of stars speckling the clear night's sky.

Her shoulders slumped as she blew out a resigned breath. This was out of her control, and she knew it. "I guess we'll tell the guests the news and send them all home." She hesitated before looking at Bo. Disappointment stung her eyes. She didn't want him to know that all she really felt like doing was sitting in one of those chairs and having a good cry on Rebecca's behalf.

"You stay here. I'll take care of the guests," he said.

"You don't have to. That's my job."

"You did your job already."

"Not really. The wedding is off. I've never let a client down before. Ever." And now she wanted to cry on her own behalf.

There was something gentle in his eyes when she looked up at him. "Stay here," he said again.

She watched him walk off toward the crowd, then she turned to face the garden. She wasn't sure exactly how long she stood there collecting herself before Bo came up behind her. When she turned, he was standing there with Pastor Phillips.

Claire started to apologize to the older man, but Bo patted the pastor's back and narrowed his gaze at her.

"Pastor Phillips is ready to go to the hospital."

Claire scrunched her brows. "What? Why?"

"Because there's a wedding to be had, and we don't have much time. If Rebecca wants to be married before my baby brother gets here, then that's what we'll make sure happens. Assuming we beat the clock."

Pastor Phillips chuckled. "My wife was in labor for twelve hours after her water broke with our first child. I think we'll be okay."

Bo reached for Claire's hand. "You've never let a client down, right? Why start now?"

"You don't even believe your father and Rebecca should be together. Why are you doing this?"

"Maybe I see things differently now. Because of you."

Chapter Six———————

Claire grabbed the wedding bouquet before climbing into Bo's car. It was an assortment of purple irises and white lilies—exactly what Rebecca had requested. In fact, aside from wanting to marry before her baby was born, the flower preferences were the only other thing Rebecca had asked for.

After a short drive, Bo parked in front of the labor and delivery wing, and they hurried inside. Claire clutched the arrangement tightly as she walked beside him toward the elevator. Pastor Phillips had driven separately. Hopefully he wasn't far behind.

"What's wrong?" Bo asked. "You were talking as fast as I could drive on the way here."

Claire shook her head. "A hospital isn't exactly my favorite place. I watched my grandmother die here." And ever since, Mount Pleasant Memorial had carried nothing but bad memories for her.

They stepped inside the elevator, and Bo reached for

her hand. He didn't let go once the door opened on the second floor. The feel of his skin against hers distracted her from the repetitive beeping sounds and the smells of disinfectant as they walked.

"Let's make a few happy memories here today, shall we?" he asked, giving her a wink that short-circuited all the negativity in her mind.

"There's nothing more joyful than a wedding. I've always thought so."

His smile wobbled just a little as they walked.

"I'm sorry. I guess weddings hold as many bad memories for you as hospitals do for me."

"I used to think I never wanted to go to another wedding again. But there's nowhere I'd rather be tonight than at this one with you."

Her heart fluttered. "Same. Even if it is at a hospital."

They stopped behind Rebecca's door, and Claire knocked softly.

A moment later, it cracked open, and Pearson Matthews peeked out at her. Claire had seen him many times over the years. His presence was always confident and commanding. Now he looked like a man juggling half a dozen emotions: excitement, fear, anxiety, exhaustion, confusion, joy.

"How is Rebecca feeling?" Claire asked.

In response, they heard Rebecca groan in the background.

"The baby is coming fast," Pearson said. "What are you two doing here?"

"You couldn't come to the wedding so we brought the wedding to you," Bo answered. "Do you think Rebecca is up for it?"

Pearson smiled at his son, a dozen new emotions popping up on his face. "I think that will probably make her really happy...Thank you, son."

Claire's eyes stung just a little as she watched the brief father-son interaction. "Great. Can we come in?"

Pearson swung the door open wider. "Becky, look who's here!"

Rebecca looked between Claire and Bo and then to Pastor Phillips, who stepped up behind them.

"Do you still want to get married before the baby arrives?" Claire asked.

"Yes." Rebecca shifted and tried to sit up in bed. She was wearing a hospital gown instead of a wedding gown. Her hair was a little disheveled, and the makeup she'd put on for tonight's ceremony needed a touch-up. Even so, she was as beautiful as any bride Claire had ever seen.

Rebecca flinched and squeezed her eyes shut, moving her hands to her lower belly. "But we better do this fast," she gritted out.

Pearson went to the head of Rebecca's bed as Pastor Phillips opened his Bible to read a short passage. Afterward, he looked up at the bride and groom and read off vows that they repeated.

Bo never let go of Claire's hand as they stood witness to the happy union. It was quick, but no less perfect. A tear slid off Claire's cheek as Rebecca said, "I do." Then Pearson dipped to press his lips to Rebecca's—their first kiss as man and wife.

Claire would've wiped her eyes, but one hand still carried the bouquet and the other was held by Bo. He squeezed it softly as he glanced over. There was something warm in his gaze that melted any leftover resolve to resist this man.

Rebecca pulled away from her husband and turned to her guests, which had expanded to include two nurses. "My bouquet, please."

Claire finally broke contact with Bo and handed the arrangement over.

"Okay, ladies. Arms up," Rebecca said. "Bouquet tossing time!"

"Oh, no. I'm already married," one of the nurses said with a laugh.

Bo stepped off to the side, leaving Claire and the second nurse in the line of fire. Claire usually removed herself from this moment at weddings too. Fighting with a bunch of single ladies over a superstition had always seemed so silly, albeit fun to watch. As the bouquet went sailing across the room though, Claire lifted her hands reflexively and snatched it from the air, much to the second nurse's disappointment.

"You're next!" Rebecca said with a laugh. Then she flinched again as another contraction hit her.

"Okay, that's it," the married nurse said. "I think your baby wants to join this party."

Rebecca opened her eyes. "Okay." She looked at Claire. "Thank you. For everything. This was absolutely perfect."

"You're welcome. But I couldn't have done this without Bo."

Rebecca looked at him with tears in her eyes. "Thank you too."

"That's what family is for, right? Welcome to the Matthews clan."

Pearson stepped over and reached out his hand for Bo to shake. He shook Claire's hand as well.

"We're going to give you two some privacy now," Bo told him.

"Don't go too far," Rebecca called from across the room. "Your baby brother will be excited to meet you."

Bo seemed a little stunned by the invitation to stay. He looked at Claire.

"I'm in no hurry to go home," she said. Nor was she in a hurry to leave Bo's side right now.

* * *

"That was amazing!" Claire said, leaning back against the headrest of Bo's car as he drove her to his home three hours later. "And your baby brother is adorable. I can't believe I got to hold a newborn who's only been on this earth for an hour. That was such a rush. And the wedding was perfect, even though we were the only ones in attendance."

He glanced over, feeling a sense of pride and accomplishment at helping to put that contented look on her face. "You pulled it off."

"*We* pulled it off."

From his peripheral vision, he saw her turn and look at him.

"You said it yesterday, and it's true. We make a pretty good couple." Her relaxed posture stiffened. "Team. We make a good team," she corrected.

"I liked it better the first way." He'd been waiting to talk to her all day. The hospital hadn't seemed like the right place, but now he couldn't wait any longer. He pulled into his driveway, parked his car, and then looked across the seat at her.

Her contented, dreamy look was gone, replaced by a look of confusion. It was just last night that they'd kissed in this very car, but it felt like a lifetime ago.

"I like you, Claire Donovan. I liked you last spring, but I was a coward. I'll admit that."

"Sounds about right," she agreed.

"I'd just watched my best friend marry the woman I thought I wanted. But I was wrong. I was so wrong. You're the woman I want, Claire. And I want you like I've never wanted anything in my entire life." His heart was thundering in his ears as he made his confession.

Her eyes became shiny for the hundredth time that night.

"The last few days have breathed new life inside me. I don't want to think about waking up tomorrow and not knowing if I'll see you." He ran a hand through his hair to keep from reaching out and touching her. "Claire, I want another chance with you. If you say yes, I promise I won't mess things up this time."

She was so still that he wondered if she was okay.

"Say something," he finally said.

"I'm hungry." After a long moment, her lips curved ever so slightly.

He cleared his throat and turned to look out at his yard. "Well, there's probably still some food left over from the reception. The guests each took some, but it'd be a shame for the rest to go to waste. I even think I saw Janice Murphy spike the punch on her way out," he said.

Claire gave a small laugh and nodded when he looked at her. "There's also a place to dance under the stars."

"The evening is set for romance," he agreed.

"So let's enjoy it and see where the night takes us. On one condition." Her expression contorted to something stern with just a touch of playfulness lighting up her eyes. "If it ends up leading somewhere nice, you have to promise you'll call me tomorrow."

He chuckled. "I promise that it will lead somewhere nice, and when it does, you might never get rid of me."

She looked up into his eyes and smiled. "I might never want to."

Epilogue———————————————

In the blink of an eye, everything could change. Or in Claire's case, one month's time. That was how long it'd been since she'd planned Rebecca and Pearson's wedding. It had all happened so fast, but everything had fallen into place perfectly.

Claire stepped out of the dressing room at Sophie's Boutique and did a twirl in front of the body-length mirror. The cotton dress was a deep rose color with tiny blue pin dots in the fabric. The hem brushed along her knees as she shifted in front of the mirror.

"That's the one," the shop owner said, stepping up beside her.

"I feel a little foolish. It's just our one-month anniversary, but Bo told me to wear something nice."

"One month together is definitely worth celebrating. Where is he taking you?" Sophie asked. "Any idea?"

Claire shook her head. "No." It didn't really matter though. It was the gesture that melted her heart like a marshmallow against an open flame. He was always doing little things for her to show her how much he cared. "Okay," she said, looking down. "This is the one. I'll take it off and let you ring it up for me."

"Do you have the right shoes?"

Claire laughed. She loved to shop as much as the next person, but she couldn't wait to get home and ready for whatever Bo had planned for them. "I do. But thanks."

An hour and a half later, Bo picked her up at her place and started driving.

"You're still not going to tell me where we're going?" she asked.

He was dressed in nice jeans with a polo top and a sport coat. She was almost disappointed to have to go out tonight because she would have rather been alone with him. They'd spent a lot of alone time together over the last month, and she wasn't sure she'd ever get enough.

"That would ruin the surprise."

She huffed playfully. "Fine. How's baby Noah?" she asked. He'd told her he was stopping by the hospital this afternoon. It had been all she could do not to invite herself along, but visitors were limited to family right now. She was just the girlfriend.

"A genius," Bo answered. "He takes after me."

This made Claire laugh out loud.

"And he'll be leaving the NICU tomorrow. The doctor says he's ready."

"That's wonderful news. I'm sure Pearson and Rebecca are so happy."

He nodded. "They are."

Claire blinked as she looked out the window, recognizing the route. Surely she hadn't gotten all dressed up just to go back to his place.

He turned the car onto Lavender Road and drove all the way to the end. After pulling into his driveway and parking, he turned to her. She blinked and kept her gaze forward. The fairy lights were turned on—they'd never taken them down—and a table was set up at the peak of the hill behind his house.

Bo stepped out of the car and walked around to open her door for her. Then they approached what he'd put together. There was a small vase of fresh flowers at the table's center, sandwiched between two candles, not yet lit. Another table was set up to the right with what appeared to be catered food from Taste of Heaven.

"A candlelit dinner under the stars." She turned and stepped into him, wrapping her arms around his neck and staring into his eyes. "All this just to celebrate one month of being together?"

He leaned in and kissed her lips, soft and slow. Nothing in her life had ever felt so right as being with him.

"No. All this is to tell you that I love you, Claire Donovan. I love you so much."

She blinked him into focus. A man had never uttered those words to her before, but they were music to her ears. She wanted to hear them again and again. "I love you too, Bo Matthews."

She laughed as he pulled her in for another kiss under the starry night sky. Then they had dinner and shared a dance before retreating to his room, where he repeated those three little words again and again.

About the Author

Annie Rains is a *USA Today* bestselling contemporary romance author who writes small-town love stories set in fictional places in her home state of North Carolina. When Annie isn't writing, she's living out her own happily ever after with her husband and three children.

Visit her online at:
  http://www.annierains.com/
  @AnnieRains_
  http://facebook.com/annierainsbooks
  https://www.bookbub.com/authors/annie-rains

Fall in love with these charming small-town romances!

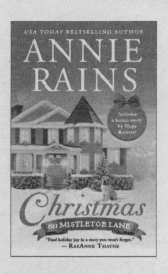

CHRISTMAS ON MISTLETOE LANE
By Annie Rains

Kaitlyn Russo thought she'd have a fresh start in Sweetwater Springs. Only one little problem: The B&B she inherited isn't entirely hers—and the ex-Marine who owns the other half isn't going anywhere.

THE CORNER OF HOLLY AND IVY
By Debbie Mason

With her dreams of being a wedding dress designer suddenly over, Arianna Bell isn't expecting a holly jolly Christmas. She thinks a run for town mayor might cheer her spirits—until she learns her opponent is her gorgeous high school sweetheart.

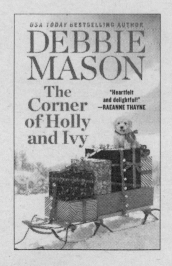

Discover exclusive content and more on forever-romance.com.

CHRISTMAS WISHES AND MISTLETOE KISSES
By Jenny Hale

Single mother Abbey Fuller doesn't regret putting her dreams on hold to raise her son. Now that Max is older, she jumps at the chance to work on a small design job. But when she arrives at the Sinclair mansion, she feels out of her element—and her gorgeous but brooding boss Nicholas Sinclair is not exactly in the holiday spirit.

THE AMISH MIDWIFE'S SECRET
By Rachel J. Good

When *Englischer* Kyle Miller is offered a medical practice in his hometown, he knows he must face the painful past he left behind. Except he's not prepared for Leah Stoltzfus, the pretty Amish midwife who refuses to compromise her traditions with his modern medicine…

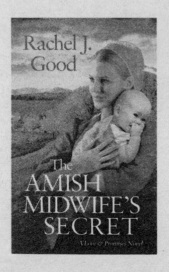

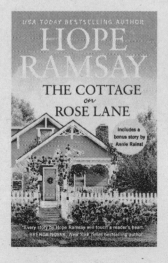

Follow @ForeverRomance and join the conversation using #ReadForever.

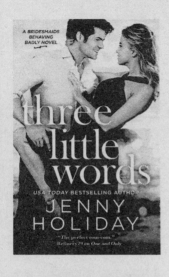

THREE LITTLE WORDS
By Jenny Holiday

Stranded in New York with her best friend's wedding dress, Gia Gallo has six days to make it to Florida in time for the ceremony. And oh-so-charming best man Bennett Buchanan has taken the last available rental car. Looks like she's in for one *long* road trip with the sexiest—and most irritating—Southern gentleman she's ever met…

THE WAY YOU LOVE ME
By Miranda Liasson

Gabby Langdon secretly dreams of being a writer, so for once she does something for herself—she signs up for a writing class taught by best-selling novelist Caden Marshall. There's only one problem: Her brooding, sexy professor is a distraction she can't afford if she's finally going to get the life she truly wants.

Visit
Facebook.com/ForeverRomance